The Wis

The Wish

Sylvia Ann Baxter

The Pentland Press Limited
Edinburgh • Cambridge • Durham

First published in 1994 by
The Pentland Press Ltd.
1 Hutton Close
South Church
Bishop Auckland
Durham

ISBN 1 85821 204 9

Typeset by CBS, Felixstowe, Suffolk
Printed and bound by Antony Rowe Ltd., Chippenham

I dedicate this book to my family,
and to the memory of my dear late mother,
Elsie Baxter.

SPECIAL THANKS

I thank my friend Muriel Bebbington, who, by showing me the inscriptions written on the windows of her Shropshire farmhouse dated 1875, inspired me to write this book.

Thanks also to my Australian friend, Adrian Nisbet, to Robin Walker, Miss Rosalie Whately and Doreen Meredith.

AUTHOR'S NOTE

On completion of this book I learnt that there is a country house in South Shropshire by the name of Netley Hall, and wish to point out that it bears no reference to the Netley Manor featured in my story. In addition, although the Long Mynd hills and the Caer Caradoc hill are both a part of the South Shropshire landscape, all other names and places mentioned in this book are fictitious.

CONTENTS

PART ONE
CATHERINE

PART TWO
ELIZABETH

God moves in mysterious ways
His wonders to perform

PART ONE

CATHERINE

CHAPTER ONE

Vancouver in the summer of 1978.

Catherine Shepherd grabbed her purse and keys and left the sixth floor city apartment she shared with Jenilee Harris. She had arranged to meet Jenilee at one of the harbour coffee bars at ten-thirty, so now she would have to get a move on. Jenilee had left early that morning to keep an appointment, and Catherine had put her absence to good use by giving the apartment a thorough clean – a chore which Jenilee evaded with the most amazing resolution.

That particular morning Catherine had promised to accompany Jenilee on a shopping expedition, for her monthly allowance from her father was already burning holes in her pockets. Paul Harris was in the shipping business and was extremely generous to his effervescent, nineteen year-old daughter, who could sweet-talk her father into giving her almost anything. He also helped Catherine financially and paid the rent on the apartment which the two girls shared.

Catherine liked Paul Harris, who was like a father to her now. He and his wife Norene had been very good to her over the last four years, fostering her after her previous foster parents had split up and gone their separate ways, neither wanting to take on the responsibility of Catherine single-handed. At three years old, she had been orphaned when her parents had been killed in an automobile accident in the Rockies, and had spent the next three years in a children's home on Vancouver Island.

Afterwards there had been a succession of foster parents who had given her a temporary home, until eventually, at the age of fourteen, she had settled down with the Harris family. She and Jenilee had grown to be like sisters, although Jenilee, the eldest by a year and a young woman who had a happy-go-lucky approach to life, could never hope to be the lady that Catherine would one day become. Catherine possessed a quality of the very rarest kind, but from whom she had inherited it she never knew.

Twelve months previously, after making a bid for independence – Jenilee's independence rather than Catherine's – they had moved into the apartment together and the arrangement had worked very well. Jenilee was a student at a nearby art college where Catherine herself was due to study in early fall.

3

Art had always interested her, although she despaired over the fact that as yet her artistic talent had still not surfaced in any marked direction, even though she knew it was there inside her.

Outside in the busy streets it was hot as she picked her way through the tourists and shoppers in Gas Town, then walked on towards the harbour. There she leaned on the handrail for a moment, gazing at the spectacular view across the bay. As usual it was a hive of activity, with craft of every size and description sailing across the sparkling water, the mountains in the background a haze of misty blue beneath the heat of the sun.

Her eyes were drawn to the water which lapped gently against the quayside below her, and as she gazed into its blue-green depths, she suddenly remembered the dream she had had the night before, the same dream she had experienced for three consecutive nights. She had found herself standing in a beautiful lawned garden looking across at an old house which stood in the near background, where tall trees and shrubs contributed towards its seclusion. She knew instinctively that it was an English house, yet how she knew was a mystery to her. And the dreams never varied; they had all been the same. There she was, standing in the garden, gazing at a house which meant nothing to her. Catherine remembered being amazed by the reality of the dreams, almost as though she were actually there in the garden. Even now, in broad daylight when she was wide-awake, she could still see it in her mind's eye – and clearly enough to remember every detail. She frowned. It was all so puzzling.

As she thought about the matter an idea occurred to her. That evening, when Jenilee went to the movies with her boyfriend and she had time to herself, she would sketch the house as she remembered it in the dreams, although she feared her limited talent would fail to do it justice. However, she would do her best. Happy with the idea, she headed towards the coffee bar where Jenilee was waiting.

That evening Catherine began the sketch, copying the house exactly as she remembered it in her dreams. Two hours later she sat and admired her work, feeling highly satisfied with her efforts. It was, without doubt, a remarkable achievement for an eighteen year-old novice who, until that day, had limited herself to sketching flowers and nothing more. At last her talent had surfaced.

She smiled. The sketch had captured her from the very beginning, as she had watched it take shape with every meticulous stroke of the pencil. It was a large period house, black and white timbered, with small mullioned windows partially obscured by the vines and creepers which clung to the walls. She ran her finger over the flight of steps which led to the studded front door surrounded by its stout wooden porch, then over the two ornamental stone statues which stood at the foot of the steps, one on either side. To the front of

4

the house she had sketched the lawns and gardens, skilfully using her pencil to shade in the tall, majestic trees, almost bringing the whole scene to life with detail.

As her finger traced the avenue of trees which lined the drive leading down to the house, she became aware of the powerful vibrations which the sketch transmitted into her flesh – a feeling which left her considerably overawed and mystified. In some uncanny way she could feel it enticing her into its midst, into its own earlier century; an era of horse drawn carriages, of elegantly dressed ladies and gentlemen of wealth and fortune who lived in magnificent country homes with their many servants. Catherine became intrigued by her imagination, aware of a strange and mystic longing for the past. It was a feeling which came from deep within her soul and which was impossible for her to understand.

Her brow was knitted in a frown as she rose to her feet and propped the sketch against the wall. She then turned to walk away, but found herself compelled to look back at it, drawn by some force she could not possibly have described. Suddenly a spark of recognition began to flicker in her eyes, a recognition which emerged from the farthest and darkest corner of her mind. Evolving from it came the conviction that behind the old house lay a courtyard; a cobbled courtyard enclosed by stone-built stables.

Catherine was naturally puzzled, for the revelation indicated that she was somehow familiar with the English house. Yet how was that possible? The place did not exist. It was all in her mind. She had dreamt it. Nevertheless the instinct doggedly persisted, convincing her that at some time or another she had seen that old house for herself. She laughed sceptically and checked her wayward thoughts. What a lot of nonsense! Why, she had never even been to England, let alone visited a place like that! Her entire life had been spent right here in British Columbia, where she would probably end her days. Perhaps she had been working too hard and had allowed her imagination to run away with her? It had to be something like that.

Satisfied with her conclusion, Catherine left the room. However, during the months which followed, the sketch continued to haunt her, filling her with a deep and passionate longing for something which it held within its midst; an obscure promise which enticed her back to it time and time again until she believed she would go mad from sheer bewilderment.

The three ensuing years had brought their changes. Catherine had blossomed into spectacular womanhood, leaving behind the gawky schoolgirl image of yesterday. She had a natural, old-fashioned beauty which her contemporaries envied, and there was a serenity about her seldom found in a woman these days. During the last three years her artistic talent had improved dramatically, and she was now a student at the Riseholme Art College in Vancouver. Professor Summers, the Art Master at the college, said she showed great promise, admitting that he found her particular type of talent rare. 'Almost extinct', he had said.

One of her earlier paintings, and in his opinion her most spectacular to date, hung on exhibition in the college gallery, a prize exhibit which continued to receive the acclaim and admiration it richly deserved. It was an oil painting of the old English country house which she had sketched three years earlier, and which had brought out every grain of potential she possessed. The professor considered Catherine his star pupil, gifted with an extraordinary ability to capture life on canvas, meticulous and conscientious to a fault.

Professor Summers was browsing through some papers when Catherine entered the room to commence her studies, radiance itself as she walked with poise towards her desk, her tall, slender figure causing several heads to turn. Heads always turned in her direction. Catherine had that effect on people. She had the most exquisite face with the very finest bone structure, cornflower blue eyes fringed by long, sweeping lashes and dark hair which fell in natural waves to her waist. She was a striking woman in every way, whose personality remained unaffected by her looks and accomplishments, her kind nature and generous spirit as true as ever.

The professor's eyes were still upon her as she began to work on her latest creation, a man astride a magnificent black horse, the scene being set in an emerald wood. He frowned. Why was it that she always chose subjects from the past? He was beginning to find it oddly disturbing that never once in the three years she had studied here had she ever painted a modern scene. Everything she had done had been old-fashioned.

In thoughtful mood, he recalled Catherine's four achievements. There was the English country house; a brilliant old-fashioned hunting scene, also English; a superb piece which featured a Victorian lady and gentleman seated in an open carriage and pair, and an exquisite and remarkably detailed bluebell wood. What was it about that country and its past which she found so intriguing? It was a complete mystery to him. And now this, her latest piece, a figure most certainly from the nineteenth century. Because of the period in which her painting was set and the fact that her work was entirely her own creation, he knew she could not possibly have seen her subject. Yet as he watched her now, he could have sworn she was painting the man from memory. It was uncanny – quite unbelievable.

Aware of the Art Master's presence beside her, Catherine inclined her head to look at him. 'Professor?'

'My apologies for disturbing you, Catherine,' he said. 'I was simply admiring your work.' He eyed the portrait keenly as he spoke. Why, even now, in its unfinished state, it would surpass her creation of the house. It was a truly remarkable piece. 'An outstanding achievement,' he acknowledged. 'Outstanding!'

'Thank you, Professor. I must admit, I feel proud of it myself. I believe it's the best work I've ever done.'

The professor smiled encouragingly. 'Yes, I believe you're right, my dear. But tell me something, Catherine: why do you always choose subjects from the last century? Why is your work always dated?'

Catherine grew thoughtful. 'I'm not exactly sure, Professor,' she began. 'Perhaps it's because scenes from the past are always the first to spring to my mind? It happens all the time, almost as though I was meant to paint them. I realise this will sound a little far-fetched, but I lack inspiration for contemporary work. I know that as an artist, my talent is limited to creating scenes which belong strictly to the past.'

Professor Summers looked decidedly shocked. 'But that's preposterous, Catherine! I've never heard anything like it! You're an artist, in my opinion the best, able to paint any subject – past or present!'

Catherine watched him pace the floor, realising how deeply she had shocked him. But it was true. She did feel incapable of contemporary work, no matter how absurd it sounded. She should know, for she had attempted it often enough and had failed miserably. It was a different matter when she embarked on scenes from the past, though. The subjects were already there imprinted in her mind; it was almost a form of second sight.

The professor returned to her desk, a father figure concerned for the welfare of his pupil. 'I believe your obsession for the past is proving unhealthy, Catherine. Your own confession that you're unable to paint modern subjects proves this to be correct.' He heaved a sigh. 'I'm concerned about you, my dear. I believe you've been working too hard and are in need of a rest. I advise you to go out and enjoy yourself more. Broaden your horizons, Catherine. Involve yourself with life as it is today and put your obsession with the past behind you.' The professor hoped she would heed his advice, for she was a brilliant student with a highly promising future and nothing should be allowed to threaten that. 'By the way, Catherine, may I ask if you've made plans for the summer vacation yet?' he concluded conversationally.

Catherine's spirits lifted. 'Yes, Professor. Jenilee and I are going to Europe to visit England and France. Oh, but I can hardly wait to see England!'

Later that morning as lunchtime approached, Jenilee pulled up a stool and sat beside Catherine's desk. The lanky red-head crossed her legs and lit up a king-size cigarette with a Lauren Bacall-like sophistication. 'Know somethin', huh? You work too hard, Cathy. Take a break and come for a coffee. I wanna discuss our vacation plans. You do realise we'll be off to Europe in only three weeks' time?'

'How could I forget?' replied Catherine rapturously. 'I'm counting the days until we go. Oh, we're going to have a wonderful time, Jenilee!'

Jenilee smiled. 'Yeah, we sure are,' she agreed. 'It'll be my last vacation as a single woman, so I guess I'd better make the most of it. Oh, that reminds me, Cathy. I was talkin' to a friend of Greg's last night who would like a date with you. I told him to give you a call. His name's Anthony Holmes. He lives at Princeton and is studying to be an architect. Anyway, I told him you were the most stunnin' woman at college, with a smile that could stop the world. Boy, was he impressed!'

Catherine laughed. 'Forget it, Jenilee. I've told you before, I'm not interested in dating. So stop match-making. I'll find myself a man when I'm ready – which isn't yet!'

'But you should go on dates, Cathy. Lord, there are enough guys queuin' up to take you out. Besides, I hate to think of you livin' all alone in the apartment after Greg and I are married at Christmas.'

'Don't worry about me, Jenilee. I'll be fine.' Catherine cast her a smile. 'But I shall miss you when you leave – especially if Greg whisks you off to some remote corner of the globe for a couple of years or so.' Jenilee's fiancé was a geologist, whose work took him to some far-off places. At the moment he was studying volcanoes in New Zealand, but would fly home to Canada in December when he and Jenilee would be married. In the meantime, Catherine looked forward to Jenilee's company in Europe, which they had planned before Jenilee had met Greg Marshall.

'I shall miss you too, Cathy,' she replied. 'But you know I'll visit when I can.' She then admired Catherine's portrait. 'Say, this is comin' on beautifully. Bet old Summers is pleased!'

'Yes, he is, although he wants me to paint more modern scenes in future. He's not happy about my always choosing old-fashioned subjects for my work projects here.'

Jenilee studied her friend for a moment and in part she couldn't help but agree with the professor. Catherine did have a somewhat strange fascination with the past. 'In my opinion you belong to an earlier age, Cathy. I picture you with your hair in ringlets, wearing a long old-fashioned dress, with a big hat and a frilly parasol in your hand. Yeah, you'd look just fine in that kinda outfit.'

Catherine gave a hoot of laughter. 'Jenilee Harris, your imagination is worse than mine! You really shouldn't encourage me with such notions. Professor Summers believes I'm too obsessed with the past for my own good. Perhaps I am,' she said reflectively. 'It really does intrigue me. Anyway, I prefer to think of myself as interested, as opposed to obsessed. Why, until I sketched the old English house I wasn't even that! Strange, but it was that which began it all really – my interest in the past, I mean.'

'Does it still haunt you in that weird kinda way, Cathy?'

'Yes. Every time I look at it. I know this will sound ridiculous, Jenilee, but it's as though it were trying to tell me something.'

Jenilee shuddered. 'Huh! It would scare the hell outa me!' she declared. 'I wouldn't have it if you paid me a thousand dollars!'

'Oh, but it doesn't frighten me,' said Catherine. 'I just find it puzzling because I'm convinced I've been there at some time or another. Yet how could I have? It's just a picture. The old house doesn't exist.'

'Sounds bizarre to me,' retorted Jenilee grimly. 'If I were you, I'd throw the damn thing in the trash bin and forget it!'

A soft smile formed on Catherine's lips. 'Ah, yes,' she said, 'but you're not me.'

After Jenilee had left, Catherine returned her attention to her portrait of the man. It was a man whom she felt she had come to know. She gazed into his crystal blue eyes, which for all the world appeared to be staring right back at her. It was uncanny the way the man's handsome image touched her heart, filling her with a warmth and feeling which she had never known before. Indeed, if it were possible to fall in love with a painted figure, then she was, without doubt, in love with him... had been from the moment she had begun it.

She traced the outline of his face with her finger, along the jaw and over his cheekbones to his eyes and forehead, coming to rest on his sleek dark hair. How proud he looked astride his horse, dominant and masterful, possessing the kind of strength which lesser men would fear and envy. He exuded wealth and importance through the canvas, and was dressed accordingly in slim-fitting black trousers tucked into high black riding boots, with a white shirt which had a ruffle of frills down the front and around each cuff to match. Had he been real, she might have imagined him to be a landowner of some kind, rich powerful and successful.

Catherine knew the portrait had an affinity with her painting of the English house, for it, too, possessed the ability to draw her with its strange magnetism. Another puzzling fact: because his image had been so clear in her mind whilst painting him, she knew she was not making up his appearance as she went along; rather she was painting him as though from memory. Initially she had found the fact disturbing, although she had come to accept it now for whatever it was.

Professor Summers wanted the painting to hang in the art gallery upon completion and Catherine agreed. She would miss it when she went away on vacation, for it had become part of her life now. But it would be here when she returned, she told herself. A thrill of excitement feathered down her spine at the thought of England. Although she never admitted the fact to anyone, not even to Jenilee, she felt that England was calling her to its far-off shore, enticing her with some mysterious promise. Catherine knew that only time would tell whether her instinct was correct.

Catherine found England a wonderful country, far in excess of her expectations. After recovering from jet-lag, she and Jenilee had spent the first two weeks exploring the famous sights of London, typical tourists, keenly photographing everything they saw. They had visited art galleries and museums by the score, had spent hours in Harrods and the very best boutiques, and had been to the theatre in Drury Lane and enjoyed another evening at the ballet. They had also spent a few days in the Cotswolds and Oxford, enjoying the river and the countryside and making friends with the local people at the inns where they had stayed. The weather had been glorious throughout the whole two weeks, and both women looked tanned and refreshed after their vacation.

Now their visit had come to an end and they were back in London, all packed and ready to leave England. They were taking the ferry to Calais that morning to begin their two-week stay in France. Jenilee had relatives in Paris and they had arranged to visit them upon their arrival. Catherine felt sad at having to leave England, disappointed that its promise had simply not materialised.

A sceptical laugh escaped her as she sat in the hotel foyer waiting for Jenilee. What had she been expecting, anyway? She just didn't know, and chided herself for being so foolish.

She picked up a copy of *Country Life*, and looked with interest at the photographs of imposing country houses featured within. Suddenly her eyes beheld a familiar picture and she turned back a page to have another look. Her expression turned to shock. Long moments ticked by as she stared at it in disbelief, for there before her eyes was a photograph of the English country house which she herself had sketched and painted. It was almost like seeing a ghost!

An age seemed to pass before she was able to gather her senses together even to think clearly. Quite by chance she had discovered something which in her heart she had known all along. The old house *did* exist; it was not just a figment of her imagination.

Beneath the photograph was a short informative write-up which she quickly read:-

Cambourne Hall in South Shropshire. Owned by the Montgomery family for over four hundred years, Cambourne Hall lies amidst the glorious setting of the Shropshire hills and its surrounding countryside. The house was built in the mid-fifteen hundreds and has great architectural interest, the chimney stacks being unique in their design. Cambourne Hall is a Grade 1 listed building which, together with its large country estate, is one of the finest country houses in Shropshire today.

Catherine felt completely overawed and mystified. She wondered why it had appeared to her in the dreams she had experienced three years ago – and clearly enough to sketch down to the last small detail. How could she, a Canadian, be connected with Cambourne Hall?

Puzzled, she stared hard at the photograph whilst endeavouring to collect her thoughts. It was not identical with the house she had depicted in her sketch because the front porch was missing. So were the two stone statues which had stood at the foot of the steps, although the studded front door was still there.

Carefully examining the structure of the house, Catherine noticed that the huge oak timbers which framed its walls corresponded precisely and in every detail to her own sketch, as did the six sets of imposing chimney stacks, unmistakably defined by their unique design. The long tree-lined drive which led to the house was still there too, although there were not as many trees as there had been years earlier. Years earlier? A shiver coursed down the length of Catherine's spine. It reminded her that she had sketched the house as it had stood perhaps a hundred years ago, a fact which she found most disturbing.

Contemplatively, she sat back in the chair trying to figure it out. But she had no success. She was at the peak of her frustration when Jenilee appeared. She was pink-faced after struggling with her heavy luggage. Heaving a sigh, she dropped it beside Catherine's.

'Bet I'm charged excess baggage with that lot!' she exclaimed. 'Lord knows why I bought so many books to give friends back home. Key rings would have been much easier to carry!' Jenilee could see that Catherine hadn't heard a word she had said, and cast her an enquiring look. 'Is anythin' wrong? You look kinda pale, as though you'd seen a ghost!'

'Perhaps I have,' replied Catherine. She handed Jenilee the magazine. 'Take a look and tell me what you think.'

Jenilee sat down. When she saw the photograph, she gave an exclamation of shock. 'But this is your–'

'–My painting? Yes, it is. I came across it quite by accident whilst waiting here for you. I don't know what to make of it at all.'

'But... but the house appeared to you in a dream, didn't it, Cathy? Then you sketched it as you remembered it. So how can it be real?'

'I don't know,' said Catherine grimly. 'But here it is in black and white, the identical house featured in my own sketch and painting. I just don't understand it.'

Equally puzzled, Jenilee stared at the photograph again. 'No, the house isn't identical to yours,' she said. 'There are features in your work which don't appear in this photograph, the porch and the two statues, for instance. The drive is different too. See?' She pointed. 'My theory is that sometime in your life, probably when you were very young, you saw this house in a book or somethin' and for some reason it remained imprinted on your memory. Years later, when you began your career as an artist, you sketched the house which your mind remembered so well – even though you yourself had forgotten all about it. That would explain how you were able to sketch it in such detail. There!' she concluded triumphantly, 'How's that for psycho-analysis?'

Despite her torment, Catherine smiled. 'You'd make a terrific shrink, Jenilee, but I'm afraid I can't go along with your theory. Do you honestly believe that the mind of a child could remember all the intricate detail which went into sketching that old house? No.' She shook her head. 'No child could possibly remember all that.'

Jenilee nodded in agreement. 'Yeah, I suppose you're right. Oh, it's all so weird! That old place always did give me the creeps, and right now it's makin' the hair on the back of my neck stand on end! Forget it, Cathy. Forget you ever saw it and let's be on our way.' She leapt to her feet as she spoke.

'Forget it?' echoed Catherine. 'I don't believe you said that, Jenilee. I want to know what's happening here. There must be a reason why I sketched the house and I want to know what it is.'

'But there's nothin' you can do about it! Besides, we have a train to catch, remember? If we don't get a move on we're gonna miss it.'

However, deep in thought, Catherine remained seated. Although she had never been much of a believer in fate and destiny, she couldn't help but wonder if perhaps she had been *meant* to see that photograph – meant to see it in the hope that she would investigate the matter further. The more she thought about it, the more convinced she became.

Suddenly it was clear to her what she must do if she ever wished to find the answers to the questions which had plagued her since completing the sketch of the house. Without further hesitation, she informed Jenilee of her decision. 'I'm sorry, Jenilee, but I can't go to France with you as arranged. I've thought the matter over and have decided to go to Shropshire to see the

12

house instead. I'd never forgive myself if I left England without seeing it. Please say you understand.'

'Oh, no! You can't!' appealed Jenilee. 'I won't let you!'

But Catherine looked determined. 'I'm sorry, Jenilee, but my mind's made up. I'm going.'

'But somethin' awful might happen to you, Cathy! I... I feel afraid for you!'

Catherine smiled reassuringly. 'But of course nothing awful will happen to me, Jenilee. After all, it's only a house.'

'Yeah, I know. But sometimes it's best to leave things as they are. Delvin' into the unknown could have disastrous consequences. Don't ask me how or why, but I have the strangest feelin' that somethin'... somethin' will happen to you if you go there.'

'But I must!' emitted Catherine, exasperated now. 'You know how the sketch has haunted me all these years! I have to go, Jenilee!'

Finally, Jenilee conceded. 'All right, then, I'll come with you. Heaven forbid I should allow you to go to that sinister old place on your own. I'll give Kevin and Josie a call and let them know we won't be going to Paris now.'

Catherine smiled and expressed her thanks, but would not allow Jenilee to change her plans. 'No, Jenilee. Your relatives would be disappointed if you didn't visit them as arranged. Anyway, with a bit of luck I should be rejoining you in a day or two. I just want the chance to see Cambourne Hall for myself and perhaps find out more about it.'

Eventually Jenilee agreed to allow Catherine to go to Shropshire on her own, although not without deep reluctance. Still looking none too happy with the arrangements, she asked, 'Anyway, how do you propose to get to Shropshire, Cathy?'

'I think I shall hire a car. It would be quicker than taking the train. Talking of trains, you're going to have to hurry if you want to catch yours, Jenilee. Have a good trip. I shall miss you!'

The two women embraced, with Catherine promising to call Jenilee in Paris to let her know she had arrived safely in Shropshire.

'Goodbye, Cathy,' she said. 'I hope you find whatever it is you're lookin' for. And please take good care of yourself!'

'Thank you and I will,' said Catherine. 'Goodbye Jenilee. See you soon.'

Once Jenilee had departed, a fleeting wave of uncertainty swept over Catherine and she felt an urge to abandon her mission to Shropshire and go after Jenilee instead. But the moment passed and it was not long before she was driving towards the west. As the miles rolled away, she wondered what lay in wait for her there.

CHAPTER TWO

Catherine arrived in Shropshire in the late afternoon, still wondering what connection she could have with Cambourne Hall. Throughout the journey her mood had been tense and thoughtful. Was she right in driving all the way up here to see the house? Or should she perhaps have taken Jenilee's advice and left things as they were? Whereas Jenilee was convinced that she was heading towards danger, Catherine felt there was nothing evil or sinister about the house. Quite the contrary, for she felt it was extending her a hand of welcome as opposed to emitting some kind of threat. No, she had no fear, only a wish to unravel the mystery and have all her questions answered. She smiled to herself. Turning her back on it and walking away wouldn't achieve that, she thought. Well, she was in Shropshire now, and one way or another she intended to learn all about Cambourne Hall and its past.

Although she had invested in an excellent road map, she had become hopelessly lost after turning off the main road into the narrow country lanes. The fact that they all looked alike confused her even further, and they were all neatly lined on either side by hawthorn hedges entwined with honeysuckle vines and wild roses. She could have sworn she was driving round in circles!

Eventually she stopped at a farmhouse to ask directions to the Hall, feeling that tight grip of tension slowly ebb away. Here beneath the ocean of clear blue sky she felt at peace with herself at last, glad now that she had decided to come to Shropshire. The lady at the farmhouse was kind and helpful, furnishing her with clear and simple directions to Cambourne Hall.

She drove carefully in order not to miss the sharp narrow turns in the lanes, and eventually arrived at the crossroads which she had been expecting. Wearing a frown, Catherine sat still and thoughtful at the wheel. Although she remembered the lady telling her to take the left turn here, for some unknown reason she felt compelled to take the road leading right. The fact left her considerably confused. She looked across the road at the signpost, wondering if she had made some kind of mistake. But the directions were clearly written there – Cambourne left, Netley right.

'Netley... Netley...' She spoke the name aloud, aware of a faint ring of familiarity. Over and over it echoed through her mind; then it was gone, leaving her wondering if she had imagined it. Perhaps she had read about a place called Netley at some time or another? It was the only explanation she could think of. After another puzzled look at the signpost, she dismissed the matter from her mind.

She took the left turn and drove on for another two miles or so, becoming aware of the strangest feeling. Her heartbeat grew disturbingly rapid and her head began to pound like a drum. Catherine wondered what was happening to her – and for no apparent reason at all. Panic instilled itself within her as the pounding persisted, and she was about to stop the car for a breath of fresh air when she saw it, there in the distance, dominating everything which stood around it – Cambourne Hall. How imposing it looked amidst its glorious country setting, playing its role in a very real world!

Every fibre of her being became filled with awe, and there was a feeling in her heart which she could only describe as reverence; a profound respect at being guided here from across the Atlantic Ocean to the house which she felt she knew so well. There were tears in her eyes as she stared at the place, wondering what great power lay concealed within its walls and which had called her from afar. It was a power she could feel right here and now, like an invisible finger summoning her long-awaited presence.

Obeying the command, she drove on, eager to take a closer look at the house. Minutes later, she drew up at the huge wrought-iron gates. Within, nestling beneath the trees, she saw a stone-built lodge, opposite a sign which read: 'Cambourne Hall. Private Estate'.

Catherine focused her eyes down the long tree-lined drive, recalling the day she had completed the sketch, remembering so well the strange way it had drawn her. Now she was here. Oh, it all seemed too incredible!

Moments later she arrived at the house itself, spellbound now with awe and admiration, for it was undeniably magnificent and so much larger than she had envisaged.

Tentatively she stepped out of the car on to the immaculate pebbled drive which circled the house, sighing with pleasure as she did so.

She looked at the features which she remembered so well from her sketch: those old mullioned windows, still partially obscured by the long vines and creepers which grew there to this day; the studded front door and the stone steps leading up to it. The old wooden porch had been removed, so had the statues. But then she already knew that, having seen the photograph earlier.

Her eyes wandered to the neatly kept gardens which fronted the house; to the velvety lawns partially dappled in shade beneath the overhanging trees, which cast their long shadows in this pre-evening hour. Catherine became captivated by the serenely beautiful setting, already feeling remarkably at home in these surroundings. Much as she was enjoying the view, she knew she couldn't stand there gazing all evening. Summoning her courage, she walked up the steps and rang the door bell. Having done so, she was unsure of what to say, deciding that the truth would be out of the question at this early stage. She would just have to play it by ear. If it came to the worst, she could always pretend she had lost her way.

The butler answered the door to her, a tall imposing man of fifty years or so, impeccably dressed in a manner befitting his status. The fellow exuded an air of self-importance which Catherine found intimidating.

'Yes?' he said, his eyebrows raised austerely.

His sombre, matter-of-fact manner rendered Catherine speechless, and she was unable to find her tongue.

Astonishingly the man suddenly smiled at her. 'Ah, I expect you have called in response to Madam's advertisement. But it is a little late,' he said, glancing at his pocket watch, 'and you really should have telephoned for an appointment.'

Catherine was about to explain that she wasn't here in response to any advertisement, when the man suddenly mouthed his most timely interruption. 'Still, perhaps Madam will see you now that you are here? If you would care to give me your name, then kindly go round to the rear door,' – he indicated the way with his finger – 'where Lynette will show you into the waiting room.' Catherine's blank expression prompted him to add, 'You are here in response to Madam's advertisement, are you not?'

Catherine had no alternative but to think extremely fast. An advertisement for an assistant, he had said? This could be just the break she needed. If she admitted to being here in response to some kind of job, then she would at least be able to see the interior of the house; perhaps be fortunate enough to meet the owner. Without further hesitation, she mouthed her reluctant lie. 'Oh yes, I most certainly am. And my name is Catherine Shepherd. Miss Catherine Shepherd.'

The man smiled. 'Very good, Miss Shepherd. If you care to proceed to the rear entrance, I will inform Madam that you are here.'

'Thank you,' said Catherine politely.

The path led Catherine past spectacular rose beds, neatly separated by lawn paths which led on to yet more lawns and gardens. Upon reaching the rear of the house, she came to an abrupt halt. Intuition had always led her to believe that behind the house lay a cobbled courtyard, its perimeter enclosed by stables. She bit her lip, knowing that this was the moment of truth. Did a cobbled courtyard and stables exist there? Or was it just her imagination? Any minute now she would know.

Apprehensive, she closed her eyes before rounding the corner, almost afraid of what she might see. When the suspense was too great she opened them again, catching her breath at the sight which confronted her now.

16

There, opening out before her, was the courtyard and stables which she had so clearly seen in her strange inner vision. Although she had half expected it, actually seeing it left her deeply shaken.

After regaining her composure, she noticed that the courtyard was not, in fact, cobbled as she had foreseen, but concreted instead. The stables were different too, for they had been modernised. Her vision had obviously depicted the courtyard and stables as they had stood in the last century. It was a fact which confused her even further. Pondering for a moment over the missing cobbles, she wondered if perhaps they lay buried beneath the layer of concrete. How interesting it would be to know. Thoughtful, she moved on.

At the rear door she was greeted by two Labrador dogs, who ran around her barking excitedly. Catherine patted their silky heads, and as she did so a chubby round-faced maid appeared in the doorway.

'Phantom! Kim! Here dogs!' she called, then to Catherine: 'Afternoon, Miss. Madam 'as agreed to see you and won't keep you waiting above a minute. Would you care to follow me, please.'

When Catherine stepped into the house, with its low beamed ceiling and timbered walls, the strangest sensation crept over her. Her heartbeat grew rapid again and she was warmed by a feeling which she was unable to interpret. Deeply fascinated, she gazed around, her eyes taking in every detail as she followed the maid along the passage, which had sturdy oak doors leading off on either side. The passage itself was really quite uninteresting. It was the feeling of being there which Catherine found so stirring.

Moments later she was shown into a waiting room, where she took a seat for a moment. Everything was happening so fast, and whilst she was grateful for the chance to be sitting here in Cambourne Hall, she still had no idea what she was going to say to the owner. She had little chance to remedy the situation, for suddenly the maid re-appeared.

'Madam will see you now, Miss,' she informed her.

Catherine cast the maid a smile. 'Thank you,' she replied.

She was led into an impressive hall which boasted many fine antiques, including an old grandfather clock which chimed the half-hour as she passed by. Opposite the studded front door was an enormous mirror, an elaborate item glorified by its intricate gilt frame. Many old oil paintings hung on the timbered walls, the paintings continuing all the way up the grand oak staircase to the panelled landing above.

Seconds later, as she was about to be shown into the drawing room, she experienced pangs of apprehension. A sudden thought: what was the name of the lady whom she was about to meet? A hasty question to the maid told her that her name was Lady Montgomery, and that Catherine must address her by her title.

'Good luck!' she said warmly.

After being announced, Catherine entered the magnificent drawing room. She had little idea as to the kind of attitude to expect from a titled lady, a member of the English aristocracy capable, or so she had heard, of some degree of snobbery and condescension towards less fortunate souls. However, one look at Lady Montgomery's kind face, softly lined by sixty or more years of gracious and compassionate living, indicated to Catherine that she need not have worried. For there, seated behind a Regency writing table, was a true English lady. She was delicately built and had an air of refined, dignified composure which aptly befitted her status. It struck Catherine that she was an extremely attractive woman for her age, tastefully dressed in tweeds and a cream silk blouse, with a row of pearls around her neck and matching earrings peeping from behind her short, wavy grey hair.

Still observing Lady Montgomery, Catherine noticed the look of surprise on her face as she walked towards her, and couldn't help but wonder what had initiated that look. Had she expected someone older or something?

Politely she proffered her hand. 'How do you do, Lady Montgomery. It's good of you to see me,' she said.

When the elder woman failed to respond, Catherine addressed her again. 'Excuse me... is there something wrong?'

Lady Montgomery immediately cast aside her thoughts and apologised for her rudeness. 'Oh, please forgive me, Miss Shepherd. I didn't intend to stare at you so. Only... only you gave me a shock when you walked in because you appeared to remind me of someone. But for the life of me I just can't think who.'

She rose to her feet, using her left hand to shake Catherine's own as her right hand was encased in plaster. 'How do you do, Miss Shepherd. As you can see, I'm somewhat incapacitated at the moment which is why I'm looking for someone to assist me. Being right-handed makes tasks so much more difficult for me.'

'Yes, I can imagine,' said Catherine. 'How did you injure your arm, Lady Montgomery?'

'Oh, I had a nasty fall. Such a dreadful nuisance – although I ought not to complain, for it could have been much worse. Anyway, please sit down, Miss Shepherd,' – she indicated the luxurious four-seater settee – 'then tell me all about yourself. I'm intrigued to know what an attractive American lady is doing in these quiet parts.' A friendly smile enhanced her features as she spoke.

'I'm Canadian, actually,' she replied, 'and am on vacation at the moment.

In fact, I've only just arrived from London. As I find Shropshire such an interesting county, I thought...'

'...Thought you'd like to stay for a while?' interposed the lady percipiently.

'Yes, exactly, Lady Montgomery.'

'So you saw my advertisement and decided to apply for the position?'

'Well... more or less,' came the hesitant reply.

'I'm so glad you did, Miss Shepherd. It's such a refreshing change meeting someone like you. The other applicants were most unsuitable, I'm afraid. '

'What exactly is the position, Lady Montgomery?' she enquired interestedly.

The elder woman smiled. 'Well, I require someone to assist me with my correspondence and so forth, and also to act as my chauffeur. The position will not be a demanding one, Miss Shepherd. Quite the contrary, for my needs are very simple really. However, I must have someone I can rely upon, you understand. I offer the use of a car, a room here at the house, and naturally an agreed remuneration. May I ask if you're interested, Miss Shepherd?'

Catherine looked taken aback by the question, marvelling at the way things had turned out for her. Why, only yesterday she'd had no idea the house existed. Yet here she was today, sitting in the drawing room being interviewed for a job by the owner. It was with careful thought that she considered the matter. The prospect of remaining in England for a while longer was viable, for she didn't have to be back at college until September. Of course, it would mean forfeiting the remainder of her vacation with Jenilee, but she would understand. Besides, anything was worth forfeiting for a chance to stay here at Cambourne Hall, and with a bit of luck she might discover her mysterious link with this house.

'Indeed I am, Lady Montgomery,' she replied enthusiastically. 'I'm very interested in the position.'

Lady Montgomery looked delighted. 'Good. I'm glad. Now, tell me more about yourself, dear. Whereabouts in Canada do you come from? I must admit, you have surprisingly little accent for a Canadian. In fact one might well mistake you for an Englishwoman.'

Catherine laughed. 'Yes, so I'm often told,' she said, 'but I was born in Vancouver and am still at college there.'

'Ah, how interesting. And do you live with your parents, Miss Shepherd?'

'No. My parents died when I was a child. I spent the first three years in a children's home, then went to various foster homes. Now I share a flat with a friend, who is a student at the same college.'

'I see,' said Lady Montgomery. After a moment, she continued. 'Allow me to tell you a little about ourselves. There are only four of us in the family now, my husband and I, our son, Alistair, and my husband's aged cousin

19

who occupies a flat upstairs and who lives quite separately from us. Emma prefers to be independent,' she said, 'and values her seclusion. But she has a nurse who lives with her, so we know she's well taken care of. In addition, there is our butler, Raymond Walker, whom you have already met, Lynette, our maid, and a gardener and several grooms who run the stables. Oh, by the way, Miss Shepherd, may I ask if you're able to type?'

'Yes, Lady Montgomery, I am.'

'Good. That will be a help. And I know you're able to drive, having seen your car parked outside.' She cast Catherine a warm smile. 'Well, you appear eminently suitable for my requirements, Miss Shepherd, and I have pleasure in offering you the position – if you feel you would like it?'

Catherine was delighted. 'Like it? Oh, I certainly would, Lady Montgomery. Thank you!'

'Excellent,' she acknowledged. 'I can't tell you how relieved I am at having found someone like you. I don't usually employ staff without first seeing their references, but in your case, Miss Shepherd, I'm prepared to make an exception. I pride myself on being a good judge of character, and feel certain that you'll fit in very well here.'

'Thank you, Lady Montgomery. I'm sure I shall.'

'Now, Miss Shepherd – or may I call you Catherine?'

'But of course,' she replied.

'What I was about to ask, Catherine, is whether you'd like a room here at the house? Or perhaps you've already found accommodation in the village?'

'Oh, no, Lady Montgomery. I would much prefer to stay here.'

'Good. Do you wish to move in immediately, dear?'

'Yes please,' she said keenly. 'I have all my stuff in the car – oh, now there's a point. I rented a car in London this morning, which I expect means a journey all the way back to return it?'

'Not necessarily, Catherine. If you give me the name of the rental company, I'll ask my son to contact them for you. I'm sure they'll be able to help. Now, I expect you'd like some tea after your journey. Or perhaps you'd prefer coffee?'

'No. Tea would be nice, thank you, Lady Montgomery.'

Whilst Lady Montgomery rang for the maid, Catherine gazed around the room with its antique furniture and ornaments. She had always cherished a fondness for antiques, but had never seen anything to match the ones in this house. A Chippendale influence was dominant, the chairs, glass cabinet and the small occasional tables all being of his particular design. It lent the room an air of distinction. There was also a wide collection of ornaments, including Wedgwood, Worcester and Chelsea porcelain, Regency cut glass and many exquisite items made from silver.

Catherine sighed with admiration. 'This is a beautiful room, Lady Montgomery. So very English,' she said.

'Thank you, dear. My husband, who is a retired diplomat, now pursues his passion for antiques. Needless to say, the house is bursting with them, including those which have been in the family for generations.'

After partaking of tea and a slice of fruit cake, Catherine was shown upstairs to her room which was situated at the entrance to the west wing.

'Dinner is at seven-thirty, Catherine,' Lady Montgomery told her. 'There will only be the three of us this evening as my husband is away on business and won't be home until tomorrow. After dinner I'll show you around the house. I'm certain it will be of interest to you.'

Catherine smiled broadly. Interest was an understatement!

'Do make yourself at home and enjoy your stay with us, Catherine. As it's only a temporary position, perhaps you could treat it as a working holiday rather than just another job. Much more fun that way!'

When Lady Montgomery had left her to settle in, Catherine walked over to the window. What a magnificent view met her eyes across the courtyard and the surrounding country estate; a view of pastures, woodland and fields of golden corn, the rolling Shropshire hills providing the backcloth to the scene. It was so soothing to the eye, and very different from the view she was familiar with back home over the busy Vancouver streets. Catherine smiled to herself, happy beyond words to be here in England and in this very house.

Afterwards she rested on the divan contemplating today's remarkable events. Was it really only this morning that she had seen the photograph of Cambourne Hall in the magazine? How well things had progressed since then – as though the whole thing had been planned in advance! She exhaled a thoughtful sigh. Perhaps it had? Perhaps she was simply following the hand of some predetermined destiny from which there was no escape? Only time would tell.

After a refreshing shower, Catherine changed into a cream linen dress, then, coiling up her hair and adding a touch of make-up to her face, she was ready to go downstairs to dinner.

As she closed the bedroom door behind her, she found herself staring down the landing towards the west wing. For some peculiar reason she felt compelled to venture down that wing, feeling drawn to it like a moth to light. Understandably puzzled, she took a step towards its entrance, wondering what strange force was attracting her so strongly. Something was calling her from that shadowy, antiquated passage; she could feel it in every fibre of her being – and whatever it was it had power. Catherine would like to have pursued the matter, but it was already seven-thirty and she didn't have time.

21

Perhaps she would have the chance to investigate later when Lady Montgomery showed her around the house. She certainly hoped so. Still feeling curious, it remained on her mind as she went downstairs.

In the hall she met the butler, Raymond Walker, who greeted her with a smile and a polite 'good evening'. 'Madam informs me that you'll be working here for a while,' he commented.

'Yes,' replied Catherine. 'I hope to stay until Lady Montgomery's arm has healed.'

He cast her another pleasant smile. 'I thought Madam would offer you the job, Miss Shepherd. I knew the moment I saw you.'

Catherine laughed. 'Really?'

'Anyway, I hope you enjoy your stay at Cambourne Hall, Miss Shepherd. Now, please allow me to show you to the dining room,' he said.

Lady Montgomery greeted her in the panelled dining room a few moments later. 'Ah, here you are, dear. Allow me to introduce you to my son, Alistair. He's been looking forward to meeting you.'

Catherine turned to the tall, sandy-haired distinguished figure by her side; an elegant man who looked the part of an aristocrat. His hair was short and worn side-parted, and he had clear green eyes which gazed at her with interest. As he bore little resemblance to his mother, Catherine concluded that he favoured his father in looks.

'How do you do, Mr Montgomery,' she said politely.

Alistair shook her hand. 'How do you do, Miss Shepherd,' he responded. 'I understand you're from Vancouver and that you're at present on holiday in England?'

'Yes, that's right, Mr Montgomery. I hope to stay here until early fall.'

'Might I enquire what brought you to Shropshire?' he asked.

His direct question caused Catherine unease, but she decided to be truthful – or as truthful as she could be, given the circumstances. 'Curiosity, Mr Montgomery,' she replied. 'Curiosity brought me to Shropshire.' She graced him with a smile. 'You see, I read an article in a magazine and decided to visit the county. I love it here, Mr Montgomery, and as I don't have to be back at college for another six weeks, I decided to stay for a while.'

'I see,' he said. 'Well, we're delighted to have you here, Miss Shepherd, and hope you'll enjoy your stay with us.'

The three continued in polite conversation, Catherine learning that Alistair was a solicitor and that he had his own practice in Marbury. He was also engaged to be married, the event due to take place in three months' time.

Later, over dinner, he said, 'Mother tells me that you're at college, Miss Shepherd. What subject are you studying exactly?'

'I'm studying art,' she replied. 'It's my passion!'

'Art – how fascinating,' said Lady Montgomery, joining in the conversation. 'We had an artist in the family. Her name was -' She broke off in mid-sentence, an incredulous expression on her face. 'Good heavens! I know who you remind me of now! Oh, why didn't I realise it earlier? Perhaps because you were wearing your hair loose this afternoon, Catherine, and I just failed to see the resemblance!'

'By jove, I do believe you're right, Mother!' interpolated Alistair keenly. 'I've been racking my brains all evening wondering who Miss Shepherd reminded me of – Elizabeth Montgomery, of course!'

The pair stared at Catherine in a fashion which clearly puzzled her.

'The likeness is incredible!' exclaimed Lady Montgomery. 'Oh, wait until I tell James. He'll never believe me!'

'Could you blame him?' murmured Alistair.

All this intrigued Catherine greatly, and she was longing to know more about the woman she resembled. 'Who exactly is Elizabeth Montgomery?' she asked interestedly.

'Was, dear,' corrected Lady Montgomery, 'for Elizabeth lived here at the Hall in the eighteen hundreds.'

Catherine felt gooseflesh rise to her skin. 'Please tell me about her, Lady Montgomery,' she asked eagerly.

'Well, Catherine, Elizabeth was the sister of my husband's late father, Edward. Had she lived, then she would have been his aunt. But that was not to be, I'm afraid.'

'Why? Did... did something happen to her?'

'Yes, it did, dear. You see, Elizabeth met with a tragic accident when she was only twenty-two years old.' She sighed, adding, 'I've always had the feeling that Cambourne Hall has never really recovered from her loss. That although it happened many years ago now, her untimely death and its repercussions still linger to this day.'

A shudder ran down Catherine's spine and the gooseflesh returned. 'How dreadful! How did it happen, Lady Montgomery?'

'I'm not exactly sure, Catherine, although I understand that Elizabeth's father, Sir Giles Montgomery, was responsible for her death after bitterly opposing her relationship with a man named Richard de Ville – Count de Ville to be correct. It was a French title, you understand.'

'Our resident ghost,' interpolated Alistair.

Catherine's mouth fell open. 'Ghost? You mean that Cambourne Hall is... is haunted?'

'Oh, yes,' he replied on a grimmer note. 'Most decidedly.' The young man turned to his mother. 'Shall I enlighten our guest, Mother? Or do you wish to tell her?'

'I shall tell her,' said Lady Montgomery. 'You see, Catherine, Elizabeth was an artist – a brilliant one, so they say. Sir Giles doted on her, loved her more than anything else in the world. But he kept her a virtual prisoner here, allowed her no personal freedom at all. Apparently he treated her as though she were still a child, refusing to acknowledge that she had grown into an exceedingly beautiful woman – probably because he was afraid of losing her to some dashing young man. Anyway, history relates that Elizabeth fell in love with Richard de Ville, who was a Frenchman by birth but who came to reside at a nearly manor. Sir Giles hated the de Villes and the trouble began when he discovered that his daughter was having a love affair with Richard. He forbade her to see the man again, although she must have disobeyed him because some time later she bore Richard's child. A few months later Elizabeth met her death and–'

–'And Richard's ghost has haunted the place ever since,' interposed Alistair, 'forever searching for his long lost love. Does the fact frighten you, Miss Shepherd?'

'No, not in the least, Mr Montgomery,' she admitted frankly. 'You see, I don't believe in ghosts.'

Alistair laughed. 'Ah, I see we have a sceptic amongst us, Mother. A disbeliever, no less. Well, Miss Shepherd, perhaps you may change your mind before you leave here. For who knows?' he said, 'perhaps one of these days you'll see him for yourself, for looking as you do, resembling his beloved Elizabeth, he might just mistake you for his long lost love!'

'Shame on you, Alistair!' rebuked his mother. 'You'll frighten Catherine with such stories.' She turned to Catherine. 'Please take no notice, dear. Besides, I doubt there is any truth in the story.'

'Just because you disbelieve, Mother, does not mean there is no truth in it,' said Alistair firmly. 'Father believes there is a spirit here and Aunt Emma most certainly does.'

'Have you ever seen it... the ghost?' asked Catherine, thoroughly intrigued by the story.

'No, never, although I have felt its presence about the Hall. I believe Father has, too.'

Catherine became lost in thought. The story of Elizabeth Montgomery had deeply fascinated her. It was amazing to think they bore a remarkable resemblance and that Elizabeth had also been an artist. She would love to know more about her.

The house was more beautiful than Catherine had envisaged, furnished with valuable antiques and oil paintings, many having been handed down over the generations. During her tour of the Hall, she learned that the house had been built in the year 1541 for William Montgomery, and that it had

24

remained in the ownership of the Montgomery family ever since.

'There are twenty-eight rooms in all,' said Lady Montgomery, 'although only a fraction of that number are in use today. Years ago, of course, many servants were employed here, so the house could afford many rooms. But those days have gone now, Catherine – at least for us,' she said.

In Catherine's opinion, the study was the most interesting room in the house. Hundreds of books, many of them leather-bound, lined the shelves, which covered three walls almost from ground to ceiling, the far wall being dominated by a huge stone fireplace. The floor was of polished oak, and rich burgundy curtains hung at the windows, which afforded unrestricted views across the lawns and gardens. A grey Chesterfield settee occupied the central position in the room, with a walnut desk and chair over in the corner inviting anyone who wished to sit and read.

'What a beautiful room, Lady Montgomery,' admired Catherine, 'and what a fine collection of books you have here.'

'Yes, indeed we have, dear. Many of them are extremely old and valuable, handed down over the years, you understand. Please feel free to look around whenever you wish. You may come across something you'd like to read.'

Some time later the two women walked up the grand staircase together, Catherine's eyes fixed on the spectacular paintings which lined the wall. At the head of the stairs they paused to look out of one of the windows, and it was here that Catherine noticed a photograph on the window ledge. Her heart missed a beat and she picked it up to examine it.

Lady Montgomery saw her interest in the picture. 'Yes, that's a photograph of the house as it stood many years ago,' she said. 'As you can see, it's very old, for there's the porch which once stood outside the front door, and the two stone statues, which even then were crumbling away with age. I believe it was taken sometime in the early nineteen-twenties,' she concluded conversationally.

Catherine was speechless. So she was right! Years ago there had been a porch and two statues here, just as she had sketched them. It was quite a discovery for her, even though it left her as confused as ever.

As they moved on towards the west wing, she asked Lady Montgomery a question. 'On my way here this afternoon I noticed a signpost which gave direction to a place called Netley. The name seemed familiar to me, although I can't think why. Does Netley have any historical interest, Lady Montgomery?' she asked.

Sarah looked thoughtful. 'No... not that I know of, Catherine. Netley is a very small village consisting of half a dozen farms, a few houses, a shop and an old church. With the exception of Netley Manor, which stands on the outskirts of the village, that is about all there is to it.'

'Netley Manor?'

'Yes. It's a very old house which has a great deal of land with it – or it did have in days gone by. At present it's owned by good friends of mine, Sir Arthur Forsythe-Jones and his wife. Years ago, of course, it belonged to the de Ville family... you remember, we talked about them at dinner. But following Richard de Ville's death, the estate was sold and the family moved back to their chateau in France.'

A thought occurred to Catherine. Could it have been Netley Manor which had enticed her so much at the crossroads? For what else was there, she asked herself? Intrigued, she began to piece the facts together in her mind. Netley Manor had once belonged to Richard de Ville, who in turn had been involved in a love affair with Elizabeth Montgomery from Cambourne Hall. That fact alone connected the two houses, if nothing else. But where did she fit into it? It had happened such a long time ago.

Another question to Lady Montgomery: 'When exactly did all that happen? In which year, I mean?'

'Let me think,' said Sarah. 'I believe it was in 1886. Yes, I'm certain it was.'

'1886,' repeated Catherine quietly. 'So long ago now. Who was Sir Giles in relation to your husband, Lady Montgomery?' she asked a moment later.

'Well, Giles was my husband's grandfather, although he died many years before James was born.' She looked at Catherine with a puzzled frown. 'You seem very interested in our family ancestors, Catherine? Is there any particular reason?'

'N... no, of course not, Lady Montgomery. I was just curious, that's all.'

'Giles was a tyrant by all accounts, a man to be avoided at the best of times. Indeed, I believe he caused the de Villes great sorrow all those years ago. Changing the subject for a moment, dear, tomorrow evening I've been invited to Netley Manor for a game of bridge and would like you to drive me.'

'Yes, of course, Lady Montgomery. I'd be delighted.' Catherine felt pleased, for it would provide her with the opportunity to see Netley Manor.

As they walked along the west wing a moment later, Catherine was suddenly overpowered by the same strange feeling which had attacked her earlier: the rapid heartbeat, the pounding in her head which grew louder with every step she took. She held her head and closed her eyes, hoping the feeling would pass. Although she heard Lady Montgomery asking her if she was all right, she was aware of something far stronger calling her from within the room outside which she was standing.

When she reached out to touch the door, the strangest sensation crept over her. Catherine could not have described how badly she wanted to enter that room, drawn by some powerful force which came from within its walls.

Unable to resist that which called her, she placed her hand on the handle and began to turn it.

Suddenly Lady Montgomery pulled her away. 'No, Catherine! No-one must enter that room! Besides,' she added on a calmer note, 'it's always kept locked.'

The sharpness of her voice brought Catherine to her senses and embarrassed, she apologised for her mysterious behaviour. 'I'm so sorry, Lady Montgomery. I... I just don't know what came over me...'

Lady Montgomery looked as shaken as Catherine herself, unable to understand her strange behaviour.

'Why is no-one allowed in there, Lady Montgomery? What's in the room?' she asked after a moment.

'Well, you see, Catherine,' began Lady Montgomery unsteadily, 'before Sir Giles Montgomery died, he stipulated that whilst this house remains in the ownership of a Montgomery no-one must ever use or disturb that room in any way. And that's precisely the way it has been to this day. Everything inside is exactly as it was left in 1887.'

Catherine looked amazed. What an incredible story! 'Whose room was it, Lady Montgomery?'

'It was Elizabeth's room,' she replied, 'left just as it was in honour of her memory. A shrine which remains to this day.'

The words hit Catherine like a bombshell. Over and over they echoed through her mind – Elizabeth's room – Elizabeth's room – Elizabeth's room! She grew faint and had to lean against the wall for support.

Lady Montgomery looked most concerned. The young woman had turned as white as a sheet. 'Catherine, what is it? Are you ill, dear?'

Catherine inhaled a long deep breath and gradually the faintness passed. 'No... no, I'm quite all right, Lady Montgomery. I just felt dizzy for a moment. I expect it's because I'm tired after my long drive today.' She managed a weak smile. 'I think I'll go for a walk in the garden. A little fresh air might do me good.'

In the garden, Catherine still felt disturbed at what had happened to her outside Elizabeth Montgomery's bedroom, unable to cast it from her mind. Darkness was beginning to descend now, so she would have to return to the house soon. She sat for a moment on a seat by the rose beds looking across at it, sombre now amidst the shadows of the approaching night. What was the secret which it held within its walls? And what exactly did it want with her?

For the umpteenth time she recalled standing outside Elizabeth's room, still in awe of the great power which had drawn her. She knew for certain that had the door been unlocked, and had she been alone, then nothing in the world would have prevented her from entering. Curiosity prompted her into wondering what the room looked like from within: old-fashioned, most certainly; grim and sombre, perhaps not. Oh, what she would give for a chance to take a look for herself, and perhaps discover what had called her! However, she realised there was little hope of that.

Weariness was beginning to catch up with her. Today had been the longest in living memory – to say nothing of the strangest. Things had happened to her today which were worthy of a science fiction movie. And wasn't that a fact!

She decided to return to the house by way of the courtyard, and had just left the path which led to the stables when her eyes were drawn towards the ground. She noticed that a small area of concrete which paved the courtyard was badly cracked and broken, resulting in it lying loose and crumbled at her feet. Bending down, she began to remove the pieces in order to expose what lay beneath. Intuition still told her that the courtyard had once been cobbled, and it was with bated breath that she hoped it would not let her down.

Once the larger pieces of concrete were out of the way, she scraped the loose bits of cement with her hands. Suddenly her fingers touched upon another kind of surface, smooth and rounded, telling her without doubt that she had found the elusive missing cobbles. Her face lit in a satisfied smile. She had been right all along. In days gone by the courtyard had been cobbled, just as intuition told her. But how had she known that, she asked herself? Oh, it was all so perplexing, and she wondered how long she would have to wait before learning the answers to her questions. A day? A week? A month? Or indeed perhaps never, she concluded. One thing was clear: she wasn't going to learn anything tonight.

After replacing the bits of concrete, she walked across the courtyard to the house. Suddenly a movement from an upstairs window caught her eye, and looking up she caught a glimpse of a dark, shadowy figure who had been watching her. Catherine felt a chill run down her spine. Thinking of the ghost which was said to haunt the Hall, at that moment she was not entirely sure that she disbelieved the story any more. So many strange and unbelievable things had happened to her today, leaving her with the conclusion that here, at Cambourne Hall in Shropshire, absolutely anything was possible.

CHAPTER THREE

Catherine found little solace in sleep that night, for the events of the day and the confusion in her mind transformed themselves into strange disturbing nightmares. She woke quite suddenly, startled by a feeling of urgency. Switching on the bedside lamp, she glanced at her wristwatch. Oh, was it really only five minutes to midnight? It felt as though she had been asleep for hours. She lay back against the padded headboard and gazed around the room, sombre now in the still of the night. It was remarkable how the atmosphere in a room could alter, depending on the hour. A short while ago it had appeared far less forbidding, when the afternoon sunshine had shone in through the window.

Catherine suddenly realised that she had forgotten to call Jenilee to let her know that she had arrived safely in Shropshire. Her mind had been too preoccupied with other things that evening. She must remember to call her tomorrow, for Jenilee was sure to be worried about her.

She ran her tongue over her lips, feeling thirsty. Earlier, Lady Montgomery had instructed her to make herself at home, so she decided to go downstairs to make herself a cup of tea. As she slipped into her robe and slippers, she wondered what had woken her so abruptly, concluding that it was probably the nightmares from which she had been suffering.

Catherine was on the point of leaving the room when she stopped in her tracks, then, almost trance-like, found herself walking over to the window. Drawing back the curtains, she saw the moon appear from behind a silver-edged cloud illuminating the courtyard and stables with its pale, silver light, lending it an eerie look. For some inexplicable reason her eyes were drawn to a small loft window in the old stable at the far corner of the courtyard. She noticed it was the only stable which had not been renovated and looked completely out of character. Indeed, it gave the impression that it was standing in an era of its own, a solid stone reminder of days gone by. Catherine was unable to tear her eyes away from that window, deeply attracted by something unseen. She felt excitement building up inside her, yet didn't have the least idea why.

Downstairs in the hall the grandfather clock struck the midnight hour. Catherine's excitement intensified and she stared all the harder at the loft window. But nothing happened – nothing at all. A few moments passed and the spell was broken, leaving her both puzzled and disappointed. What a strange experience! Tomorrow, if time permitted, she would investigate the old stable loft, for she had the distinct feeling there was something up there which she must see.

The hall was bathed in moonlight, quiet as the night itself. The only sound came from the old grandfather clock, its pendulum swinging back and forth, back and forth, pleasantly soothing amidst the silence of the night. She paused for a moment to gaze at her reflection through the mirror, looking pale and ethereal now, like a vision of her own ghost staring back at her. Her white satin dressing-gown shimmered in the moonlight, and when she raised her hands to gather her hair to the top of her head she saw herself as though for the very first time. At that particular moment there was an aura of mystery about her which even she failed to fathom. Perhaps it was just this house? Or the midnight hour? Or...? Suddenly she had the strangest feeling of being watched. Staring through the mirror, she could see there was no-one there... And yet...? Couldn't she feel the presence of... something?

A tremble feathered down her spine as she thought about the restless spirit of Richard de Ville, forever seeking his long lost love, Elizabeth. Intrigued by the story, she cast aside her fear and allowed her eyes to roam around the hall, searching every dark shadow to see if there was anything there. But she saw nothing. Only instinct warned her of a presence.

She exhaled a deep breath and decided it was time to make her tea. If Richard de Ville's spirit was here and intended to make itself known to her, then doubtless it would have done so. Perhaps it was just a story anyway. Or perhaps spirits didn't appear to disbelievers... if indeed she was a disbeliever now?

Catherine's first morning at work passed very well. Besides dealing with Lady Montgomery's correspondence, she was asked to check the guest list in preparation for the summer ball due to be held next Friday night.

At eleven o'clock two young men from the rental company called to collect her car, so she didn't have to worry about that any more. Tonight she would call Jenilee in Paris, let her know that she had acquired a temporary job here and that she would not be rejoining her after all. Poor Jenilee! She would be so disappointed, but it just could not be helped.

During her lunch hour, she decided to browse through some of the books in the study. She had intended to visit the old stable loft which had been of so much interest to her last night, but a downpour of heavy rain prevented this. It was whilst she was gazing at the many books which lined the shelves that her eyes became drawn to one book in particular. It stood on a high shelf and was difficult to reach from where she was standing. She couldn't even read its title. A frown creased her brow. She wondered why, out of the hundreds of books before her eyes, she was so interested in that one. Seeing a pair of step-ladders, Catherine eventually retrieved it.

The book was extremely old, bound with a black leather cover which had become cracked around the edges. She caught her breath upon seeing it to be an old edition of the Holy Bible, then sat down on the steps and began to examine its brown, discoloured pages. Suddenly, and quite by accident, she noticed an envelope concealed between its leaves, so she carefully removed it, curious to learn what it was. Written on the envelope was the name Miss Elizabeth Montgomery. Deeply intrigued, Catherine saw that it contained a letter and, unable to resist, she stole a peep at it. Although it was dated May 5th 1887, the handwriting was still clear enough to read. It was headed Netley Manor. Excitement coursed through her body, for one glance told her it had been written by Richard de Ville.

Curious to learn what the letter contained, she began to read the bold, masculine handwriting.

My dearest, dearest love,
No words can truly convey the feelings in my heart as I write. Where should I begin, my love? With my deepest, deepest sorrow at being parted from you for so long? With my joy, my overwhelming happiness at being home again and near you? No, my dearest Elizabeth, for of these sentiments I am certain you are already aware. But what you cannot possibly know, my love, is how very much I have missed you during my long months of absence. The longing in my heart every day for you, to touch you, to hold you, to look upon your face again and to make good my promise to return to you. Oh, Elizabeth, dearest, the thought of you kept me alive all those months, sustained my spirit, my determination to recover and come back to you. Now I am here and nothing in the world can keep me from you.
This evening, at six o'clock, I shall come for you as promised. Be waiting my love. Rid me of the ache of being without you for so long. Marry me and make my happiness complete. There is so much more I wish to say to you, Elizabeth, so much I wish to tell you, but I regret that time does not permit. Before I close, my dearest, allow me to convey how much I love you, Elizabeth. I love you. May you always be assured of that.
Until we meet this evening,
I remain your ever loving servant,
Richard

Catherine stared at the letter for ages, deeply touched by Richard de Ville's heartfelt words. It was obvious that he had loved Elizabeth very dearly. Curiosity prompted her into wondering what happened on the evening of May 5th, 1887, when Richard came to claim her. Did he take her away with him, she wondered? Or instead, had the tyrannical Sir Giles prevented him? What exactly happened to the couple that night?

She remembered being told that Elizabeth had met with a tragic accident whilst she was still very young. Could it have been here at the Hall where she had met her untimely death? As her mind wandered deeper, she found herself wondering what kind of man Richard de Ville had been; what kind of man Elizabeth had fallen in love with – and had loved enough to bear his child. There was so much she wished to know, but with no possible way of finding out. It had all happened such a long time ago. It was a part of the past, dead and buried, and she told herself that she would never know now. She sighed, then returned the letter to the Bible where it had lain concealed all those years.

Later that afternoon, Sir James Montgomery returned home. Alone with his wife in the drawing room, he listened as she related her news about their new employee, Catherine Shepherd, and her incredible likeness to Elizabeth Montgomery. 'If I hadn't seen it with my own eyes, then I would never have believed it, James,' she said. 'And another thing, dear. Catherine is an artist too. Don't you find the fact astonishing?'

James failed to look impressed. Although he did not disbelieve his wife, he did think she was exaggerating a little. 'If you say so, dear,' he replied idly.

'Oh, James,' she tutted, 'you're not listening to me! If Catherine walked into this room now wearing an old-fashioned dress, with her hair worn in an upswept style, then you'd be convinced she was Elizabeth!'

But Sir James believed nothing of the kind. No woman could possibly resemble his late father's beautiful sister. Although he had never seen Elizabeth, he had seen enough photographs of her to know she was unique. No. No-one could possibly resemble her. Not in a hundred years!

'We shall see, Sarah,' was all he said.

'You certainly will, James, because I've invited Catherine to take afternoon tea with us. Perhaps then you will acknowledge the likeness.'

There came a knock at the door and Catherine herself walked in. Sir James was seated with his back to her when she entered, but rose politely to his feet when she approached. He could not have been more startled if it had been Elizabeth Montgomery herself at whom he found himself staring. The sight of her rendered him speechless and he was forced to concede that his wife was correct. This young woman did resemble Elizabeth. And the resemblance was astounding!

James collected himself. 'How do you do, Miss Shepherd,' he said.

His eyes held hers as he spoke and he found it difficult, if not impossible, to tear them away. All the stories which his father had told him about Elizabeth came flooding back to him. Oh, but it was as though he was looking at her now... at Elizabeth!

James shook himself. This woman was not Elizabeth. She was Catherine Shepherd from Vancouver, Canada, and the resemblance was coincidental.

For her part, Catherine found herself staring back at him, stirred by a corresponding sense of recognition. She felt she had met him before somewhere. 'How do you do, Sir James,' she replied.

Still gazing at one another in a manner which baffled Lady Montgomery, the two shook hands.

'Excuse me for staring, Sir James, but have we met before somewhere? In London perhaps, for I was there recently?'

Frowning, the man shook his head. 'No, I doubt it, Miss Shepherd. I haven't been to London for almost a month, Besides, I think I would have remembered meeting a young lady like you. No, Miss Shepherd. We have never met before.'

Catherine smiled. 'Then I apologize, Sir James. It was simply that your face seemed familiar to me.'

Sir James cast his wife a knowing glance. 'Yes,' he said sombrely. 'I'm aware of the feeling, Miss Shepherd. Anyway, my dear, come and sit down and tell me all about yourself. My wife tells me you're studying art at a college in Vancouver?'

He listened with interest as she told him all about herself, and because he had once been a regular visitor to Canada, they found they had a strong talking point. Catherine had taken a liking to the tall, good-looking, silver-haired man whom she estimated to be in his sixties; the father figure whom she had been deprived of during her own childhood.

'Tell me, Catherine,' – he had dispensed with the formality of addressing her as 'Miss' – 'what do you think of my ancestral home? Frankly, I'm wondering if you'll find it a little too quiet here?'

'Oh, no, Sir James. Quite the contrary. And I think your home is beautiful, the finest house I've ever seen. I'd be content to spend the rest of my life here.'

Her remark caused James to feel uneasy. 'Well, I'm pleased you like the house, Catherine, and that you don't feel it's too quiet for you.' He looked at his wife. 'Let's have tea now, dear,' he suggested quietly.

That evening, Catherine walked over to the stables to see the loft at closer quarters. The heavy rain had ceased and the sun made a welcome return to the sky. A young, fresh-faced stable lad greeted her as she approached. Other than he, she saw no-one else around. She entered the old stable, peering through the dim light at the row of stalls which had once been used to accommodate the carriage horses. All manner of old harness hung from rusty hooks on the walls, dated and obsolete now, covered by cobwebs and the dust of many decades. It was sad to see the deterioration which had taken place here. She stood for a moment imagining the stables as they must have been years ago, spick and span, smelling pleasantly of freshly mown hay and leather polish.

One of the stalls, the last in the row, caught her interest and she stepped inside, curious to look round. An old hay rack, still displaying bits of fusty fodder, stood above the stone manger with its iron ring once used to secure the horses, and she saw that the floor was cobbled, just as the courtyard had been. When Catherine turned round she noticed an old side-saddle which stood on a wooden saddle horse in the corner of the stall and intrigued, she walked over to have a look at it.

The saddle was extremely old beneath its layer of dust, far too fragile even to think of removing it from the stand. Running her hand over the dry, cracked leather, she raised one of the flaps and saw the initials which had been engraved on the inside of the leather: the initials E.M. She didn't have to be Einstein to know they stood for Elizabeth Montgomery. So this saddle had once belonged to her, and in all probability her horse had been stabled right here in this stall. The discovery excited her.

Looking around, she noticed a door in the far corner of the stable, and instinctively knew that it led to the loft above. Her heart missed a beat as she walked over to it. Because the door was jammed, she had to use a metal bar to prise it open. Before her now was a flight of stone steps which led up to the loft and, rallying her courage, she began to make her way up. Suddenly a hand grabbed the back of her shoulder and, frightened half to death, she gave a cry.

'Sorry, Miss,' came a deep male voice. 'I didn't intend to scare you, only I don't think it's wise for you to go up there.'

Spinning round, she came face to face with an elderly man who, judging from his attire, she presumed to be one of the grooms. 'Oh, th... that's all right,' she said shakily. 'I was having a look round when I came across these steps. I... I just wondered what was up there.'

The fellow smiled in a friendly fashion. 'Ah, there's nothing up there but mouldy old 'ay and loose floorboards. That's why I 'ad to stop you from going up. Don't want you meeting with an accident now, do we?' His eyes were appraising, for it was a nice change meeting someone like her. Not many strangers came to the Hall these days, not foreigners at any rate. Ah, but it was a far cry from the old days when he had been but a lad here, for the place had been alive with all manner of comings and goings then. 'You'll be Madam's new assistant, the Canadian?' he said.

'Yes, that's right,' replied Catherine pleasantly. 'News travels fast around here.'

'Aye, that it does, Miss!' he agreed. 'My name's Ben – Ben Sykes. I'm the 'ead man around 'ere,' he told her with pride.

'How do you do, Ben. I'm Catherine Shepherd. Tell me, how long have you worked at Cambourne Hall?'

A wide grin transformed his features and his expression became full of interest, for there was nothing he enjoyed more than a good old yarn. 'Ah now, I've been 'ere since I was a nipper. My father, William Sykes, worked 'ere afore me, and 'is father, Ned, afore 'im. Guess us Sykes 'ave been 'ere for generations!' he chuckled.

'I see. How interesting,' she said.

'Per'aps you'd care for a ride out this evenin', Miss? I'd be 'appy to fix you up with an 'orse.'

'Oh, thank you, Ben, but I'm afraid I don't ride. I've never been on a horse in my life.'

Just then one of the lads brought him a message telling him he was needed elsewhere. 'Well, I'll take my leave of you now, Miss,' he said, doffing his cap in gentlemanly fashion. 'Per'aps we'll 'ave a chat another time?'

When he had gone, Catherine turned her attention to the steps again. Although Ben had warned her against going up there, curiosity got the better of her and she went up anyway, although extremely cautiously.

At the head of the stairs was another door, in a far worse condition than the one at the bottom, for its rusty old hinges had completely seized with age. At first it was impossible to open, but then by putting her shoulder to it and pushing hard she found that it began to give. When at last the gap was wide enough for her to squeeze through, she entered the loft.

She looked at the small window which had fascinated her the previous night, seeing it now for what it was, old and dirty, covered by thick cobwebs. Apart from the ventilation openings in the walls, the window provided the loft with its only source of light. Looking around, the whole place gave off an atmosphere of decay and neglect, made worse by the masses of dusty old cobwebs which hung like grubby lace curtains from the walls and roof. A mound of fusty hay was stacked against the far outer wall, and the entire floor was covered with it, concealing those dangerous loose floorboards beneath.

Catherine looked around, deciding that the place was not as eerie as she had initially believed. On the contrary, in bygone days it might well have

35

been quite pleasant up here. She wanted to walk across to the other side, but having been warned of the loose floorboards, she was understandably apprehensive. Then she noticed an old pitchfork resting against the wall by the door, and taking it began to clear a path through the hay directly in front of her, enabling her to establish the soundness of the floorboards beneath. As they all seemed safe enough, she was soon at the other side.

There she stood by the window, asking herself what she was doing up here. Was she going a little mad, or had she really been convinced there was something up here which she must see last night? She recalled the feeling in her heart when she had looked across at the loft from her bedroom window, knowing for sure that she had not imagined it. There was something up here. But what? Looking around, she saw nothing of interest at all.

Catherine considered her situation. She was all alone in a foreign country without a soul to turn to or confide in, following the hand of some unknown destiny without so much as a thought as to where it might lead her. Only now did she stop to question the reason for her being here in Shropshire. All the mysterious events which had taken place since her arrival flooded into her mind, confusing her to the point of wanting to abandon it all. Just forget it and go home! It was a moment of weakness, and in that moment she allowed herself to cry. They were tears of confusion and frustration rather than of self-pity, and because she felt alone and helpless in her search for the answers to why she was here.

It was whilst she was crying that she saw it; there through her tears on the glass pane – the writing on the window. She could hardly believe her eyes. It had been staring her in the face all the time!

She grabbed a handful of hay and cleaned away the dust and cobwebs from the glass, at last revealing the message of love which had been written there all those years ago – words which had probably been scratched on to the glass with a diamond, still there, clear and visible to this day. It was dated July 4th, 1886, and began,

> For my dearest Elizabeth
> Lest you should forget how very much I love you.

Then underneath followed a poem.

> The gift of love I give thee
> A love which will never die
> My heart is yours eternally
> Never to say goodbye.
> Richard.

Catherine read those words over and over again, inspired by each and every one. She smiled softly, for Richard de Ville's poem had filled her with an extraordinary feeling of contentment, provided her with the encouragement which she had needed so badly. Once again she was at peace with herself, prepared to accept whatever lay ahead, regardless of what it might be. She did not question the reason why the poem had been of such reassurance to her; she simply knew that it had and that she was thankful.

Before leaving the loft, she thought of Richard de Ville and Elizabeth Montgomery, wondering if this place had once been the venue of their secret meetings. Whatever it had been to them all those years ago, she herself had found peace here, and with that she walked away, remarkably contented now.

At six-thirty Catherine telephoned Jenilee in Paris.

'Are you all right?' she kept asking, followed by, 'What do you mean – you're stayin' on for a while? A temporary job? What kinda job?' came her despairing voice.

'I'm assisting Lady Montgomery, who has broken her arm,' replied Catherine. 'Oh, Jenilee. I just love it here! The house is beautiful and I've discovered so much. I believe I was meant to come here.'

'I'm not sure I like the sound of that, Cathy. It... it frightens me. Oh, I wish you'd forget it and come to Paris!'

'By the way,' Catherine continued, 'I don't want to alarm you, Jenilee, but Cambourne Hall is supposedly haunted and –'

'What?'

Catherine laughed. 'Sorry. I thought that would shock you. But it really does have a fascinating history. Many years ago an artist lived here at the Hall. Her name was Elizabeth and – wait for it – I'm told I look exactly like her.'

A long silence ensued. The hair on the back of Jenilee's neck was standing on end and prickles of alarm ran down her spine.

'Jenilee? Hello? Are you there?'

'Yeah, I'm here, Cathy. I... I just don't know what to say – except I wish you'd come away from that place! I don't like all this you're tellin' me!'

'But it's all right, Jenilee. Really it is. Please don't worry about me. Call me on Saturday evening, when perhaps there will be more to tell you.'

Jenilee sighed with frustration. 'Yeah, all right – but if you need me in the meantime, Cathy, call me. Promise?'

'I promise,' said Catherine. 'Bye, Jenilee. Talk to you again soon.'

Half an hour later, Catherine was driving Lady Montgomery to Netley Manor. She was feeling exuberant, longing to see the house which Richard de

Ville had once owned. Lady Montgomery pointed out various places of interest as they passed through the little village of Netley; the old black and white timbered cottages, the school, shop, farms and so forth.

'And across the village green is the church, Catherine. You can just about see it through the trees. Several of my husband's ancestors are buried in the churchyard.' She smiled. 'But I'm sure you don't wish to know that.'

On the contrary, Catherine would like to have known more, but was reluctant to ask. Earlier, over dinner, she had ventured to ask Sir James why the old stable had not been modernised along with the rest. He had explained to her that it was because his father, Edward Montgomery, had expressed a wish for the stable to remain as it was; another shrine in honour of his sister, Elizabeth, who had spent much of her time in that stable. Catherine felt grateful to Edward Montgomery, for the old stable and its loft had certainly endeared itself to her.

Catherine was aware they were approaching Netley Manor long before the house came into sight, for the heavy thud-thud of her heart was already telling her. A strong feeling of excitement built up inside her and she stepped a little harder on the accelerator. Moments later the house came into sight, and she gave a long sigh of pleasure upon seeing it at last. 'Oh... it's beautiful!' she said. 'Just as I imagined it!'

'Yes, dear,' said Lady Montgomery, casting her a glance. 'Indeed it is.'

Although the house was just as magnificent as Cambourne Hall, with its long tree-lined drive which led through open parkland down to the beautiful gardens and lawns which fronted it, it was in itself very different in design and construction. Built of stone, at closer quarters it appeared enormous, with large sash windows offering panoramic views across the surrounding countryside. Catherine did not believe it to be as old as Cambourne Hall, estimating it to have been built some time in the seventeenth century.

After parking the car, she followed Lady Montgomery across the gravel drive to the house, where they were shown into the drawing room by the butler. There they were greeted by Lady Forsythe-Jones, a tall, slim lady about the same age as Lady Montgomery; another privileged member of the upper classes, dressed in an exquisite grey dress and matching jacket.

She kissed her friend on the cheek in greeting. 'Good evening, Sarah. I'm so pleased you could come.' She turned to Catherine. 'This must be Miss Shepherd, whom you were telling me about?'

'Good evening, Isobel. Yes, this is Catherine, who has come all the way from Vancouver.'

The two women shook hands, with Lady Forsythe-Jones saying it was a pleasure to meet her, followed by a stream of questions which Catherine politely answered. Afterwards, seeing the Canadian's interest, Lady Forsythe-

Jones kindly showed her around the house.

She found it tremendously interesting, with its many rooms all tastefully furnished with antiques, and in a manner not unlike Cambourne Hall. Curiosity prompted her into wondering what the house looked like a century ago when Richard de Ville had occupied it, and she indulged in silent speculative enquiry as to whether Elizabeth Montgomery had ever been here. Concluding the tour, Lady Forsythe-Jones took her along to her husband's study. It was undoubtedly a man's room, which smelled pleasantly of tobacco and had an atmosphere about it which had not been apparent in the other rooms. The moment she stepped through the door she felt it, like a hand of welcome reaching out to her. She smiled to herself. It was strange how it lent her such a feeling of warmth and contentment.

The walls of the room were panelled in oak, the room itself displaying magnificent antique furniture. Before her, on the outside wall, stood a huge stone fireplace large enough to step into, and having a heavy oak shelf running across the top. Resting on the shelf were various ornaments, Wedgwood mainly, also one or two photographs in small gilt frames. Catherine's eyes became fixed to that shelf, where she concentrated hard on those few attractive ornaments.

Then it happened. The most extraordinary phenomenon imaginable. Quite suddenly she found herself gazing at entirely different objects on the shelf, seeing them through a fine hazy mist, yet seeing them clearly enough to identify what she saw. A row of books now stood in place of the Wedgwood ornaments, held in position by a pair of exquisite statuettes of horses – black horses. Occupying the central position on the shelf stood an old clock made from polished wood, its pendulum swinging gently back and forth, back and forth, rhythmically. She stared at it in amazement. It even displayed the time of day – twenty-five minutes past five. Then the phenomenon passed, leaving her staring wide-eyed at the ornaments again. The unbelievable experience had left her in awe. She had been allowed a glimpse into the past. But why?

Catherine became aware that Lady Forsythe-Jones was speaking to her. 'Well, Miss Shepherd. I hope you've enjoyed your tour of the house. Perhaps you'd care to take a stroll around the grounds before you leave?'

Catherine thanked her most kindly, adding that she would love to see the grounds. On the point of departure, she suddenly asked Lady Forsythe-Jones a question. It was a simple question, one which was asked without any prior thought. 'May I take a walk beside the lake, Lady Forsythe-Jones?'

'But of course you may. Feel free to walk wherever you wish, Catherine. Incidentally, we have a rather interesting summerhouse which you might care to see. Just follow the path and you'll eventually come to it.'

Catherine noticed that Lady Montgomery was staring at her in a highly puzzled manner. Staring back questioningly, she felt her cheeks beginning to burn.

'How on earth did you know about the lake, Catherine?' she asked.

Catherine looked blank. She had no idea at all. 'I... I'm not exactly sure, Lady Montgomery.' she began. 'Perhaps Sir James mentioned it to me before we left this evening?'

'No, Catherine.' She shook her head. 'He mentioned nothing of the kind. I was with you in the room, remember?'

'Then... then someone else? Or perhaps I even saw it from one of the upstairs windows?'

'No, that's impossible, Miss Shepherd,' said Lady Forsythe-Jones, joining in the conversation. 'You see, the lake is completely secluded by trees and is not visible from any of the windows upstairs. Anyway, why are we making such a fuss? It's obvious that someone else told you about it.' She cast Catherine a smile. 'Enjoy your walk. It's of no importance who told you.'

Lady Montgomery's eyes followed Catherine as she said goodnight and left the room. She was totally unconvinced, and felt disturbed by an inner nagging which she could not shake. There was something about Catherine Shepherd which she did not understand. She had felt it all along. But exactly what it was, Lady Montgomery did not know.

Outside in the gardens, Catherine pondered over the puzzling enigma, knowing full well that no-one had told her about the lake at Netley Manor. The information had come from within her own mind; from that same dark corner which had provided her with the insight over the cobbles in the courtyard – indeed, with the insight which had enabled her to sketch Cambourne Hall in the first place. Contemplating the incident which had happened in the study, and now the matter of the lake, she took her stroll around the garden.

Eventually she came across the summerhouse which Lady Forsythe-Jones had mentioned. It was circular in shape, quite large, and made almost entirely of glass. The door was open so she stepped inside, finding it pleasantly warm and inviting. Wooden seats ran around its perimeter and there were several comfortable lounge chairs available. She sat down for a moment relaxing. It was whilst she was looking around that she noticed scratch marks on the glass panes and went across to investigate. Closer examination revealed that the scratches were, in fact, signatures; very old signatures, probably written on the glass with a diamond – as in the loft at Cambourne Hall. Catherine was fascinated and began to read the many names, which were headed by Rachael de Ville, and continued:

22 today – June 20th 1886.

Immediately below was the name Richard de Ville, followed by that of

Elizabeth Montgomery. Smiling, Catherine breathed a long sigh. So Elizabeth had been here after all. She found the fact comforting, glad that Elizabeth had had the chance to see the manor before she died.

Catherine noticed that below Elizabeth's signature was that of Edward Montgomery, whom she knew to be Sir James' late father. More signatures followed, ending with a Bertram Hodgkiss. Catherine was enthralled, and it wasn't difficult to imagine that Rachael de Ville, Richard's sister, had held a birthday party here and that the signatures were those of her guests. She pictured them in their lace and finery; the young ladies in their fashionable bustle dresses, whilst the men perhaps wore stylish flannel trousers and sporty check jackets, with colourful bow ties around their necks. How elegant they must have looked, and how she would have loved to see them for herself. After one last look, allowing her eyes to linger on Richard de Ville's fascinating handwriting, she left the summerhouse.

In melancholy mood, she headed towards the lake, puzzled by the fact that she instinctively knew which path to take, requiring no directions to lead her beside its tranquil waters. She smiled when it came into view, stretching out before her in the distance. It was completely surrounded by woodland, which cast long dark shadows across the water at this late evening hour. The sun, a spectacular ball of molten orange, was beginning to set behind the distant hills, burning the sky with its deep, rich colour. The air was still and calm, without so much as a whisper of the breeze. Indeed, the only sound to be heard was the water gently lapping the edge of the bank, the only movement coming from a flock of wild geese which streamed out across the backcloth of the fiery evening sky.

Feeling wonderfully at peace here, she gazed at her reflection in the water, seeing shoals of tiny black fish meandering their way past the plant life which grew in abundance on the bed of the lake. Something prompted her to look out across the water, and the shock which followed her casual observation was enough to deprive her body of breath. She gasped, for there in the near distance, where only a moment ago there had been nothing but an expanse of empty water, was a rowing boat occupied by two people, a man and a woman. The vision presented itself in exactly the same way as the former one, through that same hazy mist, yet clear enough for her to see the occupants of the boat quite well. Although she was unable to make out their faces, she could see that the man was dark haired and wore a white shirt of some kind, whilst the woman was dressed in a snowy white gown, her face hidden from view by the frilly parasol which fluttered above her head.

Deeply fascinated, Catherine returned her gaze to the man, captivated by the very sight of him. A strong sense of recognition presented itself in her mind, frustrating her to a point at which she longed to cry out to him. But she couldn't speak a word, for his name eluded her. She felt wretchedly tormented, plagued by some distant nagging memory of a kind which bewildered her. Just for a moment she thought she heard their voices drifting out across the water, and strained her ears in an effort to overhear their conversation. But it was no use, although she did hear their happy, carefree laughter. A moment later, and before her very eyes, they vanished into thin air, with not even a ripple on the water to mark where they had been. Catherine was left all alone again, staring out across the empty lake.

Tears burned her eyes and her heart ached from the feelings aroused by the man in the boat. Catherine could neither shake those feelings nor explain them to herself. She could only accept what her heart was telling her. Sadly, she turned and walked away, up through the woods towards the house again.

The incident remained on her mind as she drove back to Cambourne Hall, recalling over and over again the vision of the dark haired man whom she felt she knew so well. But how could she know him? He was from the past! The parasol which the lady had been holding clearly indicated that fact. Who could they have been? And why had they appeared to her like that? Oh, but there was so much she longed to know!

Driving through Netley village, she couldn't help wondering if Elizabeth Montgomery was buried in the churchyard, although it was far too late to go searching for gravestones now. Perhaps she could look tomorrow, if time permitted.

Arriving at the Hall, Catherine parked the car by the stables in the courtyard, then made her way over to the house. A sudden cold chill coursed through the length of her spine. She stopped for a moment and, compelled to look upwards, noticed that she was standing beneath a small balcony. Strange, but she had never noticed it before. Its balustrade was made from wrought iron, and behind it was a pair of old-fashioned French windows. Curiosity prompted her to wonder whose room it was, though she knew for certain that it was situated somewhere in the west wing. Her intrigue deepening, she counted the number of windows along that particular wing, noting that the room was the fifth from the end. Before she retired to bed, she intended to establish exactly whose room that was. Catherine hugged herself as yet another shiver passed over her. A chilling premonition of some kind? After one last look at the balcony, she hurried for the safety of the back door.

By this time darkness had descended, and not wishing to draw attention to the fact that she had ventured into the west wing, Catherine crept along the landing without daring to switch on the light. She examined every dark, nebulous shadow as she counted the bedroom doors until she came to the one she was looking for. Even before she reached it she knew which room it was. She might have guessed! It was the one which had belonged to Elizabeth Montgomery. Although Elizabeth had died years ago now, there was a part of her which still lived on to this day. Indeed, it might well be argued that it was Elizabeth herself who haunted Cambourne Hall, not Richard de Ville.

An overwhelming urge to see inside the room prompted her into trying the door handle. Disappointed, she found it locked. But then she had expected it to be. She sighed with exasperation. Catherine felt that the key to this whole frustrating mystery lay within the walls of that room, and that if only she could get inside, then everything would unravel itself and provide her with an explanation as to why she was here. Discouraged, she made her way to her own room and to her bed.

For a long while sleep eluded her, her tortured mind refusing to provide her with a temporary escape from her wide-ranging thoughts. Lying in her bed, she began to turn the sequence of unexplained events over in her mind, beginning on the day she had completed her sketch of the house. Her detailed analysis of each singular event which had happened to her since terminated with that evening's unbelievable vision of the man and woman in the boat. She took into account the fact that she felt herself familiar with the man.

Afterwards she arrived at a conclusion. It was not one she readily accepted, nevertheless, one which she felt could not be denied. Was it possible she had lived on this earth before? Lived right here in Shropshire? It alarmed her even to consider such a thing, yet it was the only explanation she could think of. It would certainly explain how she knew about the cobbles in the courtyard, the porch over the front door and the two statues, also the lake at Netley Manor. Understandably, the conclusion troubled her, because she felt she had overstepped the boundaries of believability even to suppose she had been delivered back to a house where she had lived in an earlier lifetime. Catherine considered the matter. Perhaps such things were possible? Perhaps untold wonders did occur in this remarkable universe in which we live? Who was to say? After considerable thought, she allowed herself to accept that, yet in her own case was not prepared to take the matter any further. She would not allow her mind to stray beyond the point in question that she might have led an earlier existence. That was as far as it went. She then banished the matter from her mind.

Eventually she fell asleep, but woke with a start just before midnight. Compelled to leave her bed, she threw back the quilt and walked over to the window. Once again her eyes were drawn towards the loft, and for a long few moments she simply stood there watching, waiting, though for what she did not know. Just like last night, she heard the clock downstairs strike the hour of midnight, and with her eyes glued to the window she felt excitement building up inside her. But disappointment followed, and she was left with no alternative but to return to bed.

In their bedroom in the east wing, Sarah Montgomery chatted to her husband. 'Catherine is such a nice young woman, but she troubles me, James.'

'Troubles you? In what way, Sarah?'

'Well, take this evening, for instance. After Isobel had shown her around the house, Catherine suddenly asked if she might take a walk beside the lake.'

James laughed. 'But why should that trouble you, dear?'

'Ah, but you see,' his wife pointed out, 'no-one had mentioned anything about a lake at Netley Manor. She... she just seemed to know. I also find it curious that only yesterday she expressed an outright interest in Netley. Don't you think that strange for someone who has never been to England before, let alone to a tiny village in the middle of nowhere? And another thing,' she continued; 'yesterday, when I was showing her around the house, she begged me to allow her into Elizabeth's room. Begged me with a desperation which I found alarming.'

James rubbed his chin, his expression serious now. 'I see. Anything else, Sarah?'

'Yes... yes, there is something else, now that you ask. This will sound ridiculous, but when Catherine walked into our drawing room yesterday for her interview, the most peculiar feeling struck me. I felt that I was the outsider in the room, not she. That she belonged here more than I.' Sarah saw her husband's expression darken. 'I told you it would sound ridiculous, James,' she said.

'I don't think it so ridiculous, Sarah. I too have sensed something strange about Catherine. I find her resemblance to Elizabeth Montgomery astounding. Why, until I saw her for myself, I would never have believed it possible for two women to look so much alike.'

Sarah nodded in agreement. 'Yes, the likeness is remarkable. So is the fact that, like Elizabeth, Catherine is also an artist. Coincidence, I suppose.' It was more a statement than a question.

'Coincidence?'

'Why, yes, dear. What else could it be?'

Locked deep in thought, James fell silent. His mind was troubling him, taking him down a most disturbing path until he was compelled to check his thoughts. He pulled himself together. Perhaps tiredness was accounting for his illogical conclusions? 'What else indeed?' he murmured quietly. 'What else indeed?'

CHAPTER FOUR

After breakfast the following morning, Catherine was greeted by her employer. 'Did you enjoy your visit to Netley Manor, Catherine? And did it live up to your expectations?'

'Oh, yes, thank you, Lady Montgomery. I enjoyed it tremendously. I thought the house was fascinating!'

'And did you... did you manage a stroll around the lake?' she asked tentatively.

Their eyes met and held, causing Catherine mild embarrassment. 'Y... yes, I did and I found it well worth the visit. It was so quiet beside the water.' She recalled the vision of the man and woman in the rowing boat and added, 'I... I was so glad I went.'

'Yes, I'm sure,' said Lady Montgomery quietly. 'Anyway, Catherine, my husband is taking me out to lunch today so I won't be needing you this morning. Perhaps this afternoon you would assist me with the final arrangements for tomorrow evening's ball? Dear me, it hardly seems a year since the last one. How time flies when one is getting old.'

Catherine decided to make good use of her time by visiting Netley church. Just as she was preparing to leave, Alistair appeared.

'Good morning, Catherine,' he addressed her in his beautiful upper-class voice. 'I was wondering if you'd care to accompany me on a ride around the estate this morning?'

'How nice of you to ask, Alistair. But I'm afraid I don't ride. I've never been on a horse in my life.'

The young man looked surprised. 'Then we must remedy that one of these days. It's a positive disgrace to reside here at Cambourne Hall and be unable to sit on a horse proficiently.' He cracked his riding crop against the palm of his hand and smiled. 'Perhaps I shall have time to teach you next week? In the meantime, enjoy your morning, Catherine.'

It was a glorious day, warm and sunny. Had the church been nearer, then Catherine would have walked to Netley in preference to driving. She paused for a moment beside one of the rose beds to say good morning to the elderly gardener who was busy cutting roses.

'Mornin', Miss,' he replied. 'Lovely day!'

'It certainly is,' she agreed. Her eyes beheld the flowers which he had just cut and placed in a basket. 'What beautiful roses,' she commented, 'and such lovely colours, too.'

'That they are, Miss.' He cast her a smile. "Ere, I'll make you a present of one. Pick which one you'd like.'

Delighted, Catherine thanked him, then chose a rose of deepest red, its petals like velvet to the touch. She then secured it to her dress with a safety pin which she found in her purse. After saying goodbye to the old man, she continued on her way.

Halfway up the drive she slowed down the car to peer through the passenger side window. Her interest was aroused by a bridle path which led through the field adjacent to the drive. A sense of curiosity mingled with a strong feeling of familiarity prompted her into wondering where it led. Had she not been visiting the churchyard, she would certainly have taken a walk down there now. Perhaps she would be able to take a look this evening.

Sometime later she was strolling through the churchyard, past the many graves which lined each side of the path, and right up towards the church door itself. Reverently she entered the beautiful old building, where she knelt to say a prayer. Afterwards she walked up to the altar, admiring the magnificent stained glass windows which portrayed Christ with His disciples. Vases of fresh flowers decorated the window ledge beneath, all lovingly arranged by the local women.

Outside in the sunshine again, she began to examine the names on the headstones, intent on finding the Montgomery family grave. But it was nowhere to be seen amongst the graves at the front of the church, so finally she followed the path around to the rear. Here she found the headstones much older than the others, some of the names being impossible to read, the stonework having crumbled away with age. As she walked along the path towards the far corner, she suddenly froze in her tracks. Not for one moment had she expected to see the de Ville family grave here in Netley churchyard. Nevertheless, there it was before her, their names clearly written on the headstone.

Catherine's face paled as she read the two inscriptions: Robert de Ville. Died January 19th 1886. Aged 59 years. Below that, Richard de Ville. Son of Robert. Died May 6th, 1887. Aged 30 years.

The strength ebbed from her body and she suddenly felt faint. Her heart was pounding, her eyes refusing to tear themselves away from his name. Just how long she stood there staring at it she did not know. All she was aware of was a deep sense of pain and an even deeper sense of loss. Catherine wondered why she should feel that way about a man who had lived so long before her, favouring the logical explanation that perhaps it was because he had endeared himself to her after she had read his poem on the loft window; also the letter which he had written to Elizabeth. The letter! It was then she remembered the date on that letter – May 5th 1887. No. No! Richard de Ville had died the day after writing to Elizabeth promising to take her away from Cambourne Hall! Her head began to reel and she was saddened beyond words at the fate which had befallen him all those years ago.

Limply she subsided to her knees beside the grave. There were no flowers beneath the headstone. Instead, the grave had been covered by a layer of loose white chippings which looked remarkably new, considering the number of years it had been there. It puzzled Catherine. Someone must have been tending it – But who? Lady Montgomery had told her that following Richard's death, his family had returned to France. What a mystery it all was.

She noticed that a clump of grass had managed to take root amongst the chippings, and reached to unearth it. Whilst doing so, the rose she was wearing suddenly fell on to the grave. Catherine lowered her hand to retrieve it, but found herself overcome by reluctance. So instead she left it lying there beneath the headstone where it had fallen. A single red rose on the grave of a man whom she had never known. It was a simple little gesture, yet somehow it signified so much. Catherine smiled as her eyes beheld his name, feeling strangely contented now. 'You're welcome to my rose, Richard,' she murmured tenderly.

Time was getting on, and if she didn't find the Montgomery family grave soon, then she would have to leave without seeing it. Rising to her feet, her eyes strayed across the path. She jumped when she saw it there before her – the very headstone she was looking for. It had been there all the time, directly opposite where she had been kneeling.

A cold chill passed over her when she read the inscription: Helen Montgomery. Died September 6th, 1870. Aged 36 years. Another shudder upon reading the inscription below: Elizabeth Montgomery. Daughter of Helen. Died May 5th, 1887. Aged 22 years. Catherine gasped with shock. She read them again, unable to believe that which was so clearly written. Elizabeth Montgomery had died on the 5th of May, 1887, on the very day when she was to have left Cambourne Hall with Richard de Ville.

Her heart sank in her breast and she felt utterly demoralised. What had happened on that fateful day, she wondered? And what had happened to Richard only a few short hours afterwards? Something awful must have occurred to have caused their deaths within such a short time of one another.

Despite her wretchedness, she read on: Giles Montgomery. Husband of Helen. Died June 26th, 1887. Aged 60 years. Charlotte Montgomery. Sister of Giles. Died March 27th, 1907. Aged 78 years. The last inscription was that of Edward Montgomery. Son of Giles and Helen. Died November 3rd, 1940.

Aged 79 years. As there was no headstone to mark the grave of Elizabeth and Richard's child, Catherine presumed that he or she had been buried elsewhere.

Once again she stared at Elizabeth's name and shuddered. An ominous silence prevailed over the churchyard now. Even the birds had stopped singing. The sun disappeared behind a dark, heavy cloud which had suddenly appeared from nowhere, and a chilling wind sprang up rustling the trees around her. A sense of uneasiness stole over her. Catherine knew it was time to go.

At three o'clock that afternoon Sir James and Lady Montgomery returned from lunch, and for the rest of the day Catherine was busy assisting her employer with the final arrangements for the ball. 'How many years has the ball been held here, Lady Montgomery?' she asked interestedly.

'Ah, let me see. I believe James said that the first ball was held in 1862, and that it became an annual tradition after that, although it was cancelled in 1887 following Elizabeth's and Sir Giles Montgomery's deaths. Giles died only a few weeks after his daughter.'

'Yes, I know, Lady Montgomery. I visited Netley church this morning and saw the Montgomery family grave.'

'Oh, did you, dear? I wouldn't have thought it of any interest to you. Had I known you were going, I would have given you some flowers to take along.'

'I was surprised to see the de Ville family grave,' she confessed. 'I had a shock when I saw it.'

Lady Montgomery's eyes grew questioning. She found the Canadian's interest in the two families most perplexing. 'Ah, so you saw it, did you? And yes, I suppose it is ironical that the graves are so close together – considering the hatred which existed at the time... well, on Sir Giles' part, anyway.' She gave a sigh. 'What was it all for, I wonder? There was no winner in the end. No satisfaction gained by the death of a so-called enemy. What it really amounted to was the sheer waste of two young lives. So sad,' she said. 'Oh, by the way, Catherine, Cousin Emma has expressed a wish to meet you this evening. I must admit, you're very honoured. Emma doesn't take kindly to strangers these days. The old dear is so dedicated to her seclusion, you know.'

'Cousin Emma?'

'Yes. You remember, I told you about her on the afternoon you arrived. She's my husband's aged cousin who occupies the flat upstairs.'

'Oh, yes,' said Catherine, remembering. 'I shall be pleased to meet her whenever she wishes, Lady Montgomery.' She had hoped to walk along the bridle path that evening, but it would have to wait now. It was then she decided to ask Lady Montgomery where the path led.

'Well, Catherine, it just leads on through the fields and eventually terminates near the main Cambourne Road. Why do you want to know?' she asked.

'Oh, no reason really. I just happened to notice it this morning and wondered if there was anything of interest down there.'

'No, dear. There's nothing of interest at all... except fields and woodland. Of course, years ago there used to be an exquisite bluebell wood in that area. It was the highlight of the whole estate by all accounts. I wouldn't know if it's still there, though. I haven't been beyond Lower Coppice for years now.'

Lady Montgomery's statement was of great interest to Catherine. A bluebell wood? Back home she had painted a bluebell wood and it was one of her favourite pieces. Her mind ran riot again. Was it possible that it was the same wood featured in her painting? Or was it just coincidence, she wondered? It was just another puzzling enigma along with all the rest, and would remain so until she'd had the chance to see the wood for herself.

At six o'clock sharp, Catherine was shown to Miss Emma Montgomery's flat by Lady Montgomery. 'I do hope Emma won't bore you,' she remarked, leading the way up the back staircase. 'I can't think why she's asked to see you at all.'

'Oh, but I'm looking forward to it, Lady Montgomery. I'm certain we'll find something to talk about.'

'But of course!' replied Sarah, 'you could persuade her to tell you about Elizabeth and Richard. Emma is certain to know what happened to them.'

Catherine questioned the cryptic remark. 'I don't understand, Lady Montgomery. How would Miss Montgomery know what happened to them?'

'She would know what happened, Catherine, because Emma is Elizabeth and Richard's daughter,' came the reply.

'What?' Catherine's mouth fell open.

Lady Montgomery laughed. 'You look surprised, Catherine?'

'Well... well, yes I am. Why, only this morning I was searching for her grave in Netley churchyard.'

'Oh! Don't tell her that, for goodness sake. Emma is determined to outlive us all!'

The two shared a laugh. Catherine still felt incredulous of the fact that Elizabeth and Richard's daughter was still alive.

'But how old is she exactly?'

'Emma was ninety-four last birthday, but she doesn't look a day over seventy. She may be old in years, Catherine, but she's far from being senile, bless her. In fact, she's an amazingly intelligent woman for her age. I doubt anyone could pull the wool over Emma's eyes!'

Upon reaching the old lady's flat, the door was opened to them by Miss Mavis Plummer, Emma Montgomery's middle-aged nurse; she was a tall, bespectacled woman who had sharp, pointed features and small deep set eyes.

'Good evening, Mavis,' Lady Montgomery greeted her pleasantly. 'I've brought Miss Shepherd along to see Emma. I trust it's convenient for her to visit?'

Miss Plummer managed a strained smile. 'Yes, of course. But she mustn't stay too long now,' – here she wagged a pointed finger – 'for Miss Montgomery is a very old lady and -'

'Who is it, Mavis?' interrupted a questioning voice from within.

'It's Miss Shepherd to see you, Emma. I was just telling her . . .'

Again the voice interrupted her. 'Then stop wasting time and show her in. It's me she's here to see – not you!'

Mavis Plummer's thin lips curled in a humourless smile, and without further ado she showed the two guests into Emma's small living room.

'Hello, Emma,' said Lady Montgomery, 'and how are you this evening?'

Emma cast her a look which was almost grudging. 'I'm very well, thank you, Sarah. I'm as strong as an ox and you know it!' She then shuffled herself around in her armchair, focusing her attention on Catherine. Her old eyes narrowed. 'Is this the Canadian?' she asked.

'Yes. This is Miss Catherine Shepherd from Vancouver.' She turned to Catherine. 'Catherine, this is Miss Emma Montgomery.' Sarah then stepped aside enabling the two women to see each other more clearly.

A long silence prevailed whilst they stared at each other in what may well have been described as mutual fascination. Never in her life had Catherine been more conscious of another human being, and the feelings which flooded into her heart whilst gazing at Miss Montgomery were completely indescribable. Neither woman spoke, both far too aware of the other and of their own personal feelings to want to spoil it with words. Whatever Catherine had expected that evening, it certainly wasn't this.

An overwhelming urge to touch the old lady instilled itself within her and slowly, without so much as a word, she held out her hand. Emma Montgomery's bright blue eyes blurred for a moment, then, responding, she raised a shaky hand towards Catherine's. Both felt it when they touched, although the feeling they experienced was too extraordinary, too far above them, to put into words.

The silence was rudely shattered when Emma suddenly spoke, her rasping voice causing Catherine to jump. 'Leave us, Sarah!' she said.

Lady Montgomery looked hypnotised by the two women's reaction to one another and was staring at them, transfixed.

50

'I said leave us, Sarah!'

Meekly, the younger woman obeyed. 'See you at dinner, Catherine,' she said, then quickly left the room.

Catherine collected herself. The last few moments had been like a dream. She couldn't imagine what had come over her. 'Please forgive me, Miss Montgomery. I'm forgetting my manners. I'm very pleased to meet you.'

The old lady smiled, showing worn, creamy teeth. 'And I'm pleased to meet you, Miss Shepherd. Very pleased. Now, come and sit beside me. I want to know all about you.'

Whilst chatting together, Catherine's eyes were drawn to the cameo brooch pinned to Emma's black woollen dress. It stirred an odd feeling inside her. She was convinced she had seen it before somewhere.

'What are you looking at?' demanded Emma, although not unkindly.

'I... I apologise, Miss Montgomery. I didn't mean to stare. Only... only it's your brooch. I'm certain I've seen one exactly like it. But I can't think where.'

Miss Montgomery raised her eyebrows. 'Are you sure? This is a very unusual brooch,' she said, 'and it's old.'

'Oh, yes, I'm quite sure. I recognise the design; the lady's head in the centrepiece and the fine gold filigree setting. So beautiful!' she said.

'Indeed it is,' agreed the elder woman quietly.

Miss Montgomery proceeded to ask question after question, beginning with Catherine's childhood in Vancouver. Although Catherine was not averse to her lengthy inquisition into her background, she was unable to understand the avid curiosity with which it was conducted. Eventually she formed the opinion that Miss Montgomery was probably a curious old soul by nature and nothing more. Her eyes travelled over her whilst she was talking. How amazingly well she looked considering her age! Indeed, it was difficult to believe that she was ninety-four years old. Although her face was lined, she had very good skin, her remarkable bone structure indicating her to be a lady of fine breeding. Yet wasn't that understandable? After all, Emma was the daughter of Elizabeth Montgomery and Richard de Ville. She had also been blessed with a good head of hair, long and thick and as white as the driven snow, now neatly coiled around her head. Her eyes, almost as blue as Catherine's own, displayed an amazing alertness for a woman of her years, and they gazed back at her in a look of reflective interest.

'I understand you're an artist, Miss Shepherd. Tell me, is your work contemporary, or...?'

'Oh, no, Miss Montgomery. Definitely not. All my work is set in the last century.'

The old lady smiled. 'How very interesting. Do tell me about it, please.'

Obligingly, Catherine began to describe her paintings, naturally omitting the one of the house. All ears and interest, Miss Montgomery sat on the edge of her seat hanging on to every word.

'Incredible!' she exclaimed at last. 'Quite incredible! But are there not one or two which you have failed to mention, Miss Shepherd? Those which are perhaps... special to you in some way?'

Catherine could not have looked more shocked. Why, it was as if Miss Montgomery knew. Actually knew! Bordering on uneasiness, her voice faltered when she spoke. 'Sp... special to me? I... I don't understand...?'

Again the old lady smiled. 'Then let me put it to you another way, Miss Shepherd. Have you ever painted anything else besides those which you have already described?'

The question had been clear enough, and Miss Montgomery sat waiting for an answer.

'Well... well, I have painted a portrait,' she confessed, still unable to understand the old lady's remarkable insight.

'Ah... a portrait!' she echoed, then raised a frail old arm and pointed directly past Catherine's head. 'You mean something like that?'

A silence filled the air, broken only by Catherine's gasp as she turned to see the painting which hung on the wall behind her. Mesmerized, she moved to stand before it, beholding the captivating vision with both wonder and awe. It was exactly like looking at herself! Had she been wearing the same pink gown, and had her hair been worn in that upswept style, then the two would have been identical. She required no-one to tell her the name of the woman featured in the portrait, for wasn't it pounding through her head with the most disturbing clarity?

Overwhelmed, she studied it more closely, taking in every detail of Elizabeth Montgomery's exquisite beauty. That lovely oval face with its smooth, creamy skin; the high aristocratic cheek bones, the cheeks softly flushed with colour, so exact in every detail to her own. All her thick, dark hair with its long wispy tendrils; those captivating cornflower blue eyes fringed by long thick lashes and arched by delicate brows. There was an aura of mystery about her, as though she were in possession of some wonderful secret, and she exuded a happiness which her admirer could almost feel; one which came directly from the heart and which straight away told Catherine that she had already met and fallen in love with Richard de Ville. The artist, a certain Frederick Llani, had not only captured her beauty and serenity, but had also succeeded in capturing her mood. That was something which would live forever in the painting and which nothing, not even time itself, could destroy.

The sound of Miss Montgomery's voice suddenly broke the electric silence in the room. 'Do you know who she is, Miss Shepherd?'

'Yes, I know,' replied Catherine. 'It's Elizabeth, isn't it?'

'Yes, Miss Shepherd. It's Elizabeth. Are you shocked? At the likeness you bear her, I mean?'

'Yes... yes I am, Miss Montgomery. The likeness is remarkable.'

'Yes, remarkable, Miss Shepherd,' she agreed disconcertingly, as Catherine returned to her seat.

After a short silence, Catherine plucked up courage to ask Emma about the couple. 'What happened to cause their deaths within a day of each other, Miss Montgomery?'

'Who told you that?' came the sharp reply.

'Why, no-one, Miss Montgomery. I visited Netley church this morning and saw the family graves.'

That appeared to please her. 'Ah, I see. Tell me, dear, were they tidy?'

'Oh, yes, most certainly. In fact, your father's grave appeared as though it had been tended recently. It puzzled me at the time.'

Miss Montgomery smiled. 'That's because I arranged to have it tended, Miss Shepherd. You see, I am his last living relative in England. Although I was born out of wedlock and was unable to take his name, I am still his daughter – and have never forgotten it. Oh, it was no fault of his that he and my mother never married. No, that was my grandfather's doing. I dare say things would have turned out quite differently had he been a kinder, more sympathetic man. But as things turned out, I was orphaned at a very early age, whilst he was unable to live with the burden of his guilt.'

Catherine listened to the story with eagerness. 'But what happened, Miss Montgomery? Why was your grandfather so opposed to your parents' relationship?'

'You appear very interested in my parents, Miss Shepherd?' she said, raising an enquiring eyebrow.

'Yes, I am, Miss Montgomery. I'm very interested. Won't you please tell me all about them? About your mother and her life here.'

'Why? What do you want to know?'

Emma's question caused Catherine unease and she directed her reply somewhat flippantly. 'Oh, just idle curiosity. Call it a foreigner's interest in the history of an old English country house. A story to tell the folks back home.'

Miss Montgomery's gaze grew more disconcerting and Catherine felt that she wasn't fooling her in the least. She believed that the reticent old lady was in possession of more truths and answers than she had confessed to during their conversation. Besides, how had she known about the existence of her other two paintings? How could she have known? There was something about her which Catherine could not fathom. She had felt it the moment she had seen Miss Montgomery, knowing for certain that she had felt it too.

Miss Montgomery was speaking again. 'Very well, Miss – oh, fiddlesticks to all this 'Miss' business. My name is Emma. And I shall call you . . . ?'

'Catherine.'

'Very well, Catherine. I'll tell you everything you want to know.' Her eyes began to twinkle with amusement. 'A story to tell the folks back home!'

Catherine listened intently as Emma began her story.

'Elizabeth was a wilful woman with a tremendous capacity for life and happiness. Following her mother's death whilst she was still a child, she was brought up by her father, Sir Giles. Oh, he thought the world of her, and showered all his love and devotion upon her whilst ignoring the needs of his son, Edward. I understand Sir Giles made poor Edward's life a misery, always complaining that he was too soft and gullible. But Edward and Elizabeth were very close and I believe she made up for Giles' insensitive behaviour. Anyway, to get on with the story. Although my grandfather gave Elizabeth everything a father could give, when she came of age, he deprived her of the thing she wanted most – Count de Ville, my father. It arose from the fact that in his younger days my grandfather had been desperately in love with Rebecca Pascal, who later became Richard's mother, you understand. But Rebecca turned him down, and some time later married the Marquis de Ville, a Frenchman.'

'Robert de Ville?'

'Yes, that's right. Anyway, Giles grew bitter and hateful, and it was then that the feud between the two families began. Oh, it was all Sir Giles' fault. He behaved despicably towards Rebecca and her husband and caused them a great deal of trouble. Eventually matters became so bad that the two men fought a duel, and although Giles did not kill Robert outright, he did succeed in crippling him for life. Shortly afterwards the de Villes left England for their chateau. It was there that Richard and his sister Rachel were born.'

'Was Netley Manor sold then, Miss Montgomery? Sorry, Emma.'

'Oh, no, Catherine. It was left in the care of the steward until they returned many years later. Sadly Robert died, and soon afterwards Giles learned of his daughter's love affair with Richard. My grandfather turned mad with rage and forbade Elizabeth to see him again. But as I told you, Catherine, my mother was wilful and pursued the callings of her heart. Something which caused a good deal of trouble in the household, by all accounts!' She chuckled.

'During the summer of 1886, my father was called away to France. Unfortunately this occurred only a short time after Sir Giles' heart attack. I'm told that although my father pleaded with Elizabeth to accompany him, she refused. Uncle Edward said it was because she had promised to nurse her father back to recovery and that she would not break her word. So Richard went alone, promising to return a few weeks later. Sadly, during that time he suffered a dreadful accident which left him paralysed for months, thus preventing his return to England and to my mother.'

'How dreadful, ' said Catherine. 'That must have been terrible for them.'

'Yes, apparently it was. You see, not long after my father had left for France, my mother found that she was expecting me. She had a very difficult time during those months, having to face up to my grandfather and, of course, the shame and disgrace of it all.' She raised her eyebrows and smiled. 'It was the Victorian era, remember. Things were very different in those days. It was considered most improper for a woman of breeding to give birth outside wedlock. Indeed, my grandfather stated that I was to be adopted after making my entrance into the world, although for some reason he changed his mind and allowed my mother to keep me.'

Catherine listened with fascinated interest, although she was still to learn how the unfortunate couple met their untimely deaths. 'What happened after that, Emma?' she enquired eagerly.

The old lady clasped her hands together in her lap and continued. 'Well, in the spring of 1887, my father suddenly returned to England, and one night he came to the Hall to take my mother and me away with him.'

Catherine thought of Richard de Ville's letter in the library and smiled. Of that she already knew.

'Unfortunately,' said Emma, 'my grandfather was present in the house and refused to allow us to be taken from him. Apparently there was a dreadful scene in the hall downstairs, whereupon my father was ordered from the house. Determined to leave with him, my mother ran upstairs for the valise which had been left behind in the bedroom. I understand it contained my clothes and that she would not leave without it. Anyway, my grandfather followed her, and upstairs in her room an argument broke out between them. No-one could say what happened after that, for my grandfather refused to speak of it. But somehow my mother fell to her death from the balcony window.'

Catherine felt her blood run cold. 'Elizabeth actually fell from the balcony? And to her death?'

'Yes, she did,' said Emma. 'It was a dreadful tragedy which left its mark upon the house throughout the years which followed – right up until now, in fact.'

There was a painful tightness in Catherine's throat and her mind was whirling chaotically. Elizabeth Montgomery met her demise after falling from her balcony on to the courtyard below – on the very spot where she herself had experienced that strange chill. It was as though she had shared the same kiss of death which Elizabeth had experienced all those years ago.

The thought of it chilled her to the bone.

'You're very quiet, Catherine,' observed Emma. 'What is it?'

'N... nothing,' she lied. 'It just came as a shock to me to learn about your mother. What happened the following day?'

'Well, the following day my father and grandfather fought a duel, and it was then that my grandfather shot and killed him.'

Emma saw the grief which swept Catherine's face. 'Do you wish me to continue?' she asked quietly.

Catherine could barely speak, shocked into silence by Emma's statement. Her heart was aching too, and she wondered why she should feel such pain upon learning of the fate of Richard de Ville, a man she had never known. 'Y... yes, please do,' she said at last.

'Very well,' said Emma. 'Now, where was I? Oh yes, after the duel had taken place, Edward vowed never to speak to Sir Giles again – and I'm told he kept that vow. So my grandfather found himself living in sorrow and seclusion, plagued by guilt at what he had done. Eventually, unable to live with that guilt, he hanged himself from Hangman's Tree a few weeks later.' The old lady sighed. 'Well, Catherine, there you have it. Now you know.'

It seemed an age before Catherine was able to snap herself out of the deep sense of sadness brought on by the story she had heard. What a tragic waste of three lives: Elizabeth, Richard and then Sir Giles himself! Had Giles been a more sympathetic man, then history might well have recorded an entirely different story. But as it was, his hatred had destroyed them all.

'How sad that your parents died the way they did, Emma, and that you were orphaned so young in life! Who looked after you when Sir Giles died?'

'I was brought up by Charlotte and Edward,' she replied, 'who told me about my parents. They were marvellous to me. Edward was just like a father, and I suspect it was I who prevented him from marrying until he was forty-eight years old. He was far too dedicated to my upbringing to consider his own life and pursuits.' A sudden twinkle lit her eyes. 'Great-aunt Charlotte told me that he had cherished à fondness for Rachael de Ville. However, after my father's death, Rebecca took Rachael to their chateau in France where she eventually married a Frenchman. Edward married a widow, Jennifer Thornton-Taylor, who was thirteen years his junior. They had only one child, James. When Edward died, Jennifer went to America to visit relatives, and there she became ill and died. It was all very sad. By the way, I spent a great deal of time at the chateau in Bordeaux and... and...' Emma began to yawn, looking sleepy now.

Catherine felt guilty. She realised the old lady must be tired and that she was outstaying her welcome. 'I must be going now, Emma. I've already taken up far too much of your time this evening.'

'No, not at all, Catherine.' I've enjoyed talking to you so much, and...' – she began to yawn again – 'and there's still so much I want to say to you. Promise you will visit me again when you have time? Promise, Catherine?'

Catherine squeezed her frail old hand. 'Yes, I promise, Emma. Thank you for telling me about your parents. You'll never know how grateful...' The words faded from her lips. Emma Montgomery had fallen asleep.

With a few minutes to spare before dinner, Catherine took a stroll around the gardens, where she turned matters over in her mind. Her visit to Miss Montgomery had proved more enlightening than she would ever have believed, and thanks to her she was now in possession of many more facts. She thought of Sir Giles and how his hatred had destroyed two young lives, wondering how he must have felt upon seeing his beloved daughter fall to her death from the balcony. What had caused Elizabeth to fall like that, she wondered? Had the two been struggling or something? Only Sir Giles and Elizabeth knew that secret, and it had been taken to the grave with them. No-one would ever know now.

The following morning brought a flurry of excitement to Cambourne Hall. The Grand Ball was considered the most important social occasion of the year, with every upper-class family in the county in attendance. Many guests would be arriving from as far away as London, titled aristocrats, the very cream of society, all gathered together for this annual event.

Not one pair of hands lay idle, and every member of the household was busy with his or her own appointed task. The whole place was a hive of activity now, with delivery vans arriving throughout the morning, adding to the hustle and bustle which already filled the house. Catherine's time was occupied in assisting anyone who looked in need of a helping hand. At the moment she was with Lady Montgomery in the kitchen annexe, surrounded by garlands of beautiful flowers just delivered by the florist. Each woman was armed with a pair of secateurs, artistically arranging the blooms into vases and baskets, with nothing left but a pile of stalks and leaves when they had finished.

'This is a very exciting occasion for me,' remarked Catherine cheerfully. 'I've never been to a ball before. I hope my little black dress is worthy of the occasion, for I'm afraid that's all I have with me.'

Lady Montgomery cast her a warm smile. 'I'm sure you'll look beautiful whatever you wear, Catherine. I just want you to enjoy yourself, dear. Had there been more time, I daresay I could have arranged a partner for you. But as it is...'

'Please don't worry, Lady Montgomery. I understand. Besides, Alistair said I'd be welcome to join him and his fiancée. I'm looking forward to meeting Caroline,' she added.

'Yes, I think you'll like her, Catherine. Incidentally, may I ask if you have a young man in Canada? Someone special, I mean?'

Catherine's thoughts strayed to her portrait of the man on horseback. He was special to her. Very special. But there was no way she could explain that to Lady Montgomery. 'No... not that I can speak of,' she replied. 'I guess I must be hard to please.'

Sarah laughed. 'Well, I think it's better to be certain, Catherine. James and I have been extremely happy together. I couldn't have wished for a finer man.' She smiled encouragingly. 'Perhaps you'll be as lucky as me, dear. Perhaps one day you'll meet a man who will change your life.'

It was evening and the first guests began to arrive at the Hall. Upstairs, Catherine watched from her window as yet another Rolls arrived. The drive was already lined with limousines, with the courtyard taking the overflow. Enthralled by the splendour of the occasion, she wished that Jenilee was here to share these privileged moments. She'd be able to tell her all about it when she telephoned the following evening.

Before moving away from the window, she glanced across at the stable loft. Only then did she remember waking up the previous night a few minutes before midnight, seemingly for the sole purpose of leaving her bed to stare out of the window at the loft – just as she had every night since her arrival. As on previous occasions, after the clock downstairs had struck the hour of twelve, she had returned to her bed experiencing that same feeling of disappointment. This strange recurring event was beginning to frustrate her. How long would she have to contend with it, she wondered?

Before going downstairs, she glanced at herself through the full-length mirror. Although the black cocktail dress looked nice, especially with her hair worn in an upsweep of curls, she knew she would look out of place amongst the other ladies in their long ball gowns. But it could not be helped. They would just have to take her as they found her.

Downstairs she found the ballroom already packed with couples who danced to the music of the orchestra. How very grand it all was, and how proud she felt at being allowed to attend a social function graced only by the privileged few.

Catherine felt self-conscious as she mingled with the well-to-do guests, aware that she was being appraised by many pairs of curious eyes. Several of the gentlemen greeted her with a smile and a polite 'good evening', whilst their ladies merely eyed her with cool indifference – and some of them with frank envy. Catherine couldn't imagine why. They were the ones wearing diamonds and designer clothes, not she!

A short while later she found herself standing at the back of the room feeling like the proverbial wallflower. She was rescued from her own company when Alistair appeared and invited her to join him and his fiancée. She found Caroline Dalton a friendly woman, who immediately put her at ease. Being five years her senior, she was tall and willowy, with short blonde hair which had been expertly cut to suit her attractive oval face. During conversation, Caroline told Catherine that she was a horsewoman who bred Welsh Mountain ponies for the show ring.

Shortly afterwards, the trio was joined by Andrew McFarlane, a good friend of Alistair's, who reminisced with Catherine over his six months' stay in Vancouver. It was whilst she was talking to Andrew that she began to feel strange; almost light-headed. The music from the orchestra seemed to be growing fainter, and Andrew's voice became nothing but a whisper, his mouth performing the function of speaking but with no real sound issuing from it. It happened so gradually that she had hardly been aware of it. But now the very atmosphere in the room had changed. Even the light which filtered in from the windows, assisted by the brightly lit crystal chandeliers, had altered. It suddenly seemed much later in the evening now, almost as though two hours or so had become lost in time.

Dazed, she looked around, aware of an amazing transformation in the ballroom. She found herself staring through a fine, hazy mist at a gathering of people who were not of her time, overhearing snippets of conversation which had taken place right here in this room almost one hundred years ago. Had she been asked to describe what had just taken place, Catherine would have said that she felt as though she had been gently drawn out of the twentieth century, to be carefully replaced in the nineteenth. Absurd, but for some reason she did not feel out of place here. On the contrary, she felt quite at home. Although Catherine acknowledged her presence in that bygone era, knowing for certain that she was there and that it was not just her imagination playing tricks, she felt there was no actual reality to it all; that she could well have been dreaming the experience. All around were smiling faces acknowledging her; old-fashioned figures dressed in their elegant Victorian clothes. Oh, it was all so astonishing!

Suddenly her eyes were drawn to the far corner of the ballroom. It was then she saw him, actually saw him, standing with his back to her talking with a small group of guests. Her heart leaped with excitement, her whole being filled with joy. A warm flush of heat softly coloured her skin and the emotion, the very feeling which coursed through her body, was enough to deprive her of breath.

Smiling now, blissfully happy, she moved gracefully across the room to the music of a Strauss waltz being played in the background by the orchestra. The sparkle in her clear blue eyes, the very way in which she gazed at him, gave clear indication of her love, bringing smiles to the faces of those who witnessed her memorable walk across the ballroom floor. She held her breath as she came to stand behind him, aching, bursting with joy at being near him again. For a long moment she allowed herself to look at the man whom she loved so dearly; a man who had occupied her every thought from the first moment they had met. Her worshipping eyes beheld his sleek dark hair, its length at the back just brushing the collar of his black tail coat; his tall, attractive handsomeness and those strong broad shoulders! There was not another man on the face of the earth who could hold a candle to him – and he was hers. Hers!

Gently she placed her hand upon his shoulder, her spirit rocketed by the explosion of feeling which followed. Just to touch him felt wonderful. Smiling, her lips parted to speak his name, but to her sheer horror no sound was heard at all. Sudden panic instilled itself within her. She couldn't remember it. Couldn't remember it!

At that moment the man turned to face her. Oh, she had a colossal shock. He was not the one! He was not the same man he had been only a moment ago! The vision had abruptly ended, rudely returning her to the reality of the twentieth century again. A gasp escaped her. Her face had turned white and she suddenly felt sick and light-headed. Unable to bear the pain of such bitter disappointment, the torture and anguish in her heart after believing she had found him again, she gave way to the nausea which swamped her and fainted at the gentleman's feet.

The next thing she knew was that someone was reviving her with smelling salts, asking if she felt better. The voice sounded dim and distant, overshadowed by the ringing in her ears. All around her was a sea of eyes belonging to the inquisitive guests, who were no doubt wondering what had caused her to faint at Lord Marbury's feet. Thankfully Alistair and Caroline arrived on the scene, Alistair authoritatively asking the guests to move back and allow her room to breathe. Soon afterwards Catherine began to come round.

Suddenly everyone was addressing her at once, demanding to know what had happened. Overcome by the whole experience, she longed for the privacy of her own quiet room. After Alistair had assisted her to her feet, she blurted an apology to the man at whose feet she had fallen, then accompanied by her friends, quickly retreated from the ballroom.

Upon reaching the hall, she succumbed to emotion and burst into tears. The incident had completely devastated her and left her feeling wretched. Offering their comfort, the couple were curious, as well as concerned at what had happened.

'What on earth caused you to faint, Catherine?' questioned Alistair with a frown. 'And what possessed you to approach Lord Marbury like that?'

'I... I thought I recognised him,' she blurted. 'But when he turned around I realised I'd made a mistake! Oh, I had such a shock! I could have sworn he was... was someone else...'

'But I don't understand, Catherine. How could you know anyone from these parts? You've never been to Shropshire before.' After a thoughtful silence, he added, 'Who did you believe him to be, anyway?'

'I... I don't know...' she began. She couldn't very well admit to Alistair that she had been momentarily transported back in time! He would think she had completely lost her senses.

She recalled the feeling she had experienced in her heart upon seeing the man. It had been so strong that it had completely overpowered her. Catherine wondered where that feeling had been born and where it had thrived. Had it been some time in the eighteen hundreds? The answers were still out of reach, frustrating her almost to screaming point. Seeing the man had disturbed her in a way she would never forget. How could she? Even now, in her mind's eye, she could see him standing there, faceless, nameless and tantalizing.

Close to tears again, she covered her face with her hands. It had all been too much. This evening's strange happening had topped the balance of her endurance and she knew she couldn't take any more. Thankfully, neither Alistair or Caroline pressured her with further questions. Both could see how distraught she was and, clearly worried, they suggested she retire to her room. She agreed and was grateful when Caroline offered to accompany her upstairs.

Halfway up the staircase they encountered Mavis Plummer, whose curiosity was aroused by Catherine's distress. 'Is anything wrong?' she asked.

Neither woman wished to become involved in lengthy conversation and moved quickly past her on the stairs, Caroline simply explaining that the heat in the ballroom had proved too much for Catherine.

'I see,' said Miss Plummer, then continued on her way.

Shortly afterwards, Catherine sat in bed drinking hot sweet tea which Caroline had kindly made her. 'Oh, I'll never never be able to face Sir James and Lady Montgomery tomorrow after they hear what happened to me tonight. I shall probably be asked to leave.'

Caroline smiled. 'No, of course you won't, Catherine. My future parents-in-law are the nicest people you could wish to meet. They'll understand. Besides, we're all capable of making mistakes, you know. Oh, I bet this is one occasion Lord Marbury won't forget in a hurry. Having a beautiful woman swoon at his feet must have done wonders for his ego!'

When Caroline had left her, Catherine fell asleep. But it provided little solace, for her mind became tormented by wild, outrageous nightmares. Time and time again she re-lived those moments when she had walked across the ballroom floor, straining her memory in an effort to remember the name of the man whom she had approached. In the dreams he actually turned around to face her, startling her half to death when she saw he had no face at all, just an outline of a shape which meant nothing to her. Besides being haunted by nightmares, she woke with a start just before midnight again, compelled to leave her bed to gaze through the window at the stable loft. As usual, nothing happened. When she returned to her bed, she cried herself to sleep, her spirits at their lowest ebb yet. She knew she couldn't continue like this any longer.

CHAPTER FIVE

Next morning, Catherine was joined by her employer in the office. Lady Montgomery looked uneasy and Catherine knew she was troubled.

'Good morning, Catherine,' she said. She hovered beside the desk for a moment. 'Catherine . . . Catherine, I'm concerned about what happened to you last night. Alistair explained it to me, but whatever caused the incident, dear?'

Catherine blushed, knowing she couldn't possibly relate the true facts. Although she hated lying, there was no alternative. 'Oh, I expect it was the heat, Lady Montgomery,' she replied flippantly, 'and naturally the excitement of the occasion. I . . . I do apologise for making such a fool of myself. I didn't intend to cause you embarrassment.'

Sarah smiled kindly. 'There's no need for you to apologise. My concern was for you, not the incident.' Still wearing a troubled frown, she began to pace the floor. 'I must admit, Catherine, I sometimes have the feeling that you're . . . well, hiding something from me. In fact, there are several things about you which clearly puzzle me. Your avid interest in this house and its past, for instance, and the strange way you acted outside Elizabeth's bedroom that evening.' Lady Montgomery turned and looked Catherine straight in the face. 'Catherine . . . what is it? What is it about you that I just don't understand?'

Catherine felt decidedly uneasy. What should she say? What could she say? She was searching her brain for a suitable reply, when suddenly the door opened and Sir James entered. The man was obviously in a hurry.

'Come along, Sarah!' he said, 'I've been waiting for you, dear. You know we arranged to be in Marbury before nine-thirty!'

'I'm coming, James,' she replied, then to Catherine. 'I'm afraid I must go, dear. Perhaps . . . perhaps we could have a chat this evening before dinner? Goodbye, Catherine. Have a nice morning.'

Emma was nodding in her armchair when Miss Plummer showed Catherine into the room early that evening. She was soon wide awake, however, delighted to see her young guest.

'I hope I haven't called at an inconvenient time, Emma?'

'No, not at all, Catherine. It's only five-thirty, so there's still half an hour until supper time. Come and sit down. I want to know what upset you last night. Mavis said you had been crying and that Caroline Dalton had to help you to your room.'

Catherine rolled her eyes. Miss Plummer hadn't wasted much time in relating that. Once again she decided to blame her condition on the heat. However, Miss Montgomery wasn't in the least bit fooled and, with a pointed finger wagging insistently in her direction, warned her guest that she had not been taken in. 'I want the truth now, if you please!'

Catherine heaved a sigh. Miss Montgomery might be very old, but she hadn't lost an ounce of her intelligence. 'Very well, Emma. I will tell you the truth.' She clasped her hands tightly together in her lap and began. 'I was upset because I thought I recognised someone. But when I approached the person in question, I realised I'd made a mistake.' She gave a constrained laugh. 'I'm afraid the shock caused me to faint. The whole incident was most embarrassing,' she admitted.

'Who was the man whom you thought you recognised, Catherine? What did he look like?' question Emma interestedly.

Catherine's eyebrows rose. 'Man? How did you know it was a man, Emma?'

'Because I'm not stupid!' replied the old lady. 'Just who did you believe him to be?'

'I . . . I don't know . . .'

'You don't know – or you don't want to know?' she asked with deliberation.

Catherine's unease intensified. 'I don't know who I thought he was, Emma, and that's the truth! Although I felt I knew him well, I just couldn't remember his name! I'd give anything to know, I truly would!' The words came bursting from her mouth in a rush.

'Very well, dear. Then describe him to me. Tell me exactly what he looked like.'

'Emma, I—'

'Please, Catherine!' she entreated. 'It's important to me!'

'Very well, Emma. He was tall, about six feet two I would say, and dark haired. In fact it was almost black.'

'Was it curly or . . .?'

'No, Emma. His hair was straight and sleek.'

'And how about his eyes? What colour were they?'

'I have no idea. I didn't see his face because he was standing with his back to me.'

'I see. Yet you still believed you knew him?'

'Oh, yes – without a doubt.'

Emma's next question was far more difficult to answer. 'What was he wearing?' she asked.

'W . . . wearing?'

'Yes, dear. Wearing!'

Catherine closed her eyes and sighed. The man had been from another time and had not been wearing modern clothes. How could she possibly convey that to Emma? 'Emma . . . Emma, this is very difficult for me. I really don't know how to—'

'—How to tell me that he was wearing old-fashioned clothes?' She finished the sentence on her behalf.

Catherine's eyes grew wide and incredulous. 'How on earth did you know that?' she blurted.

Emma smiled. 'Well, I must admit I was guessing, Catherine. But I deduce I was correct?'

'Y . . . yes, you are,' she admitted, awed.

Emma sat back in her chair, her expression complacent. 'What you saw was not actually real, was it, dear? In fact, what you have been privileged to see was something which happened many years ago – and in this very house. Am I right?'

Catherine was speechless. Emma Montgomery was the most amazing woman she had ever known.

'I see I have shocked you, Catherine,' she said. 'I'm sorry. It was not my intention.'

'You're amazing, Emma. And yes, you're right. But how did you know all this?'

'Oh, intuition, dear, intuition.' She shuffled herself to the edge of her seat. 'I'm aware of so much more besides, Catherine. More than you could possibly imagine. Allow me to ask you another question, one which I know you will answer truthfully. Why are you here? The real reason, I mean?'

Once again Catherine was astounded by the old lady's remarkable insight, acknowledging that Lady Montgomery had been right when she had said that no-one could pull the wool over Emma's eyes.

Miss Montgomery saw her reluctance and quickly reassured her. 'You can trust me, Catherine, I promise you can trust me.'

Relief flooded into Catherine, for now she had the chance to unburden herself to someone who appeared to understand, someone capable of believing the unbelievable. 'You're an incredible lady, Emma. How long have you known?'

'Oh, I knew from the start that you weren't here in connection with any job. Another reason brought you to Cambourne Hall, didn't it, Catherine?' she asked percipiently.

'Yes, Emma, it did. I'll tell you why I came here, and although it will sound too far-fetched for words, I'm certain you'll believe me.

She then began her story, beginning with the sketch she had done of the house, telling how it had haunted her during the three years which followed. Miss Montgomery listened intently to every word, never questioning, never interrupting, just allowing her simply to talk. Catherine omitted nothing in the story, conveying everything which had happened to her since arriving at Cambourne Hall, concluding with the incident at the ball. Judging by her expression of abounding interest, it was clear that Emma believed every word. Indeed, the way she was sitting on the edge of her chair with her hands clasped tightly together, and the way her eyes were twinkling with excitement, gave a clear indication that she was having difficulty in containing her elation.

'Oh, my dear! What a remarkable story!' she exclaimed at last. 'Truly remarkable!'

'You . . . you believe me, Emma?'

'Believe you? Oh, I most certainly do, Catherine!'

'What do you make of it all, Emma? I've reached the stage where I can't think straight any more. What do you think guided me here?'

Emma's old eyes held hers for a moment, her expression reverent now; a profound respect for something which was way above them. 'Who can say? Perhaps it was a gift.' she said, her voice edged with meaning. 'I believe I can help you with your other queries, though. For instance, would you like me to tell you the name of the man whom you saw last night? The same man you witnessed in the rowing boat at Netley Manor?'

'You know who he was?'

Emma smiled and lowered her voice to a whisper. 'Yes . . . I know who he was. You see, Catherine, the man you saw was my father – Richard de Ville.'

Catherine looked astounded. The statement had left her speechless and it was a good few moments before she found her tongue. 'Richard de Ville! But . . . but that's impossible! I don't believe it!'

Quietly, Emma insisted. 'But it was, dear. Believe me – I do know what I'm talking about.'

Incredible as it was, Catherine did believe her. However, the implication that the man she had approached yesterday evening at the ball was none other than Richard de Ville himself, and remembering her feeling for him, her love, left her burning with another knowledge. 'But if the man in the boat was Richard de Ville, then . . . then the woman with him must have been . . .'

'. . . Elizabeth Montgomery.' Emma spoke the name which Catherine had been fearful to utter. 'You, dear. You,' she repeated. 'What you witnessed on the lake was a vision of yourself and my father in your earlier lifetime. Believe me, Catherine! It's true!'

Catherine's head was reeling. Her legs turned weak and she suddenly felt faint. Emma's words were pounding through her mind, demanding that she should acknowledge that which she already knew in her heart. She had lived on this earth before – lived right here in this very house in the late eighteen hundreds. Furthermore, she had been Elizabeth Montgomery herself. Acknowledge it, Shepherd! Acknowledge it! You know you felt it all along!

Slowly her mind came to terms with it until she eventually acknowledged the fact. It was true, and, like it or not, there was nothing in the world she could do about it. 'I know,' she murmured. 'I . . . I felt it.' The knowledge became too great to bear and she fell weeping at Miss Montgomery's feet. 'Oh, Emma, I knew it in my heart all along! I was convinced of it after I left my rose lying on Richard's grave that morning! But . . . but I wouldn't admit it to myself! I was afraid to!' Coming to terms with the fact that she had once been Elizabeth Montgomery had been the most difficult acceptance of all.

Still on her knees, she continued to sob emotionally for him, for herself, for everything. Tears sprang into Emma's eyes and she placed her hand on Catherine's head. Catherine looked up into her face, incredulous of the present unbelievable circumstances. She was gazing at her own daughter from an earlier lifetime; Emma at the mother she had lost. The two had been allowed to meet again after death had separated them all those years ago. That had been the feeling they had shared when they had first met each other; a deep inner instinct which not even the passing of time could destroy. They smiled, then clung to each other for a moment.

'This is the most precious moment of my life,' murmured Emma. 'Oh, but I shall die contented now, for I have been more than compensated for the tragedy which took place in my childhood. You know, Catherine, I've always had the unfailing belief that there is justice in the afterworld, and that one's life on earth and the manner in which it is led is eventually accountable to God Himself to be judged accordingly. That belief, and the fact that you're here with me today, has made me the happiest woman in the world. Whatever the reason for your being here, dear, you can rest assured it has been blessed by God and is something which you need have no fear of.'

Emma's heartfelt words were of great reassurance to Catherine and, returning to her seat, she began to feel much better. 'It all seems so incredible,' she whispered.

'Yes, I agree it does, Catherine. But who are we to question the works of the Almighty? For some reason known only to Him, you have been allowed to return again, although to serve what purpose I really do not know.'

'Perhaps it has something to do with Richard,' said Catherine thoughtfully. 'Does that make sense to you, Emma?'

'Yes, I believe it does. You realise he still waits for you? Waits right here at

Cambourne Hall where you were taken away from him all those years ago. I expect you've already heard the story that his spirit haunts the Hall? Believe it, Catherine. It's true!'

Catherine cast her mind back to the night of her arrival, when she had ventured downstairs to make herself some tea. She recalled the feeling of being watched by some invisible presence in the hall. Catherine did believe it. Miss Montgomery spoke the truth. She wanted to know all there was to know about him and asked Emma to tell her everything. Where they first met – everything.

Emma smiled keenly. 'I shall be glad to!'

Sitting back in her chair, she began to relate the story. 'Uncle Edward told me that you met my father in Bluebell Wood.' She chuckled with amusement. 'Apparently he caught you bathing in the stream dressed in nothing but your underwear. Most unladylike!' she teased.

'Bluebell Wood,' murmured Catherine. 'Some time ago I painted a bluebell wood. I was always so fond of it.' She smiled tenderly. 'Now I know why.' Realisation suddenly dawned on her. 'Emma, I also painted a portrait of a man on horseback, a handsome, dark haired man. It's him, isn't it? It's Richard?'

Emma smiled. 'Yes, dear, it's Richard. Allow me to explain that when Elizabeth was eighteen years old, she began her artistic calling by sketching this house. Later she painted it in oils – just as you did, Catherine. I understand it was a brilliant piece of work which won the acclaim of a famous artist, Mr Frederick Llani, who arranged to have it exhibited in a London art gallery. After Giles' death, the painting was given to Mr Llani by Edward and Aunt Charlotte in remembrance of Elizabeth. I understand he had been very fond of her. Anyway, she undertook several other paintings after the one of Cambourne Hall, all identical to the ones you painted in Vancouver.'

Catherine looked astonished. 'You mean . . . mean I painted the exact replicas? Recreated the identical pieces of art?'

'Yes, dear, you did. My father's portrait was Elizabeth's last accomplishment.'

'What became of all the paintings?' Catherine questioned, absorbing the remarkable facts.

'I'm afraid I don't know, Catherine. After Elizabeth died, my grandfather took charge of all her possessions. But I did inherit her portrait and cameo brooch. Aunt Charlotte kept the brooch in safe keeping for me until I was old enough to have it.' Emma proceeded to unfasten the cameo which had been of such fascination to Catherine the other day. 'For you, dear,' she said, squeezing it into her hand. 'You recognised it because it had been given to Elizabeth by my father. I was told she never let it out of her possession and

68

that it was pinned to her dress when she died. She must have been very fond of it. Take it,' she urged. 'It belongs to you!'

Deeply touched, Catherine gazed at the cameo, desperately wishing she could remember the man who had given it to her all those years ago. But she had no memory of him at all. Although she had loved Richard de Ville dearly, she was unable to recall him to her mind. The only fragment of remembrance she had been allowed to retain was how he looked in the portrait. That was all.

She pinned the brooch to her blouse. 'Thank you so much, Emma,' she said. 'I shall treasure it always . . . wear it always, and every time I look at it I shall think of him.'

Afterwards, Emma told her about her own life and how she had spent it. 'I was once betrothed to a Frenchman,' she said, 'but sadly he was killed on the battlefield. I never fell in love again after that.'

'Where did you meet him, Emma?'

'Well, it was whilst I was staying at my father's chateau. You remember, I told you I spent a great deal of time there when I was young. It was there I became an exceedingly efficient business woman.' She smiled broadly. 'My father would have been so proud of me, because eventually I ran the business along with Rachael's two sons – whose own sons run the place to this day.'

Catherine was pleased, glad that Emma had been accepted into her father's family and that through her they had at last become united. 'What kind of business is it, Emma?' she enquired interestedly.

'Oh, the wine business, dear, established by the de Ville family many generations ago. The chateau is one of the finest in Bordeaux now.'

She remembered the photograph albums, and delighted Catherine by showing her pictures of the place. Besides the chateau, Catherine saw many photographs of Emma during her various stages of growing up. She had been such a pretty child, but oh, that was nothing to the tall, dark haired beauty she had eventually developed into. A real stunner, inheriting her looks from both parents equally. She smiled as she examined the photographs. In her earlier lifetime she had been robbed of the chance to see her daughter grow up. Now, ninety-four years later, she saw what she had missed. Astonishing! It was all so astonishing.

The old lady began to speak about her father again, flooding Catherine with nostalgia. Again she searched her mind for a fragment of memory, but all to no avail. Feeling deeply frustrated, she covered her face with her hands. 'Oh, Emma, I've tried so hard to remember Richard, but nothing will come! Why can't I remember him? Why? Have I been brought back here simply to be tormented by his memory?'

Emma reached out to her, her voice encouraging. 'Oh, no, Catherine. No!

You mustn't believe that. I'm certain God has allowed you to return for a very special reason. I'm convinced of it!'

'Then why can't I remember anything, Emma? Why is the past such a mystery to me?'

'Perhaps you're not meant to remember,' said the old lady wisely. 'At least, not in the way you would expect.'

Her cryptic remark puzzled Catherine. 'Not in the way I would expect?'

Emma continued. 'Perhaps you were meant to search for the reason as to why you are here, Catherine.'

'But I have searched, Emma. I've done my utmost!'

'Then perhaps you've been looking in the wrong places. Think about it for a moment.'

Catherine obeyed, and it was then she remembered Elizabeth's bedroom. She grew excited. 'Emma, I need to see Elizabeth's room. I feel there's something in there . . . calling me. I felt it when Lady Montgomery showed me around the house on my first evening here. But I don't have the key,' she added despondently.

A sudden twinkle lit Emma's eyes. 'But I do,' she admitted. 'I have the key, and furthermore, I'm prepared to take the responsibility of lending it to you.'

'You have the key?'

'Yes. So what do you say, Catherine? Are you prepared to venture into the room which once belonged to you?'

'Oh, yes, Emma! I am!'

'And are you prepared to accept whatever may arise from it? A great power has made it possible for you to be here today, Catherine, a power which may already have predetermined your destiny – and your fate. Are you convinced – really convinced – that this is what you want? To follow the path, wherever it may lead you?'

'Oh, yes, Emma, yes!'

Miss Montgomery then reached into her pocket and brought out a key. 'Then go with my blessing,' she said.

The key to Elizabeth's room was now in Catherine's hand; a key which could well unlock the door to the past and allow her to know why she had been called here from the far distant shore of Canada. Catherine saw a look of sadness sweep over Emma's face. 'Please don't worry about me, Emma. Everything will be all right. I'm not afraid,' she assured her.

Emma managed a smile. 'I know you aren't. I know.'

The two women embraced. 'I thought I was seeing things the first time I saw you, Catherine. You were walking across the courtyard on the evening you arrived. I was watching from the window. You saw me, didn't you?'

Catherine recalled the incident, when she had linked the mysterious figure with the ghost. 'That was you?' she asked.

'Yes, it was me. Even then I knew who you were . . . really were, that is. Don't ask me how, though. In a million years I would never be able to tell you. God be with you, Catherine. I hope you find what you're looking for.'

'Thank you, Emma. And thank you for lending me the key.' She kissed the old lady's cheek. 'See you soon.'

Reaching the door, she turned to look at Emma, frail and aged in her black woollen dress with a shawl around her shoulders. Gracing her face was a look of pure contentment. It was as though she had never felt happier. Catherine cast her an affectionate smile and waved goodbye.

The house was silent. There was not a soul around when Catherine entered the west wing after leaving Emma's flat. It was the first occasion she had ventured into this particular part of the wing, and as she walked along the landing several paintings attracted her eyes. Curious, she paused to look at them. Amongst various landscapes were three portraits, the first being of a man. Her heart missed a beat when she read the nameplate below. So this was Sir Giles Montgomery – her very own father in an earlier existence; a man who had been responsible for countless misdeeds during his lifetime. He had stood between Elizabeth and Richard de Ville, destroying them both with his unyielding hatred.

Catherine studied his image with fascination. How formidable he looked, proud and arrogant, seated on a high-backed chair holding a cane in his right hand. His cold grey eyes, set deep beneath thick bushy eyebrows, gave the impression of dominance and austerity, his hard, rugged features and strong determined jaw appearing as though they had been roughly chiselled out of granite itself. The proud tilt of his chin surrounded by its mass of whiskers lent him a look of defiance. He was unmistakably a man who refused to yield to his fellow men and who had paid the price by being despised for it. Oh, what a strange man he must have been! What a paragon of peculiarity! Yet instinct told her that she had loved him dearly all those years ago.

As Catherine studied the portrait, it struck her that it looked oddly unfinished, as though the artist had abandoned it prematurely for some reason or another. She could see that he was a genius, so why hadn't he given it its final touch? Being an artist herself, she couldn't help but wonder why.

On the left hand side of Sir Giles' portrait was that of his sister, Charlotte Montgomery. In stark contrast to her brother, Charlotte looked kind and genteel, a woman who possessed an abundance of love and understanding. She appeared a refined and dignified lady, demure in her deep mauve dress, her thick grey hair coiled neatly around her head. Once again, intuition told her that she had thought the world of Aunt Charlotte when they had all lived together here.

Hanging beside Charlotte's portrait was another. Catherine smiled, for this was, without doubt, Sir James Montgomery's father, Edward, Elizabeth's own dear brother. She stared at it for ages, knowing for certain that she had loved Edward very dearly. How blue-eyed and handsome he had been, possessing a knight-in-shining-armour quality and he was so fair in comparison to his beautiful dark sister. He had the kind of face which promoted trust and reliability; a modest man who had gained the respect of others by his ability to show compassion and understanding. It was a far cry from his father's approach, which consisted in inflicting fear and intimidation. Oh, how she wished she could remember Edward now! How desperately she wished she could remember them all! But none of the portraits had succeeded in sparking off even a flicker of recognition.

After one more glance at each of them, Catherine proceeded on her way. Shortly afterwards she was standing outside Elizabeth's bedroom door, experiencing the same erratic heartbeat as on the first occasion she had stood here. A variety of emotions ran riot through her body. Apprehension, curiosity, excitement and a deep sense of respect all presented themselves within her at once. There was no telling what was in there; no telling what lay in wait for her inside. But if she wished to learn the reason for her being here, then she must cast aside any last-minute doubts and proceed as planned.

Slowly and deliberately she placed the key in the lock, then with trembling hands turned the old brass key. After ensuring that no-one was around to see her, she inhaled a long deep breath and cautiously pushed open the stiff oak door. Upon entering, she found she might have been stepping back into time – almost a century, in fact. Long moments passed before her eyes adjusted themselves to the sombre, semi-darkness which prevailed in the room. When at last she could see, she stared at her remarkable surroundings. The fact that she was standing in a room which had once belonged to her completely overawed her. Furthermore, it had remained exactly as she had left it on that fateful evening in 1887.

Minutes later she drew back the heavy dove-grey curtains at the French windows and rolled up the old linen blind, thereby enabling her to see out on to the balcony. She shuddered when she saw it, the very place where she had fallen to her death all those years ago. It was ironical to think that ninety-four years later she had returned to the very same place.

The light which filtered in from the window had considerably brightened the room, transforming the initial impression of gloom and ushering in a pleasanter, more interesting atmosphere. She was able to see the Persian carpet which covered the floor, the items of dark, old-fashioned furniture which occupied the room and the various pieces of bric-a-brac which long ago had given Elizabeth's bedroom its lived-in appearance. Beside the bed was a small writing table; scattered around were various chairs, Thomas Chippendale by the look of them. In one corner of the room stood a large oak wardrobe, with a matching dresser and stool in the opposite corner. Displayed on the dresser top were an assortment of jars and bottles containing perfumes and other toiletries once used by herself. Among them was an exquisite silver-backed brush and comb together with a matching hand-mirror. She moved to examine them, intrigued to think that they had once been her own.

Deeply fascinated, she stole a peep inside the dresser drawers containing Elizabeth's undergarments, all carefully wrapped in tissue paper and giving off the odour of mothballs. In one of the drawers, carefully wrapped as was everything, she discovered a beautiful ostrich feather fan, exquisite garlands of silk flowers once used to decorate her hair, and many items of assorted costume jewellery. She fingered them lovingly, barely able to comprehend that she had worn them in a century long since past; an era which had taken with it its own particular style and fashion. A glance inside the wardrobe revealed many beautiful dresses, mantles, skirts and blouses, leaving Catherine of the opinion that Elizabeth Montgomery had possessed an admirable taste in clothes.

Suddenly her interest was aroused by the photographs which stood in gilt frames on a table near the bed, made drab by its faded dove-grey quilt. Closer examination revealed them to be pictures of Elizabeth's family, Giles, Charlotte and Edward, but there was also one of a woman whom Catherine failed to recognise. Perhaps it was Elizabeth's mother, Helen Montgomery? Whoever she was, she had certainly been beautiful. Standing between the photographs was a paraffin lamp, below it a Charles Dickens novel and an ancient edition of the Holy Bible. Eagerly she picked up the latter, hoping to discover more hidden letters. But she found nothing. She did find several pressed flowers concealed within the discoloured pages of the Dickens novel, though, all carefully wrapped in tissue paper to preserve them. Among them was a rose, an orchid and several bluebells which she presumed had come from the wood. Catherine wondered what special significance the flowers had held for Elizabeth, for surely she had preserved them for a reason. It was frustrating to know that although she stood amongst everything which had one been her own – clothes, trinkets and suchlike – nothing had succeeded in triggering even a hint of familiarity.

Just then she noticed a tapestry-weave valise on the floor by the bed, its condition frail and dilapidated. Carefully she opened it. To her delight, she discovered delicate baby clothes, again carefully wrapped and smelling of mothballs. She knew they had been Emma's, and that the valise had been packed in readiness for Elizabeth's departure with Richard – which had never taken place. How sad that it had all been in vain. Instead of leaving Cambourne Hall to begin her new life with the man she loved, Elizabeth had left it to go to her grave. She returned the clothes to the valise. Let them remain where they had been all those years.

Catherine gazed at the four walls which enclosed her, restless, burdened by a deep sense of sorrow for the past and its elusive memories. As yet, nothing had transpired to give her so much as a clue as to why she was here, and a nagging doubt lurked in her mind that perhaps she had made a mistake about this room. Desperately her eyes searched for anything that might help her discover the secrets which she was aching to unravel, and in their avid search they came to rest upon a small door handle in the very wall beside which she was standing. It had not been apparent to her earlier because the door was covered by the same drab wallpaper which decorated the walls. Curious, she stole a peep inside.

It appeared to be a large cupboard of some kind, built deep into the wall and large enough for her to step inside. There were shelves occupied by boxes of hats, boots, shoes and a fine selection of handbags all carefully wrapped up. On the floor were several large brown paper packages which Catherine quickly untied. To her delight, she discovered the original paintings done by Elizabeth in the eighteen hundreds. The sight of them left her breathless and, feeling much happier now, she studied each one. Here was the painting of the lady and gentleman seated in the open carriage, none other than Sir Giles Montgomery and his sister, Charlotte; the old fashioned hunting scene, undertaken on this very estate, ah . . . and the one of Bluebell Wood itself, a paradise rife with flowers and tall, majestic trees. She could almost feel its tranquillity and sensed that it had been a very special place to Elizabeth and Richard all those years ago. As yet, it was the only place she had still not seen. Catherine promised herself a walk there as soon as time allowed.

Wrapped up between the paintings was a smaller package. Opening it, she found it to be the original sketch of Cambourne Hall, corresponding in every detail to the one which had sparked off this whole amazing episode in her life. Awed, she fingered it, recalling how it had enticed her with its promise of the past. A reverent tear trickled down her cheek, for now she was here in this very house. It all seemed so unbelievable.

Only one more package remained unopened. It just had to be the one she was longing to see, for where else could it be, she wondered? With bated breath she untied the string, closing her eyes as she removed the stiff brown paper which covered it. Her fingers touched it long before her eyes were graced. When she saw it, she was filled with joy at seeing him again; the man whose handsome image had remained with her throughout the long span of time which had so cruelly separated them. A man she had never stopped loving. It was a love which had survived the test of time, living on in her heart until this very day.

Tears trickled down her cheeks in quick succession, stirred by a feeling which in truth no words could describe. Richard de Ville had meant everything to her. Everything. Yet she still could not remember him or a single moment of their time together. Catherine felt she was being cruelly tormented, for she wanted him now as she had wanted him then – but he was gone and she was here.

Deeply frustrated, she gazed at his image through tear-filled eyes, wondering if this was the reason why she had been allowed to return to Cambourne Hall. To be tortured by the memory of a man whom she would never know again, and subjected to the knowledge that she had led a previous existence in this very house and that she had died here because of the one she loved. Was that it? Was it? For nothing else had happened to lead her to believe otherwise.

She grew angry and felt she had been cheated, knowing she would have to live the rest of her life yearning for a man whom she would never see again. Although she had been reborn, her heart had remained in the past. Oh, but it was just too much to bear!

Overcome by emotion and blinded by tears, she ran into the bedroom and towards the French windows. Uncaring of her actions, she turned the stiff old key, and with the windows unlocked she then opened the doors which led out onto the balcony. There she clung to the balustrade, weeping pitifully. Nothing in the world mattered any more, and in those moments she despised her own existence. Catherine hated herself and everything else for inflicting this misery upon her. But above all she hated God.

Below her in the courtyard, Ben Sykes rounded the corner of the house. Armed with a brush and shovel, he began to sweep up, whistling cheerfully as he went about his work. Had Ben looked upwards, he would have seen a young woman who had come to the end of the road, seemingly with no way back and no way forward. Ben didn't even hear her cry out to the Lord in bitterness and resentment.

'You've cheated me, God! Cheated me! You've only brought me back here to be punished! Oh, and to think I had such faith in you! Such trust!'

A light breeze rustled the trees around the Hall, and it was then it happened. The reason why she had been reborn and allowed to return to the house which had once been her home was about to unfold. It was a simple reason. It was to grant her the wish which she had uttered with her last dying breath whilst lying on the cobbles in the courtyard on that fateful evening in

1887. A wish she had prayed for with such unfailing belief that it had touched God's mercy and been allowed to come true. It was by way of recompense for the tragedy which had befallen her, caused by Sir Giles Montgomery's broken promise to the Lord; a promise known only to himself and God. It was also to reward Elizabeth for her undying love and devotion.

Catherine Shepherd knew nothing of the miracle which was beginning to take place. The very last thing she saw before closing her eyes on that warm July evening in 1981 was old Ben sweeping up the courtyard below her. And the very last thing she felt was the soft caressing wind, like the touch of silk upon her face, transporting her back through the passage of time. When she opened her eyes she was Elizabeth again, with no recollection of Catherine Shepherd or her life in the twentieth century. Time had taken her back to the 25th of May, 1886, to enable her to re-live almost one year of her life in the eighteen hundreds; days which had been so special to her; days which she had spent with her beloved Richard.

PART TWO

ELIZABETH

CHAPTER SIX

The first thing she saw on that hot sunny morning in May was old Ned sweeping up the courtyard below her. He was whistling cheerfully as he went about his work, happy this morning and with good reason. Elizabeth's spirits were also high, for had she not a whole day's painting in Bluebell Wood to look forward to?

She called out to him in greeting. 'Good morning, Ned! 'Tis a beautiful day, is it not?'

The tall, grey-whiskered old man with his rosy, weathered cheeks and bright hazel eyes looked up at her and smiled, doffing his battered old cap as he did so. 'Good mornin', Miss Elizabeth! Aye, 'tis indeed a lovely day! Will ye be wantin' your mare this mornin', Miss?'

'Oh, yes, most certainly, Ned – but not until Papa has left for London. If you would be so good as to have her ready for ten o'clock.'

'Yes Miss.' The groom tugged his forelock. 'I shall see she is ready for ye!'

Elizabeth and Ned were not the only ones in high spirits that morning. Far from it. The entire staff at Cambourne Hall was in a state of secret elation, overjoyed at the prospect of one whole week's absence of their dominating master, Sir Giles. Trouble had been brewing on the estate of late, and there was unrest and discontentment amongst the overburdened labourers. This had added fuel to Sir Giles' temper and blackened his darkest moods. Oh, but he had earned their enmity with his high-handed and unchristian attitude, ruling them with a rod of iron, winning his way with threats, demands and punishment! Giles Montgomery deserved their contempt.

Elizabeth stole a peep at herself through the mirror in her bedroom before going downstairs to join her family for breakfast. The pale primrose morning dress she was wearing showed off her shapely figure to perfection, with its fashionable draped bustle, slim-fitting bodice, high collar and long slender cuffs. She patted her hair, which was styled in an upsweep of curls, with wispy tendrils falling loose upon her collar. After breakfast she would change into her riding habit, for her father forbade her to attend the table in clothes which gave off the odour of horses. He said it was not befitting for a young lady of breeding to smell of the stables.

Elizabeth smiled at herself in the mirror. Intuition told her that today was going to be wonderful. Simply wonderful!

Downstairs, Sir Giles and his sister were already seated at the breakfast table, Charlotte having fallen into contemplative silence after listening to her brother dictate his customary orders concerning Elizabeth's welfare during his absence. Charlotte Montgomery made a handsome figure of a woman for her fifty-seven years, tall in stature and of ample build, with kind grey eyes and gentle features. She exuded mature elegance in her mulberry brocade dress, her thick grey hair coiled neatly around the back of her head. Miss Montgomery was a refined lady of admirable equanimity and virtue who, unlike so many of her contemporaries, did not allow herself to be bound by the dictates of fashion or the snobbery of high society living. She was a homely lady with simple tastes, who firmly believed that the secret of good breeding was never to deviate from calmness and moderation. However, her inner strength was periodically tested by her autocratic elder brother who, unlike herself, possessed very few virtues at all.

Charlotte was weary of him, for it was the same every time he went away – orders, orders, orders. It was as though the man knew nothing else. Had she not been told on past occasions that Elizabeth must not leave the estate during his absence? It was a procedure she knew by heart. She did not require telling at all.

Sir Giles rose politely to his feet when Elizabeth entered the room. He was a stockily built man of average height who carried himself with proud dignity and an air of self-importance. Now he smiled tenderly at the daughter who was so dear to him. She looked radiant this morning. Indeed, he conceded, she was growing more beautiful with every passing day. It troubled him; troubled him to think that she had grown into a woman and that one day soon she might wish to leave him. That was something which he could not bring himself to face, for life without Elizabeth would be no life at all.

'Ah, so here you are, my sweet! I was wondering what had become of you!' he said cheerfully.

'Good morning, Papa. Good morning, Aunt Charlotte.' She kissed their cheeks in turn. 'I apologise for being late for breakfast, only I was talking to Ned from my balcony.'

Giles' expression soured. 'Ah, 'tis beneath you to converse with the stable staff, my dear. You should exercise your conversation with more worthwhile souls, Elizabeth.'

'Oh, Papa! What a dreadful thing to say! I am ashamed of you. Ned has been like a grandfather to me. I think the world of him and you know it!'

Noting her brother's harsh expression, Charlotte was wise enough to change the subject. 'What time do you intend leaving for London, Giles?' she asked.

'Immediately following breakfast,' he replied, helping himself to another plate of kidneys. 'You know I always catch the morning train, Charlotte.'

Elizabeth broached the subject which her father usually managed to avoid, today being no exception. 'Papa, when are you going to take me to London with you? You have been promising me for so long. Surely you realise I am of age when I must be introduced into society? Besides—'

'Hush, child,' he interrupted. 'Perhaps next year. You are still only twenty-one years of age and—'

'—And what, Papa?' she entreated. 'Tell me, is it your intention to wait until I am an old maid? Until I am so old and ugly that no self-respecting man would want to marry me, anyway?'

Embarrassed, Giles diverted his eyes away from her. 'Pray calm yourself, Elizabeth. You have all the time in the world yet. You are still a mere child, my dear.'

It was with rising indignation that Elizabeth told him otherwise. 'But I am not, Papa! I am not! Why, most young ladies of my age have already acquired suitors and are contemplating marriage. But I will never find a husband if you continue to hide me away here!'

'Elizabeth, shame on you!' he retaliated. 'I am your father, and I do know what is best for you. Pray do not offend my ears with such wayward talk again!' His cheeks had turned into a shade of deep purple, just as they always did when he become irate. Giles suffered from high blood pressure brought on by his inability to deal with troublesome situations with equanimity. He always had to shout and lose his temper.

'Have I not given you everything you ever wanted, Elizabeth? Clothes, jewellery and now your new mare? I ask you in all earnest – what else must a father do to bring about his daughter's pleasure?'

Elizabeth looked contrite, sorry for having offended him now. Moments later she was by his side imploring forgiveness. 'Oh, I do beg your pardon, Papa! Please forgive my rudeness. It was not my intention to distress you so.'

The master's expression softened. 'Hush, my dear, let us forget the matter. You know how dearly I love you, Elizabeth, and you must learn to trust my judgment, child. Believe me when I say I know what is best for you.'

'Yes, I know, Papa. But I wish you would try to understand me a little better. Understand that I am no longer a child . . . but a woman.'

'Yes, yes, Elizabeth!' he said with some agitation. 'Now please return to the breakfast table and let that be the end of the matter.'

Charlotte heaved a sigh. Once again her brother had won the day – but then did he not always? It was the same every time the two became involved in verbal conflict. Giles always belittled Elizabeth into submission. But things would change! The day would come when she would fight back; fight him with the same stubbornness which he extended towards her. When that day arrived, they would all have to look to their laurels. And arrive it surely would.

'How do you intend to pass your time during my absence, Elizabeth?' asked Giles, turning to his daughter again.

'Oh, I expect to be kept busy in Bluebell Wood, Papa. I hear the bluebells are at their best now. I do hope so, for I plan on making a start on my painting this morning.' Painting was her life. It was really all she had to call her own.

Giles ran a hand around his Dundreary whiskers, then nodded his approval. 'Yes, very commendable, my dear. Work diligently, Elizabeth. Conduct yourself with propriety at all times – and remember the rules. You must not—'

'—Go beyond the boundary of the estate.' She spoke the words on his behalf, for she had heard them so many times before. 'I know, Papa, and I will not,' she told him quietly.

Charlotte pursed her lips. Even in Giles' absence his authority lived on. Poor Elizabeth! She was not allowed to travel beyond the boundaries of her father's estate. Although he behaved towards her with love, he ruled her with the same rod of iron as he did everyone else. He would not allow her to attend social functions of any kind: parties, musical evenings, the Sunday afternoon picnics organised by the church, indeed, to go anywhere where she might meet people of her own age. And more to the point – meet young men. He was afraid of losing her, although it might be asked whether his very principles were not enough to drive her away. Charlotte believed so. Oh, she had warned him on more occasions than she could remember about the possible consequences of his folly. Warned him that if he failed to change his attitude, then the day would come when his daughter would rebel against him and go her own way. Moreover, he would have no-one to blame but himself. But being Sir Giles Montgomery, he had stubbornly refused to listen to her warnings, and would no doubt have to live with the result of his mistakes one day.

Some time later he made his departure from the Hall, driven to the station in his fine carriage and pair by the Montgomery coachman. His long-suffering valet smiled with relief from one of the upstairs windows, along with the rest of the staff who witnessed his welcome departure. Jovial laughter would replace their customary solemnity as they proceeded about their daily business, and a pleasant, friendly atmosphere would prevail during the next few days.

Among those delighted to see the back of him was none other than his own son, Edward, who had purposely remained well out of his father's way after he had sent him on an early morning errand to Squire Ridley's home. Dissatisfaction had broken out amongst the labourers employed on Sir Giles' estate, and placing himself above such menial and distasteful matters, Giles had chosen to evade his duties by sending his son to deal with the matter on his behalf.

Edward waited patiently behind one of the oak trees until his father's carriage had disappeared out of sight. Then, smiling to himself, he urged his horse into a brisk canter as he headed down the drive towards the house. At twenty-five years of age, standing six feet tall and slender in build, Edward made a fine figure of a man. Blue-eyed, fair and dashing, he was by nature kindly disposed and carried himself well amongst others. He was held in high esteem and respected by all who knew him; the kind of man whose trust could be counted upon at all times. Edward would make an admirable master when the time arrived – and for many that time could not come soon enough.

Elizabeth was on her way out when he came striding through the front door. Now dressed in a jade green riding habit, black button-up boots and a wide-brimmed hat adorned by colourful feathers, she was all set for her ride to the wood. Her face lit up on seeing her handsome brother. 'Oh, there you are, Edward! I missed you at breakfast. Did you manage to see Papa before he left for London?'

Edward gave her a brotherly hug. She looked beautiful this morning – but then did she not always? 'Good morning, my dear sister! No, I did not see Father. He sent me to Markham Lodge with a view to discussing our latest problems with Squire Ridley.' He threw down his hat and riding crop on to one of the chairs and heaved a sigh. 'I am afraid we have trouble, Elizabeth, and needless to say the matter has been left in the hands of the good squire and myself.'

'What kind of trouble, Edward?' she asked.

'Oh, the kind which Father has brought upon himself,' he replied in a long-suffering voice. 'The man continues to allow those impoverished families to live in uncivilised squalor in appalling tumbledown cottages without so much as the most meagre of comforts to console them. Why, the places are nothing but hovels! Cold, damp, filthy hovels! I tell you, Elizabeth, it makes me feel ashamed!'

Elizabeth had never seen her brother so angry. Normally Edward was controlled and placid, but all the recent trouble had infuriated him. There was no need for it. A little more of the milk of human kindness from the master and the matter would soon be resolved. But that would be the day when pigs took to flight, no doubt.

'How Father can stand by and watch them starve and suffer as they do is beyond me!' he exclaimed, striding up and down the hall with his hands clasped behind his back. ''Tis a well known fact that other profitable estates allow the workers to share in the fruits of the land. They are given an annual allowance of potatoes, milk, wheat and cider, and above all are given decent homes in which to live and bring up their families. But not here!' he sneered. 'Not here!'

Helpless, Elizabeth stood quietly listening.

'Oh, there are other problems, too,' he continued. 'Many of our tenants have got seriously behind with their rent and father has demanded that they either pay up or get out. Ah, he cares not that they have nowhere to go; have nothing to their names but a few sticks of old furniture and the rags upon their backs. His indifference to their plight appals me, Elizabeth – especially when I see him driving off in his fine carriage, and to what? To fritter away his money on his high society friends in London. Oh! 'Tis nothing but wasteful expenditure, and in my opinion both his time and money could be put to far better use right here! Anyway,' he sighed, 'I fear the problem will not remain for much longer. Keep this to yourself, Elizabeth, but Squire Ridley informed me on good authority that a nearby estate is offering good wages and housing to any decent hard-working man in need of employment. Moreover, many of our labourers are being considered. If the fellows desert us, then we shall have no men left to undertake the work on our own estate, and with harvest time approaching, well . . . heaven knows what will happen then.'

'Oh, Edward, Papa will be furious!' exclaimed Elizabeth.

'Hah, furious is an understatement, my dear sister! Just wait until he discovers the identity of the landowner. The very name of our labourers' highly respected new saviour will be enough to guarantee him a seizure!'

'Who is he, Edward?' she asked, wondering who would have the audacity to cross her father's path in such a manner. 'Do we know him?'

Edward's laugh held a touch of irony. 'Well, we certainly know of him, although as yet, we have not had the pleasure of meeting him in person.'

Elizabeth looked greatly puzzled. 'But who is he, Edward? Who?'

'You will never guess in a hundred years, Elizabeth. Would you believe me when I tell you he is—'

Poor Elizabeth! She never did learn the name of the man, for at that moment Aunt Charlotte appeared from the morning room interrupting Edward. She was surprised to see Elizabeth in the hall. 'I thought you had already left for the wood, dear,' she said. 'Be off with you before it becomes too hot to paint.'

'Yes, I am going, Aunt Charlotte. I have just been exchanging a word with Edward.' She smiled at each of them. 'Until later, then. I promise to be home in time for tea.'

'Enjoy yourself, Elizabeth,' said Aunt Charlotte.

'Yes, enjoy yourself, my dear sister – and make the most of your freedom!' called Edward teasingly.

Rhapsody, Elizabeth's mare, was all saddled and waiting when her mistress arrived at the stables, and nuzzled her soft velvet nose against her hand in affection. Elizabeth patted her and, before leaving for her ride, thanked Ned for all his hard work.

Pleased, the old man straightened himself and smiled. 'Why, thank ye, Miss Elizabeth. But then, anything is a pleasure for ye!'

Soon horse and rider were trotting along the path which led to Bluebell Wood, the sky clear and blue above them. It was hot today, without so much as a whisper of a breeze to cool the air. Oh, but it felt so good to get away from the house! So good to be alive and free!

Elizabeth reflected on her earlier conversation with her father, frustrated by his failure to understand her problems. After all, it was his duty to introduce her into society, was it not? Also to find her a suitor? But he appeared to have no wish to show her off at all. He adamantly refused to take her to London with him – indeed, anywhere else for that matter. Besides that, he allowed her no personal freedom at all. It was beyond her comprehension why he acted in such a way and may God forgive her, but it often provoked her to rebellion. She sighed to herself as she rode along, for there was no point in worrying about it now. Besides, the eligible young men whom she had already met had been most unprepossessing, half of them afflicted by an unsavoury amount of spots and pimples, whilst the others bored her to death with their self-centred conversation. Perhaps her father was doing her a favour after all. If they were an example of what men had to offer, then perhaps she was better off without!

The wood looked magnificent, proudly displaying the most spectacular carpet of bluebells she had ever seen. The sight of it left her breathless. If only her talent as an artist could do it justice, then it would make the most impressive picture on canvas. Eager to begin, she found the ideal spot to sit and work. Rhapsody nibbled at the grass, now relieved of the encumbrance of Elizabeth's canvas, paints and easel, which Ned had placed in a linen bag and secured firmly to her saddle.

Despite the shade of the overhanging trees, the sun filtered with ever-increasing power through the branches, eventually causing Elizabeth discomforture. She felt hot and sticky and her clothes were damp from perspiration.

Eventually she decided to take a stroll through the wood to cool down.

The sound of a trickling stream meandering close by was like music to her ears. She smiled and, abandoning her modesty, removed her clothes until she was wearing nothing but her camisole and drawers. Next she stepped into the cool, inviting water, wading in until she was standing knee-high in the centre of the stream. Her eyes closed as she raised her face towards the sky, wallowing in the pleasure of the moment. Oh, how wonderfully refreshing it felt standing there with her hands submerged in the water! Her peace and enjoyment were short-lived, however, for a moment later a sound from the bank broke the silence. Startled, she was horrified to see a man astride a horse only a few short yards away on the bank. Oh, the shame! The disgrace of it! Being caught in such an unladylike manner dressed in nothing but her underwear, her hair in a state of disarray!

Deeply embarrassed, she began to make as dignified a retreat from the stream as circumstances would allow, blushing crimson and aware of the man's eyes focused upon her. Elizabeth raised her head to look up at him, totally unprepared for the flood of feeling which followed. Whatever else she had expected on that glorious May afternoon, it could not compare with the overwhelming sensation she experienced when her eyes met his. She was instantly spellbound, held captive in a long look of what appeared to be mutual fascination. Oh, how exceedingly handsome he was, far more handsome than any man had a right to be; the kind which every woman dreamed about in the deepest, most secret reaches of her heart! He looked a tall man astride his black stallion, dark haired, blue-eyed, possessing the finest bone structure she had ever seen. In fact, she conceded, he looked foreign, for he exuded a certain air which was by no means English. On any showing, he was enough to put the rest of them to shame; mere mortals in the presence of a god.

Their eyes travelled over one another; he, dressed in a fine black coat, a white shirt which had a ruffle of frills down the front and around each cuff, black riding breeches which hugged his legs, and high black boots; she, dressed in her cotton broderie anglaise underwear. The stranger was having a disturbing effect on Elizabeth's senses. She grew shy and bashful, cowering behind a cloak of femininity, whilst he just sat and smiled.

They remained gazing at each other, and when they spoke, the first words came from him.'Ummm . . . how very nice! A water baby, I presume? Or are you perhaps a wood nymph?'

The sound of his warm, vibrant voice with its hint of French accent sent tingles of delight running down Elizabeth's spine, and the intimate way in which his eyes were gazing down at her brought a flush of colour to her cheeks. His mouth curved into a gentle smile. It was clear that he was aware of her embarrassment. Indeed, it could be said he was enjoying it.

Her voice betrayed a tremor as she replied, 'Y . . . you have me at a clear disadvantage, Sir, so . . . so if you would kindly turn your back whilst I step out of the water . . .'

His broad smile made him even more appealing. 'But of course,' he said in a gentlemanly manner. Obligingly, he turned his horse around until both were facing the other way. When she was safely standing on the bank, he reversed the motion.

Her hair hung loose down her back and she was standing with her arms crossed in front of her, hiding the cleavage which he had already seen. 'I was not aware you were riding through the wood, Sir, or you would not have found me . . .'

'. . . Found you enjoying a dip in the stream dressed in nothing but your undergarments?' He finished the sentence for her.

Elizabeth blushed crimson. His eyes were twinkling with amusement at her dilemma – but worse than that – they were so personal!

He threw back his head and laughed, then removed his coat and handed it down to her. 'Here, put this on,' he said, 'although, personally speaking I prefer to look at you as you are.'

Oh, such boldness! And coming from a gentleman like himself! Elizabeth cast him a reproachful look, but the man chose to ignore it. She placed his coat around her. The feel of it felt warm against her skin, and the very knowledge that it was his warmth caused a flurry of excitement within her. Secretly, she conceded against all shame that wearing his garment was the next best thing to – dare she even think it? – actually touching him! She chided herself for such a reckless thought, for it seemed her heart had suddenly sprung alive with a boldness of its own. Curiosity prompted her into wondering who he was. A stranger, most certainly, for no man who resided in these parts would have had the audacity to ride across her father's land.

'May I enquire what your business is in my father's wood, Sir? And did it not occur to you that you might be trespassing?'

'Your father's wood?' he said with a frown.

'Yes, it surely is, Sir. And I hasten to add that he takes an exceedingly poor view of trespassers whom he finds on his property.'

He did not seem in the least perturbed by her statement, and she was left with the impression that nothing would disturb a man of his considerable consequence. He surely looked the part of an aristocrat astride his horse, and simply replied by saying that he believed the path through the wood would serve as a short cut to Netley.

'Do you require an apology for my unlawful intrusion?' he asked, smiling in a most disarming manner.

'Of course not. 'Tis just that . . . that you surprised me whilst I was bathing. No-one from these parts would dare venture on to my father's property. No man in the county possesses the nerve.'

'Ah, yes. Your father! Who exactly might he be?' asked the stranger.

Elizabeth patted his gentle horse, then was compelled to rub her own neck, for she was getting a crick in it having to look up at him like that. Seeing her dilemma, he dismounted. He was taller than she had envisaged, six feet two inches at least, slim in figure yet powerfully built, a man who exuded a masculinity which made her head reel. She drew a breath, held it, overpowered by excitement at his closeness.

'I asked you who your father might be?' he repeated softly.

'Oh, yes,' she replied, hastily collecting her senses. 'My father is Sir Giles Montgomery of Cambourne Hall. Perhaps you have heard of him?'

The man's features instantly hardened and a long silence ensued. Elizabeth looked puzzled. 'Might something be wrong, Sir? Was it perchance something I said?'

Marginally his expression softened. ''Tis just the name,' he said, then, 'Oh, how fitting that I should choose *his* particular land on which to trespass!' He stared at her with an unfathomable look on his face. 'You must be Elizabeth? Elizabeth Montgomery?'

'Yes. I am Elizabeth. But how did you know?'

'My dear young woman, being the daughter of the infamous Sir Giles Montgomery, I ask you in all sincerity – how would I *not* know who you were?'

His eyes were burning into her, and the feelings which flooded into her heart exploded into thrills of wild excitement. She was unsure of how to master such emotion, for was she not a stranger to the tender passions?

'I believe it is time I introduced myself,' he said, 'although perhaps you might wish I had kept silent when you come to learn my name. I am Count de Ville – Richard de Ville. I expect the name is familiar to you, matters being what they are between our families?'

Elizabeth could not have looked more shocked if he had told her his name was Robin Hood! She gasped and stood before him in frozen silence. Oh, the man was none other than the son of her father's late, hated enemy! He was a de Ville! A de Ville! Lord, but if Sir Giles could see her now, he would already be travelling back on the first train to Shropshire!

'I see my identity has shocked you, Miss Montgomery,' he commented. 'Tell me in all truth, does the name disturb you so much?'

Elizabeth stared at him. 'Disturb her' was an understatement!

''Tis . . . 'tis just that you were the last person I expected to meet, Count de Ville. Naturally, I have heard your name mentioned many times but . . . but presumed you still resided at your chateau in France.' Deep colour suffused her cheeks, for finding oneself in the company of a de Ville was enough to throw even the most level-headed of Montgomerys off balance. For as long as she could remember, her father had insisted that she too must despise the family whom he hated so much. But, being a woman of her own mind, she had always refused. The animosity which existed was his and his alone. She would have no part of it.

He caused her heart to flutter madly when he suddenly placed a finger beneath her chin and gently raised her face towards his, melting her beneath his tender gaze.

'As a matter of fact, Miss Montgomery, I was unprepared to meet you too . . . the beautiful daughter of my late father's enemy. Perhaps now you wish our paths had not crossed? Am I correct?'

She smiled nervously. Was it the fact that he was a de Ville that unnerved her so? Or was it that he was a man who had the power to bring alive in her a passion previously unknown to her? It was the latter, and she knew it.

'Not at all, Monsieur de Ville. On the contrary, I am exceedingly pleased to make your acquaintance at last.'

He smiled. 'Are you indeed? And you are not afraid of me?'

'Afraid of you? Why should I be?'

'Ah, well, I thought perhaps your father might have warned you what an unspeakable monster I am and who knows what else, in an attempt to poison your mind against me and my family.'

Elizabeth squared her shoulders and proceeded to make quite clear her feelings regarding their family feud. 'Monsieur de Ville, I stress that I play no part in my father's vendetta against your family. I abhor his behaviour towards you and speak not only for myself, but also for my aunt and brother. None of us bears you any ill will. We never have.'

The Count looked pleased. 'Bravo, Miss Montgomery! I find your sentiments commendable. We are also tired of the animosity which exists between us and believe it time that it was ended.'

Elizabeth sighed. If only her father shared the same enthusiasm for peace, then all would be well indeed! But in all probability he would take his hatred to the grave with him. 'Unfortunately, Monsieur, I am unable to speak for my father. I fear he will never extend a hand of friendship towards you, regardless of our wishes.'

'Quite so,' he replied quietly. 'But we can always live in hope, Miss Montgomery.'

After a moment's silence, Elizabeth said, 'Well, Monsieur, I fear I must return to my painting, although I believe there is little more I can achieve this afternoon.'

'Painting?' His eyes widened with interest. 'You mean you are an artist, Miss Montgomery?'

She smiled. 'Oh, a mere amateur, Count de Ville. That is why I am here, to paint the wood whilst the bluebells are in flower. Unfortunately the weather became too hot and I . . .'

'. . . You took a bathe in the stream instead. But then I came along and spoiled it for you, did I not?'

'Oh, no, Monsieur! No—' She blushed profusely, fearing she had spoken with indecent promptitude. 'I . . . I must return your coat,' she said hurriedly. 'If you would care to wait a moment whilst I change . . .'

His mouth curved in a smile. 'I would be delighted, Miss Montgomery. Besides, I would dearly love to see your painting.'

They walked to the clearing, where he sat on a fallen log admiring her work whilst she proceeded to dress behind a sturdy oak. She took off his coat, then held it against her face, breathing in that unforgettable aroma. His aroma. Afterwards she rejoined him, shy as she sat beside him on the log. Being a lady of rectitude, she was careful not to sit too close.

He appeared most knowledgeable on the subject of art and admired her work. 'It is plain to see you possess remarkable talent, Miss Montgomery, for even at this early stage your painting exudes great promise. Perhaps I shall commission you to paint one for me one day.'

Elizabeth smiled warmly. 'It would be a pleasure, Monsieur de Ville.' Afterwards she fell into timid silence, unsure of what to say to him.

The Count sensed her shyness and asked, 'May I stay for a while, Miss Montgomery? My business of the day has been completed. Besides, I find it so peaceful here in the wood . . . and with such charming company, too.'

'Certainly,' she replied, carefully hiding her enthusiasm. 'Your company would be most pleasing, Sir. Perhaps you would entertain me by telling me all about yourself.' An idea occurred to her. Perhaps she could sketch him whilst he was talking? That way she would be able to look at him until her eyes wore out. Obtaining his permission, she proceeded.

He was a delight to listen to, explaining that he had returned to England a few weeks ago to run the estate which his late father, Robert de Ville, had left. But he told her that he intended to retain their family chateau in Bordeaux, planning to divide his time between the two.

'Anyway, enough of myself, Miss Montgomery,' he said eventually. 'It is your turn now. I wish to hear about you. You obviously gain a great deal of enjoyment from painting, but tell me, what else gives you pleasure in life? Are you perhaps a lover of the theatre or . . .?'

'No . . . no, I am afraid not, Monsieur,' she replied. 'I have never been to the theatre. Papa . . . Papa will not permit it, you see.'

'Will not permit it?' he repeated questioningly. 'But why, may I ask?'

Elizabeth grew embarrassed. 'I . . . I really do not know, Monsieur. 'Tis just the way he is.'

'And how about musical evenings and other social functions? Does he permit you to attend those?'

Her silence was as good as a reply, and it was with unfeigned annoyance that he suddenly rose to his feet to stand before her. 'Just what will he permit you to do, Miss Montgomery?' he asked brusquely, then replied to his own question by adding, 'Precious little, if my knowledge of your father is correct! Why, I do believe he rules your life as he would once have ruled my mother's! Oh, but the fellow never changes, does he?'

Indignation prompted Elizabeth into jumping to her feet before him. 'Monsieur, I deplore your remarks! Might I remind you that you are speaking about my father!'

Penitent was the last thing he looked. 'Nevertheless, it is true, is it not? He rules you exactly as he rules everyone else. Admit it, Miss Montgomery – unless you are afraid to!'

His remarks had angered Elizabeth but, worse than that, she burned with another kind of passion, one which was far more difficult to contain. She wanted to slap that arrogant handsome face of his, but at the same time longed to throw her arms around his neck and hold him. These strange new feelings disturbed her and, tormented by conflicting emotions, she turned quickly away in an effort to escape him. But there was no escape, for he reached out and grasped her wrist. The touch of his fingers against her skin sent an explosion of feeling rushing through her body, exciting every part of her. Looking up, she saw his eyes smouldering into her own, unashamedly displaying the same fiery passion.

The next thing she knew he was pulling her against him, his free arm entwining itself around her tiny waist. She struggled vainly, but eventually yielded and allowed herself to be held captive in his arms. Her own arms were up about his shoulders, but for all the world she could not remember placing them there. Trembling, she raised her face to his. Oh . . . but there was no sign of laughter in those eyes of his now. Instead, they burned from the feelings which possessed his heart, searching her own in a manner which totally consumed her. She saw them linger upon her mouth and for one wonderful moment believed he was about to kiss her. Her eyes closed and her lips parted expectantly. But he must have thought better of it for, instead of kissing her, he moved to hold her at arm's length. Disappointed, she opened her eyes and stared at him. He looked just as shaken as she.

'Please forgive me, Miss Montgomery. I had no right to speak of your father that way.'

Elizabeth gasped. She had completely forgotten about their earlier words; those which had initiated the embrace which had just taken place between them. Had she expected an apology, then she would have thought it more likely to be in consequence of his behaviour. But apparently not. It seemed he did not see fit to apologise for that.

'It simply angered me to learn that your father treats you so selfishly, Miss Montgomery. However, I realise it is no concern of mine. Please do forgive me.'

'Y . . . you are forgiven, Monsieur,' she uttered shakily. 'There is enough bad feeling between our families without you and me adding to it.'

He smiled. 'Thank you. Incidentally, I would prefer you to address me by my Christian name . . . Richard. And I shall call you Elizabeth.'

She felt herself melting again, for when it came to charm, the man had certainly been endowed with more than his fair share. 'I am afraid it is time for me to go, Mon . . . Richard. I promised my aunt I would be home for tea.'

'I see. Then I must not detain you, Elizabeth.'

She adored the way he spoke her name. Although his accent was not a strong one, due to the fact that he had been educated in England, she found it most delightful. He assisted her with her belongings, then accompanied her to where Rhapsody was tethered. It seemed he was not at all happy about her riding a horse which was so encumbered by equipment, and said as much.

'Are you certain you want to ride all the way home like that, Elizabeth? I shudder to think what would happen if your mare took fright and bolted with you. Would you not agree that a pony and trap would be more suitable for transporting your equipment?'

'Yes, I expect it would, Richard. But Rhapsody is used to it now. Besides, she rarely takes fright at anything.'

He emitted a sigh. 'Very well, Elizabeth. But if you were mine . . .'

Boldly, she gazed up into the potent depth of his eyes. 'Yes? If I were yours . . .?' she asked, allowing her voice to trail away invitingly.

Smiling, he took the bait and stepped a little closer. 'If you were mine, I would forbid you to travel in such a precarious manner. Instead, I would insist that you used a pony and trap – whether you were in favour of the idea or not.'

Amused, Elizabeth began to laugh. This was obviously his dominating side emerging. It reminded her of someone else. 'Oh, but you sound exactly like my father! I do believe there is little or nothing to choose between you!'

Her remark came as an invitation to deny any such thing. Placing his arms around her waist, he drew her gently against him. Her gasp was one of pleasure rather than of shock.

'Is that so?' he murmured. 'Well, my dear young woman, allow me to convey that at this very moment I feel less like your father than I would ever have you know. Do I make myself clear?'

Elizabeth's cheeks turned pink. She understood him only too well!

Releasing her, he bent to pick a handful of bluebells. 'For you,' he said. 'A small keepsake of today.' He then kissed her hand in gentlemanly fashion. 'Thank you for a most delightful afternoon, Elizabeth. May I ask if you will be in the wood tomorrow morning?'

'But of course. I have my painting to complete, have I not?'

'Good! Then with your permission, so shall I. Would ten o'clock be too early?'

Elizabeth felt rapturous. He wanted to see her again tomorrow! Oh, what bliss! 'Not at all,' she said with detectable enthusiasm. 'I shall look forward to it!'

He smiled. 'And so shall I. Au revoir, Elizabeth. Until tomorrow, then.'

'Au revoir, Richard. Until tomorrow.'

Spellbound, Richard watched her ride away. What a fascinating creature Elizabeth Montgomery was! Her beauty left him breathless, and never before had he met a woman who came remotely close to equalling her. Oh, there had been women in France who had pursued his affections, but his heart had remained closed to them, kept in his own possession until Elizabeth Montgomery had suddenly entered his life and stolen it from him. Richard smiled to himself. He would never have believed it possible to lose his heart to a woman so quickly and completely. It had happened the first moment he had seen her, when she had been standing in the stream with her face raised towards the sky. She had made the most bewitching picture.

Richard knew he would never be the same man again. On this glorious day in May, he had met the woman with whom he wished to share the rest of his life, to love and cherish always; a woman who would bear his children. The thought filled his heart with tremendous joy, although he sensed it would not be easy, she being who she was. Oh, dear God, why out of all the women in the world did she have to be Sir Giles Montgomery's daughter?

That evening at dinner, Elizabeth's behaviour was a source of bewilderment to Charlotte and Edward. She seemed barely able to contain herself, smiling as though she were in possession of some wonderful inner secret. After watching her dispose of an ample serving of game soup, a sizable portion of saddle of mutton with all the trimmings *and* asking for a second helping of cook's special sherry trifle, Edward found he could bear the suspense no longer.

'Elizabeth, your appetite astounds me! Pray what has brought on the urge to consume so much food? And why, my dear sister, have you been unable to refrain from smiling to yourself all the way through dinner?' He clasped his hands together looking brotherly. 'I perceive you are hiding something, Elizabeth. Is it likely you are ever going to tell us what it is?'

Elizabeth suddenly poured forth her new-found happiness. 'Oh, Edward, something wonderful happened to me today! Something which may well alter the whole course of my life!'

The two onlookers exchanged puzzled glances. What did Elizabeth mean?

'You see . . . I met a man today!'

Charlotte's eyebrows shot up in astonishment. 'A man?' she exclaimed. 'But where? And how?'

'It was in the wood, Aunt Charlotte. I was bathing in the stream dressed in my underwear when . . .'

'Your underwear!' gasped her horrified aunt. 'Oh, shame on you, Elizabeth! I fear you must have been overcome by too much sun!'

Edward burst into a fit of uncontrollable laughter. He simply threw back his head and roared.

Eventually his sister rebuked him for such ungentlemanly behaviour. 'Is it your intention to sit there laughing for the rest of the evening, Edward? Or do you wish to know what happened to me next?'

Edward's laugh grew more raucous. 'Hah! Hah! Under the circumstances perhaps I ought to refrain from listening, Elizabeth! As you know, my dear sister, I am a man of modesty myself, and have no wish for my tender young ears to be offended by confessions of what befell you in the wood whilst dressed only in your underwear!'

'Edward! What a dreadful beast you are! I am ashamed of you!'

'Oh, forgive me, Elizabeth, but your behaviour never fails to shock me. Indeed, only you could be so shameful!' The words had been punctuated by laughter. Edward then addressed his aunt. 'Oh, Aunt Charlotte, I fear my sister lacks refinement, and suspect she is in need of a little tuition on how to conduct herself when out painting in Bluebell Wood!'

Aunt Charlotte rolled her eyes, whilst Elizabeth took retributory action by throwing her napkin at him. Grinning with good humour, Edward then apologised. 'I was only teasing you, my dear. Pray continue with your story.'

Elizabeth proceeded to tell them how she had met the stranger; told them everything with the exception of his name. She would confound them with that in a moment.

'What an extraordinary occurrence, Elizabeth,' said her aunt thoughtfully. 'But who was he? And of what appearance was he, might I add?'

'Oh . . .' Her niece breathed the longest sigh. 'He was of wonderful appearance, tall . . . prodigiously handsome. A most elegant figure of a man.'

'But *who was he*, Elizabeth?' Her aunt was growing exasperated.

Elizabeth squared herself. It was time to confound them with her surprise. Confound them was exactly what she did.

'Count de Ville? Oh, bless my life!' cried Aunt Charlotte. 'Tell me you are jesting, Elizabeth?'

'She is not jesting,' interpolated Edward seriously. 'Elizabeth's description fits the Count most admirably. 'Twas he she met this afternoon, I am certain of it.'

Elizabeth gazed from one to the other. 'But of course it was! Is it your belief I would deceive you?'

'Of course not,' said her aunt grimly, 'although I doubted that even you could be foolish enough to spend the entire afternoon in the company of a man named de Ville.' She gave a sigh of despair before continuing. 'Did you not consider what would happen if your father found out, Elizabeth? You acted imprudently, and I fear that—'

'I am not wishful to upset you, Aunt Charlotte,' interrupted her niece, 'but I fear I did no such thing. Indeed, I saw nothing imprudent in spending a simply perfect afternoon in the company of a most charming man – one, I might add, of pleasing manners and propriety. A man who treated me with both respect and courtesy.'

'But he is a *de Ville*, Elizabeth!'

'It matters not to me, Aunt Charlotte! I have already informed Richard that I play no part in Papa's vendetta against his family. That none of us do.'

Consumed with anxiety, Charlotte endeavoured to make Elizabeth see sense. 'Yes, I understand, my dear. But you know how your father hates that family, and with a bitterness which is beyond me! He would never allow you any kind of relationship with Rebecca de Ville's son. Never! Take heed, Elizabeth, you must not cherish feelings for this man. The result would be catastrophic for us all. Can you not see that, pray?'

'But that is ridiculous! I refuse to share Papa's wicked feelings and will not endorse his hatred or take part in his objectionable feud! I will not!' declared Elizabeth rebelliously.

Charlotte Montgomery bowed her head and sighed. 'Oh Elizabeth, you are so impetuous, child. I agree with you in part. But your father expects your loyalty – even though it is misplaced.'

'But it is wrong of Papa to hand down his hatred to his family and expect it to live on in the hearts of his children!'

'I wholeheartedly agree,' said Edward, joining in the conversation. 'The old man is wrong to assume such liberties. Besides, it is time the feud with the de Villes was brought to an end, and I for one will be delighted to extend a hand of friendship towards the Count. 'Tis high time one of us did!'

'You appear to know him, Edward?' said Elizabeth, grateful for his support.

'Indeed, I do, my dear. He is the man of whom I was speaking this morning. The landowner who is willing to offer good housing and wages to any able-bodied fellow in need of work.'

'Oh, 'tis he?' Elizabeth gasped.

'Yes. I made it my business to make discreet enquiries about the man, and what I learned is most admirable. Count de Ville is a gentleman of upstanding character and of some considerable means, and suffice it to say, will make a far better master than our own misguided father. Our men will be richer in both means and security. Good luck to them, I say!'

'Saints preserve us!' groaned Aunt Charlotte. 'Giles will be demented when he hears about this. If only the Count had remained in France, then none of this would have happened!'

'Shame on you, Aunt Charlotte!' chided Elizabeth. 'Were you to know him, then I am certain you would change your opinion and hold him in great esteem. Speaking for myself, I can hardly wait to see him again tomorrow.'

'See him again tomorrow?' echoed her aunt. 'Oh, no, Elizabeth! No! It would be folly even to think of such a thing!'

Elizabeth looked defiant. 'But I promised, Aunt Charlotte. And it is a promise I intend to keep.'

Charlotte turned to her nephew in desperation. 'Oh, Edward! Please talk some sense into your sister before disaster befalls us all! Dissuade her from this meeting with the Count tomorrow!'

Edward slapped his hand against his thigh and heaved a sigh. 'My dear Aunt Charlotte, you are as aware of my sister's stubbornness as I. Why, I would have more success in persuading pigs to fly! Besides, I believe Elizabeth is old enough to determine her own friends. So grant her your consent, Aunt Charlotte, and allow her to enjoy a little happiness.' After casting Elizabeth an understanding smile, he strode from the room leaving the women alone together.

Following a careful inward debate, Charlotte rose to her feet and approached Elizabeth. 'Very well, Elizabeth, you may meet Count de Ville tomorrow – but I beg you, dear, do not allow yourself to grow fond of him. Nothing can come of it.'

Elizabeth kissed her in gratitude. 'Thank you, Aunt Charlotte. I do appreciate your kindness. But as for my growing fond of him, I am afraid it is too late. You see, I love him. I loved him the very first moment I saw him, and nothing in the world can change that.'

CHAPTER SEVEN

Richard was waiting in the wood for Elizabeth next morning, sitting on the fallen log where they had sat together the day before, his horse tethered nearby. Elizabeth was in high spirits. She had longed for this moment and had missed him desperately since their initial meeting. The sound of his deep, vibrant voice sent raptures of delight running down her spine as he bid her a cheerful good morning.

'Good morning, Richard!' she called. 'You are early!'

Smiling broadly, he covered the distance between them in four long strides. Their eyes met as he lowered her from her horse, and when her feet touched the ground he wrapped his arms around her waist and drew her against him, his expression remarkably tender. 'You look beautiful, Elizabeth,' he murmured. 'I cannot tell you how much I have looked forward to today . . . to seeing you again.'

Elizabeth's heart pounded as she gazed into his face and she felt lost in the nearness of him. Her hands were resting on his shoulders and she could feel the heat which radiated from his body. Those crystal blue eyes of his burned into hers, bringing a flush of colour to her cheeks.

He cast her a sensual smile. 'Do I make you nervous, Elizabeth?'

'N . . . nervous? N . . . no, of course not,' she fibbed. 'Why should you?'

She withdrew from his arms, afraid he would guess the feelings which possessed her heart.

Amused, he gave a laugh, then reached for her hand and pressed it against his lips. 'Forgive me if I do not altogether believe you, Elizabeth,' he mocked.

Later they sat together on the log. 'I see you have brought your equipment with you,' he said. 'You are hoping to continue your painting of the wood, no doubt?'

Elizabeth cast him a smile. 'No, not exactly. As a matter of fact, Richard, I had hoped to paint something rather special today – whilst I have the chance, you understand.'

'I see. And what would that be?'

'You.'

'Me? You wish to paint a likeness of me?'

'You do not wish me to?' The words were spoken sweetly.

He laughed. 'Now, I did not say that, Elizabeth. Naturally I find it flattering—'

'Then you will allow it! Oh, please Richard! You would make a wonderful subject. Besides, I have never done a portrait before and confess you would make perfect practice for me.'

'Perfect practice?' He pulled a face. 'Is that really all I amount to?'

'Of course not.' She laughed.

'Very well, I will allow it, Elizabeth. Where would you like me to sit?'

'Oh, thank you, Richard. I do appreciate it. And I would like you to sit on your horse, then I shall always be reminded of our first meeting yesterday.'

Shortly afterwards, after the preparations had been completed, Elizabeth began. Richard's horse, Black Shadow, was remarkably patient for an animal of his high spirit and stood long enough for her to accomplish the outline she desired. She had made a good start on the portrait, and yesterday's sketches of Richard would be of tremendous value. Hopefully she would be able to undertake much of the work at home.

Never had she put so much love, so much of herself, into her work; her creativity was at its best today. She rested for a moment, her eyes upon him. What a handsome figure of a man he made! Dressed in the identical clothes he wore yesterday, his hair side-parted with the front bit falling softly across his forehead, he made the kind of picture she would never forget. The image of him as he was now would live on in her mind forever.

At midday they took a well deserved break, and sat together by the trickling stream eating fresh bread and paté and enjoying the Chateau de Ville wine which Richard had brought. During conversation, he admitted that although he had no liking for Elizabeth's father, he would be prepared to meet him half-way in friendship. 'But I do it only for you, Elizabeth,' he confessed, 'for in the light of our new-found friendship and the fact that I wish to see more of you, I feel it only prudent to gain your father's consent.'

Elizabeth was delighted. 'Oh, Richard, I am so pleased! I will do everything I can to help you gain his friendship. Papa and I get along exceedingly well together, and I feel certain I can persuade him to see you.' It reassured Elizabeth to think positively rather that negatively. Her father must be allowed his chance.

'I understand he is absent from home at the present time, Elizabeth. When do you expect his return?'

'Oh, not until next week,' she replied, her voice edged with relief. 'He is busy visiting in London, as he does every summer about this time.'

Richard smiled. 'Good. Then we still have a little time left together.' He reached for her hand and gave it a squeeze. 'Would you accompany me on a drive to the river next Sunday, Elizabeth? We could perhaps take a picnic with us and make it a special afternoon.'

Elizabeth's expression turned downcast. 'I fear such an outing is out of the question, Richard,' she replied. 'My aunt would never allow it. Please allow me to explain that Aunt Charlotte is responsible for me during Papa's absence. He gave orders that I am not to travel beyond the estate. I know she would not venture to deceive him on such a matter.'

'I see,' he murmured thoughtfully. 'Then perhaps it would be to our advantage if I spoke to your aunt myself, for 'tis only common courtesy, is it not? Besides, after presenting myself in person, perhaps I might gain her as an ally?'

Elizabeth immediately brightened. 'Oh, would you, Richard? You would charm all her fears away, I just know it!'

Her remark provoked him to laughter. 'Oh, how you flatter me with confidence, Elizabeth! Tomorrow morning I shall put it to the test. I intend to call at the Hall for the purpose of introducing myself to your aunt, so let us hope I make a good impression upon her judgment.'

The following morning, Elizabeth stood by the drawing room window eagerly awaiting Richard's arrival. Poor Aunt Charlotte had been consumed with alarm at hearing that Count de Ville would be calling at the Hall to make her acquaintance. 'Upon my soul!' she had declared, 'Whatever would Giles say if he knew that a de Ville was planning to cross the threshold of his home?'

Elizabeth had told her not to concern herself so, for her father was away in London and would never know of Richard's visit. She said that the Count wished to make peace with her father, and would it not be wonderful if they shook hands and agreed to forget the past and all their differences?

Although Charlotte had agreed, in her wisdom she knew that day would never come. 'Your father is too set in his determined ways ever to change now, Elizabeth,' she said.

Now Charlotte was seated on the tapestry-weave sofa in the drawing room in readiness to receive her distinguished guest. Dressed in her mauve silk dress with its white lace collar, she made a picture of charm and elegance, and Elizabeth knew she could rely upon her to make Richard feel both welcome and at ease whilst in the house of his enemy. Edward had expressed a keen wish to meet him, and arranged to make a timely appearance after the business at hand had been concluded.

'Oh, he is here! He is here!' cried Elizabeth.

'Elizabeth! Pray calm yourself, child! Might I remind you that a lady of breeding never shows such wanton enthusiasm,' scolded Charlotte. 'Come and sit beside·me on the sofa. And stop fidgeting. He will be here in a moment.'

Two minutes later, Granville Stokes, who for the past twenty-two years had been employed as butler to the household, entered the room in a state of panic. Count de Ville had condescended to make a personal call at the Hall in the absence of the master, and under the circumstances the astonished fellow was uncertain what to do.

'Calm yourself, Stokes,' said Charlotte quietly. 'It escaped my attention to tell you that the Count was expected here this morning.'

Stokes' jaw dropped open and, looking as puzzled as a man could be, he did as he was bid.

Moments later Richard de Ville made his entrance into the drawing room; the first occasion that a de Ville had crossed the threshold of the Montgomery family home since Sir Giles had been betrothed to Rebecca over thirty years ago.

Smiling, dashingly handsome in his black morning suit, he approached the two ladies, whereupon he politely introduced himself to the elder. 'How do you do, Miss Montgomery. It is a pleasure to meet you.'

Charlotte was immediately captivated by his striking appearance and charming manner, and extended her hand in greeting. 'How do you do, Count de Ville. 'Tis a pleasure to meet you, too.'

After he had kissed Elizabeth's hand in greeting, Charlotte begged him to take a seat and, wearing a smile on her face, eyed him whilst his gaze was averted to Elizabeth. Oh, it was no wonder she was so taken by him! Even her detailed description of the man failed to do him justice. He was devastatingly handsome, a most elegant figure of a man, enough to turn any woman's head. Besides his good looks, he possessed charm and a pleasing disposition. Suffice it to say, she had taken an immediate liking to him. In truth, how could she have done otherwise, she wondered?

'Elizabeth tells me that you wish to end the hostility between our families, Count de Ville?' She smiled warmly. 'How it gladdens my heart to know that you, at least, are prepared to let bygones be bygones – especially considering my brother's past misdeeds towards your family. I speak with sincerity when I say that I have never shared Giles' bitter feelings, and pray we all have a much brighter and friendlier future to look forward to.'

'Thank you most kindly, Miss Montgomery,' he said appreciatively. 'Your support is of great value to me. May we indeed look forward to better times.'

Later, when the three were partaking of sherry and biscuits, Charlotte raised her glass to the Count. 'I make a toast to the future and to the long-awaited peace between our families.'

'I second that, Miss Montgomery. To the future!' said the Count.

Afterwards, Richard was able to exchange a private word with Elizabeth.

'You look lovely this morning, Elizabeth. Your dress is beautiful . . . as indeed are you,' he murmured softly.

She smiled sweetly. Of course, this was the first time he had seen her wearing a dress. On their previous meetings she had been wearing her riding habit – and might the memory fade quickly of their first encounter, when she had been wearing nothing but her underwear! Perhaps the apricot bustle dress she was wearing now would compensate for that.

'Thank you, Richard,' she said graciously. The two gazed at one another in reflective fascination, both oblivious to Aunt Charlotte's presence in the room.

The old lady saw the exchange of feelings being transmitted between the couple and her heart took a worried turn. Oh, but this was love and no mistake – and love at its most powerful! She doubted that anyone would have the strength to part these two, not even Sir Giles Montgomery. After clearing her throat, she addressed Elizabeth. 'Dear, would you mind leaving the room for a moment? I wish to speak to the Count alone.'

Following her niece's departure, Charlotte was unsure of what to say. She had never been faced with this kind of situation before. 'Count de Ville,' she began, 'please understand that I am responsible for Elizabeth during my brother's absence, and under the circumstances feel I must enquire as to . . . to . . .'

'. . . To my intentions, Miss Montgomery?' He completed the sentence on her behalf. His disarming smile put her at ease. 'Miss Montgomery, you have my assurance as a gentleman that my intentions are strictly honourable. I would never do anything to harm Elizabeth.' A serious expression replaced his smile. 'To be frank, your niece has succeeded in capturing my heart, Miss Montgomery. Does that perhaps answer your question?'

Charlotte smiled at his honesty. 'Yes, it does,' she replied, 'and I extend you both my blessing and good wishes. But there is my brother to consider, you understand. He is a bitter, stubborn man who over the years has allowed his hatred of your family to consume him. I warn you, Count de Ville, he will make an awesome obstacle to overcome in your path to Elizabeth.'

The Count's face clouded. Oh, he knew full well that any confrontation with Sir Giles Montgomery would not be easy; that obtaining his friendship would possibly be the greatest challenge which had ever presented itself to him. But he would not allow that to daunt him! 'Yes, I do acknowledge that, Miss Montgomery, but steadfastly refuse to allow the fact to sway me. Forgive my boldness, but nothing which your brother sees fit either to say or to do will keep me from Elizabeth – nothing! May I assure you of that.'

Charlotte raised her eyebrows. The fellow certainly possessed determination and admirable strength of character. Moreover, she did believe that Giles had met his match in this particular man. Her brother was indeed in for a rude awakening upon his return from London. 'I admire your honesty and determination, Count de Ville,' she said, 'and pledge you my support in the matter.'

'Thank you, Miss Montgomery,' he replied, then putting his good fortune to the test he asked, 'I wonder if I might be allowed the honour of taking Elizabeth on a drive to the river next Sunday? I promise to take good care of her.'

Charlotte smiled. She had heard all about the Sunday afternoon outing from her niece and had given the matter considerable thought. Despite her promise to Giles, she was of the opinion that Elizabeth deserved a little happiness; therefore she would grant her permission. 'You may take Elizabeth to the river, Count de Ville,' she said, 'but I am afraid there is a stipulation which I must insist upon.'

'Name it, Miss Montgomery. I shall be most happy to agree.'

'Good. It is that my nephew, Edward, accompany you as chaperon. I have no knowledge concerning the customs in France, Count de Ville, but in this country it is considered improper for a young lady of breeding to step out with a gentleman unescorted.'

Richard was quite familiar with English customs and gladly extended his agreement. 'I do hope your nephew will not object to playing the role of chaperon, though?' he added.

'No. Not at all,' Charlotte assured him. 'Like Elizabeth, Edward has very little fun in life, and I am certain he will enjoy the outing. Speaking of Edward, he has expressed a wish to meet you, Count de Ville. Perhaps now would be a fitting time to introduce you?'

'I would consider it an honour, Miss Montgomery. Incidentally, I have an idea which might meet with your approval. Would you consider it impertinent of me if I suggested bringing my sister along next Sunday? She would make an admirable companion for Edward.'

'Why, no,' replied Charlotte. 'As a matter of fact I think it a splendid idea. Now you all have an afternoon to look forward to!'

Sunday afternoon, and upstairs in her room Elizabeth looked radiant in her pale blue bustle dress with its jacket bodice and pleated hemline, the skirts attractively drawn up at the sides by elaborate bows made from the same material. Her hair had been styled in fashionable ringlets, which looked perfect beneath the wide-brimmed blue hat she wore.

Downstairs, Edward waited in the drawing room. He looked dashing himself this afternoon in his grey flannel trousers and sports jacket, beneath it a white shirt with its butterfly collar and a yellow bow tie. It had reassured

Elizabeth to know that he had not objected to playing the role of chaperon. Indeed, he had told her it was an honour. Edward had certainly established a firm and friendly relationship with the Count after being introduced to him the other day. The two had talked together at some length, discussing the tender matter of Sir Giles' rebellious labourers. In an effort to ease the situation, Richard had agreed not to hire any more men until he had talked the matter over with Sir Giles himself, although Edward despaired of his father's willingness to grace the Count with the time of day. Several of the labourers had already established themselves at Netley Manor; something which would no doubt infuriate the master when he came to learn of it.

Moments later, Elizabeth floated into the drawing room to the rustle of silk, where Edward greeted her with brotherly praise. 'You look magnificent, Elizabeth! In fact, my dear, words fail me!'

Elizabeth laughed. 'You look dashing yourself, Edward. I had almost forgotten what a handsome brother you are.'

'Ah, such flattery, Elizabeth. I only hope my appearance befits a young lady of Miss de Ville's high standing. I must say, I am really looking forward to our outing. 'Tis such a long while since I was at the river. I would never have believed that one day I would be accompanying Count de Ville and his sister. Oh, if only Father could see us now. Eat your heart out, old man!' he cried mockingly. 'My sister and I are enjoying your absence!'

Noting Elizabeth's disapproving face, he immediately apologised. 'You know I did not mean it, my dear!'

The de Villes' carriage arrived. Shortly afterwards, Richard introduced his lovely fair-haired sister to the Montgomery family. Rachael was indeed of striking appearance: almost the same height and build as Elizabeth, with high cheek bones, a small aristocratic nose and sapphire eyes which shone beneath long fair lashes. She looked elegant in her pale yellow dress, with hat, gloves and parasol to match. Elizabeth took an immediate liking to her – and to judge from the way Edward's eyes were appraising her, it seemed that he did, too!

Rachael had very little accent for, like Richard, she too had been educated in England. 'I am delighted to meet you all,' she said, 'especially you, Elizabeth. I have heard so much about you from my brother. I confess he has talked of very little else lately!'

Richard cast her a warning glance. 'That will do, Rachael,' he chided good-humouredly. 'Besides, who was it who took almost four hours to prepare herself for our outing today? I simply fail to understand what a woman finds to do in so long a time. I was beginning to think I would have to wait the entire day for you!'

Everyone laughed and then, after saying their goodbyes to Aunt Charlotte, the two couples went on their way. In no time at all they were driving through the sleepy little hamlets and villages, tranquillity itself on this hot Sunday afternoon.

On arriving at the river, they left the carriage in the hands of the trusty de Ville coachman, then spread the rugs beneath a shady oak and sat down together. Soon Edward and Rachael became absorbed in private conversation, leaving the other two to do the same. After expressing how much he had missed her during the last few days, Richard then enquired after Elizabeth's paintings.

'The woodland scene is coming along most pleasingly,' she replied. 'So well that I hope to complete it soon.'

'And the portrait? Or have you abandoned it?' he asked, his blue eyes teasing.

'Richard!' she scolded. 'You know I would never do that! As a matter of fact, I have been working on it in my room. The sketches were of such value – although I will never complete it unless you agree to sit for me again.'

'Is that an invitation?'

'Do you wish it to be?'

He smiled. 'But of course.'

'Then it is!'

They laughed together, after which he took her hand and squeezed it into his own. 'You are so lovely, Elizabeth,' he murmured. 'A breathtaking sight for any man's eyes.' He saw her blush, smiled, then rose to his feet.

Towering above her, he made a fascinating picture to the woman who loved him. He was dressed in brown today: brown coat, trousers, shoes and a white shirt, his hair side-parted as usual. He looked wonderful!

Richard held out his hand to her. 'Would you care for a stroll beside the river, Elizabeth? I recall you have an affinity for water.'

His eyes were teasing, reminding her of the incident which any proper young lady would prefer to forget.

'Richard! How ungentlemanly! Pray do not remind me of what was undoubtedly the most embarrassing moment of my life!'

Edward's attention was captured by the sound of Richard's laughter. 'Is it a private joke, old fellow, or may we all join in?' he asked good-humouredly.

Elizabeth's colour deepened when the Count proceeded to enlighten her inquisitive brother. 'Ah, well you see, Edward, when I first met your delightful sister, she was standing knee-high in water dressed, I might add, in nothing but her underwear.' He grinned broadly. 'Naturally she was blushing from the embarrassment of her plight – just as she is now, in fact! At the time, I recall, I was unable to decide whether she was a wood nymph or a water baby. But now I know her better, I would say she is a combination of the two!'

The air became filled with the sound of Edward's laughter, who shook his head in firm agreement with the Count. 'Yes, I wholeheartedly agree, Richard. Your description of my sister is most fitting.' He glanced at Elizabeth and smiled. 'She has no shame at all, you know. Suffice to say, her behaviour often leaves me wondering if perhaps a mistake had been made at her birth. That far from being a Montgomery, she is really the daughter of some vagabond gypsy fellow who resides in one of those travelling caravan contraptions. The kind who prefers to bathe in running streams and run barefoot and half clad across the land.'

Poor Elizabeth! Her cheeks had turned crimson and, brandishing her parasol, she rose quickly to her feet and gave chase after Edward, who had been wise enough to flee from her. Richard and Rachael laughed as they looked on, everyone enjoying their light-hearted moments of frivolity.

'Elizabeth and Edward are such fun!' said Rachael. 'I am so pleased we are friends with them. Edward is a charming man.'

'Yes, I agree he is,' nodded Richard. 'Were his father only like him, then our problems would be at an end, Rachael. But I fear he is not,' he added flatly.

Because everyone was hungry, Richard and Elizabeth postponed their stroll until after their picnic tea, all four enjoying the food which their respective cooks had provided. Later, all that remained on the tablecloth were a few crumbs which they duly passed on to the birds.

Afterwards, Richard and Elizabeth took their stroll and, arm in arm, they exchanged polite smiles with other young couples who walked beside the weeping willow trees which lined the water's edge. It was beneath one of those willows that they eventually found themselves alone. Elizabeth grew shy as she stood before the man who had occupied her every thought since meeting him last week. Slowly she raised her eyes and looked up into his face, her heart missing a beat from the way he was gazing back at her in reciprocal fascination. She caught her breath when he clasped hold of her waist, his arms drawing her closer.

'Elizabeth . . . oh, Elizabeth!' he uttered.

Enraptured, she closed her eyes when he lowered his head to kiss her lips, feeling herself drowning in ecstasy. Abandoning her shyness, she put her arms around his neck and clung to him, unashamedly responding to the fervour of his kiss. She became completely intoxicated, uncaring of the fact that she was being foolishly reckless in the arms of a man whom she had only known for a matter of days.

Several kisses later, Richard raised his head to look down into her face, the words pouring from his mouth in an emotional torrent. 'Oh, Elizabeth . . .

Elizabeth, I love you! I love you! You stole my heart the first moment I saw you! God knows, but I shall not rest until the day you are mine!'

His admission filled her with happiness and, uncertain of whether she was laughing or crying, spilled out her own love in return. 'And I love you, Richard! Oh, I do! I do! I had no idea it was possible to love someone so much!'

They held each other close, then Richard asked, 'Marry me, Elizabeth? Marry me? I want to spend my life with you, have children with you, grow old with you . . . I love you!'

Elizabeth was overjoyed and replied without hesitation. 'Oh, yes! Yes! I will marry you, Richard! Oh . . . you have made me so happy!'

'No more than you have made me, Elizabeth,' he replied with a kiss. 'We must marry soon, my love, for I cannot bear to be parted from you. I think I would die if I ever lost you!'

Elizabeth clung to him tighter. 'You will never lose me, Richard! Never in a hundred years! I promise!'

Later that afternoon, Richard announced the news to Edward and Rachael, who were delighted for the couple.

'Congratulations to you both!' said Edward. 'That is wonderful news indeed!' After shaking hands with Richard, he hugged his sister. 'Elizabeth, I cannot tell you how pleased I am. I wish you every happiness, my dear.'

'Thank you, Edward. And I shall be happy, for how could I be otherwise, wed to the man I love?'

'You were made for each other,' sighed Rachael. 'One only has to see you together to know that.'

The couple smiled, for that was certainly true.

Everyone was in high spirits as they travelled back to Cambourne, all discussing the impending marriage which they believed would at last unite their respective families. Elizabeth and Rachael exchanged ideas for the forthcoming event: the guest list, the gowns they would wear and so forth. Richard and Edward exchanged bemused smiles, for being men, they would no doubt be relieved when the whole affair was over! No-one mentioned Sir Giles or his part in the matter. If anyone had spared him a thought, then it had remained a private one.

Upon arriving at the Hall, Rachael suggested that they have a picnic next Sunday afternoon, compelling Edward to explain about his father. 'You see, Rachael, Father will have returned from London by then, making any future outing very difficult.'

'When is he due home, Edward?' asked Richard soberly.

'Oh, some time late Thursday evening, old boy. He is sure to have returned by then, otherwise he will miss the annual summer ball next Friday night.'

'Oh, the summer ball!' interpolated Rachael. 'I have heard so much about it from my friends. It is reputed to be the most prodigious social event of the season.' She sighed wistfully. 'How I would love to attend – although I realise it is out of the question, Sir Giles disliking us so.'

Elizabeth felt ashamed, for Rachael was yet another innocent victim of Sir Giles' hatred of her family. She also felt angry, for he blatantly snubbed the de Villes, whilst every other landowner of consequence was invited to the ball. Oh, why was he so bitter and unkind? Why could he not forget the past and make peace with his enemy?

Elizabeth's compassion prompted her into a somewhat rash decision. She would invite the de Villes to the ball. After all, she had accepted Richard's proposal of marriage, and the sooner he met her father and discussed the matter, the better it would be for them all.

'I invite you to the ball as my guests,' she said. 'I will inform Papa when her returns from London. When he hears that you wish to speak with him Richard, make peace with him, then I am sure he will not object.'

Edward looked shocked. Lord, had Elizabeth lost her senses? Their father would have a fit if he knew what she had done!

'Thank you most kindly, Elizabeth,' said Richard, 'but for your own sake I must decline the invitation. I cannot allow you to take such a risk. No,' he shook his head. 'I must contact your father myself.'

Elizabeth grew determined. 'I care not about the risk involved, Richard. Indeed, I am tired of worrying about what Papa will either think, say or do, and must stand up to him in defence of my principles. I have a life and a mind of my own, and consider it my duty to ask him to end his vendetta against your family. You shall come to the ball as my guests, and let that be the end of the matter.'

'Bravo, Elizabeth!' said Edward. 'I admire your courage, my dear. Moreover, I pledge my support.' He turned to Richard and Rachael. 'I also invite you to the ball, and should Father see fit to object, then he will have me to contend with, too.'

The de Villes smiled. It seemed they had no say in the matter any more. However, Richard still had strong reservations about accepting, and had it not been for Rachael, then he would undoubtedly have refused. He heaved a defeated sigh. 'Very well, I accept your kind invitation Elizabeth. But having agreed, I hope it will not result in trouble for you. That is the last thing I would want.'

'Well,' began Edward, 'let us hope the old man is in an agreeable mood upon his return. I will certainly do my best to sweeten him.'

Richard smiled. 'At least the occasion will allow me the opportunity of meeting your father, Edward. Indeed, perhaps the informality of the occasion will be to my advantage.' He reached for Elizabeth's hand. 'The sooner I ask Sir Giles for Elizabeth's hand in marriage, then the sooner she will be mine.'

'. . . And the sooner we shall all enjoy your wedding day!' said Rachael enthusiastically.

'Hear! Hear!' agreed Edward. 'That is a day we shall all look forward to in future!'

It was Thursday evening and Sir Giles had returned home from his visit to London. His presence created a nervous hustle amongst the household staff, who jumped when his loud, authoritative voice suddenly shattered the silence which had been so golden. It boomed out across the landing at his long-suffering valet. 'Simkins! Simkins! Bless my life, I have just found a stain on my dinner jacket!' He thrust it into the arms of the quivering man. 'Take it out of my sight and bring me another at once. Deuce!' he uttered with irritation, 'I cannot tolerate incompetent fools!'

Elizabeth was already seated at the dinner table when her father made his appearance some fifteen minutes later. She rose to her feet to kiss his cheek in affection 'Papa! How pleased I am to see you! Come and sit down and tell me all about your visit to London. I trust you had an enjoyable stay?'

'Indeed I did, my dear,' he replied, taking his seat at the head of the table, Charlotte and Edward looking on. 'I found it most beneficial.' He smiled. 'Naturally I missed your company, Elizabeth, but was consoled by the thought that you would be here to welcome me upon my return.' The man spread his napkin across his lap and gazed at his beloved daughter. 'So, my dear, how have you spent your time during my absence? Did you paint the scene in the wood as you intended?'

'I most certainly did, Papa, and consider you will be delighted with it!'

'Good,' said Giles. 'Most commendable. Perhaps you would care to show it to me after dinner?'

'But of course, Papa. I shall be happy to.'

'By the by, Elizabeth, speaking of paintings. Whilst in London I commissioned a prominent artist of some prodigious renown to undertake our family portraits. The fellow's name is Frederick Llani, and he is expected to arrive here next week.'

Elizabeth looked pleased. 'An artist. How wonderful! Which one of us is to sit for him first, Papa?'

Giles laughed at her enthusiasm. 'You, my dear,' he said kindly. 'We shall take our turn when your portrait is completed. 'Tis my wish that you have a new gown for the occasion, Elizabeth. Something special. Perhaps your aunt would help you to choose something appropriate?'

'But I already have a new gown, made especially for the ball, Papa. I am certain you will approve of it for my sitting.'

'Good. I am delighted. I shall give you my opinion when I see you wearing it tomorrow evening.' The man's face softened in a smile. 'Are you looking forward to the ball, my dear?'

Elizabeth's expression became one of dreamy bliss. 'Oh, indeed I am, Papa. More than I can possibly convey.'

Edward gave a discreet cough, fearful his sister would divulge too much. Since informing Aunt Charlotte of the invitation which they had extended to the de Villes, the ball had become an extremely tender subject. Charlotte had been deeply shocked at her niece and nephew's impetuous behaviour, telling them that it had been sheer folly even to think of inviting their friends into the house of their enemy, and that their father would never grant his permission. Although Edward and Elizabeth had frequently experienced Giles' foul temper, they could not possibly know of the deep-rooted hatred which had slowly consumed him over the years in the aftermath of his love for Rebecca Pascal. But Charlotte knew. The two had remained adamant, however, and try as she might she had been unable to persuade them into retracting the invitation – if only for their guests' sake. So, in an effort to help, she had suggested that perhaps it would be wise if she informed Giles of the invitation. Although they had initially disagreed, not wishing to involve their aunt, they eventually consented to her suggestion. Charlotte knew the moment would have to be hand-picked and opportune. A moment when Giles was approachable.

Heeding Edward's warning cough, Elizabeth made light of the matter. 'But then I always look forward to the ball, Papa,' she continued. 'Moreover, I am proud to know that such an important function is held here in our very own home and that we ourselves play host to so many influential people. I think it prudent to invite our neighbours too, for how else can we gain their friendship if not by extending them a welcome to our home?' She fixed her eyes upon his. 'Would you not agree with me, Papa?'

'In part, Elizabeth,' he said briskly. 'Although we do have certain unmentionable neighbours who, suffice to say, I would never allow to set foot here. That kind we can well do without!'

Elizabeth was unsure as to whether he was referring to the de Villes or not, for they had several neighbours whom Sir Giles was unable to tolerate. Immediately after dinner, Edward quickly excused himself, saying that he had a pressing engagement in Cambourne. The truth of the matter was that Edward had no wish to be summoned to his father's study, where he would, no doubt, be obliged to relate the fact that several of his labourers had deserted him in favour of employment at Netley Manor and that the rest were planning to follow suit. He would wisely leave the matter until tomorrow, when he hoped his father's mood would be civil. Poor Edward was not to know that one of his father's interfering friends would call at the Hall that very night and relate the story on his behalf, divulging everything with the exception of the name of the establishment where the deserters had taken up residence. No fellow who valued his skin would dare impart that information to the notorious Sir Giles Montgomery. Not on his life!

The master was in a foul, uncivil mood the following morning, easy to anger and quick to find fault, it being attributed to last night's informative gossip on the part of his friend. Breakfast proved an unpleasant occasion for everyone, and even his beloved Elizabeth could say nothing to please him. She worried in silence. Why did all this trouble concerning the labourers have to escalate before the ball? It was the worst possible time. It came as a relief when Giles abruptly excused himself from the table, saying he had business to attend to and that it was unlikely he would be home for luncheon.

Following the master's departure, Edward made his entrance into the breakfast room, having purposely stayed well out of his father's way that morning after being warned of his anger by Aunt Charlotte. He threw himself into a chair and heaved a sigh. 'Ah, 'tis a bad day for us all, I fear. Father is on his way to inflict his abominable temper on Squire Ridley, blaming him for our present predicament, no doubt. Well, no-one can say that father was not warned. I myself warned him of the consequences if he continued to treat his men like dogs, riding rough-shod over them for all these years, driving the poor beggars into rebellion! Soon we will be left with only a handful of stable staff to run the place, and with several hundred acres of hay to harvest, to say nothing of the corn which is already ripening in the fields, well, Lord only knows how we shall manage. Bless me if the old man has not brought the place to its knees!' he emitted bitterly. Edward jumped to his feet. 'I will go and have another talk with the men – see if I can dissuade them from leaving us – although I doubt if my efforts will meet with much success. Their hearts and minds are set now!'

Alone with her niece and deeply concerned about the Count's impending visit to the Hall that evening, Charlotte endeavoured to make Elizabeth see sense. 'You must get word to Richard. Implore him not to come here tonight, Elizabeth! Due to all this trouble with the labourers, you must see that your father's hatred of the de Villes will have substantially increased. 'Tis the very worst time to let him know of your involvement with his enemy,' she said grimly.

'I refuse to do any such thing!' cried Elizabeth, looking mutinous. 'My relationship with Richard has no bearing on the matter concerning Papa's labourers, and I will not allow it to rob me of an evening which I have been looking forward to all week!'

Charlotte tutted with despair at her nieces's mulish obstinacy. Her stubbornness would be the downfall of them all. She rallied her defences and pursued her case. 'Elizabeth . . . I beg you child, allow matters to calm down a little. Be patient—'

'Patient? Hah!' she snapped. 'Considering my father and his cast-iron principles, I fear my patience would have to be extended to the rest of my life! No, Aunt Charlotte, matters must be allowed to stand as they are. Edward and I are willing to take full responsibility for the de Villes' invitation here tonight, and wish that to be the end of the matter.'

Charlotte cast her a withering glance, then moved quietly towards the door. She had done her best, but to no avail. 'Very well, dear,' she conceded wearily. 'Have it your own way – but Elizabeth, please do not say I did not warn you.'

It was almost six o'clock when Sir Giles returned home. Charlotte was enjoying a few well-deserved moments of rest in the sitting room when her angry brother suddenly stormed in. A tremor passed over her upon seeing his face, distorted into ugliness by his rampant rage. His skin was purple and his eyes shone with hate. Charlotte had never seen him so incensed with anger, and his presence filled her with trepidation and alarm. 'Giles . . . Giles, in heaven's name what is wrong?' she questioned cautiously.

He ignored her question and strode over to the oak cabinet, where he poured himself a stiff drink. After swallowing the liquid, he immediately topped up the glass. 'Wrong?' he replied at last, 'I shall tell you what is wrong! Yesterday evening I discovered from a friend that my labourers are intent on leaving here to seek employment elsewhere – that indeed, many of them have already deserted me. Aagh,' he sneered, 'I knew the scoundrels were up to something behind my back, but no-one, including my own wretched son, was prepared to tell me just where they intended to go! Today I am informed that the rest of them are on the brink of desertion, putting my absence to good use by preparing to sneak away behind my back. Well, I managed to persuade Ridley into divulging their well-kept secret, and what do I learn? That they intend to reside in comfort and complacency at Netley Manor, no less!' His eyes widened from sheer disbelief. 'Would you credit it, but the beggars are being enticed from under my nose by that . . . that unspeakable scoundrel, de Ville! Gad!' he cried scathingly, slamming his fist down hard upon the table top. 'I do believe that name will pursue me to my grave! First the father and now the son. Is there no end to them, I wonder?'

Concerned about his blood-pressure, Charlotte tried to calm him. 'Oh, Giles, pray control yourself! Such fury is certain to bring on an attack!'

'Attack!' he echoed. 'Indeed it will! But I vouch it will be of a vastly different nature to the one which you have in mind! I intend to pay that French blackguard a little visit. Perhaps my shotgun will teach him a lesson against poaching his neighbours' men!'

Charlotte looked aghast. 'Oh, Giles, do not be so foolish! Pray gave a little thought to the consequence of such folly. Besides,' she said placatingly, 'Count de Ville is not poaching your men. He is simply—'

'But of course he is!' came the savage interruption. 'Not even they would be reckless enough to leave my employ without first ensuring that they had somewhere to go! Anyway, what would you know of the matter?' he asked suspiciously.

'Very little, Giles. But I do know that your men are leaving you because you are unjust to them – not because they are being enticed away. You are to blame for the trouble which is upon your head today, and you cannot rectify it by breaking the law.'

'Law? Humph!' he scoffed. 'I am my own law when it comes to such matters! Tell me what other law will protect me against such a despicable underhanded deal?' Enraged, he paced the floor, his hands clasped together behind his back. 'Oh, de Ville knows full well his actions in stealing my men away from me. The fellow is intent on ruining me, carrying out his father's legacy of revenge against me!'

'Stuff and nonsense, Giles! Can you not see that you are ruining yourself? You are your own worst enemy, and always have been. You do not seem to realise what all this hatred has done to you. Why, over the years I have watched you turn into a bitter, twisted man, heartless and uncaring even to those of us who love you. Tell me, Giles,' she asked earnestly, 'what has it all been for? What have your misgivings gained you in life, except loneliness?'

Contemplative, Giles paused for a moment, then lowered his head until he was staring at the carpet. 'Perhaps I have grown hard,' he acknowledged. 'But I have always acted as I saw fit, dealing with matters with the courage of my convictions. Gad, Charlotte, would you prefer I were the type of man who allowed the world to wipe its boots on me?' He looked at her. 'Anyway, what right have you to criticise my actions? I confess, how would you know how I felt after Rebecca Pascal deserted me? Why, the woman left me with nothing but a broken heart after casting me aside like some . . . some unwanted garment! And for what, pray? For some Frenchman named de Ville!' An ugly sneer distorted his features again. 'Well, they shall pay. All of them! You will see!'

Charlotte heaved a long-suffering sigh. 'They have been paying for well over three decades, Giles – as have we all. Must it continue until there are none of us left?'

'If need be,' he growled. 'If need be!'

Charlotte stared at him wearily. Oh, what an obstinate man he was! She suddenly remembered that she must inform him of the de Villes' invitation to the ball tonight. Lord, what a thankless task that was in his present objectionable mood!

Rallying her courage, she said, 'Giles . . . Giles I am not wishful to trouble you, but before you retire upstairs there is a pressing matter which I must discuss with you. One which I really ought to have mentioned earlier, had you been at home.'

'Well? What is it?' he asked impatiently. 'The hour is late and I must rest before the ball tonight.'

'Yes, indeed, and it is a matter concerning the ball and the guest list which compel me to speak to you. Please do not lose your temper again, Giles, but during your absence I . . . I . . .' she faltered, her heart quaking.

'Well? You what?' he demanded.

Charlotte collected herself. Faint heart never won the day. 'I took it upon myself to invite a further two guests whom you—'

'Upon my soul!' he interrupted. 'Is that the pressing matter, pray? Oh, do not burden me with such petty trivia, Charlotte! The guest list is your concern, not mine! Kindly deal with the problem yourself!'

'But Giles, I prevail upon you to listen! If you will allow me but a moment to tell you—'

Enraged by her persistence, the old man's voice became a snarl. 'Desist! I declare I am growing weary of you, Charlotte! Do you not know I have more important matters on my mind? Deal with the problem yourself!' He then strode from the room slamming the door behind him.

Charlotte closed her eyes and sighed. She had tried, but she had failed. Her high-handed brother had refused to listen to a word she had to say. Well, doubtless he was in for a rude awakening at the ball that night, and he had nobody to blame but himself!

CHAPTER EIGHT

The guests were beginning to arrive in considerable numbers now, filling the ballroom with their lively chatter and gay, contagious laughter. The house looked spectacular on this most special occasion, the downstairs rooms lit by the magnificent crystal chandeliers with their scores of yellow candles. Two smartly dressed footmen occupied their positions at the front door, with two more servants in the hall, their task being to relieve the gentlemen of their canes, white gloves, cloaks and top hats, the ladies of their cloaks and mantles.

Upstairs, Annie Fosdyke, Elizabeth's young fair-haired maid, fussed over her mistress's appearance. She had just finished styling her hair into fashionable ringlets and was now adorning it with pink and white silk flowers. Elizabeth's gown looked a dream, a sensation of pale pink satin and lace, its design suiting her figure to perfection. A tasteful amount of cleavage peeped from above the bodice with its deep lace frill designed to be worn off the shoulder, whilst the full skirt was enriched by the lace overskirts which draped the bustle, its scalloped edges cut away at the front of the dress allowing a wide panel of satin to be shown off.

Moments later Elizabeth swirled before the mirror, delighted with her appearance this evening. She smiled, for it was only natural she wished to look her loveliest for Richard on this auspicious occasion. She clipped on her diamond earrings, whilst Annie secured the matching necklace around her throat, then applying a little rose-water to her neck and wrists and pulling on her elbow-length fingerless gloves, she was finally ready to grace the ball.

Annie passed her the ostrich-feather fan and her pink-beaded evening bag. 'Don't forget these, Miss,' she said. The maid stepped back a pace to admire her mistress. 'Oh, you do look beautiful, Miss Elizabeth. You'll be the belle of the ball and no mistake!'

Elizabeth smiled graciously, then thanked Annie for helping to prepare her. The maid bobbed a polite curtsey, hoping she would have a wonderful time that evening.

Her ensemble now complete, Elizabeth proceeded downstairs. Before attending the ball, she stole a peep at the long line of carriages which stretched all the way down the drive, but was unable to see whether Richard's was amongst them, for there were so many. Besides, darkness had fallen now, making it difficult to see.

She found the ballroom alive with gaiety and laughter, extending a gracious welcome to her father's well-to-do guests. Oh, what a picture of elegance they made! The ladies in their clouds of floating tulle, dripping with jewellery, some unrecognisable beneath their highly adorned hairstyles; the gentleman in white bow ties, white waistcoats, starched shirts with their butterfly collars, black tail coats and trousers, their hair sleeked and parted down the centre. Many sported handlebar moustaches, so popular in the Victorian era.

Amidst them all now, Elizabeth began to feel uncontainably excited. Lord Carruthers, a distinguished barrister-at-law and a long-term friend of her father's, a man of the most prodigious presence, was the first to address her.

'Ah, Elizabeth! Good evening, my dear. My, my,' he said, raising his eyebrows, 'how delightful you look! Delightful! Indeed, my dear, I confess you grow more beautiful with every passing year!'

Elizabeth smiled and extended her hand, which he suavely raised to his lips. 'Thank you, Lord Carruthers. 'Tis so kind of you to say so.'

The gentleman was fingering the end of his moustache when his possessive wife appeared. Lady Carruthers was a woman of ample proportions, with huge bosoms which had been squeezed into a gown which was far too tight, her throat, ears, wrists and fingers all glittering with the sparkle of diamonds. Tight-lipped and austere, she bid Elizabeth the briefest 'good evening', then tugged her husband's arm in an effort to relieve him of the younger woman's company. Maud Carruthers was firmly convinced that all men were unprincipled rakes where pretty young women were concerned, and that it was a wife's duty to keep them well away from that which they found so alluring. She determinedly proceeded to put her convictions into practice.

Elizabeth's entrance into the ballroom caused quite a stir amongst the guests, the young men in particular, who were all eager to sign her card. During polite conversation with one of them, Elizabeth's eyes strayed around the room in search of Richard and Rachael. But to her disappointment they were nowhere to be seen. She thought it strange that they were so late, for Richard had promised to be early.

Whilst looking around, she caught a glimpse of Edward, who was detained in conversation with Percival Bromhead, and cast him a sympathetic smile. Acknowledging his sister, Edward rolled his eyes, looking exceedingly bored in the company of this pompous, irksome man. Indeed, very few fellows of Edward's generation could tolerate Bromhead at all, understandably so since his entire topic of conversation never once extended beyond that of his own stable of expensive horses, which became tedious after a while to the ears of the listener. Even from this distance, Elizabeth could hear his loud, assertive voice above the heads of the other guests . . . 'Oh, come, come my dear fellow! You must surely admit that I own the best pair of greys in the county, to say nothing of the finest Hackney carriage horse . . .'

Poor Edward, Elizabeth commiserated with his plight. How tedious, having to listen to such a bore!

The evening steadily progressed. Elizabeth was seen dancing with Bertram Hodgkiss to the music of the orchestra, her spirits dampened by the de Villes' continued absence. Even her own father had failed to grace the function with his appearance and, feeling worried, she excused herself from Hodgkiss to go in search of Aunt Charlotte. Upon finding her, Elizabeth enquired as to her father's whereabouts.

'In all probability he is still upstairs resting, Elizabeth,' she replied. 'As you know, the ball never finishes until the first light of day, so there is still plenty of time for him to make his appearance.' Charlotte decided against burdening her niece with details of her conversation with the master earlier. She also refrained from mentioning that she had been unsuccessful in informing him of the Count's visit here tonight. Charlotte hoped that Richard would decide against attending the ball, understandably postponing his visit until matters regarding the labourers had improved.

But even as the two women were speaking together in the dining room, the de Ville carriage was already making its way down the drive towards the house. Rachael peered through the carriage window, all eyes and interest as they approached the Hall, so proud to be a guest at the Montgomery ball. Richard's response to the occasion was far less enthusiastic, however, and he was feeling understandably uneasy at the prospect of entering the home of his enemy. Before leaving Netley Manor, he had exchanged heated words with his mother, who was apprehensive about her son and daughter's invitation to the ball. Rebecca knew Sir Giles Montgomery for what he was, an unprincipled tyrant, a man who would never succumb to forgiveness nor allow himself to forget the past and extend a hand of friendship towards the enemy. Therefore, she had endeavoured to dissuade her son from visiting Cambourne Hall that evening.

However, being a man of his word, Richard honoured his promise and escorted his sister to the ball as arranged. He had his reservations though, conceding his mother to be wise in her words. But, in all fairness, Sir Giles must be allowed his chance, and now Richard took his sister's hand as she alighted from the carriage outside the house.

Soon afterwards the couple were introduced into the ballroom. Upon hearing their name a sudden hush prevailed across the room, with many of the guests left wide-eyed and staring, incredulous as to the identity of the strangers. Count de Ville and Miss Rachael de Ville here in the house of Sir

116

Giles Montgomery? Why, it was enough to leave them dumbstruck! However, many preoccupied guests missed the announcement and were left speculating as to the name of the tall, handsome man who mingled amongst them now.

Richard looked around in the hope of seeing Elizabeth, but she was nowhere to be seen. Fortunately Rachael spotted a group of her friends so the couple walked over to join them.

It was at that moment that Elizabeth returned to the ballroom after speaking with her aunt and wandered aimlessly amongst the guests, her heart filled with despondency. She believed Richard had decided against coming here after all. Suddenly she saw him at the far side of the room, standing with his back to her talking with a group of guests. Her heart gave a leap of joy. Oh, he was here!

Smiling now, blissfully happy, she walked gracefully across the floor towards him, past the many couples who swirled to the music of a Strauss waltz. There came a sudden lull when all eyes were upon her; smiling faces who witnessed her memorable walk across the ballroom floor. In the eyes of her beholder, there was something very special, very magical about her now, for she exuded an aura of mystery, also an extraordinary beauty which instilled a breathless admiration into every man and woman who watched her sweep by. In her preoccupied state of mind, even the music from the orchestra appeared to fade into the distance, the only sound coming from her own thudding heart. Indeed, she conceded that she might well be in a dream; a deep, unforgettable magic dream where nothing was impossible and no-one else existed but herself and he.

She held her breath when she came to stand behind him, filled with happiness upon seeing him again. Pausing, she allowed herself to gaze at this elegant profile then, raising her arm, reached to touch him gently on his shoulder. Her lips parted, her voice a whisper as she spoke his name. 'Richard . . .'

He turned around to face her, smiling as he reached for her hand. His touch filled her heart with elation and the look in his eyes reflected her own, worshipping with passion and deep unspoken love. 'Elizabeth . . . oh, you look enchanting!' He pressed her hand against his lips, his eyes never leaving her face.

Bewitched, she smiled at him radiantly, a smile which captured not only him, but many other pairs of eyes as they looked on. One had to be blind not to see the love which was being exchanged between the two.

Realising they were being watched, Elizabeth collected herself and extended a polite welcome to her guests. 'Miss de Ville, Count de Ville, welcome to Cambourne Hall.' She spoke loud enough for the inquisitive guests to overhear, wanting everyone to know that the couple were her guests and that they must be treated with respect.

Following Elizabeth's greeting, many of the guests turned to one another and began to converse in whispered tones, no doubt wondering what had transpired between the two most influential families in the county to bring them together this evening. After the initial fuss had died down, the three were allowed some privacy.

'Oh, Richard . . . Rachael, I am so happy you are here! I was convinced you had decided against coming tonight!'

'My apologies for being so late, my love. I . . . I was unavoidably detained at home.' Richard wisely declined from saying more.

'Oh, it matters not, Richard. You are here now and that is all that matters. And Rachael,' she said, her eyes admiring Miss de Ville's ball gown, 'how lovely you look! Your dress is beautiful!'

'Thank you, Elizabeth,' she said graciously. 'You are looking beautiful yourself.' Rachael was bubbling with happiness, longing to see Edward, who suddenly made his timely appearance at their side.

After greetings had been exchanged, Edward whisked Rachael away to the dance floor, leaving the other two alone.

'I have missed you so much, Elizabeth,' murmured Richard tenderly. 'Have you missed me?'

'Missed you? Oh, but of course I have, Richard! I could hardly wait for this evening to arrive!'

'I have looked forward to the occasion myself,' he responded, 'despite my reservations about meeting your father. By the bye, Elizabeth, where is he?'

'He is still in his room, resting. I expect he will be down shortly.'

Whilst conversing, they became aware that they were being watched again by curious eyes. Richard smiled as he gazed around, then turned to Elizabeth. 'May I have the pleasure of this dance, Elizabeth? If the gossips are to have their day, then we must provide them with something which is worthy of their wagging tongues.'

Elizabeth laughed and accepted his arm, proud at being in the company of the handsomest man to grace the occasion. They made an elegant picture as they swirled across the floor in full view of everyone, their togetherness being discussed at some length.

'Bless me, but if my eyes do not deceive me!' exclaimed Sir James Denby. 'I do believe Montgomery's daughter is dancing with the new master of Netley Manor!' He turned to the stout, silver-haired man at his side. 'What do you say, Jennings, old chap?'

Jennings shrugged his shoulders. 'Blessed if I know,' he replied. 'Never set eyes on the fellow before. Besides,' he tittered, 'I doubt you or I will see the day when a de Ville is welcome in this house, let alone see him dance with Montgomery's daughter.'

'But it is he! I know it!' insisted Sir James with profound conviction. 'I saw him in Cambourne only a week ago. Oh, he was dressed quite differently then, of course, but there is still no mistaking his devilish good looks.' Perplexed, he rubbed his clean-shaven chin. 'Wonder what the deuce is going on?' he muttered. 'Rumour has it that Montgomery is out for his blood after the fellow supposedly poached his men from him. Yet here he is at the old man's ball. Gad, but Montgomery is a strange old stick. There is no crediting what he will do next!' The words had been punctuated by ridiculing laughter, after which Sir James nudged the other man with his elbow. 'Perhaps the master is going soft in his old age, what? Say you the same, Jennings, eh?'

Jennings' reply was sceptical. 'Yes, and pigs will fly,' he remarked dispassionately.

During the interlude the two couples took a stroll outside for a breath of air. The ballroom had become stuffy, but out there the air was cool and refreshing, the navy sky speckled with the light of a thousand stars. Cascades of pretty Chinese lanterns, all the colours of the rainbow, hung along the terrace which overlooked the lawns and gardens. It was here that Rachael extended to Elizabeth and Edward an invitation to her twenty-second birthday party, which was to be held at Netley Manor on the twentieth of June. 'Do say you will come! All my other friends will be there. Besides, I would love you to visit my home. Mamma has given her permission, and assures us she is looking forward to making your acquaintance at last.'

'Elizabeth and I would be honoured to accept your invitation, Rachael. However, until we gain Father's permission, I regret I cannot make our acceptance a definite one,' said Edward.

'I see,' replied Rachael. 'But you will come if you are able?'

Edward cast her an encouraging smile. 'Elizabeth and I would be delighted to, Rachael.'

The two couples went their separate ways. Alone together now, Elizabeth and Richard strolled arm in arm through the gardens. It was beneath one of the trees there that he took her into his arms and clasped her in a loving embrace. Following a tender kiss, he reached into his pocket and brought out a small gift box which he handed to Elizabeth. 'For you,' he said. 'I bought it whilst I was in London last week. I hope it is to your liking, Elizabeth.'

Shyly, she accepted the gift. 'Thank you, Richard,' she said.

It was the most beautiful cameo brooch, its centrepiece set with the finest gold filigree. Elizabeth breathed a sigh of delight when she saw it. 'Oh, Richard, it is beautiful! I adore it! Thank you so much. I shall treasure it always . . . wear it always, and every time I look at it I shall be reminded of you. I love you!'

He lowered his head to kiss her. 'And I love you.'

One kiss led to another, and soon they were lost to everything but each other as they stood in the shadows locked in each others arms. Their privacy was short-lived, however, for the sound of voices disturbed them. Reluctantly they released each other, Richard suggesting that they return to the ball in case Sir Giles had made his appearance. As things turned out, he was nowhere to be seen, his absence giving every indication that he did not intend to grace the ball that evening after all. Although it surprised Elizabeth, she was not unduly troubled.

'Never mind, Richard,' she said, 'there will be other occasions when you will be able to meet Papa. Indeed, perhaps he will agree to a private meeting between you.' She smiled as she took his arm. 'Anyway, let us forget about him, shall we? The evening has been so heavenly and there is a feast of food awaiting us in the dining room. Afterwards the orchestra will play again and there will be dancing for us to enjoy, so . . .'

Richard returned her smile. 'So let us proceed, my dear Elizabeth!'

Following a delicious supper, the couple resumed their place on the dance floor, with not a man or woman in the room able to hold a candle to their happiness. Unknown to them, Sir Giles had made his overdue appearance whilst the couple had been occupied in the dining room. He stood in the company of a small group of guests, looking paler than usual and somewhat terse in mood. His behaviour indicated irritability, and sharp warning glances were being exchanged between guests. Sir Giles Montgomery was well known for his volatile moods. Indeed, to judge from his austere expression, it could be said that the master of Cambourne Hall was not enjoying the occasion. The truth of the matter was that the man was only there under sufferance. He would have preferred to stay in his bedchamber where the peace had brought some solace to his troubled mind. Giles felt unwell. He was worried over the trouble concerning his labourers, hating the man whom he regarded as responsible for it all. Well, he would make sure that de Ville regretted his mistake. Be it the last thing he ever did, Giles promised he would make the fellow pay.

Suddenly he caught sight of Elizabeth across the room, dancing in the arms of a dark, dashing stranger. His breath caught in his throat. Oh, she made a beautiful sight . . . sheer radiance itself. The image of Helen came flooding back to him and for a moment he was possessed by a wave of nostalgia. But the image was soon overshadowed by another, that of a woman who had scorned him many years ago. He flinched from the pain of bitter memory, then closed his eyes and cast her from his mind. Years ago he had vowed never to think of Rebecca again. It was a promise he intended to keep.

When the couple neared him, he gazed at the man in whose arms Elizabeth danced. His old heart missed a beat and he felt oddly uneasy. His sharp eyes narrowed, studying the man until the hair on the back of his neck stood on end. Visibly, Giles stiffened. Who was the fellow, he wondered curiously? Who was the stranger who made him feel so ill at ease? Giles knew there was something familiar about him . . . that proud, handsome profile and his tall, athletic build. But it was his eyes which caused the strongest sense of familiarity, plucking at some far-off string of recognition.

Whilst pondering over the problem, Giles became aware of an atmosphere in the room, tense and heavy, charged with feelings of unease and apprehension. The cause of it puzzled him. He rubbed his chin as he glanced around. It seemed that his guests were watching Elizabeth, and he had to be blind not to see how their tongues wagged in their wide, aristocratic mouths. But for what reason?

His eyes followed their gaze and he saw his daughter and her partner laughing and smiling at each other. Anger boiled inside him, transforming his complexion into a shade of purple. Who was the stranger who danced with Elizabeth? Who was he? His identity was there to be grasped and Giles knew it; it throbbed at his mind with malicious scorn.

Just then he was joined by his friend, James Denby, and an acquaintance, Darwin Jennings. Denby was renowned for his sharp wit and humour. However, when it came to tact and diplomacy, he was less well endowed. 'I say, Giles, thought for a moment you had lost your mind, old chap. I confess I did not expect to see yon fellow,' – he wagged a pointed finger at the Count – 'here tonight, what?' He laughed heartily. 'I declare his presence in your home has caused quite a stir, Sir, considering the circumstances, eh?' His remarks were followed by a series of nudges against the master's ribs. 'Hah! Decided to be a good sport about it, have you? 'Tis your intention to bury the hatchet after all these years, what?' Denby threw back his head and laughed again. 'Well, old chap, judging by the way he is eyeing your daughter, perhaps your friendship will be extended into welcoming him into the family! Oh, upon my soul, whoever would have believed it, ending with *him* as your son-in-law!'

Giles was outraged, his expression thunderous. His eyes flashed with contempt at the man who stood beside him, conceivably a sorry man for having spoken without thought of the consequences.

Darwin Jennings flinched when his friend was suddenly shaken by Montgomery's strong hands. 'You babbling clown! Confound you, Sir, how dare you speak to me in that way!' Ignoring the gasps emitted by the group of guests, Giles shook him again. 'I demand to know the meaning of your unseemly remarks. Speak up, man – I am waiting!'

121

Unspeakably alarmed, Denby choked on his reply. 'I . . . I say old boy . . . st . . . steady on! I . . . I meant no harm. Just jesting, old chap!'

'Jesting?' emitted Giles. 'The deuce you were, Sir! Explain yourself, man! Who is yon fellow with my daughter, pray?'

Shocked, inquisitive guests had begun to mill around the three men, all anxious to know what was going on. Although Sir Giles was well known for his foul temper, he had not been known to air it quite so publicly before – at least not for a good many years. Denby and Jennings exchanged confused glances, neither able to understand Giles' question.

'Well? I am waiting!' roared Montgomery. 'Or must I thrash the information out of you?'

'B . . . but I thought you knew, Giles . . .' uttered Denby nervously. 'The fellow is a guest at your ball, is he not?'

'I said *who is he*, Denby?' repeated his persecutor, losing all patience now.

'W . . . why, the man is d . . . de Ville, Giles. Count de Ville from Netley Manor.'

A shattering silence followed. All eyes were on Sir Giles' mortified face, his features transformed into a mask of granite. He stood statue-like before the crowd, his eyes wide and staring, paling before everyone who bore witness to this temporary seizure of his senses. Barely a breath passed the lips of those who watched, and not a sound was heard to break the silence.

When Giles recovered himself, there was no mistaking the anger which burned in his eyes. Fists clenched, he stiffened, then squared his shoulders resolutely. No-one stood in his path as he made his move. No fellow was quite so foolhardy. A gangway of guests formed two lines before him as he slowly and deliberately made his way across the floor towards his daughter, then crowded behind him, all anxious to see what transpired.

Charlotte, Edward and Rachael had been conversing together at the far side of the room when the incident had occurred, and were now inching their way through the crowd towards Elizabeth. Ignorant of the scene around them, having eyes only for each other, she and Richard danced on. Neither noticed that the orchestra had stopped playing or the sea of eyes which were upon them now.

Moments later, Sir Giles approached them, his disparaging eyes coming to rest on de Ville. Of course! Gad, but why had he not seen it earlier – the resemblance which the man bore to his strikingly beautiful mother! No wonder the sight of him had aroused his unease!

Elizabeth felt Richard suddenly stiffen as the two men looked at each other, their eyes reflecting their mutual hostility. She followed his gaze, startled at seeing her father standing but a few paces away. Her countenance paled and she was stunned by the awesome expression on his face and the crowd which gathered behind him. 'P . . . Papa!' she exclaimed.

Montgomery spoke, his coarse voice breaking the years of silence between himself and his enemy, for any de Ville was his enemy. 'Unhand my daughter at once, Sir!'

But Richard did not comply, antagonising the man into repeating himself. 'Are you deaf, Sir? I said unhand her!'

Richard then released Elizabeth, but remained staunch and unintimidated by her side.

'Your presence in my home astounds me, Sir! I demand to know the reason for such intrusion! Confess to me what audacity has brought you here tonight!'

'The Count is here because I invited him, Papa!' interpolated Elizabeth.

Giles' jaw dropped open. 'Y . . . you invited him? You invited a de Ville into my home? I do not believe it, Elizabeth!'

Rallying her dignity, Elizabeth continued. 'I invited the Count here this evening because he wished to meet you, Papa!'

Giles' expression turned to one of horror. 'How dare you, Elizabeth! How dare you assume such a liberty!'

Edward's voice suddenly rose above his father's angry tones. 'I would be obliged if you would kindly direct your recriminations at me, Father, for 'twas I, not Elizabeth who invited the Count and his sister to the ball this evening.'

The old man swung around to stare at his son, who stood tall and unflinching before the steel-grey eyes which had so often daunted him into submission. 'You? You invited a de Ville to cross the threshold of my home? But why?' he reiterated. 'Why?'

'Because the Count and Miss de Ville are my friends, Sir, and because I feel it is time that one of us ends the feud which has existed between us for so long.'

'Do you indeed?' roared Giles. 'And who are you to question my judgment and authority?'

'If I might be allowed to speak, Sir,' intervened Richard, 'I entered your home not merely in response to the invitation, but because I wished to speak with you man to man. You and I are neighbours now, Sir Giles, and I feel we should let bygones be bygones. Thirty years is a long time to hold a grudge, so let us bury the past and look forward to the future. I am prepared to take the first step by offering you my hand in friendship. I trust you will accept it in good faith.'

A hush prevailed throughout the room. This was indeed history in the making; a possible truce between the two most powerful families in the county. The silence was rudely shattered when the master's voice boomed out across the room.

'Your offer invites nothing but my contempt, Sir. I would not accept your hand if my very life were dependent on it! Your time has been wasted. I despised your father as I now despise you! So kindly leave my home before I have you thrown out!'

A cry of shame passed Elizabeth's lips and distressed, she caught hold of her father's arm. 'Oh, Papa! What a wicked thing to say! I am ashamed of you!'

Purple-faced and bitterly angry, he shrugged off her hand and ordered her to be silent. 'I shall deal with you later, Elizabeth. Upon that you have my word!'

'I would be obliged if you would confine your dealings to me,' protested Richard, 'and leave Elizabeth out of the matter!'

'Allow me to remind you that my daughter is my concern – not yours!' Giles retaliated. 'I will thank you to stay out of the matter!'

'I hasten to correct you, Sir Giles, for she is also mine. Oh, I had hoped for an amicable discussion with you this evening. Hoped the informality of the occasion would have mellowed your mood. But knowing you for what you are, Sir, I should have known that my hopes were futile.'

Richard turned his attention to the throng of awe-struck guests who hung on his every word, addressing them with the dignity of a gentleman. 'It was not my wish to cause a scene here tonight. Indeed, I had hoped that my business with Sir Giles would take place in the privacy of his study. But as that is out of the question now, I have no alternative but to inform him of my intentions right here where I stand.' The audience hung with bated breath as Richard turned to address a tight-lipped Montgomery. 'I advise you that your daughter has engaged my affections, Sir, and that with or without your consent it is my intention to marry her.'

Montgomery looked dumbfounded. Then, with fists clenched, he attacked the Count with loud, verbal abuse. 'Marry my daughter? Why, you impudent scoundrel!' He ventured a step nearer. 'Damn you for what you are, Sir, for not content with enticing my men from my employ, you are now after my daughter too! Get out before I thrash you!'

Richard's lips curled with contempt. 'Oh, I am proof against your anger, Sir Giles. You do not intimidate me. Furthermore, your men required no enticing from me.' He heaved an angry sigh. 'I promised Edward that I would do nothing until I had spoken to you in person. But all that business is now at an end. I shall be more than glad to offer them employment!'

'No!' cried Montgomery, 'I protest!'

'You may protest all you wish, because I confess I am in sympathy with your men. Plainly speaking, Sir Giles, you are a tyrant. A heartless, uncharitable tyrant, well deserving the contempt which is associated with your name.'

Sir Giles flew at his adversary in an almighty explosion of fury, directing his clenched fist at de Ville's jaw. But the Count's agility proved too quick for him and the blow fell short. Undeterred, he swung at him again, but Edward jumped forward and grabbed his father's shoulder pulling him backwards, just as Richard darted sideways to avoid another flying fist.

'Control yourself, Father! Your behaviour is disgracing us all!'

'Let me go! Let me go, you young upstart!' growled Giles, uncaring of the scene he was creating. A succession of foul curses passed his lips, causing many of the ladies to gasp with shock. Suddenly he wrenched himself free and with infinite menace approached the Count again. 'You shall never have her, de Ville! Never as the day is long. Why, I would rather see her dead and in her grave than married to the likes of you!'

Gasps of outrage were emitted from the mouths of every Christian lady and gentleman of principle, and a sea of sympathetic eyes rested on Elizabeth. Tears filled her eyes. She could not understand how her father could be so cruel.

Unheeding the savage look which Giles cast him, Richard placed a protective arm around her shoulders. 'I find the measure of your hatred astounding and declare your last remark to be unforgivable. Furthermore, I vow to waste no time in taking Elizabeth from you.' He turned to address the guests again. 'I apologise for the disgraceful scene which you have been subjected to tonight, and assure you that it was not my intention to air my differences with Sir Giles in such a public manner. I hope you will all forgive me.'

There came a response of respectful acknowledgement from every fellow in the room, the ladies smiling compassionately at both himself and Elizabeth.

'Gad, but the fellow has pluck!' said Lord Carruthers. 'There is not another man in the county who would have had the spunk to stand up to Montgomery in that way!'

'Yes, a most gallant fellow!' his companion agreed.

Count de Ville had won everyone's heart with his honour and principles, gaining their respect and admiration into the bargain. Montgomery, on the other hand, looked lost and alone, incredulous in the face of his opponent's popularity. A contemptuous sneer crossed his face. Well, the man was welcome to it. Was welcome to the lot of them, his supposed good friends. The pompous, self-opinionated asses that they were!

He was still sneering as he directed one last threat at de Ville. 'You have spoken your piece, Sir. Now kindly leave my house – or as God is my judge, I shall kill you!'

'Most certainly,' said Richard with dignity. 'But I warn you, one day I shall return for Elizabeth. Upon that you have my word.' He then turned to leave, politely nodding his head to Charlotte and Edward. Elizabeth took his arm. Rachael was already clinging to the other. She then proceeded to accompany him to the door.

'Elizabeth! Let them make their own way out!' called Sir Giles.

She turned to face him, chilling him with her icy stare. 'If nothing else, you might at least allow me to exercise good manners, Papa.'

'You bring shame on me, Elizabeth. Nothing but shame!' he cried.

'I beg to disagree with you, Papa, for in my opinion you have managed to do that for yourself!'

Edward joined in the show of supportive loyalty and accompanied the others to the door. Warm smiles of encouragement went with them on their way, and never again would the name de Ville go unrespected by those to whom the Count had endeared himself that night. Sir Giles was left alone to stand and watch, a morally defeated man.

Sometime later he paced the floor of his study. He was still brooding over the incident when he was joined by his sister. 'Were you aware of the de Villes' invitation here tonight?' he questioned savagely.

'Indeed I was, Giles. Perhaps you recall my effort to bring the matter to your attention? But you had "more important matters on your mind", did you not?'

'Deuce, woman!' he cried. 'You should have made me listen! Made me!'

'Made you, Giles?' Charlotte laughed cynically. 'Since when has anyone been able to make you listen to something which you did not wish to hear? Well, my dear brother, you succeeded in thoroughly disgracing yourself tonight, and without a modicum of decorum managed to perform it before half the population of Shropshire! It will take years to live this down, Giles, to say nothing of the damage which you have undoubtedly caused between yourself and Elizabeth. 'Tis my belief you have lost her, Giles. Moreover, lost her through your own evil disposition. Pray tell me how long you can live with that?'

CHAPTER NINE

The following morning Elizabeth took breakfast in her room. She had no wish to join her father or his weekend guests in the dining room that morning, still feeling angry and humiliated after his shocking behaviour the previous night. Charlotte and Edward stole a few moments to visit her, where the three of them discussed the incident.

'I am so sorry, Aunt Charlotte,' Elizabeth apologised, 'you warned me of the consequences and I should have listened to you. I confess it serves me right for being so headstrong!'

'Do not blame yourself, Elizabeth,' said Charlotte, 'your father behaved disgracefully last night, and I fear it will be a long while before his society friends allow him to forget it.'

'It has certainly put the damper on us attending Rachael's birthday party,' said Edward gloomily. 'Father will never give us his permission now.'

'Oh, why does Papa have to be so unkind?' exclaimed Elizabeth. 'Why must we be made to suffer for his hatred?'

'Do not take on so, Elizabeth,' said Edward. 'You know Father and what he is. Nothing you or I can do will change him.'

Charlotte looked thoughtful. 'When is Rachael's party?' she asked.

'The twentieth of June,' said Edward. 'Although I fear the day will mean nothing to us now.'

'You know, dears, I believe that is the weekend your father visits Carleton Grange. Perhaps if it is . . .?' A glint appeared in her kind old eyes and a captivating smile lit her face.

Elizabeth and Edward exchanged hopeful glances. 'Do you mean . . . mean you would allow us to go?' asked Elizabeth eagerly.

Charlotte smiled. 'Yes, I would, Elizabeth. I deplored your father's behaviour last night, and in the light of Richard's proposal of marriage and the fact that you deserve a little happiness in life, I promise to help you all I can.'

'Oh, Aunt Charlotte, I . . . I hardly know what to say! Thank you so much!' she said, moving to hug her aunt.

'I, too!' said Edward, brightening. ''Tis jolly decent of you, Aunt Charlotte. How kind you are to us.'

The old lady laughed. 'Do not become too eager, for I have no wish to disappoint you. Still, let us be optimistic and hope your father is absent from home on Rachael's birthday. Then you can both enjoy yourselves!'

Sir Giles Montgomery's mood remained distant and brooding. He was still absorbing the shock of meeting Count de Ville last night, left almost demented by the fellow's confounded admission that Elizabeth had 'engaged his affections,' and that with or without his consent he intended to marry her. Oh, but what a cursed statement that had been by Gad! Giles wondered how Elizabeth had come to know him so well. Where had she met him? And where had these so-called 'affections' been engaged? Deuce, but there was so much he wished to know!

The old man lowered his weary body into one of the wicker chairs in the garden, staring blankly into space. He would never be in possession of the facts unless he swallowed his pride and confronted Elizabeth directly. The man shuddered. Oh, but he would never forget the look on her face last night, one of such contempt for him, her own father.

Deeply tortured, he wrung his hands in his lap. Aagh, but it was all the fault of that blackguard de Ville. The man was out to destroy him any way he could, first his labourers, the disloyal wretches that they were, and now his beloved daughter. It was the scoundrel's intention to rob him of the most precious thing in his life. The very thought was like a knife in his heart, thrusting and twisting until it almost drove him mad. Well, he would never allow de Ville to have her. He would willingly shoot the fellow first!

The sound of gay, laughing voices suddenly disturbed his murderous thoughts. 'Ah, so here you are, Giles. We have been searching everywhere for you!'

The sight of Lady Florence Stroud, her parasol a-twirling, was enough to send him leaping to his feet. His eyes shrank from the loudness of her dress, those gaudy scarlet and yellow stripes which ran vertically across its vulgar, billowing skirts. Monstrous!

Her squeaky, irritating voice addressed him again. 'Giles, dear, we are about to have a game of croquet. Do say you will join us?'

Giles shook his head and declined the invitation, longing to flee from her company, her offending gown. Several more weekend guests appeared, filling the air with their jovial laughter. Muttering his apologies, Giles strode off, saying he would see them at dinner. His self-enclosed mood was all too apparent to his perceptive guests. Indeed, his role of host had undergone a certain amount of criticism that day, for he had failed to entertain them in his usual grand style. The previous night's ignominious events were most certainly the cause of his negligence today, although no fellow in possession of his right mind was wishful to involve himself in the master's self-inflicted dilemma. His obdurate disposition had initiated his problems, now he must live with the consequences.

Giles hastened along to Elizabeth's room. He must enquire as to her relationship with de Ville; pluck it at the bud before it blossomed. The man promised himself that under no circumstances would he lose patience with her, for he did not wish to worsen matters by antagonising her. It was imperative that he speak with her, though.

Outside her bedchamber, he straightened his bow tie before knocking.

'Who is it?' came the voice from within.

"Tis I, Elizabeth. May I enter? I wish to speak with you.'

'The door is open.' Her voice was curt.

She was sitting by the balcony gazing out across the hills, and failed to greet her father when he entered. Giles pulled up a chair and sat beside her, chilled by her aloofness, her indifference.

He patted her hand in a conciliatory manner. 'Have you no word of greeting for your papa, Elizabeth? I confess your frigid demeanour leaves me feeling wretched. You must know that I wish to speak with you, my dear.'

'About what, Papa? Your disgraceful behaviour last night? The deplorable way in which you treated Count de Ville and his sister?'

Giles stiffened. 'I beg your forgiveness for the unfortunate incident, Elizabeth, but you must realise that what you did was wrong. Inviting the de Villes to my home without first gaining my permission was nothing short of sinful!'

'Yes, I agree, Papa. But you were not here, and I invited them to our home in an act of friendship. The Count wished to meet you, make peace with you, but you received him with hate in your heart and humiliated him in front of everyone. Oh, I was so ashamed of you!' Deeply angry, she rose to her feet and moved away from him.

He stood up and followed her. 'But he is my enemy, Elizabeth! My enemy! Can you not see that, pray?'

She turned to face him, her eyes defiant. 'It makes no difference to me what he is, Papa. Nor who he is. Because I love him. I love him and I want to marry him!'

'Oh, Elizabeth!' he cried, deeply stung by her confession. 'You do not know what you are saying! Love – for him? You cannot be serious, child!'

'But I am serious, Papa!' she told him earnestly. 'Is it really so difficult for you to comprehend?'

'Indeed it is! I am quite unable to comprehend any of it!' He moved to grip her arms. 'Kindly inform me how you met the man, Elizabeth. How did you come to know him as you do?'

'I met him whilst out riding, Papa,' – she omitted to mention that the meeting took place in the wood – 'and we fell in love.'

'You fell in love?' he repeated, astonished. 'Just as quickly and as simply as that?'

'Yes, we did. I fell in love with Count de Ville the moment I saw him . . . and he with me.'

'Gad!' he exclaimed, dropping his hands to his sides. 'I confess I have never heard anything like it in my life!' A stony silence ensued, after which he asked, 'And when did this . . . this exchange of affection take place, if I might ask?'

'It was whilst you were away in London, Papa.' She saw his face harden into granite. 'And before you begin to rant and rave, please allow me to assure you that our meeting took place purely by accident. The Count had . . . had lost his way, you see, and neither of us knew with whom we were conversing.'

Sir Giles' promise to maintain his patience was cast to the wind. 'I declare I have never heard such poppycock! You allowed your affections to be robbed by a complete stranger? You . . . such a mistress of virtue, Elizabeth? What rubbish!' Shoulders rounded, his chest heaving from the burden of his sighs, he began to pace the floor. 'Your admission offends my intelligence, Elizabeth. Can you not see that your feelings for this man are but mere infatuation? A passing fancy for an admittedly striking young Frenchman? Why, you probably see him as some . . . some knight in shining armour. Well, fairy stories are for children, Elizabeth. You are an adult and must be realistic. The man is our enemy! The son of the vilest, most loathsome—'

'Papa, please!' she objected. 'I refuse to listen to such wickedness! Indeed, your hatred astounds me! Oh, and to think I held you in such high esteem!'

'But, Elizabeth, please—'

Impervious, she hardened her heart and turned away from him. 'I do not want to listen to any more, Papa. Please leave my room. I wish to be alone.'

Sir Giles hung his head. 'I am deeply hurt to know you think such ill of me, Elizabeth,' he said. 'But regardless of your feelings, I consider it my duty to advise you that your affection for this man is futile.' He looked at her through narrowed eyes. 'I shall never allow him to have you, Elizabeth. Never! Moreover, I demand that you never see him again. If you practise deceit against me then I shall see to it that you pay the price of your folly. Now, if you will excuse me, I have guests to entertain. Good day, Elizabeth,' he concluded curtly, then strode from the room.

Rebellion rose within her, and her father's demand that she must never see Richard again was challenged by her heart. She had always loved and honoured her father, complied with his every wish without dispute. But on this occasion he asked too much of her. Nothing in the world would ever rob her of her love for Richard de Ville, and equally, nothing or no-one would ever prevent her from seeing him. She hoped God would forgive her and, moreover, that He would understand.

On Monday morning Giles encountered his daughter in the hall dressed in her riding habit. 'Where are you going, Elizabeth?' he questioned suspiciously.

'I am going to the wood, Papa. I wish to finish my painting before the bluebells die off.' She addressed him with cool dignity.

Sir Giles' eyes narrowed. Due to their conflict, he felt he could not trust her now; not even within the boundary of his estate. 'Very well, Elizabeth, then I shall accompany you. If you will kindly wait but a moment whilst I go upstairs and change.'

Aunt Charlotte appeared from the drawing room and saw her niece's dismay. She knew Elizabeth had planned a secret rendezvous with Richard in the wood, for Elizabeth had confessed the fact yesterday. The old lady endeavoured to console her. 'Oh, Elizabeth, there will be other occasions, my dear. Perhaps your father will allow you to ride alone tomorrow. Not even he can spare the time to accompany you every day.'

'But I promised Richard I would meet him today, Aunt Charlotte!' she said with exasperation. 'I doubt that his time will be extended into waiting until tomorrow for me! Besides, all the tomorrows in the world will not alter Papa, nor his wretched principles! I hate myself for deceiving him, Aunt Charlotte, but he leaves me no alternative. As it is, I lay awake all night wondering how I would escape him this morning. Wondering if I would be allowed a few short hours to call my own!' Her expression grew alarmingly determined. 'Well, I do not intend to wait forever for my freedom. One of these days I shall—'

Just then Giles appeared on the landing dressed for his morning ride. His brown leather boots squeaked from newness as he descended the stairs, and the sound of his whip being slapped against the palm of his hand was altogether irritating. 'I am ready, Elizabeth. Shall we go?' he said briskly.

Fifteen minutes later saw them riding through the courtyard, Elizabeth filled with despair, whilst her father rode with his usual air of self-importance. As they were riding past the house, a timely miracle occurred. Charlotte suddenly appeared at the front porch, where she called out to her brother. 'Giles! Giles! Squire Ridley has called on a matter of some importance. He awaits you in your study, where he begs a few moments of your time!'

'Deuce!' exclaimed Giles in vexation. 'Blessed nuisance of the fellow to call just now! Aagh, bringing me tales of further rebellion, no doubt!'

Elizabeth sat her horse with bated breath, praying her father would see fit to grace the good squire with his time.

'Very well!' he shouted. 'Tell the fellow I shall be but a moment, Charlotte!' He turned to Elizabeth. 'You go on ahead, my dear. I shall endeavour to keep the matter brief and rejoin you as soon as I can.'

Oh, praise be! It was all Elizabeth needed, and she lost no time in making for the wood. She must warn Richard that her father was but minutes behind and that he must depart forthwith.

Horse and rider were soon speeding along the cart track which led to Lower Coppice. Rhapsody sensed the urgency of the occasion, for soon it became difficult to restrain her eager spirit, the pair of them flying across the land as though on wings. Reining her back, Elizabeth set her at the hedge which enclosed her father's cattle, for the meadow beyond would prove a substantial short cut to the wood. They took it magnificently, a leap which would undoubtedly have been the envy of many a huntsman.

Upon reaching the wood, she found Richard already there waiting for her in their usual meeting place. Elizabeth rushed into his outstretched arms. 'Oh, Richard! It is so good to see you, my dearest! But I must warn you that Papa is following. He is but minutes behind! You must go!' The words came spilling from her mouth in a rush. Already as she spoke she was ushering him towards his horse.

He dug in his toes and halted her. 'Steady, steady, Elizabeth!' he said. 'Now, explain what is amiss.'

Quickly she told him what had happened, whereupon his expression grew contemptuous. 'Oh! Were it not for you, I would be sorely tempted to stay and face the man! Thrash the matter out with him – this time without an audience to overhear us!'

But Elizabeth would not hear of it. 'No, Richard, please! I . . . I fear for you! I am convinced Papa would shoot you if he found you here!'

Her remark caused him to smile. 'Do not worry so, for I am able to take care of myself.' He drew her into his arms as he spoke, where she curled her own around his neck and clung to him. 'When can I see you again, Elizabeth? There is so much we must discuss. We must meet again soon!'

'I do not know, Richard. Papa has become obsessed with my every move and allows me to go nowhere on my own. However,' she added, after careful thought, 'I may be able to meet you on Friday. Papa always rides to Cambourne on Friday mornings. If I am able, I will slip away and meet you in the wood at ten o'clock.' She looked at him with eager eyes. 'Say you will be here, my love?'

His kiss was answer enough. 'The devil himself could not keep me from you!' he responded.

Reluctantly she drew away from him. 'Goodbye!' she whispered. 'With all

132

my heart I look forward to seeing you soon, Richard!'

'I, too,' he acknowledged. 'Elizabeth, if by chance you cannot keep our rendezvous, then I shall wait for you the following Friday at the same hour. Be assured of it!'

Mounting his stallion, he sat for a moment gazing down at her. Their meeting had been so brief, he had barely had the chance to look at her. He smiled. She made the loveliest picture in her plum-coloured riding habit, with a matching hat adorned by plumes and feathers, her feet tucked into black button-up boots which peeped from beneath her skirts. Rosy-cheeked after her exhilarating ride, wisps of dark wavy hair fell upon the collar of her jacket, and at her throat, pinned to her silk cravat, was her treasured cameo brooch. She looked adorable!

His intimate gaze brought a blush rising to her cheeks. 'You sit there as though you had all the time in the world, Richard!' she scolded. 'Be off with you before my heart stops beating altogether!'

He leaned over the side of his horse to kiss her lips. 'Very well, my love. Until Friday. I love you Elizabeth!'

Horse and rider then galloped away, leaving Elizabeth with a tender smile on her face. 'And I love you,' she murmured.

The days which followed were long and tedious for Elizabeth, made more so by her father's persistence in accompanying her everywhere. Shameful as it was, his continuous company had become too monotonous for words. He escorted her around the gardens, on her walks and rides; even to visit old Mrs Potter in one of the cottages. Her patience had been maintained only by the hope of being able to relieve herself of his company on Friday morning. Now it was Thursday, and the man himself made his entrance into the drawing room where the family sat together for their usual glass of sherry before dinner.

In civil mood this evening, he poured himself a drink, then joined his daughter on the sofa. His eyes admired her lilac gown. 'You look most fetching in that colour, Elizabeth,' he said, 'you should wear it more often, my dear. By the by, speaking of gowns, it escaped my attention to inform you that Mr Llani is expected here tomorrow morning. You remember, Elizabeth, he is the artist fellow from London.' Casting her a warm smile, he added, 'So tomorrow I look forward to seeing you in that fine pink dress of yours. A most befitting garment for the occasion.'

Elizabeth's expression clouded. Tomorrow morning? But tomorrow was Friday! She had arranged to meet Richard in the wood at ten o'clock! Fretful, she turned to Giles. 'Mr Llani is expected here tomorrow morning, you say?'

'Indeed he is,' came the firm reply. 'So I trust you will prepare yourself accordingly, Elizabeth.'

Elizabeth's heart sank. Of all the days to arrive, the artist had to come tomorrow. 'What time is he expected in the morning, Papa?' she asked with bated breath.

'Ten o'clock.'

Ten o'clock! Oh, no! It must be a conspiracy! Her father had enlisted another to thwart her now! As if one minder were not bad enough, she would have two of them to contend with in future! Mr Llani, drat him, was arriving here tomorrow, and to add insult to injury, at the precise time of her meeting with Richard. Oh, how she loathed this man for robbing her of the chance to be with her beloved!

Sir Giles addressed her again. 'I myself will be present throughout your sittings, my dear, for I intend your portrait to be undertaken exactly to my specification.'

That was the last straw for Elizabeth, who leapt angrily to her feet. Oh! Was there no escape from the man? Could she not even have her portrait painted in peace? Rebellion flooded into her. She longed to tell him that she had made her own arrangements for tomorrow morning and that she had no wish to have her wretched portrait painted! But instead she kept silent.

Frowning, Sir Giles rose to his feet, wondering what was amiss with his daughter. She looked so vexed all of a sudden. 'Elizabeth, what is wrong? Have I said something to upset you?'

She fled from the room, saying she wished to be alone. Three pairs of eyes stared after her disappearing figure, her father unable to understand her capricious mood.

Next morning, Frederick Llani arrived punctually at ten o'clock, where he was greeted in the hall by Sir Giles. Elizabeth awaited him upstairs, abhorring the man for having cheated her out of her meeting with Richard. Sometime later, she made her feelings clear by greeting him with icy coolness – if not with obvious dislike. Unable to understand her attitude, Sir Giles cringed at her lack of manners, although Mr Llani himself appeared proof against her frosty disposition by taking not the slightest notice. Heated words were exchanged between the two men upon entering the room allocated for the sittings, for being a professional, Mr Llani adamantly refused to allow Sir Giles to sit in attendance. The master put up a fierce argument but eventually conceded, allowing the artist to have his own way. The fellow was, after all, a member of the professional field, notorious for their unpredictable moods and tantrums. Ah, should the portrait fail to meet Giles' requirements, then he would send him back to London where he came from!

Elizabeth, seated on a high-backed chair, watched the man as he painstakingly prepared the equipment, laying it out on the table made available for his use. She found herself assessing his somewhat unorthodox appearance. To begin with, his silver-grey hair was worn much longer than was considered fashionable for today's upstanding gentlemen, although the way it was styled, brushed backwards off his forehead, suited, she conceded, his pleasing, aristocratic features. His eyes, which displayed kindness, were a shade of darkest brown, and below his mouth with its straight white teeth was a neat beard cut into a point below the chin, which suited him perfectly. Of medium height and slender in build, he was dressed in a brown velvet day suit, with a flamboyant scarlet cravat around his neck. All in all, Elizabeth conceded that the artist exuded a certain appeal, although she still refused to warm to him.

She watched him remove his jacket, fold it, place it carefully down on to a chair, then don his artist's smock. The procedure had been conducted without so much as batting an eyelid, speaking a word, or directing a passing glance in her direction, for that matter. Nervously she shuffled in her chair. She had the distinct feeling that he was giving her a dose of her own medicine; treating her with the indifference which she had bestowed upon him. After what seemed like an age, he politely asked if she was ready. 'Of course I am ready, Mr Llani,' she snapped. 'I have been ready and waiting all morning!'

His lips curled in the vestige of a smile, but remained sealed against speech. In true artistic fashion, he instructed her to sit this way, that way, upright, then sideways, first from left, then to right angles, until she became monumentally bored with the whole tedious business. He objected to her tight, immaculate hairstyle, and proceeded to tease loose several strands with his fingers, allowing them to fall into wispy curls on her neck, thus achieving a more natural, more flattering effect, he said. Her skirts had been pulled and spread in an effort to achieve the desired effect, her hands placed just so upon her lap.

Just when she thought there was little else he could do to her, he threw down his brushes and strode over to her. 'No, no, no!' he said. 'It simply will not do!' In thoughtful manner, he rubbed his chin. 'Your posture is too rigid. That high-backed chair must go.' He eyed one of the plush velvet stools, deciding to use that in preference to the chair. 'Would you mind, Miss Montgomery?' he asked.

Elizabeth gave a long exasperated sigh. 'Not at all, Mr Llani. Anything to oblige!'

He used one of the sapphire blue velvet curtains as a backcloth to the portrait, her pink satin dress contrasting beautifully with its colour. Wisely, he decided that nothing else was needed in the picture. When at last everything was in order, Mr Llani began his work.

In no time at all Elizabeth's thoughts strayed to Richard again, for she had been unable to dispel him from her mind. The knowledge that he was waiting in the wood for her whilst she was here conceding to Mr Llani's artistic whims was more than she could bear. She grew irritable and found it increasingly difficult to sit still. Moreover, it did not occur to her that she was frowning and that there was an unbecoming pout on her lips.

Calmly the artist placed down his brush, removed his smock and put on his jacket, then politely asked if she was ready.

'Ready? Ready for what, pray?'

'Ready to show me around your beautiful gardens, Miss Montgomery,' he replied. Her puzzled expression made him smile. He placed his hands upon his hips and approached her. 'My dear young lady, it is patently clear that something troubles you, and that you are neither in mood nor spirit to undergo the burdensome task of having your portrait painted. Were I to continue my work regardless of your state, then I assure you most profoundly that the result would be something which your audience would flee from. Shall we go?' he added briskly.

Astonished by one so enigmatic, Elizabeth led the way like a lamb. She conceded that perhaps her opinion of him had, after all, been a hasty one, for she was actually growing to like Mr Llani!

They were on the point of leaving the house when Sir Giles suddenly appeared from his study. He frowned when he saw the couple. 'What is going on? May I ask where the pair of you are going?'

Mr Llani proceeded to relate that Miss Montgomery and himself were about to take a stroll around the gardens, adding, and with a certain air of nonchalance, 'Is there anything wrong with that?'

Giles' cheeks reddened. 'Indeed there is!' he replied curtly. 'Bless my life, Mr Llani, but I am not paying you to walk my daughter around the gardens. I am paying you to paint her portrait, if you please!'

'On the contrary, Sir Giles, I feel compelled to remind you that you have not paid me anything yet, and neither will you if I choose to cancel my appointment here. Our agreement can be rescinded at any time, you understand.' He raised his eyebrows. 'Now, Sir, was there anything else . . .?'

'But . . .?' began Sir Giles, confounded.

Mr Llani sighed. 'The reason for our stroll is not to waste valuable time, Sir, but to refresh your daughter with a breath of fresh air. To put a little colour into her cheeks. Encourage her spirit, so to speak.'

'Encourage her spirit!' mocked the master sarcastically, then retreated to his study, defeated.

Smiling, Mr Llani turned to Elizabeth, offering his arm. He had won her admiration just now by standing up to her father like that, and accepting the proffered assistance, they took their stroll together.

Soon her tension ebbed away and she felt more at ease in his company. Moreover, her dislike of the man was rapidly waning. They sat together beside the rhododendron bushes, where he proceeded to endear himself further by telling her tales of his remarkable adventures in foreign lands. The fellow was indeed an enigma, for gazing at his prim, gentlemanly person, who would have thought that he had led such a colourful, often dangerous, life? Soon Elizabeth's new-found respect for him had blossomed into open admiration.

'Did you ever marry, Mr Llani?' she enquired interestedly.

He sighed wistfully. 'No, my dear, I did not. Although there was a certain Viennese lady who engaged my affections many years ago. But it was never to be,' he said. He turned to her. 'Anyway, enough of me. What about you, Miss Montgomery? Who occupies your heart on this glorious summer's day?'

The fellow's bold question shocked her. 'Mr Llani . . . please . . .'

He smiled. 'Ah, I see I have embarrassed you. I apologise, for that was not my intention.' In fatherly fashion, he tapped her hand with his fingers. 'I wish you would allow yourself to trust me, my dear. 'Tis plain that something troubles you, and the wisdom which my age affords tells me it has something to do with a man. Am I correct?' He raised an enquiring eyebrow, adding, 'Incidentally, Miss Montgomery, may I ask why you dislike me so?'

Astounded by his outspokenness, Elizabeth was unable to refrain from laughing. Instinctively she felt she could trust him, and without further ado proceeded to pour out her troubles into his listening ear. She told him everything, including the reason for venting her dislike upon him earlier.

The man was sympathy itself and, friends at last, the two got along famously during the days which followed, as encouraged by his warmth and compassion and his never-ending patience, Elizabeth's portrait began to take shape. The man possessed an amazing aptitude for art and beauty, his unique skill gaining Elizabeth's admiration, who learned much from his experience and advice. Never once did he weary of her endless questions, always taking the trouble to sit and listen, encourage and advise, eventually praise, once she had allowed him to view her own achievements. Judging by his enthusiastic response, it seemed he had not expected such admirable works of art.

'Oh, Elizabeth, these are splendid. Splendid! Naturally your father told me you possessed artistic talent, but I had no idea it extended to this!'

Elizabeth was warmed and excited by his response to each and every one, certain now that she really did possess a talent for art. It was difficult to know which one inspired him the most, although he did appear to favour her first achievement, the painting of Cambourne Hall.

'This is remarkable, Elizabeth,' he said. 'Indeed, they all are! Oh, but such works must not go unseen. You must exhibit them, my dear. Have them displayed in an art gallery.'

'I am afraid my father would never allow it, Mr Llani,' she said sadly.

'Is that so,' he replied. 'Well, we shall see, for I intend to approach the man myself. 'Tis a crime to allow such pieces to go unseen.'

Elizabeth decided to show him her unfinished portrait of Richard. He gasped when he saw it, his eyes filled with admiration.

'Do you like it, Mr Llani?'

'Like it? Why, words fail me, Elizabeth. Fail me!'

The artist proceeded to examine the work, his eyes following those careful, meticulous lines which shaped the subject's head, the warmth which was revealed in his eyes, instinctively knowing by the love and care which had been put into the portrait just who the gentleman was. 'This is the Count, is it not, Elizabeth? The man you are in love with?'

Elizabeth smiled. 'Yes, Mr Llani. It is he.'

'Well, Elizabeth, it is a fine piece of work indeed. In fact, I find it inconceivable that a young woman of your limited experience could produce such a masterpiece of skill and beauty. You have brought your subject to life with a depth that truly amazes me, my dear, and can only conclude that you have been blessed with a remarkable gift. Treasure it, Elizabeth, for there is not an artist in the world who would not give his all to possess your talent.'

'Thank you, Mr Llani,' she acknowledged. 'And I will treasure it . . . always!'

CHAPTER TEN

It was Friday, and the first meal of the day found Elizabeth irritable. Richard had promised to wait in the wood for her today. She had not seen him for two whole weeks and prayed her father would be gracing Cambourne with his usual weekly presence that morning. She had missed Richard dreadfully and her happiness today was hanging on a thread, all too dependent on her father's changeable schedule.

Mr Llani, who was to remain a guest until all the portraits had been completed, gazed at her from across the breakfast table. Being a man of percipience, he had watched her spirits sink with increasing despair of late, knowing all too well the reason why. Elizabeth was missing her beloved, living only for the moments when she would be with him again. His heart went out to her, an innocent victim of her father's hatred.

Mr Llani was aware that she and the Count had arranged a secret rendezvous in the wood that morning, for Elizabeth had trusted him enough to divulge the fact. Folding his arms in front of him, he put on an exaggerated frown as he addressed her. 'You look decidedly peaky this morning, Miss Montgomery. Indeed, considering your pale countenance, I declare this morning's sitting to be out of the question. Perhaps a ride around the estate would be beneficial? I am certain that would put a little colour back into your cheeks.'

Elizabeth saw the twinkle in his eyes and knew straight away that he was trying to help her.

The man smiled broadly. 'Well, shall we go, Miss Montgomery? It is already past nine o'clock.'

Elizabeth jumped to her feet, eagerness itself now. 'Yes, indeed, Mr Llani! If you would kindly wait but a moment whilst I go upstairs to change.'

But Sir Giles was present at the table and he had other ideas. He was growing weary of the man who had persistently robbed him of his daughter's company of late. In fact, he had barely seen anything of her since the artist had arrived. When the two of them were not involved with the sittings, they were either walking, taking tea together in the summerhouse, or paying one of their endless visits to the stables. Well, he was monumentally tired of the whole situation and would be relieved to see the back of the fellow!

'I think not,' he said sternly. 'I believe too much time is being wasted on frivolous activities, Mr Llani, and would be obliged if you would kindly proceed with the matter in hand – your work, Sir, if you please!'

Undeterred, the artist composed an equable reply. 'Most certainly, Sir Giles. And whilst you kindly remind me that I am here to paint your daughter's portrait, I point out that it is with all our interests in mind that I insist she appears at her sittings looking her best – not a seedy shadow of her true self. Do I make my case clear, Sir? Or would you rather I present you with a second-rate portrait of your daughter?'

Unspeakably angry and feeling himself disparaged, Sir Giles threw down his napkin and stormed from the room, leaving the onlookers with smiles upon their faces.

'Bravo, Mr Llani!' cheered Aunt Charlotte, who was also present. 'I do believe my brother has met his match in you!'

Soon Elizabeth and Mr Llani were riding towards Bluebell Wood. Richard was already waiting, surprised to see his beloved riding towards him with a companion. After dismounting, Elizabeth introduced the two men.

'Thank you for bringing Elizabeth to me, Mr Llani,' said Richard afterwards. 'You are a gentleman and I am in your debt.'

Frederick Llani smiled. 'It was my pleasure, Count de Ville. It pains me to see Elizabeth so unhappy, and I am only too glad to be of assistance.' He glanced at her, still smiling broadly. 'Ah, I see an improvement already, her pink cheeks and sparkling eyes. Just what I like to see!' He gave a laugh. 'I do, after all, have a vested interest in Elizabeth's appearance, Count de Ville.'

'You do indeed,' agreed Richard amiably.

Frederick mounted his horse. 'I will take my leave of you now,' he said, 'and promise to return for Elizabeth in an hour or so. It has been a pleasure to meet you, Count de Ville. I hope we shall meet again one day. Enjoy yourselves!'

Following his departure, the couple fell into each others arms, uttering endearments which rolled from their lips in a breathless torrent. The kisses they exchanged required no words of accompaniment to convey how much they had missed one another, hungry kisses, loving kisses, kisses which lost them to the rest of the world. Later they took a stroll beside the stream.

'I have good news, Richard!' said Elizabeth eagerly. 'Edward and I shall be attending Rachael's birthday party on the twentieth of June, as Papa is visiting Carleton Grange that weekend. Oh, I cannot tell you how very much I am looking forward to the occasion!'

Richard smiled as he took her into his arms again. 'That is good news indeed, Elizabeth,' he responded. 'Ah, but we shall have a wonderful afternoon! I long for you to see Netley Manor . . . our home together when we

140

are man and wife. Oh, but I can hardly wait . . .' His words trailed away and his lips met hers in a long kiss.

Elizabeth curled her arms around his neck, her fingers straying upwards through his dark, silky hair. His own arms were around her back, drawing her closer against him. Desire swept her body and she clung to him in response, overwhelmed by the strength of her feelings. Both were being swept away on a tidal wave of passion when the sound of a snapping twig alerted them. Elizabeth jumped, fearful that her father had followed her and Mr Llani to the wood. But she need not have worried, for it was only two playful rabbits chasing one another through the trees. The couple looked at each other and laughed with relief.

'Let us hope that at my sister's party we shall be able to relax and enjoy ourselves without fear of being confronted by your father,' said Richard.

'Oh, yes. It will be wonderful to know that he is far away and that he cannot spoil our afternoon together.'

'Amen to that, my dear Elizabeth. Now,' he said, taking her into his arms again, 'where were we . . .?'

That same afternoon Elizabeth sat for Mr Llani. Although her meeting with the Count had been a short one, it had been enough to revitalise her, put colour back into her cheeks and give her the sparkle and vitality which the artist saw in her now. Oh, but it was like looking at an entirely different person, for she had sprung into new life, glowing with a radiance which would be captured forever by the skill of his hand and the keenness of his eye, contributing towards the finest painting he had ever undertaken. Indeed, it could be acknowledged that this was Mr Llani's 'pièce de résistance', his very own Mona Lisa. He was tremendously proud of it, for it had the power to draw the eyes of the beholder, holding him or her spellbound with its incredible depth and beauty.

Sir Giles was enthralled by it, and as the portrait progressed towards completion, he would sit before it, utterly captivated. The allure which shone from her eyes alone was altogether riveting, and the way Llani had captured her glow, her radiance, was completely beyond his understanding. Giles made no attempt to hide the fact that as a man, he disliked Mr Llani intensely; but as an artist he held him in the highest esteem. Although he flatly refused the fellow the honour of exhibiting Elizabeth's portrait in one of the London art galleries, due, one might suspect, to his overbearing possessiveness of her, he did, in fact, grant his permission for Elizabeth's painting of Cambourne Hall to go on show. Both she and Mr Llani were overjoyed by the news, and soon the canvas was packed and transported off to London for a twelve-month showing. No-one could then have foreseen the tragic events which would transpire during those months, and that eventually

141

the painting would be presented as a gift to Mr Llani by Edward and Charlotte in memory of Elizabeth.

Friday the nineteenth of June brought near-disaster when Sir Giles suddenly changed his mind about visiting Carleton Grange that weekend. His change of heart was calculated to dismay others besides his family. The entire staff at the Hall was upset into the bargain. Sir Giles had been exceptionally irritable of late, and three days' peace and quiet would have been most welcome to them all.

In the drawing room, the old man proceeded to explain matters to his woebegone sister. 'I am really unwilling to go visiting just now, Charlotte,' he said. ''Tis a bad time, you understand, considering the scene between myself and de Ville at the ball.' He groaned at the memory of that eventful night. 'I have become a laughing stock, Charlotte, a source of entertainment to everyone. I simply cannot face them all at Carleton Grange this weekend. I cannot!'

Charlotte would have liked to tell him that he had only himself to blame for his predicament, but wisely restrained her feelings, for no purpose would be served by antagonising him. All the same, she did her utmost to sway him from his decision. 'But do you not see that hiding only worsens the matter, Giles? If you wish to regain respect, then you must face your friends. Rally your dignity and face them.'

The master's face creased with distaste. 'No . . . no, I cannot do it, Charlotte, knowing how they hold me in contempt.'

Charlotte grew vexed. She thought of Elizabeth and Edward; how dreadfully disappointed they would be if they were unable to attend Rachael's party tomorrow. In a supreme effort to change his mind, she summoned up all her persuasion. 'Giles . . . Giles you must proceed with your visit to Carleton Grange. By joining your friends, facing them with dignity, you will allow them no time for gossip, for that is something which is usually undertaken behind one's back, is it not?'

Giles looked thoughtful, and for a moment Charlotte believed she had swayed him. But she was mistaken.

'No . . . no, I think not,' he said. 'There will be other times.' He rose to his feet. 'I must write a note of apology to the Granvilles, for 'tis only common courtesy to let them know I will not be there.' The man had already reached the writing desk, the pen poised in his hand awaiting its task.

It was then that Charlotte inhaled a deep breath and aimed her few well chosen words. 'Very well, Giles. Pray proceed – if it is your wish to be called a coward.'

Outraged, Sir Giles swung around to face her. 'Coward? How dare you!

And woe betide the fellow who refers to me as that!'

'Maybe so, Giles,' said Charlotte, shrugging her shoulders with indifference, 'but that will not prevent them from speaking their minds.'

The man began to snort with indignation, appalled at the very thought of being labelled the unmentionable, for being referred to as a coward was the greatest disgrace one could suffer. Charlotte could see the cogs of his mind turning away. She had touched a nerve there; the underlying implication had offended her brother's self-esteem.

He suddenly threw the pen onto the notepaper. 'Bless my soul, but if I have not changed my mind!' he cried. 'I will not have the likes of that lot call me a coward behind my back!' Another angry snort, then, 'I intend to visit the Granvilles' with my head held high – and heaven help the first fellow fool enough to mention either my daughter or de Ville!'

So Charlotte had won the day, as well as the hearts of all those who watched the master depart the Hall in his carriage and pair a short while later. When he had gone, she slumped into one of the armchairs, for the last hour had been considerably gruelling. Giles had laid down the law in no uncertain terms, demanding his sister's promise to ensure that Elizabeth remained confined to the house that weekend; that under no circumstances was she to leave the Hall. Grim-faced , she recalled his warning and those dark, menacing looks which he had cast at her. Inflicting fear and intimidation was Giles' business and he had had no qualms about administering them to his sister. His final warning rang loudly in her ears: 'Take note, Charlotte, for should my wishes go unheeded, then I shall make you suffer the consequences of your foolishness.'

Looking determined now, Charlotte cast all thoughts of her brother from her mind. Elizabeth and Edward would have their afternoon's enjoyment at Netley Manor – and to blazes with Giles and his rules!

The following afternoon the couple proceeded to the party in their carriage and pair, travelling at a brisk pace to the steady clip-clop of the horses' hooves. Elizabeth had never looked more beautiful. Her gown was made from white lace; fashionably bustled, its overskirts were deeply scalloped, as was the hem of the dress. The sleeves were tastefully rouched, their long slim cuffs fastened by a row of lace-covered buttons. The neckline was high and heavily laced, and secured to it, just below the throat, was her cameo brooch. Finishing off the dress was a satin bow sash worn around the waist, its colour being of delicate peach. Upon her head was a wide-brimmed lace hat adorned with matching silk flowers, her hair styled in ringlets beneath. Her hands were slipped into white lace gloves, one clutching her parasol with its fine crystal knob.

Edward looked equally splendid in a brown check jacket, white shirt and yellow bow tie, with cream flannel trousers and leather shoes, and a saucy straw boater to complete his sporty image.

Both were in exceedingly high spirits as they travelled on their way, politely acknowledged by the hard-working farmers who tended their fields, and who doffed their caps in respect as the carriage passed by.

Upon reaching the crossroads, Elizabeth's eyes were drawn to the small stone sign which pointed to Netley. Her heart gave a leap of excitement. They were heading towards forbidden territory now, Netley and its surrounding vicinity being strictly out of bounds to anyone who went by the name of Montgomery. But today was different. Her father was many miles away and she had been invited to Netley Manor as a guest, no less! The thought lifted her effervescent spirits even higher.

Soon they were travelling along the gravel drive which led down to the house, magnificence itself in the near distance. Elizabeth was unable to contain her delight, for it far exceeded her expectations and was much larger than she had envisaged. 'Oh, Edward, how impressive it all is! The house, the parkland, the gardens . . . Oh, I love it already! I can hardly believe it will be my home one day!'

When the carriage had drawn to a halt behind the many others, they saw Richard come striding from the house, his sister in close pursuit. 'Welcome! Welcome to Netley Manor!' he said, his eyes resting upon Elizabeth. He reached for her hand and, after assisting her from the carriage, pressed it against his lips. 'You look beautiful, Elizabeth. Enough to take my breath away!'

Elizabeth's heart began to flutter madly. It was wonderful to see him again; to know that she was free to spend the entire afternoon in his company untroubled by thoughts of her father. Her eyes shone with happiness as she smiled into his handsome face.

'Thank you, Richard. I am so happy to be here this afternoon.'

The couple were barely able to exchange a word after that, for Rachael took command of the conversation, monopolising Elizabeth and Edward, whilst Richard stood quietly by her side. She was vivaciousness itself today, her twenty-second birthday. The last time Elizabeth and Edward had seen her was at the ball, when she had left the house weeping and demoralised at her brother's side. But now she was radiance itself, her cheeks aglow with a colour which matched her rose pink dress. She presented a picture of natural beauty, her blonde, ribboned hair worn in fashionable ringlets today. Edward eyed her with undisguised admiration, something which did not go unnoticed by the two bystanders. Elizabeth and Edward presented her with their birthday gifts and wished her many happy returns of the day.

'Thank you so much,' she said, 'and thank you for coming here today. My party would not have been the same without you to grace it.'

The two couples then walked over to the house, where the Marquise de Ville awaited their company.

In the sitting room, Rebecca stood with her back to the door, gazing thoughtfully through the open sash window at her daughter's party, which was already in full swing. She knew Elizabeth and Edward had arrived, having seen their carriage draw up outside the house. Rebecca politely awaited them now. Her thoughts strayed to Sir Giles and the dark days of their betrothal, once again experiencing that deep-rooted fear which over the years had become immovable. For over three decades both she and her family had been plagued by Giles' hatred of them, mellowed only when she and her late husband Robert had left England's shores for France. Those years had been relatively kind to them, but now Robert was gone and she was back in the house where they had begun their married life together. It had been Richard's decision to return to England. Following his father's death, he had dogmatically refused to be exiled from their English country home a moment longer. Robert had died whilst on a visit to England and had been buried in the churchyard at Netley. Afterwards his family had taken up residence in their old home again. Their peace had been short-lived, however, for now Richard had lost his heart to Giles' daughter and the old man's wrath had been incurred all over again. Rebecca knew Giles would never allow a marriage to take place between them; knew he would do his utmost to separate the two. But how far would he venture to achieve it, she wondered? How far would his immeasurable hatred take him?

Her thoughts and fears were interrupted when the door opened and the two couples entered the room. Richard then proceeded with the introductions.

'Mother, may I present Miss Elizabeth Montgomery and Mr Edward Montgomery?'

Elizabeth felt dreadfully nervous. Throughout her life she had been compelled to listen to disparaging stories concerning the woman who stood before her now, a woman who had scorned her father, thereby initiating the feud which had followed.

Slowly the Marquise turned around to face her, and only then did Elizabeth acknowledge her rare and incredible beauty. Oh, but Rebecca de Ville was exquisite, far beyond the vague, misty image which over the years Elizabeth had depicted in her mind! Dressed in a fetching blue crepe gown, she was taller than Elizabeth herself, and had retained both her sylph-like figure and looks. An ageless goddess who had been blessed with the gift of eternal youth. Her face, defiant of worthy description, with its flawless opaque skin, fine arched brows, high cheek bones and aristocratic nose, was in itself an inspiration to behold. But it was her eyes, her captivating violet coloured eyes, vivid from beneath their long black eyelashes, which were by far her most alluring feature. They were spectacular! Elizabeth knew she was staring at the Marquise, but found herself unable to do otherwise.

Her eyes wandered to her thick black hair which was worn in a pleat at the back of her head. Oh, no wonder her father had been so besotted by her! Only now was she able to understand how devastated he must have been upon losing her.

Rebecca's voice was friendly when she spoke, and without accent, for she was English by birth. 'Miss Montgomery . . . Mr Montgomery, I am delighted to meet you at last.'

'Marquise.' The two addressed her, took turns to shake her hand. ''Tis a pleasure, indeed, an honour to meet you, too,' stressed Edward.

After formalities were over, she invited them to take a seat. Elizabeth felt more at ease now, for the Marquise was so friendly, making it patently clear that she did not bear Sir Giles Montgomery's family any grudge.

She smiled from one to the other. 'And how is dear Charlotte?' she enquired. 'I cannot remember the last time I saw her.'

'She is very well, thank you, Marquise,' replied Elizabeth, passing on her aunt's good wishes in return.

Everyone was careful not to mention Sir Giles, no-one wishing to darken the friendship and goodwill which existed between them now. Elizabeth realised that the Marquise would want to speak privately with Richard and herself for, considering his proposal of marriage, it was only fitting for her to do so. As though the issue were in her own mind, she graciously asked the couple if they would spare her a few minutes of their time after the party had concluded.

'But of course,' replied Elizabeth. 'We shall look forward to it.'

Rebecca smiled. 'Thank you, Elizabeth. Well, I expect you are longing to join the party. Have fun all of you, and I look forward to seeing you this evening.'

Outside they found the party in full swing. A number of guests were already taking advantage of the croquet lawn, where flirtations took place between the young ladies and gentlemen. Some of the more successful flirtations had led to a row across the lake in one of the rowing boats, or to a leisurely stroll around the gardens and botanical greenhouses, which boasted some of the finest blooms one could ever wish to see. For the more athletically inclined male guests who wished to show off their skills, there was the tennis court, made popular by its audience of delectable ladies, who laughed and teased the players beneath their twirling parasols. Others sat in small groups around the tables on the lawn, content to sit and chat and watch the rest of them.

Rachael was busy introducing Elizabeth and Edward to her friends, many of whom were clearly unable to comprehend the situation. Sir Giles Montgomery's son and daughter here at Netley Manor! That was an enigma which had to be seen to be believed, and it aroused a great deal of speculation amongst them.

It was whilst Elizabeth was chatting to Evelyn Filingdale and Richard to one of his friends, that their eyes met and held each other in a long engulfing look of love. Deeply stirred by that look, Elizabeth was claimed by a surge of feeling which ran rampant through her body. Her legs turned to jelly beneath her and she suddenly felt light-headed, for his eyes were giving so much away. Like the pages of a book, she could read them so clearly, seeing his love for her, his manly need. Hers unashamedly reciprocated their passion, unable to conceal her own love for him. Those intimate, consuming looks continued throughout the afternoon, adding fuel to the fire which blazed within their hearts. Although they remained close at one another's sides, they were denied an opportunity to be alone together. Even now as they walked arm in arm through one of the greenhouses, several other couples were there to watch and overhear them.

Richard reached to pick one of the orchids, then handed it to her. 'A beautiful flower for a beautiful woman – and you are very beautiful, Elizabeth.' He smiled tenderly. 'I am ashamed to admit that from the moment you arrived I have been unable to tear my eyes away from you.'

Elizabeth grew coy, for of that she was already aware. 'Thank you, Richard. I shall keep the orchid forever as a reminder of today . . . for it has been truly wonderful.'

He gave a laugh. 'I do not believe the flower will keep forever, Elizabeth.'

'Oh, but it will, for I intend to press it, just as I did the bluebells you gave me. I shall keep them always . . . always.'

Her words faded beneath his searching gaze, and suddenly she was in his arms, responding to his kiss. It was a kiss they had hungered for all afternoon, aching for each other's nearness.

They were interrupted by a loud crow of laughter from the far side of the greenhouse. Bertram Hodgkiss was telling a saucy tale to his two female companions, who shrieked with laughter in response, thereby putting an end to Richard and Elizabeth's privacy.

Richard groaned his frustration and released her. He had missed her so much lately and would give all he possessed for a chance to be alone with her. There was so much he wished to say, plans they must discuss regarding their future. But there was never any time, their stolen moments passing all too soon. A thought occurred to him. 'Perhaps I could take you for a row across the lake after the party, Elizabeth? Would you like that?' he asked.

Her face lit with eagerness. 'Oh, indeed I would, Richard. That would be wonderful. Thank you.'

'Good!' he responded with a smile. 'We shall certainly not be disturbed by the likes of Hodgkiss and his screeching friends, for there is nothing but wildlife out there to overhear us.' His eyes grew intimate again. 'Idyllic bliss, would you not agree?'

A tremor of excitement ran down Elizabeth's spine and her eyes grew misty. 'Mmm . . . idyllic bliss most certainly,' she agreed.

A little later, Rachael announced that tea was being served in the marquee, upon which the rowing boats, tennis court, greenhouses and croquet lawn were instantly vacated. Much jesting and frivolity took place at the table, where there was a feast of food to be enjoyed by them all. Elizabeth noticed that Edward had become inseparable from their exuberant hostess and wondered if anything would come of their relationship. The two certainly appeared to enjoy each other's company – indeed, she suspected that Edward had lost his heart to Richard's lovely sister at a very early stage. She suddenly wanted to laugh. Their father would be beside himself if he discovered that both his children had fallen in love with de Villes. Perhaps he would be doubly outraged! But it mattered not, for Edward was old enough to lead his own life – and choose the woman he wished to spend it with. Good luck to him, she thought.

After tea someone suggested they all walk over to the summerhouse, where they gathered together inside the circular glass building.

'What a fascinating place!' exclaimed Muriel Downes.

'Yes, it certainly is,' interpolated Royland Kitchiner. 'I attended a party once where all the guests scratched their names on the host's drawing room window with a diamond.' He gave a hearty laugh. 'Suffice to say, my good friend's father was not at all amused by our antics. But short of removing the entire pane of glass, there was very little the poor fellow could do about it. The inscriptions are still there to this day. Always will be, I suppose,' he reflected.

Rachael's eyes lit. 'Oh, but what fun! Perhaps we could do the same here? Make our mark on the glass for posterity?' Having conceived the idea, she turned to her brother for permission. 'Could we, Richard . . . please?'

All eyes were upon him awaiting his reply. He smiled. 'I do not see why not, if that is what you want. Yes, you have my permission, Rachael.'

A cry of delight passed her lips. 'Oh, thank you, Richard! I knew you would agree!' She turned to her guests. 'Now, does anyone have a diamond we could use?' No-one had, it seemed, so she approached her brother again. Her eyes were twinkling and she was smiling wickedly. 'Richard . . . dear? I see you are wearing your diamond studs. Could we . . .?' Her voice was pure honey now.

He laughed as he placed a hand upon his black trousered hip. 'I protest you will be wanting the shirt off my back next, Rachael. Here,' he handed her the required item. 'Be sure it is returned.'

She kissed his cheek in gratitude, then became the first to inscribe her name on the window pane. Everyone cheered when she had accomplished the task.

Rachael de Ville

22 today

June 20th, 1886

Afterwards, Richard was persuaded to follow suit, then Elizabeth, Edward and so on until everyone had written their name.

Miss Elsie Ward ran her finger over the long list of inscriptions, which had taken quite a while to accomplish. She sighed wistfully. 'I wonder what future generations will make of this?' she said. 'Who knows, perhaps in a hundred years' time someone will read our names and wonder what it was like for us today, maybe wishing they could have been here too.'

Elizabeth moved forward to touch her own signature and that of Richard's, her voice edged with sadness. 'Perhaps, but we shall never know. We will simply be forgotten names written by forgotten people.'

'Oh, so dismal, Miss Montgomery!' chided Bertram. 'Might I remind you that this is a party and we are here to enjoy ourselves? What say you all to a game of blind man's buff?'

Whilst the rest of the guests proceeded to enjoy themselves, Richard and Edward begged to be excused for a short while, saying they had business to discuss in the study. Rather than be parted from Richard, even for an instant, Elizabeth asked if she might accompany them.

'But of course,' said Richard. 'Need you ask?'

Both men realised this was not a time to conduct business, but the matter was pressing and could not be delayed.

Shortly afterwards they sat together at Richard's oak desk, leaving Elizabeth to browse through the study. She thought it a fascinating room, for it exuded a warm, inviting atmosphere. Everywhere she looked she found an intimate reflection of the man she loved, in his books, his paintings, the exotic ornaments displayed on the oak furniture; even the desk behind which he was now sitting. The room relayed volumes of information about Richard which until now she could not possibly have gathered. A pleasant aroma of cigar smoke lingered in the air, mingling with the smell of polished furniture and the scent from the vase of yellow roses which stood on one of the tables.

Moving forward, she stood before the huge stone fireplace, which displayed many horse brasses, copper plates and pewter mugs. Eventually her eyes came to rest on the row of leather-bound books on the shelf above, held in position by a pair of exquisite statuettes of horses. They looked familiar, and closer examination revealed them to be carvings of Richard's own stallion, Black Shadow. She smiled. They were magnificent.

A heavy wooden clock occupied the central position on the shelf, its brass pendulum swinging rhythmically back and forth, back and forth. Its movements had a restful effect on her mind, and for a moment she felt hypnotised, possessed by some distant realm of fantasy.

'Elizabeth . . . you are very quiet? Are you all right?' asked Richard suddenly.

She snapped out of her daydreams and walked over to him. 'Yes, perfectly, Richard, I was simply admiring your study.' Her eyes wandered around again. 'Strange, but I feel so at home in this room. It has a certain atmosphere . . . an air of infinity which not even time could destroy. It is a place where one's spirit could happily linger.'

Edward burst into a fit of laughter, although in comparison, Richard's expression remained serious. 'Oh, Elizabeth! What a peculiar woman you are! Lingering spirits, indeed! I agree, Richard's study is very pleasant, but I fail to recognise anything infinite about it.' He turned to the other man for support. 'What say you, old fellow?'

Richard's reply surprised Edward. 'I am afraid I cannot agree with you, Edward, for like Elizabeth, I also believe one's spirit could happily remain here forever.'

Edward's expression was one of disbelief. 'Oh, what a strange couple you are – all this talk of forever! 'Tis my belief that when you die, you die. And that, my dear fellow, is the end of it! Why, 'tis inconceivable that one's spirit could remain here on earth after the death of the body has taken place. Inconceivable!'

Richard smiled. 'Well, we are all entitled to our opinion, are we not?'

Soon afterwards, Edward rose to his feet and approached his sister. 'I suggest we go along to see the Marquise now, Elizabeth, for time is getting on and I regret we must be leaving shortly.'

'Leaving?' echoed Elizabeth. 'Oh, no, Edward, not yet!' She glanced at the clock above the fireplace. 'Why, 'tis only twenty-five minutes past five. Far too early even to think of going home! Besides, Richard is going to take me for a row across the lake this evening. Please let us stay a little longer, Edward. Please.!'

'Heaven knows, I would like to, my dear. But I cannot. Father has left me a list of tasks to undertake before tomorrow. If I fail to conduct my duties then I do nothing but invite his wrath . . . and matters are already bad enough. We must leave soon, Elizabeth.'

'Might I make a suggestion?' asked Richard, intervening.

'If you grant Elizabeth permission to stay, Edward, then I will convey her home this evening in my own carriage. You know she is safe with me and that no harm will come to her.'

Elizabeth immediately brightened. 'Oh, yes! Do please agree, Edward!' she pleaded.

Edward looked thoughtful. He knew Elizabeth would be safe enough with Richard; that his father was absent from home and would never know a thing. Besides, Elizabeth deserved all the happiness she could get. It might be weeks before she had an opportunity of seeing her beloved again.

'Very well,' he said pleasantly. 'Elizabeth has my permission to stay until this evening.'

Rebecca poured tea for herself and Elizabeth whilst the two men partook of something a little stronger. Some time afterwards, Edward excused himself, saying he must return home forthwith, but not before spending a few minutes alone with Rachael in the garden. It was there he agreed to escort her to Miss Simmon's musical evening held at Netley Lodge next Saturday night, dismissing the consequences should his father come to learn of it. Life was looking up for Edward and he intended to make the most of it.

Back in the sitting room, Rebecca was conversing with Elizabeth and Richard. 'Your plans to marry meet with my heartfelt approval and good wishes,' she said. 'But I fear Elizabeth's father will never extend you the same.'

'Well, we shall see,' said Richard grimly, 'for tomorrow evening I intend to call on him to thrash the matter out once and for all. If he refuses to grant Elizabeth and me permission to marry, then I shall take her from him without his consent! God, but it will serve him right for being so damned disagreeable!'

A wave of unease swept over Rebecca. She knew Richard would have a fight on his hands, for his adversary, Sir Giles, would never stand by and watch his beloved daughter being taken from him. The man would die first – or see to it that others did. The thought chilled her cold.

Sometime later, in response to Elizabeth's curiosity as to why the Marquise had terminated her engagement to Sir Giles, Rebecca began to speak of those past days. 'Although our betrothal had been arranged by our respective families – as was customary in those days – I did, in fact, grow very fond of Giles. In the beginning I found him a kind, considerate man and admit I was happy with the arrangement. Indeed, had it not been for the fact that my mother passed away the day before our wedding, I would most certainly have gone ahead and married him. But because of that, I decided to postpone the wedding for a while, and it was during that time that Giles' character began to change.'

—'Or perhaps it was his true character surfacing!' interjected Richard scathingly.

'Perhaps,' admitted Rebecca. 'Anyway, I began to see a side of him which frightened me. He grew possessive, and became insanely jealous of anyone who paid me the slightest attention, sinking into deep, dark moods and disgracing himself at parties if I so much as conversed with another man. Oh, he became intolerable! Moreover, his ungentlemanly behaviour cost him many friends, for they refused to tolerate his appalling bad temper and manners. Eventually my respect for him diminished and I was left with serious doubts about marrying him. It became clear to me that he was demented, and I believed the balance of his mind was at fault. The matter was brought to a head whilst we were attending a dinner party at the home of Giles' last remaining friend. He accused me and our host of flirting together – utter rubbish of course – but convincing Giles of that was another matter. He began to rant and rave in front of everyone, thoroughly disgracing himself by picking a brawl with the man. Giles hit him on the chin and knocked out two of his teeth. Our host was deeply humiliated and threw Giles out into the street, where he lay sprawled on the pavement like some . . . some common drunkard. I realised I could take no more and brought our relationship to an end.'

'Did he accept that it was all over between you, Marquise?' questioned Elizabeth.

'Oh, no, my dear – far from it. He called on me constantly, begging my forgiveness, pleading with me to take him back. But I dare not, realising that a marriage between us would only bring unhappiness and misery. Then his attitude completely changed. He caused dreadful scenes at my home, promising that I would live to regret what I had done to him.'

'What happened then?' asked Richard.

'Well, a few months later I met your father and we fell in love. That is when the trouble really began. Giles refused to accept that he had lost me through his own behaviour and accused Robert of stealing me away from him, threatening to make him suffer for his crime. His persecution continued until our wedding day, when Giles appeared at the ceremony and caused an embarrassing scene. Robert, acting in defence of my honour, agreed to meet Giles in a duel the following morning. During the duel he . . . he shot and crippled my husband for life.' Rebecca's voice began to falter now. 'A . . . after that Robert and I left England to live at our chateau in France, where we spent many happy years together before Robert died. Now, through no fault of his own, my son has inherited Sir Giles' hatred and the misery begins all over again.'

Rebecca turned to Elizabeth, who was deeply saddened by the story. 'It was not my intention to speak disparagingly of your father, my dear, only to relate the facts as they happened all those years ago. I feel you are entitled to know the truth.'

'I know,' said Elizabeth quietly, 'and am truly sorry that Papa saw fit to treat you so despicably. You have my sympathy, Marquise, and my regret at what happened to you and your husband at my father's hand.'

'Thank you,' she said. 'Now, enough of this morbid talk. I believe Richard wishes to take you for a row across the lake. Go and enjoy yourselves. Live for today and let tomorrow take care of itself.'

The air was warm and still when the couple took their row across the lake, and not a soul was to be seen anywhere. The guests had departed, Rebecca and Rachael had left the manor to visit friends, and peace was in abundance all around. The only sound to fill the air was the gentle splashing of the oars against the water and the far-off cry of a pheasant in the dense woodland which surrounded the lake. Elizabeth thought it was the nearest place to heaven she had ever known, and that she had never felt happier than she did right here and now with Richard.

Smiling contentedly, she watched him as he sat before her rowing. He had removed his black jacket, turned back the cuffs on his frilly white shirt, and now looked a picture of perfect manliness. Undisputedly happy himself, he began to whistle a merry tune, relaxed and carefree this evening.

They gazed at each other and smiled. 'You make a charming picture, Elizabeth,' he murmured. 'So lovely beneath your parasol. Were I an artist, I would paint your likeness. But as it is,' – he gave a sigh of mock despair – 'such talent is beyond me. All I am good for is rowing, it would seem!'

Their laughter echoed out across the glassy water, their happiness filling the air.

'Oh, Richard, I feel so happy! Today has been the most wonderful day of my life. I shall remember it always . . . especially now . . . here on the lake with you. These moments will live in my heart forever, for how could I possibly forget the joy which I am feeling now. I love you!'

He smiled. 'And I love you . . . more than you will ever know, Elizabeth.'

Their row took them to the farthest corner of the lake, a lonely area of wooded forest, its undergrowth alive with the wildlife which lived there undisturbed, its backcloth the rolling Shropshire hills. Elizabeth noticed an intriguing pathway which led through the forest and asked if they might moor the boat and take a stroll on this glorious evening.

'But of course, ' he replied. 'If you have the time, Elizabeth?'

'I have all the time in the world,' she told him cheerfully. 'Papa is far away and I intend to make the most of his absence.'

Arm in arm they took that pathway through the trees, stopping occasionally to steal a loving kiss. As free as the birds which soared above, neither gave thought to tomorrow or the future, both living for today and the moments they were sharing together now.

'There is a clearing up ahead where we can sit for a while,' said Richard. 'I often go there when I need to be alone . . . to meditate, you understand.'

'Yes, I understand, for Bluebell Wood serves as a retreat for me. Strange how I happened to meet you there that day, for I might never have known you otherwise. Might never have known what it is to love you . . . to need you . . .'

He moved to hold her in his arms, where she nestled her head against his shoulder and held him in return. 'You do not really believe that, do you, Elizabeth? That we just happened to meet, I mean?' He looked at her and smiled. 'We were meant to meet each other, my love, to know one another as we do. It was destined. Believe it.'

Elizabeth grew thoughtful. 'Yes, perhaps you are right, Richard. Perhaps we are the means to end the feud which Papa began all those years ago, for it has to end somehow, has it not?'

'Indeed so,' he agreed. 'We must believe that whatever happens to us in the future is meant to be, Elizabeth. Nothing you or I can do will change it. Anyway,' he said on a brighter note, 'enough of such talk. This evening is far too special to spoil with all that.' His arms tightened around her, then he lowered his head and explored her lips with his own. Stirred by her hungry response and the way she clung to him, his mouth grew hard and demanding and for one beautiful moment he allowed his feelings to overpower him as he crushed her against him, his fingers biting into her flesh.

Consumed with a passion of her own, Elizabeth responded kiss for kiss, touch for touch, allowing her pent-up emotion to be blissfully released in his arms. She had awaited this moment for so long. Just when it seemed there was no restraining the love, the passion which flowed between them, Richard suddenly released her and moved away.

Bewildered, Elizabeth stared after him, then began to understand. Richard did not trust himself. Although he wanted her desperately, wanted to possess her in every sense of the word, he refrained. Richard de Ville was a man of rectitude and principle and refused to take advantage of a situation simply because it presented itself in his favour. For that she regarded him highly.

They continued along their way in silence, each with their own private thoughts. Would she ever have the honour of becoming his wife, she

154

wondered? Would she ever lie beside him at night? And would she ever be the mother of his children? Because of her father's hatred, she often thought not. Considering that, perhaps she should take the Marquise's advice, live for today and let tomorrow take care of itself. She conceded it was not such bad advice.

The clearing which Richard had spoken of was beautiful, the ground a colourful carpet of wild flowers, the whites, pinks, blues and yellows all mingling with the rich green grass. A semi-circle of pine trees lent it privacy, the open side offering a spectacular panoramic view across the rugged, bracken covered hills where sheep and ponies grazed contentedly, undisturbed by man.

Elizabeth looked around with delight. It really was a lovely place. 'What a marvellous hideaway, Richard! I love it. I can see why you enjoy coming here so much.'

He smiled at her enthusiasm. 'I am pleased you like it, Elizabeth.'

She sat down on the grass, expecting Richard to join her. He hovered above her for a moment or so, then moved away and gazed across the distant hills. Elizabeth thought he seemed a little tense following their embrace a short while ago. She shifted to a kneeling position, her hands plucking at the flowers which surrounded her, her eyes upon him as he stood with his back to her. Her heart gave a wild, uncontrollable flutter. Richard de Ville was the epitome of manliness, possessing more appeal than a score of others put together. His image rendered her breathless, her entire body aching with love. She closed her eyes and breathed the longest sigh, every fibre of her being alive with the most delicious feelings. Never in her wildest dreams had she imagined that love could feel like this.

He turned around to look at her. Oh . . . Elizabeth made an inspiring picture in her white virgin's dress, its skirts spread out around her on the grass. She was the most bewitching woman he had ever known and he loved her more than life itself. His heart began to pound. Just looking at her drove him almost mad with desire!

Their eyes met and held across the clearing, each reflecting the other's deep, smouldering look. Elizabeth smiled bewitchingly. It seemed the most natural thing in the world to go to him . . . offer herself completely.

Hypnotised, his heart on fire, he watched her rise slowly to her feet. She then walked across to him and halted but a few paces before him. His breath caught in his throat and for a long moment he believed his eyes to be deceiving him. Elizabeth was untying her hair, shaking it free of the combs which held it.

Breathless now, he saw those long dark ringlets fall loose upon her shoulders and, captivated beyond words, he stood in silent awe as she moved to stand

155

in front of him, sheer radiance itself, her eyes burning with love. His senses reeled. She was offering herself to him. Offering herself completely.

'Oh, Elizabeth . . . Elizabeth!' he uttered.

They were in each other's arms, holding, clinging, aching from their need of one another. His kisses took her breath away, whilst his fingers moved with urgency to unhook the back of her dress. The white lace gown and petticoats fell upon the grass, and with a deep groan his mouth moved to wander over her neck and her soft white shoulders, his lips tender against her skin.

Elizabeth arched herself against him, her arms locked tightly around his back. She yielded, moaned with pleasure when he untied her camisole and allowed his hands to explore the contours of her body, the firm, rounded breasts, her tiny waist and the slim hips beneath, every inch of her alive from his touch. She whispered his name as he drew her down onto the grass, where their passion was released in a succession of long engulfing kisses.

Before their union took place, he gazed into her face, into the potent depths of her eyes, which shone bright with the passion which possessed her. His words were a caress against her skin.

'Oh, Elizabeth Montgomery . . . how I love you . . .'

CHAPTER ELEVEN

Charlotte glanced at the clock on the mantelpiece and frowned. It was almost eleven o'clock and Elizabeth had not returned home. Her voice was anxious when she addressed Edward. 'I wonder where on earth she can be? Did Elizabeth not say what time she would return, Edward?'

'No, she did not,' he replied. 'Do not worry so, Aunt Charlotte. My sister will come home when she is ready. Be assured of it.'

'But I cannot help it, Edward. You know I am responsible for her during your father's absence. What if she and Richard have decided to elope together? What, pray, would I say to your father then?'

Edward laughed. He believed it most unlikely, although he did suspect the day would come when the couple would be left with no alternative. Serve the old man right, too, he thought. He had certainly invited their rebellion.

Suddenly they heard the sound of a carriage drawing up outside the house and a look of relief swept over Charlotte's face. 'Oh, listen, Edward – I do believe she is here!'

Edward grinned complacently. 'Of course she is. I said she would be along in her own good time. Anyway, I suggest you prepare your ears in readiness for my sister's chatter, Aunt Charlotte, for she is bound to keep us from our beds with tales of her afternoon at the manor!'

The two were smiling now, awaiting Elizabeth's entrance into the sitting room. But their smiles faded a moment later, for it was not Elizabeth who walked through the door, but Sir Giles. Neither could have been more startled, Charlotte's expression one of horror, whilst Edward simply froze from sheer mortification.

'G... Giles! W... whatever are you doing here? I understood you were staying at Carleton Grange until tomorrow?'

'Did you indeed?' he snorted. 'Well, so I was! But I changed my mind. I am allowed to do that, am I not?' It was more a statement than a question. He then strode over to the cabinet where he poured himself a drink. After swallowing the measure, he turned to stare at his family, his eyes narrowed. 'And what, pray, are you gaping at? By the looks of you it would seem that I was the last person you expected to see tonight! Could it be you were expecting a visitor at this late hour on a Saturday night?'

'C...certainly not, Giles,' stammered Charlotte nervously. ''Tis just a shock to see you, that is all.' She cast Edward an anxious look, desperately hoping Elizabeth would not choose that particular hour to return home.

Edward looked equally troubled. 'May I ask what prompted you into returning home this evening, Father? Were you not enjoying yourself with your friends?'

'Friends? What friends?' he ejaculated angrily. 'I will be blessed if the likes of that lot deserve the title! Why, with friends like them I would need no enemies. Indeed, I could put name to enemies who would make me more loyal friends!'

Charlotte gave an exasperated sigh. Two days at Carleton Grange and he was back, grumbling that people disliked him. 'What happened, Giles?' she asked limply, then under her breath, 'As if I did not know.'

'Happened? Hah! I shall tell you what happened. The entire topic of conversation between my so-called 'friends' this weekend was myself! All the beggars could talk about was my contention with de Ville, my labourers deserting me in favour of working at Netley Manor, and, to cap it all, they insulted me further by asking when the fellow intended to marry my daughter!' He was pacing the floor as he spoke, his voice reduced to a savage snarl. 'Well, I told them a thing or two, made it clear that neither I nor any of mine would grace their wretched homes again! That will teach them. Yes, by Gad it will!' His sneering expression grew uglier. 'And that... that unspeakable blackguard, de Ville – may the devil curse him – has made me, Sir Giles Montgomery, into a laughing-stock! But every dog has its day, and I live in wait of mine. Revenge will be sweet when it comes – and it surely will!'

'Yes, indeed it will, Giles – but be sure it does not come upon yourself,' Charlotte told him shrewdly. 'You initiated all this hatred, and intuition tells me that upon your head it will end. Think about it, Giles, unless it is your wish to end your days a lonely, broken man.'

Giles, however, was impervious to her warning and did not intend to be intimidated by the likes of his sister. 'Poppycock!' he growled. 'When I want your opinion I shall ask for it! Now,' he said, placing down his empty glass, 'where is Elizabeth? Her greeting is sure to be warm and welcoming. I confess she is the only blessed thing worth coming home to!'

Consternation flooded into Charlotte, draining her cheeks of colour. She had been dreading that question. What should she say? What should she tell him? The poor soul was lost for words.

Seeing her plight, Edward came to the rescue with his timely reply. 'Elizabeth was tired, Father, and retired to bed sometime ago. I doubt she would wish to be disturbed.'

'I see,' said the old man, shaking his head in acceptance. 'Then I shall not wake her.' He turned to Charlotte again. 'I trust you have honoured my wishes and kept a close eye on Elizabeth this weekend? Seen to it that she has remained indoors during my absence?'

Charlotte froze. She made an appalling fibber, convinced her brother would see the deceit in her eyes. 'I... I...' she began falteringly.

Once again, Edward intervened. 'Oh, for heavens sake, Father!' he said exasperatedly. 'Does not Aunt Charlotte always look after Elizabeth? Does she not always adhere to your wishes?'

Sir Giles cast his son a contemptuous glance. 'I was not addressing you, Edward – so kindly refrain from interfering in something which does not concern you. Allow your aunt to make her own reply, if you please!'

Agitated by his dogged persistence, Charlotte's reply was emitted with unbridled asperity. 'Yes! I have done as you asked! Elizabeth has remained indoors this weekend exactly as you wished! Now are you satisfied, Giles?'

'Yes,' he said, impervious to her displeasure. 'Well, I suggest we all retire upstairs, for I am tired after my journey home tonight.'

Charlotte and Edward exchanged relieved glances, then all three began to make their way upstairs.

Just five more minutes would have made all the difference; all the difference between getting away with the lies they had told and being found out. Unfortunately they were found out, for at that precise moment Elizabeth returned home. They had not even reached the head of the stairs when they heard the carriage draw up outside the house. Laughter and muffled voices were heard to follow, sending Charlotte and Edward's spirits plummeting into despair. Would Elizabeth invite Richard into the house, they wondered? She could not possibly know that her father had returned home. They waited with bated breath.

Sir Giles muttered with irritation. 'Bless me, who on earth can be calling at this hour?' he said, turning to make his descent of the stairs.

'Heaven help us now!' exclaimed Charlotte, paling before her nephew's eyes.

Edward placed a supportive hand beneath her elbow as they turned to follow Giles. 'Leave matters to me, Aunt Charlotte. Do not say a word!' he whispered. 'I will take the blame for Elizabeth's outing.'

There was no time to reply, as the front door opened and Elizabeth breezed in, sheer radiance itself. Thank God she was alone.

Unaware of her father's return, she failed to see him standing in the shadows preparing to light the oil lamp. But there was enough light shining from the landing lamp to see her aunt and brother. 'Aunt Charlotte... Edward! I was hoping you had not retired to bed.' She placed her bag and parasol on one of the chairs as she spoke. 'Please forgive me for being so late, but... but time passed quickly and...' She stared at their sharp, unsmiling faces wondering if her late return had angered them. They had failed to offer her even the curtest of greeting. And why was Edward indicating with his finger like that? An atmosphere of unease was engendered and Elizabeth's smile and vivacity faded.

On the point of enquiring as to what was amiss, the hall was suddenly lit by a pool of yellow light. The colour drained from her cheeks for there, standing in the corner, his features distorted in pure disbelief, was the foreboding figure of her father.

'P... Papa! Papa... what are you doing home?' she questioned, her face sharp with fright. 'We... we were not expecting you home until tomorrow!'

The old man looked as startled as herself. He thought it was Squire Ridley who was calling on them at this unsociable hour; had actually prepared a few choice words with which to burn the fellow's ears. But when he saw it to be Elizabeth... Elizabeth who was supposedly sleeping upstairs...

His breath was ragged as he placed a hand upon his pounding heart, once again experiencing that same painful tightness in his chest which he had suffered so frequently that weekend. He felt his breath being squeezed from his body and stood rigid and motionless. Thankfully the pain passed and he proceeded to take command of the situation.

Straightening his back and squaring his shoulders, he faced his daughter with a look of disdain. 'Apparently not!' he spat. Sneering, he took a step forward, the light in the background lending him a sinister look. 'Well,' he continued, rolling his eyes sideways in their sockets at Charlotte and Edward, 'I confess the three of you never fail to amaze me. Elizabeth is "upstairs sleeping" is she? She has "remained indoors" this weekend as I wished, eh? Oh, but what unspeakable liars you are! What deceitful, underhanded creatures I leave in charge here! How you both offend me! Traitors! Traitors, the pair of you!' His lips were compressed into a thin harsh line and he was waving a clenched fist as he spoke.

Elizabeth, who stood in immobilised silence, rushed forward to protect her family. It was she who must be punished, not they. 'Papa... Papa, please! If you will just allow me to explain -'

Giles allowed her nothing. Instead he grasped her arms, squeezing until her flesh turned white beneath his fingers. 'Where have you been, Elizabeth? I demand to know! Tell me! Tell me, or as God is my judge I shall shake the information out of you!'

Elizabeth cried out, for he was inflicting pain on her.

Edward rushed forward offering his protection. He caught hold of the furious old man and pulled him away from his sister. 'Do that, Father, and I

160

shall make you a very sorry man! 'Tis not Elizabeth to whom you should address your questions – but me. Me! Do you hear?'

Surprised, Giles stared at his son. 'And what in God's name have you got to do with it?'

'Because Elizabeth has been in my company today, Father. So you can direct your comments to me.'

'You, indeed!' rasped Sir Giles. 'Why, you must think I am a simpleton! How dare you insult my intelligence with such a confounded lie!' He turned to stare at his daughter. ''Tis plain to see that Elizabeth's source of company lies elsewhere than yourself, for did she not return whilst you were here in the presence of your aunt? I am no nincompoop to have the wool pulled over my eyes, Edward! Stay out of the matter! Your punishment will come – of that you may be sure!'

'Leave Edward alone!' cried Elizabeth. 'He is not to blame!'

'Elizabeth... I implore you, do not say a word!' cried Edward.

With one swift movement Giles caught him by the scruff of the neck and began to shake him violently. 'I said stay out of it!' he hissed.

A scuffle broke out between them, with Giles hitting and pushing, Edward fighting him off. The two women ran forward beseeching Giles to control himself.

'Stop it! Stop it, Papa! I will tell you where I have been! I have been to Netley Manor, attending a birthday party to which I was invited! Now, proceed to thrash me if you have a mind to!'

Giles' arm was suspended in mid-air, his eyes like staring marbles in his head. 'Y... you have been where?' he exclaimed.

'Netley Manor, Papa. I believe you heard me the first time.'

'Netley Manor? I cannot believe it! Who allowed such a thing, pray?'

'I did,' said Charlotte, speaking up. 'I gave permission for Elizabeth and Edward to attend the party.' She had spoken with calmness and conviction, too proud to let her brother know how much she quaked. Although Giles' face was black with fury, she continued impenitently. 'Furthermore, I am not sorry, and would do it again if the occasion arose.' Charlotte's eyes held his. 'Do not glare at me like that, Giles. Is it beyond your comprehension to conceive that you have brought all this upon yourself? You and your ruling rod of iron!'

'Y... you traitor!' He flew at her in rage. 'I trusted you and you betrayed me! You and this... this wretch beside me!' He indicated his son. 'But you shall pay! Both of you! I shall make the pair of you sorry for undermining my authority! I shall make you wish you had never been born!'

Charlotte raised her chin defiantly. 'It will have been worth it, Giles. If Elizabeth and Edward have enjoyed a little happiness today, then it will have been worth all the punishment you see fit to inflict.'

Giles scorned her audacity. 'Hah! But we shall see! We shall see!' Eyes blazing with fury, he turned to address his weeping daughter. 'Whose carriage conveyed you home tonight, Elizabeth? And why was your brother not with you as he asserted?'

'Because...' she began evasively, deeply reluctant to cause Edward further trouble.

'Well? I am waiting?' he boomed.

'C... Count de Ville's carriage conveyed me home tonight, Papa, because...'

'... Because I allowed her to stay on at the manor!' interpolated Edward. 'So make what you will of it!'

'You did what? Upon my soul, but I can hardly believe my ears! You mean to say that you actually allowed your own sister to remain unchaperoned at the home of that... that unscrupulous French braggart? Had you completely taken leave of your senses, man? Do you have any conception as to what might have befallen her whilst in his hands?'

'That is a ridiculous question, Father! Do you honestly believe I have such little regard for my sister as to allow something to befall her? Your regard for the Count is biassed. She is safer in his company than with anyone!'

'Never!' returned Giles. 'Besides which, you acted irresponsibly, Edward, and for that you will suffer the consequences!' Smouldering with helpless rage, he turned to Elizabeth again. 'You have dishonoured me by practising deceit against my generous spirit, Elizabeth – you, the one person I thought I could trust.'

'Oh, Papa... please listen...'

'Silence, Elizabeth. Go to your room. I find your presence offensive!' He glared at them all. 'Get out of my sight the lot of you! Tomorrow you will regret the mischief you have done!'

Elizabeth's family failed to grace the breakfast table with their presence the following morning, and seeing Stokes busying himself in the morning room, she enquired as to their whereabouts. Being Sunday, it was customary for the family to attend church together and time was getting on.

'Well, Miss Elizabeth,' began Stokes, grim-faced, 'your aunt and Master Edward have been confined to their rooms – and without breakfast, I am told.'

'Confined to their rooms? But on whose orders, pray?'

'Upon your father's orders, Miss. He stated that neither of them were to leave their rooms and that they were allowed no visitors... including yourself.'

'But that is preposterous!' she cried. 'When did all this take place, Stokes?'

'Early this morning, Miss. There was an unpleasant scene between the master and your aunt, whereupon she was ordered to her room. The young master, also,' he added.

Elizabeth looked furious. How wicked of her father to punish Aunt Charlotte and Edward instead of herself! 'And Papa?' she asked. 'Would you know where he is this morning, Stokes?'

'He is in the gunroom, Miss Elizabeth. I... I heard him say something about riding to Netley Manor.'

'Netley Manor?' she echoed, then rushed from the room in a flurry of rustling petticoats. Knowing her father's reputation with his pistols, she was fearful for Richard's safety.

True enough, Sir Giles was examining the armoury of weapons which lay ready to hand for the ardent hunter – or perhaps murderer in this case. There was certainly a look of murder in his eyes as he peered down the barrel of the shotgun he was holding.

Moments later Elizabeth burst into the room. 'Papa! Have you completely lost your senses?' Her eyes were drawn to the gun. 'And what, pray, do you intend to do with that?'

'This, my dear Elizabeth,' he began in a calculating voice, 'is the means which will end your relationship with de Ville. I warned him of the consequences should our paths cross again. Warned him to leave me and mine alone!'

She hurried over to him. 'Oh, what foolishness, Papa! Why, Richard would have you thrown off the place if he saw you approaching with a shotgun!'

'Ah, he is not man enough to do it himself, then?' he asked mockingly.

'Oh, he is man enough, Papa – although I suggest you never put him to the test. Although Richard is not as ruthless as you, I doubt he will forget the diabolical way in which you treated his mother all those years ago.' She eyed him derisively. 'Oh, I know all about it. I know why Rebecca de Ville deserted you. I confess I would have done the same, had I been in her shoes!'

'Desist!' cried Sir Giles. 'Might I remind you that you are speaking to your father, Elizabeth? Tell me, is that the kind of influence de Ville has upon you?'

'I believe you know me better than that, Papa! I have a mind of my own – when you care to remember it!'

'Really? Then I beseech you to use it now, Elizabeth. Use it before it is too late!' He placed the shotgun on the table and clasped her arms with grim determination. 'This man is no good for you, Elizabeth. Believe me, I know him for what he is. Do you not see that he is trifling with your affections simply to spite me? Why, the fellow is intent on revenging himself any way he can. He cherishes no feelings for you!'

Deeply offended by the implication, Elizabeth shook away his hands, vigorously protesting. 'Oh, stop, Papa! Stop! I refuse to listen to such wicked lies! Richard loves me and he is going to make me very happy. Happy, Papa! Happy! Do you have any conception of the meaning of the word? You are so consumed with hatred that you cannot see farther than the end of your own nose!' Unheeding his savage expression, she continued. 'In all sincerity, Papa, is it any wonder I have become so rebellious? It was not my intention to deceive you yesterday, but you must realise that I am entitled to a life of my own. You cannot keep me a prisoner here forever!'

'Far better I keep you a prisoner than give you to that unscrupulous French thief, Elizabeth!' he retaliated. 'Because that is what he is! A common low-down thief! Not content with robbing me of my men, now the scoundrel intends to steal you too! Well,' he sneered, reaching to retrieve his shotgun, 'over my dead body or his!'

Elizabeth grabbed the gun by its barrel and pointed it towards herself. 'Or perhaps mine!' she cried. 'Tell me, Papa, is that what it would take to bring you to your senses? Is it? Is it?'

Giles pulled the gun away from her. 'Do not be so foolish, Elizabeth! 'Tis de Ville's death I seek – not yours!'

'It would be the same thing, Papa, because I would not wish to live in a world without Richard!'

'Humbug! Utter humbug!' he retorted. 'Besides, I am dealing with de Ville as I see fit. The honourable way. Like a man!'

'Like a man!' she mimicked. ''Tis a poor specimen of a man who hides behind a loaded gun! If you must face him, then do it. Do it tonight when he comes to call on you! But in heaven's name do it like a real man, face to face, and without the aid of your weapon!'

Sir Giles looked flabbergasted. 'T... tonight? You... you mean to tell me he is coming here tonight?'

'Indeed he is,' she replied. 'Richard intends to ask you for my hand in marriage. If you refuse -'

'Refuse! Refuse! By Gad, I certainly will! Of all the audacity! Hah, the very nerve of the fellow astounds me! Well, I shall prepare him a welcome he will never forget. I must... m.. must...' Giles suddenly began to sway and had to cling to the table for support.

'Papa... Papa, what is it? Are you ill?'

''Tis n... nothing... mere in... indigestion, I expect,' he struggled to reply. He hid his face, afraid she would see his pain. His left arm was aching like a bad tooth and his chest felt tight, robbing him of breath. The attacks were beginning to alarm him now, for they were becoming so regular, each one more frightening than the last. Gradually the pain eased and he managed to straighten himself, although not without some degree of caution.

Elizabeth looked worried. She had never seen her father like this before. His furrowed brow and upper lip glistened with perspiration and suffering shone in his steely eyes.

'Papa... Papa, please allow me fetch Aunt Charlotte! She will know what to do for you...'

Although ailing, the master's anger was quickly rekindled. 'I will be blessed if you will! That interfering woman will stay where she is until I see fit to let her out! I will never forgive her for disobeying me. Never!' His face creased in an ugly sneer. 'Still, perhaps a little hardship will bring about her obedience in future, because as of today she will receive no further financial assistance from me. I intend to cut her off without a penny. Let her make her own way in future!'

Elizabeth looked horrified. 'Oh, Papa! Shame on you! You cannot mean it?'

'But I do mean it, Elizabeth. Your aunt must be punished for defying my wishes yesterday – Edward also. He too must suffer for his blatant lies and impudence. Granting you permission to stay at Netley Manor unchaperoned was nothing short of sinful, and I shall see to it that he pays dearly for his mistake. In future he will hold no authority regarding the administration of this estate. You see, my dear,' he began shrewdly, 'I intend to see my solicitor with a view to changing my will. Your brother will be disinherited within the week – of that you have my word!'

Elizabeth could hardly believe her ears. Edward disinherited? 'Oh, no, Papa! No! You would not do that to your own son. Even you could not be so vindictive!'

Sir Giles was smirking complacently, and when he spoke, the inexorable tone of his voice warned Elizabeth that he was in total earnest. 'You think not, Elizabeth? Well, allow me to remind you that I am master here. Your brother's behaviour yesterday forfeited him his right to heirship of this estate. Furthermore, your aunt will be cut off without a farthing to her name – and all because of you. Your failure to sever your connections with de Ville has cost them that!'

He stepped closer, glowering into her startled face, his final cruel remark coming as a bitter blow to her. 'Now, I ask you in all sincerity, Elizabeth – were your stolen moments with him yesterday really worth it?'

Appalled by his vindictiveness, she shrank away from him. 'You have shocked me beyond words, Papa! To dishonour your own family like that is beyond all forgiveness. I am ashamed of you! Ashamed!'

'The shame is upon yourself, Elizabeth,' he said, passing the blame. 'You have brought all this contention upon us. 'Tis you who is responsible for the rift in our family, not me!'

Abandoning her pride, Elizabeth began to weep before him. 'Oh, Papa, that is n... not f... fair.' Poor Edward and Aunt Charlotte, disgraced and disinherited, when it was she who was deserving of her father's punishment! Crying bitterly, she begged him to reconsider; pleaded with him to punish her instead of them.

Sir Giles stiffened, his expression that of unyielding granite. Normally he would have done anything for Elizabeth. All she had to do was look at him in that beguiling way and he would give her the world if it pleased her. But he would never, never give her de Ville. Bracing himself, he hardened his heart and informed her with unbending determination that he intended to remain as good as his word. Edward and Charlotte's future were now beyond his care.

Obdurate to her pleas, he watched her fall upon her knees before him, weeping bitterly. 'I lay awake all night wondering how to punish you, Elizabeth. Wondering how best to deal with your misconduct. Initially, I decided to send you to relatives in the south of England. However, not wishing to deprive myself of your company, I changed my mind.' He gazed at her pitiful figure. 'I do not intend to punish you at all, Elizabeth. I do not need to,' he said.

Puzzled by the statement, Elizabeth looked up at him, the tears still streaming down her cheeks. The smug expression on his face sent prickles of alarm running down her spine, knowing he was withholding something from her.

'You see, my dear, witnessing the downfall of your family, watching them become paupers before your eyes and knowing it was you who brought about their misfortune that will surely be punishment enough. Every day of your life, simply seeing them for what they have become – outcasts, socially rejected by their former friends, will shame you out of ever wishing to see de Ville again!'

Elizabeth's hand flew to her mouth stifling a gasp. Oh, what shrewd, calculating vindictiveness! What a master of hatefulness her father was! She quickly lifted herself off her knees, staring at the man as though seeing him for the very first time. All her life she had loved and respected him, held him in high esteem and stood by him in moments of crisis. But to do this to her beloved family... to herself, was unforgivable!

A wave of anger consumed her. Oh, how he must have enjoyed watching her grovel at his feet! How he must have relished his superiority, flaunting Edward and Aunt Charlotte's predicament before her, knowing how deeply it distressed her. The man was a monster! She stood before him, eying him with scorn. He had done all this to bring about her compliance; to force her

166

into rejecting the man she loved! Mutiny rose within her. Well, like the devil she would!

Her contemptuous expression disconcerted Giles, who had insufficiently armed himself against her furious rebuke.

'You monster!' she hissed. 'You vindictive, hateful monster! You would ruin Edward and Aunt Charlotte's lives, tear them to shreds without a grain of remorse, and all to get at me – at Richard. Oh, how you disgust me... feeding your revenge upon their downfall!'

She turned her back on him and walked across to the window, unheeding the anguish which her words had caused him. 'Well, Papa, I shall not allow you to do it. You see, when Richard comes to the house this evening I intend to leave with him. Furthermore, when I convey to him your intentions concerning Edward and my aunt, I am certain his generous spirit will suggest a home for them at Netley Manor. For unlike you, Papa, I find the de Villes caring, Christian people – the kind who put the likes of you to shame!'

Sir Giles' mouth fell open in shock. He had not comprehended the strength of his daughter's enmity. He would never have believed that she would take matters so far as to undermine his authority and leave him for de Ville.

Her anger dispelled, Elizabeth stood quietly gazing through the window at the surrounding estate. 'I shall miss this house,' she murmured, 'the gardens, the horses, the...' Her voice trailed away and there was silence. It did not occur to her that her outburst had gone unchallenged. That her father had not uttered a word for at least five minutes.

Not aware of the pain in his chest which had robbed him of breath, she continued, oblivious. 'It was never my intention to hurt or disobey you, Papa. In fact I had hoped you would charitably put the past behind you and allow the de Villes and ourselves to become united.' She laughed sardonically. 'Oh how naive I was to think you would ever change! Well, may the good Lord forgive your sins, Papa. There are certainly enough of them to forgive!'

With that she gathered her skirts and headed for the door, informing him, without so much as a glance in his direction, that it was time she began packing. Reaching the door, she heard his deep muffled groans and, swinging around, could barely believe the change in his appearance. He was all but on his knees, clutching the table as though desperately trying to hold on to life itself. His gaunt, pain-stricken face was ashen, his eyes sunk deep into their sockets, and he was groaning from whatever it was that ailed him.

She was by his side in seconds, terrified as to what had befallen him. 'Papa! What is it?' she entreated.

He clutched her sleeve. 'H... help me, Elizabeth! H... help me...'

She tried to lift him to his feet, but her efforts were futile because he was so heavy. Besides, it caused his pain to worsen. 'What ails you, Papa? Tell me!' Her voice was filled with desperation.

'H... heart ... 'tis my... my heart!' he gasped, every word an effort.

'Your heart? Oh, no! Why did you not tell me? Why did you allow me to continue in that way?' She was panic-stricken now, despising herself for bringing all this upon him. 'I must go for help, Papa! The doctor must be sent for at once!'

He clutched her arm, fearful she might leave him. 'N... no! Do not...do not go, Elizabeth. Do not leave me here... like this...'

'But I must, Papa! I must go for help!'

Suddenly his knees buckled and he fell to the floor with a pitiful groan. Falling to her own knees, Elizabeth loosened the neckcloth from around his throat, crying out for help. Giles appeared to be deteriorating rapidly, for his face was grey, his lips were blue and he was fighting for every breath.

'Oh, Papa... Papa please forgive me for the wicked things I said to you! I did not mean them! I was just so angry ...'

The old man inclined his head to look at her. Tears had sprung into his eyes and he looked a pitiful figure now. 'I... I beg you, Elizabeth...do not leave me for de Ville. If I die, then... then you must do as you will. But I implore you not to l... leave me whilst I still live. P...promise me, Elizabeth? Promise me?'

Elizabeth's kind, forgiving heart went out to him. At that moment she would have promised him anything if it resulted in his recovery. 'I promise, Papa! I promise!'

Satisfied, Giles laid back his head and slipped into oblivion.

Later that morning, Doctor John Blundell announced his verdict to Sir Giles' family as they stood outside his bedchamber. He was a kindly, sympathetic fellow of some sixty years or so, apart from his professional role, a long standing friend of the family, having shared their joys and troubles for over thirty years now.

'I regret to tell you that Sir Giles has suffered a severe seizure and that his condition is critical,' he said grimly.

Gasps of shock were exchanged between them, although the doctor's verdict had been one they had all expected. Aunt Charlotte was the first to speak. 'I see,' she said. 'Thank you, John.'

'I will visit your brother twice daily until he is out of danger, Charlotte. May I comfort you by adding that Giles is one of the strongest men I have ever known. Indeed, such an attack on a weaker man would undoubtedly have proved fatal.' He smiled encouragingly. 'I believe he has a good chance of recovery.'

'Oh, thank goodness!' ejaculated Elizabeth emotionally.

Concerned, Edward placed a comforting arm around her shoulders. She looked so ill, shouldering the blame for their father's condition personally as she did. He turned to the doctor. 'Please assure my sister that father's illness is not her fault. She wrongly holds herself responsible – believes it was she who brought on his seizure.'

'But it *was* my fault, Edward!' she blurted out. 'You were not there! You did not hear the dreadful things I said to Papa! I called him a monster and told him I was leaving home this evening with Richard! Oh, I was so cruel to him!'

'Elizabeth, listen to me,' said Doctor Blundell sympathetically. 'Your father has been ill for some time now, his problem having begun in the early part of last year. I warned him then to take things easy, to mellow a little, not to become so irate at every little thing.' He shook his head and tutted. 'But he would not listen. He just ignored my warnings and carried on in his own inimitable way. So do not hold yourself responsible, my dear. Your father's way of life was his downfall, not you.'

Throughout the rest of the day Elizabeth remained at her father's bedside, refusing to leave him for an instant. At six-thirty she was joined by Edward, who had been attending to business matters. Despite his impending disinheritance, he was still the legal heir to Cambourne Hall and would act accordingly until the time came when he would be removed from his position.

'How is he, Elizabeth?' he asked, grim-faced. 'Has he spoken at all?'

Elizabeth shook her head. 'No. He has not spoken. I expect it is the potion the doctor administered.'

Deep in thought, Edward sat gazing at the old man, whilst Elizabeth poured herself a glass of water. When she turned round to ask if he would care for a drink, she caught an expression on his face which visibly shook her. Edward was gazing at his father with such despair, such pitiful sadness, that her heart cried out to him. Yet despite that, she saw a look of love there, too; love and overflowing compassion for a man who had treated him so abominably. Afterwards she saw his tears and inner torture, the conflict which was tearing him apart.

Placing down the glass, she went across to him and put her arms around his shoulders in comfort. 'You love Papa very dearly, Edward? Despite everything he has done to you, all the years in which his heart remained closed to you, you still love him?'

Suddenly he began to weep without shame, releasing years of frustrated despair. Ever since he could remember, his father had shunned him, cast him aside unloved, blatantly showering all his affection upon his daughter instead. Yet never had this rejection affected his own love for Elizabeth. Oddly enough, it had brought them closer, for each had always idolised the other.

Edward's thoughts strayed to his late mother. His tears were for her too, that sweet, gentle lady who had known her place in life and had accepted it without question. Helen Montgomery had also been ruled by Sir Giles' harsh, dictatorial will, never complaining, accepting her lot until it had eventually killed her. Thinking about her now, he could not help but wonder if perhaps she had been the lucky one, for by dying, she had been released from her self-sacrificing bondage to her husband; allowed to live a heavenly existence in the world beyond this.

'Yes... yes, I love him,' he admitted, 'although God only knows why, for he never cherished any fondness for me. Indeed, I often think I would be better off far away from here. My servitude has never met with any thanks or gratitude, merely a blithe acceptance in response to all I have achieved.' He heaved a sigh, then pulled himself together and apologised for his weakness.

Elizabeth gave him an affectionate squeeze, assuring him that no apologies were necessary.

'Thank you,' he said. 'Anyway, it is my turn to sit with father now, Elizabeth. It is almost seven o'clock and Richard will be arriving shortly.' He smiled. 'So run along, my dear, and forget your troubles for a while. Trust me to take over here.'

When she had gone, Edward studied the man who lay sleeping in the bed on which he sat; that arrogant whiskered face, the hollowed eyes beneath thick, bushy grey brows, those furrowed frown-lines which cut deep into his forehead, and the cruel, thin-lipped mouth which had shattered the lives of so many, mercilessly spitting out orders which would punish and destroy. A vestige of a smile appeared on Edward's lips, for now the tables had turned.

'Well, old man, now I hold your life in my hands. What would you say to that if you could speak, eh? It would be hard for you to swallow, would it not, you old devil?' He gave a low laugh. 'Ah, but it matters not – although I know many a fellow who would give their soul to be in my shoes; be in a position to put an end to you.' Gently he reached to touch that pale, still face from which barely a breath was heard, experiencing overwhelming pity for the man. 'Rest easy, Father,' he said quietly. 'Rest easy. I am here.'

Downstairs in the drawing room, Elizabeth burst into a flood of emotional tears upon seeing Richard waiting for her. She ran to him, relieved beyond words to see him again. Knowing he had come to the Hall to confront Sir Giles, Aunt Charlotte had already informed him of the master's seizure and that Elizabeth held herself responsible. The news had shocked him and, being the gentleman he was, he had expressed genuine concern for the man, offering his services in any capacity.

The three sat together conversing until Mr Llani entered the room after returning from his weekend visit to Wales. He looked most concerned after being told the facts by Stokes. 'A dreadful business. Dreadful!' he tutted. 'Rest assured that I place myself at your disposal during this grave time, Charlotte, so please feel free to avail yourself of my services.'

'Thank you, Frederick,' said Charlotte graciously. 'It is reassuring to know that you are here.'

Stokes brought in a decanter of port wine for the four, who remained together in the drawing room for another hour or so. When Richard announced it was time for him to leave, Elizabeth accompanied him to the front door.

In the privacy of the porch, she rested her head against his chest and clung to him, the tears trickling down her cheeks. She felt wretchedly unhappy, plagued by guilt at causing her father's seizure, yet longing to make her escape from here with Richard. Sir Giles' fate was their fate, and she knew it, although they did not wish their happiness to be gained at the expense of his life. They would have to wait and see which way the pendulum would swing – whether he would live or whether he would die. It was as simple as that.

Richard saw her sadness and besought her not to worry. 'The good Lord will make matters right,' he assured her. 'We must have faith and trust, Elizabeth.'

'I know,' she murmured. 'I know.'

He lowered his head to kiss her lips, evoking treasured memories of yesterday. It had been the most wonderful day of Elizabeth's life, despite the fact that she was having to pay for it today.

'Oh, I do love you, Richard. And I want to be with you so much!'

His arms tightened around her drawing her close against him. 'And I want to be with you, my love.' He held her away from him and looked into her tear-stained face, his voice an urgent whisper. 'When can I see you again, Elizabeth? I know it will be difficult for you, but perhaps we could meet in the wood one morning? Tomorrow, if you are able?'

Elizabeth bit her lip. Although she desperately wanted to meet him, she knew it was impossible. 'I am afraid I cannot, Richard. I have promised to look after Papa until he recovers. Considering all the dreadful things I said to him, I think it the least I can do. No,' she concluded sadly, 'mornings would be out of the question.'

'I see. Then how about evenings? Could you perhaps meet me one evening?'

Elizabeth's face took on a thoughtful expression. Acting as nurse to her father could well extend into the evening hours. It would be dreadful if he suddenly needed her and she was not there. On the other hand, she had no wish to deprive herself of Richard's company. She needed him now, his love, his comfort. There had to be a compromise somewhere. A sudden thought. 'Night-time would be better,' she said, 'after I have settled Papa for the night. Aunt Charlotte said she would sit with him during the night until he is better

171

– if he gets better,' she added grimly.

Richard gave her an encouraging squeeze. 'Of course he will get better, my love. Why, he will be pursuing me with his pistols in no time!' It had been said to make her laugh, but he could see by her expression that it had alarmed her. 'I apologise, Elizabeth. That was tactless of me. Now, what hour of night do you wish me to meet you? And where? I will certainly not allow you to ride to the wood under the cover of darkness. No, it will have to be somewhere much closer to the house.'

After a moment's thought, Elizabeth came up with a bright idea. 'I could meet you in one of the stables – or perhaps the loft would be safer. Yes, you could wait in the loft above Rhapsody's stall. No-one would ever discover you up there, and you could tether your horse in the adjacent stall. The hour would have to be late, though, Richard, as the stable staff might still be about.'

He smiled. 'I believe it a good idea, Elizabeth. Perhaps I could signal to let you know I had arrived, for I would not want to keep you waiting in the darkness if by some chance I was unable to keep our rendezvous.'

Elizabeth nodded her agreement. 'There is a small window in the loft which overlooks the rear of the house. Perhaps you could light the oil lamp showing that you are there? Or better still, simply pass it twice across the window.'

'An excellent idea,' he agreed. 'Now, about the time. Would midnight be too late?'

'No, not at all. Midnight sounds just perfect, Richard. Everyone will be asleep by then, and none of the stable staff will be there at that hour.'

'Then tomorrow?' he asked hopefully.

'Tomorrow,' she replied, her spirits already lifting.

Throughout the night, Sir Giles Montgomery's condition remained critical and, following a sudden decline shortly before midnight, Doctor Blundell had to be sent for again. Suspecting that death was close at hand, he remained at Sir Giles' bedside until the early hours of the morning. Then, believing the immediate danger to be over, he left the Hall to return home.

All the family had remained by the bedside, Elizabeth mopping her father's brow, Edward clutching his hand with grim determination, while Charlotte sat quietly by. Giles began to come round a little, muttering deliriously, very few words being intelligible at all. Those which were understandable were beseeching words, still imploring Elizabeth not to leave him for de Ville. After the worst was over, he slept, although none too peacefully. Elizabeth and Edward slept in chairs beside his bed, too exhausted to stay awake any longer.

Dawn broke heralding a new day, and when the cock began to crow Sir Giles opened his eyes and looked around. He saw his son and daughter asleep in their chairs beside his bed..... Elizabeth, her head resting on her arm at the edge of the bed as she lay stretched from her armchair. With some degree of difficulty, he reached out his hand and placed it gently upon her head. Smiling softly, he then slipped back into deep, restful sleep, finding her presence deeply reassuring.

It was almost eight o'clock when he woke. Edward had managed to slip quietly from the room to attend to business, leaving Elizabeth sleeping by his side. Dear Elizabeth! She had remained good to her promise and stayed with him, forsaking de Ville and her vow to leave with him. Oh, Giles knew she had not meant the things she had said! She would never leave him – not she! Not Elizabeth! Grateful, he smiled. His brush with death had been a close one and he knew it. But he had pulled through and life was worth living again, for Elizabeth had chosen him.

In her chair, Elizabeth stirred. Remembrance flooded into her mind and her head shot up to look at her father, fearful he had passed away while she had been sleeping. But no... instead he was gazing back at her, smiling. Oh, praise be! He was alive! Alive!

Relieved beyond words, she threw her arms around him and sobbed unashamedly on his shoulder. 'Oh, Papa! Papa! How happy I am that you are better! I... I was convinced you were going to die!'

The old man managed a weak, responsive squeeze. 'And I am happy to know you stayed with me, Elizabeth. Thank you... thank you, my dear. I knew you would never forsake me. Not you... not my own dear Elizabeth.'

Unseen by him, her expression clouded. How could she tell him that her leaving had merely been postponed? That when he had recovered, she would surely go to Richard? Elizabeth knew she could not. It would kill him. Instead, she must bide her time and wait until he was well and strong again. The day would come.

Later that morning, Doctor Blundell announced that Sir Giles' condition had improved. 'Of course, he will require constant nursing and supervision for several weeks yet,' he informed the gathered family, 'for the man is still very ill.' The doctor smiled. 'Giles is certainly a fighter, I will say that for him. There came a moment last night when I sincerely believed we were going to lose him. Oh, I have left digitalis to help his condition, so please see he takes it. Good day to you all,' he said pleasantly. 'I will return to see Giles this evening.'

Charlotte and Edward visited the sickroom throughout the day. Although neither adopted a placatory attitude towards Giles, both being too proud to beg his forgiveness, their dispositions were kind and sympathetic. Moreover, both expressed their sincere relief that he had survived his ordeal. Surprisingly, the master's manner had been pleasantly civil towards them, which had eased the tension and created a more tolerable atmosphere.

Alone with her father, Elizabeth tactfully broached the tender subject of her family's future, although she was careful not to upset him.

The old man gave her hand an encouraging squeeze. 'Do not worry, Elizabeth,' he said weakly, 'for I have already decided to give them both another chance. You stayed with me as promised. You chose me in preference to de Ville and for that I am sincerely grateful.' His tired old eyes were beginning to close and he looked exhausted now. 'The... the fellow has gone from our lives forever, my dear. Things will be better now. You will see... you will see...' The words faded on his lips as he drifted into sleep.

Elizabeth closed her eyes and gave a long, trembling sigh. Her father mistakenly believed that her love affair with Richard de Ville was over. But Richard would never be gone from her life. Only death could part her from the man she loved.

At five minutes to midnight, Elizabeth suddenly woke from her short, restful sleep. She had stayed with her father until ten o'clock, when Aunt Charlotte had insisted upon relieving her. The child looked exhausted, completely worn out after nursing her father all day. Why, she was so stiff and weary she could hardly stand on her feet, having sat with him for over twenty-five hours. If it was self-inflicted punishment in response to Giles' attack, then Elizabeth was certainly doing a good job. One week of this and she would be the one in need of a nurse, not he.

A blissful hot bath had eased her aching bones, and after changing her clothes and brushing her hair, she had drifted into heavenly sleep in the armchair. Not for an instant had she worried about oversleeping and missing Richard's signal at midnight – quite the contrary. Elizabeth knew she would wake in time, and she did.

A tremble of excitement coursed through her body, for it was almost time. Seconds later she was standing at the window, watching, waiting, listening for the grandfather clock downstairs to chime the midnight hour. Peering out, she saw the moon appear from behind a silver-edged cloud illuminating the courtyard, and beyond, the dark, nebulous shadows which stretched from the stables like huge black cloaks. How eerie it looked at this, the witching hour, with not a soul around to witness it but herself.

Suddenly it was there – the signal she was expecting; the dim yellow flame from the oil lamp as it was passed twice across the loft window, and at precisely the moment when the clock had struck. A wave of excitement consumed her. Richard was in the loft awaiting her. He was there! He was there!

Wrapped snugly in her warm brown cloak, she left her room to tiptoe along the landing, down the stairs, then along the back hall which led past the kitchens, finally to the safety of the back door. The handle creaked annoyingly as she turned it, a harsh sound in the still of the night. Then she was gone, her dark figure quickly disappearing into the shadows of the night. It took only moments to reach the loft, less to rush into the arms which awaited her. His welcoming kiss took her breath away, robbed her of the words she had been about to utter.

In the warmth of his arms all her troubles and cares began to fade; all the traumas of the weekend and her anxiety were forgotten. She was with him now and there was no room in her heart for anything but the love which overflowed within. They drew apart and gazed at each other for a moment, the semi-darkness and the late hour increasing their awareness of one another. A tender smile was exchanged between them, Richard acknowledging the picture of loveliness she made. Elizabeth wore her hair loose tonight, free and flowing as it fell in gentle waves to her waist, her eyes shining like gems into his. Captivated, he drew a trembled breath, his heart already ablaze.

In turn, Elizabeth's feelings were close to overpowering her. Richard's dark, exotic handsomeness was having the most disturbing effect on her, and as she gazed into the potent depths of his eyes she could think of nothing but belonging to him again.

'How long can you stay, Elizabeth?' he asked softly.

She smiled as she unfastened her cloak and allowed it to fall on to the hay, the pale gown she wore and her long flowing hair transforming her into a fairytale princess. The light from the lamp picked up the sparkle in her eyes, and altogether she had a look about her which he found riveting. 'Until dawn,' came her whispered reply.

Enraptured, he gave a groan of joy, then succumbed to the passion which refused to be subdued a moment longer. Picking her up into his arms, he carried her to the far side of the loft where he placed her unprotesting upon the hay.

The rest of the night belonged to them. A night when love flowed free with no thought of tomorrow. Only when the first light of day gently filtered through the small loft window, did it end.

CHAPTER TWELVE

The week passed steadily by. Every day saw a marked improvement in Sir Giles' health, bringing relief to some, despair to others. News of his illness had spread rapidly among his friends and acquaintances, and throughout the neighbourhood in general, including labourers, tenants and suchlike. It had caused quite a stir amongst them all and a great deal of speculation had been aroused as to what would transpire if the old man died. Many knew that such an event would be a blessing, indeed, less Christian souls even hoped for it, setting wagers on it at the alehouse in the village. But as time passed, the likelihood of that began to fade, along with their hopes of a more civilised existence in the employ of the master's young son.

At the Hall, Elizabeth continued to nurse her father back to health, every hour of the day spent at his bedside. Edward proceeded to run the estate with his usual efficiency, once more the heir after his father's change of heart. Mr Llani's presence in the house was most useful and reassuring, and Aunt Charlotte admitted that she would never have been able to cope without his invaluable help. During the afternoons he continued with the family portraits, Charlotte's coming along most pleasingly.

Elizabeth had grown to love the man as though a father, their close relationship remaining as staunch as ever. They would miss him when the time came for him to leave, although he still had Edward and Giles' portrait to undertake before then.

It was Saturday already, and following Doctor Blundell's customary visit, Elizabeth stole a few moments from the sickroom to find her brother. Had Edward remembered that it was tonight he had agreed to escort Rachael to Miss Simmons' musical evening, she wondered? Edward had confided the information to his sister some days ago now. Being Edward, of course he had remembered, and she found him in a state of elation in the sitting room.

'Forgotten?' he cried with mock outrage. 'I will say I have not forgotten! Why, 'tis the only thing which has kept my spirits up of late!'

Elizabeth laughed. 'Good for you, Edward. I hope you have a wonderful time. Do not worry, for I will sit with Papa this evening. He will not know you have gone.' She reached to kiss his cheek in affection. 'Have fun – and remember me to Rachael, please.'

Later that night, when Elizabeth lay in her lover's arms in the loft, they heard Edward return home; heard his cheerful whistle in the courtyard below. It certainly sounded as though his evening had been a success, for a moment later he broke into song!

Wednesday the first of July saw Elizabeth growing tired. Charlotte was concerned for her because she had nursed her father for eleven days now without a rest. Although she was understandably exhausted, she glowed with a remarkable radiance, her aunt's intuition telling her that somehow or another Elizabeth was seeing Richard. The old lady could not think how the couple were managing it, for all her niece's time was spent at Giles' bedside. But Edward knew. Unable to sleep one night, he had seen the oil lamp being passed across the loft window at midnight and, deeply puzzled, he had watched until he saw Elizabeth run across the courtyard to the stables. Returning home late one night, he had also seen Richard's stallion tethered in one of the stalls and knew his sister was keeping a late rendezvous with the Count. Being Edward, he had said nothing to anyone, believing it was no-one's business but their own.

That evening, Charlotte suggested to Giles that Elizabeth take a rest. Surprisingly he agreed without hesitation, knowing his daughter had gone above and beyond the call of duty of late. And so, with her welfare in mind, he ordered her to spend a day in the fresh air and sunshine.

'I suggest you go for a ride. It will exhilarate you, my dear,' he said. 'But do not—'

'—Leave the estate.' She finished the sentence on his behalf. Ah, he never changed. After all he had suffered, he was still the same. She bent to kiss his whiskered cheek. 'I know, Papa. And I will not,' she promised.

Not for one moment did Giles worry that she might see de Ville, for he believed all that nonsense over and done with. He believed she had forgotten him. The old man smiled smugly to himself, for de Ville had gone from their lives for good. Sir Giles Montgomery was living in a fool's paradise. But the day of reckoning would come.

Suffice it to say, Elizabeth's day of freedom was spent with Richard in Bluebell Wood. The weather was glorious, just perfect for a picnic by the stream. Richard had brought her a single red rose, its petals like velvet to the touch.

'Oh, it smells heavenly, Richard,' she said. 'I adore roses. Thank you so much. I shall keep it always... always...'

He laughed. 'Ah, then it is destined to lie between the pages of some book, for I presume you intend to press it?'

'Yes, of course I do, – but not whilst it is so beautiful.' Idyllically happy, she added, 'Perhaps I shall give you a rose one day, Richard – a red one, just like this.'

Still laughing, he picked her up in his arms and held her against him, her nearness utterly enrapturing. 'Perhaps one day you will, my love – but at this very moment I will be content with an early luncheon. I am ravenous!'

Some time later he lay full length on the grass, one hand shielding his eyes from the strong afternoon sunshine. Elizabeth was busy packing the picnic basket following their lunch. Her eyes strayed across to him, where she studied that long familiar body with undisguised fascination. Here was masculinity at its greatest; he was a prize amongst men. Why, there was not another in the county who held a candle to Richard de Ville – and he was hers – hers! She smiled softly, recalling their moments together. During the act of lovemaking he possessed a tenderness, a sensitivity which often left her weeping. Somehow Elizabeth doubted that other men were endowed with the same gift.

He stirred when she teased his earlobe with a blade of grass, his mouth curving in a smile. 'You little minx, I was almost asleep!' he scolded, then pulled her down across his chest and kissed her.

Elizabeth curled her arms around him. 'Never fear, Richard, for should you slip into sleep, then no doubt I would find a way to wake you.'

'Mmmm... with a kiss?'

She wriggled to her feet and stood above him, laughing with impish mischief. 'No, my love – with this cup of cold water I hold!'

He jumped when she playfully splashed a few drops over him, then sat himself upright, his eyes glinting with revenge. 'Ah hah! So that is what you would do to me, is it? Well, young woman, with cold water it is, then!'

He jumped to his feet and gave chase, pursuing her disappearing figure as she ran amongst the trees. She was laughing uncontrollably, her heavy petticoats gathered above her ankles as she ran. Being a gentleman, he allowed her a few moments to escape, then, hiding behind one of the trees, suddenly jumped out at her. He flung her across his shoulder and carried her towards the stream, yelling for all she was worth. Boots and all, he waded in and, holding her tight, began to lower her struggling body towards the water, refusing to heed her loud objections.

'Now, my beauty, let us see which one of us ends up getting wet!' He lowered her to within an inch of the water's surface, then allowed himself a moment's thought.

'Is it to be head first or feet first, I wonder? Better still, all of you at once, I think!'

Red-faced from all her laughter, she cried out to him to stop. 'Richard de Ville, I defy you to do it! I will scream if you do – I will!'

He frowned in mock puzzlement. 'But I understood you had a fondness for water, my love? Indeed, were you not bathing in this very stream like some abandoned creature of the woods when I first met you?'

'Indeed I was!' she recalled. 'But not fully dressed as I am now!'

Remembering the incident, his eyes began to twinkle with amusement. 'Ah, yes... that is so. As I recall, you were wearing nothing but a little camisole and drawers... pretty drawers, with lace and frills around the -'

'Richard de Ville!'

He laughed at her embarrassment. 'I apologise,' he said. 'Anyway, if you object to a ducking, I feel I must issue you with an alternative fate, for one way or another I must punish you for wetting me, Elizabeth.'

'Anything!' she promised.

'Anything?'

'Yes!'

'Good!' His eyes lit. 'Then I shall ravish you instead. Perhaps that will teach you -'

'Ravish me? Oh, no!' she interrupted with mock alarm. 'Pray, anything but that!' She cast him a playful look, then stole a glance at her watery alternative. 'To be ravished is unspeakable, I am told. No, I beg you, I prefer the stream, Sir, if you please!'

He threw back his head and laughed again, then pulled her up into his arms, his voice intimate now. 'Is it now? In that case, perhaps I should stay away from you in future?'

'Oh, don't you ever dare!' she protested, entwining her arms round his neck and clinging to him. 'Don't you ever dare!'

Afterwards they sat together on the grass, Elizabeth's head upon his shoulder. 'What a heavenly day this has been. It reminds me of the day we met. Oh, I am so glad it was here, Richard. Bluebell Wood is our own special place now, is it not?'

'Yes, indeed it is,' he murmured. 'Our own special place.'

Had he left it at that, then Elizabeth would have been quite happy. But he chose to add something which made the hair on the back of her neck stand on end. 'If for some reason I ever lose you, Elizabeth, I promise I shall wait here in the wood for you, remaining for as long as it takes for you to come to me.'

Disturbed by the remark, she stared at him, wondering what had possessed him to say such a thing – 'If he should ever lose her'. A shudder ran down her spine and she felt as though someone were walking over her grave. 'Lose me? In what way, Richard?'

He inclined his head to look into her eyes. 'In any way, Elizabeth. In any way at all.'

A cold chill passed over her and she moved a little closer in his arms.

'What is it?' he asked.

'I... I really do not know. Something you said frightened me.'

'About my waiting here for you?'

'No.' She shook her head. 'About you losing me. It made my blood run cold.'

His arms tightened around her reassuringly. 'But I shall never lose you, my love. Never! Whatever happened, I would find you again. Why, not even in death would I rest without you.'

There – he had done it again – awakened some awesome distant echo from beyond. It reminded her of the dreams she had been experiencing lately; bad dreams, the kind which dispelled her illusions and hopes of future happiness. On these occasions she was often left wondering if, indeed, she had a future. But they were only dreams, were they not? Fears which implanted themselves in her mind while she was sleeping.

Richard saw her troubled expression. 'I apologise if my remark distressed you, Elizabeth. I simply wished to assure you that I would always be here waiting for you, should the occasion arise.'

'I know, and I shall remember that always,' she said.

His lips found hers and they became lost in the kiss which followed. Her fears forgotten, Elizabeth abandoned herself to the feelings which swept her body, drawing her lover closer in her arms. He eased her back on to the grass, making her moan when his lips gently feathered her ear. 'Now, what was that I said earlier... about ravishing you?' he whispered.

When the couple met in the loft the following night, Elizabeth knew immediately that something was wrong. 'What is it, Richard? What is the matter?' she asked, alarmed by the dark expression on his face.

He drew a deep breath before replying. 'I have bad news, Elizabeth. I regret I have been summoned to France on a matter of importance and expect to be away for at least six weeks. Moreover, I must leave at first light in the morning.'

Elizabeth looked devastated, the expression on her face tearing his heartstrings unmercifully.

'Y... you are going away?' she uttered limply.

'Elizabeth... Elizabeth listen to me,' he urged. 'I want you to come with me! I want you to leave with me in the morning for Bordeaux! Do you understand?' He was gripping her arms, his eyes imploring.

'But I cannot come with you, Richard! I cannot! You know I promised to nurse Papa until he is well again! He needs me, Richard. I dare not leave him yet. It would kill him!'

'But I need you too, Elizabeth! Can you not see that?'

She moved away from him. 'I... I know you do. But he needs me more, Richard! If I left with you tomorrow, the shock would undoubtedly cause my father to have another seizure. I simply cannot do that to him!' Tears of anguish were streaming down her face, her shoulders shaking from her weeping.

He rushed to clasp hold of her again. 'Oh, Elizabeth... please do not do this to me! Please! I beg you – I implore you to come away with me tomorrow!'

Tortured blue eyes met his. 'But I cannot – I gave my promise! I must stay with Papa!'

They faced each other in agony, overcome by frustration and despair. Elizabeth's eyes were imploring him to understand; his were simply pleading. Unable to bear her pain, her inner torture a moment longer, she gave an anguished sob and fled from him.

At the head of the stairs he caught her in his arms. Sobbing emotionally, she spun round and clung to him desperately. 'Oh, Richard...I...I am so s... sorry! I beg you to forgive me!'

'Don't,' he murmured tenderly. 'I understand, Elizabeth... truly I do.'

She was still weeping wretchedly as he lifted her up into his arms and carried her across the loft, only superficially consoled by his words. Inside she ached unbearably, hating herself for placing her father above him. But she had no alternative. She must stay at the Hall and honour her promise. She must!

While they lay together in the hay, Richard endeavoured to console her. 'I shall return as soon as my business is completed, Elizabeth. Then I shall come for you as I always promised. I swear to you, upon arriving home in England I shall take you away from here, regardless of your father's wishes!' His arms tightened around her. 'Promise you will be waiting? Promise me, Elizabeth?'

'Oh, I promise, Richard! I promise!'

That night their lovemaking was intense and urgent, Richard's love flooding into her body as never before. Recklessness came easy when their hearts and minds were so full of thoughts of parting next day. Every kiss, every touch, every whispered word was meaningful and lasting, every precious moment assuring one another of their love. It was almost dawn when sleep eventually claimed them.

When Elizabeth opened her eyes to face the cold light of day, she knew she was alone. Heavy-hearted and unable to face their farewell, Richard had left her there sleeping. Desolation masked her face as she rose wearily to her feet, her heart aching like sin in her breast. Shrouded in misery, she walked across to the window where she stared limply at the rain-swept courtyard. Tears began to stream down her face, her unhappiness too much to bear. Never as far back as she could remember, had she felt so low and despondent.

Just how long she stood there engulfed in her own sorrow, she did not know... did not care. But then suddenly through her tears she saw it, the writing on the window pane; Richard's loving poem which he had scratched on to the glass while she had been sleeping. Joy replaced the ache in her heart when she read the words –

> July 4th 1886
> For my dearest Elizabeth
> Lest you should forget how very much I love you.
>
> The gift of love I give thee
> A love which will never die
> My heart is yours eternally
> Never to say goodbye.
> Richard

A wave of happiness swept over her and she felt inspired beyond words. Although Richard had left her, he loved her dearly; promised in those few heartfelt words that he always would. It meant everything to her – everything! Elizabeth was certain now that she would survive the weeks without him, living for his return and the promise of their new life together. 'And I love you. I always will...'

It was the first day of September and Richard had been away for eight long weeks. No word had been heard from him since his departure on that wet, dismal morning last July, although no written word had been expected. Sir Giles opened every letter which arrived at the house and would undoubtedly have destroyed any correspondence from Richard. Therefore it had been agreed not to write. The old man still believed the couple's relationship had been terminated; believed it all the more after learning of the fellow's sudden departure to France. Indeed, the news had contributed towards his amazing recovery, one which had astounded everyone. His strength and fitness had returned with a vengeance, leaving him flourishing in his new lease of life. Back in his stride again, his illness behind him, he once again took his stand in his war against society, directing it at any poor soul who saw fit to cross his path.

During the last few weeks a change had come over Elizabeth. She had grown quiet and pensive and was lost in the unfathomable depths of loneliness. Inwardly she felt cheated, bitterly so. Because of her father's illness and her promise to nurse him, she had forfeited the chance to be with Richard in

France, having firmly believed that it would be many weeks before her father could hope for full recovery. Yet here he was, strutting about the house in perfect health, whilst she grew increasingly lonely. It simply was not fair and she felt there was no justice at all. She needed Richard more than ever, whilst her father needed no-one. It was a bitter pill to swallow and every day without Richard made it harder.

A physical change had also taken place in her. This had brought about the concern of her family, for her appetite, normally the subject of much teasing on the part of Edward, had dwindled into non-existence. Her refusal to take breakfast, and often lunch and dinner too, had become a source of worry to them all. Charlotte and Edward assumed it was Richard's continued absence which accounted for her distressing malaise. Sir Giles had no idea at all what ailed her.

It was at breakfast one morning that he put forward what he considered an excellent suggestion.

'Elizabeth, I feel concerned for you, my dear. 'Tis plain to see you have become run down after nursing me through my illness.' He smiled encouragingly. 'I think it time you and I took a holiday. What say you to an ocean voyage on one of the steamers? I believe it would be beneficial to your health.'

Charlotte and Edward's mouths fell open in shock. It was the first time in living memory that Giles had offered to take her anywhere. Such benevolence, thought Charlotte acidly. He ought to have suggested it years ago!

Elizabeth was clearly unmoved by her father's benign act of charity. To think of all the years she had pleaded to accompany him on his trips and now, when it suited him to take her, she had no wish to go! 'Thank you, Papa, but no,' she said laconically.

Giles cast her an uncomprehending look. 'But... but why ever not, my dear? I thought you would be delighted.'

Elizabeth rose to her feet, her expression full of disdain. 'Because you have left it too late, Papa. You should have taken me with you years ago – it was not for want of my asking.' Without further comment she walked from the room, leaving him plainly disconcerted by her coolness and rejection.

Giles tutted to himself for a moment, then, feeling disparaged, threw down his napkin and strode towards the door, calling to Edward to 'get a move on'. The old man did not understand his daughter any more. She had changed – changed dramatically. He doubted it had anything to do with de Ville leaving the country, for why should she be concerned about him after all this time? No. Something else was amiss with her. But what it was he did not know.

Later, Elizabeth stood on her balcony gazing at the hills beyond the estate.

They were spectacular now, a mass of purple colour with the heather in its full glory, the wide areas of bracken a breathtaking hue of gold. Soon the glorious summer would be over, then winter would be upon them, bringing its changes. She only hoped she would be spending it with Richard. Every new day brought the hope that today might be the one when he would return for her as promised; every night she spent alone brought disappointment. Despondency came easy after watching and waiting each day to no avail. But the day would come, she reminded herself. There was little work to keep her mind occupied these days, too. All her paintings, including her portrait of Richard, had long since been completed and she lacked the inspiration to begin another. Mr Llani's own portrait of Sir Giles was coming along nicely after all the artist's hard work and patience. It saddened her to know that he would be leaving them soon. She would miss him so much when he was gone.

She decided to take a stroll around the garden, hoping the fresh air would dispel her melancholy mood. Whilst sitting on one of the seats by the rose beds contemplating matters of the heart, she was pleasantly surprised to see Edward.

'Ah, so here you are, Elizabeth!' he called cheerfully. 'I have been looking for you everywhere.'

She smiled in greeting. 'Hello, Edward. Come and sit beside me for a while. 'Tis a beautiful day for September, do you not think?'

'Yes, it is indeed,' he acknowledged. 'I wondered if you might like to join me on a ride around the estate this morning, Elizabeth? I have a list of tenants to call upon, including Mrs Turpin and her brood of young scallywags!' He laughed heartily. 'I confess I shall be in need of some support there. The last time I visited their abode, the rascals tied my horse's legs together – monsters!'

Elizabeth laughed, but refused his invitation.

'But why not?' he entreated. 'It would be good for you, my dear.' A frown creased his brow as he gazed into her eyes. 'You have been looking poorly lately, Elizabeth. Is it because you are missing Richard?'

'Oh, Edward, I am missing him dreadfully and can hardly wait for his return. Otherwise... otherwise I am perfectly all right.'

'But you are not,' he argued, 'I can tell.'

She grew embarrassed and turned away from him. 'Well, except for a little nausea and dizziness. But it will pass, I expect. I am sorry about the ride, Edward. Perhaps another day.'

Edward heaved a sigh and rose to his feet. 'Very well, Elizabeth, if you say so. Now, if you will excuse me, I must go in search of Father. There are some documents which require his signature before I leave. I expect Doctor Blundell will have finished examining him by now.'

'Doctor Blundell? Is he here?'

'Yes, giving Father one final examination. Well, duty calls, Elizabeth. I shall see you this afternoon, my dear.'

The doctor was just departing Sir Giles' study when Elizabeth entered the house. She smiled as she bade him a polite good day.

He strode over to her with his brown leather bag. 'Good morning, my dear. And how are you today?'

Nervously, Elizabeth cleared her throat. 'I was hoping to have a word with you, Doctor, if you can kindly spare me the time?'

'But of course I can, Elizabeth – although if it concerns your father, please allow me to tell you that he is now remarkably well.'

'No, Doctor Blundell, it does not concern Papa. I am the patient on this occasion.'

October brought a chill to the air and an east wind which rustled the trees, bringing down a flurry of dry, golden leaves. The sky was dark and sombre this afternoon, with black forbidding storm clouds gathering over the hills and valleys; an ominous sign of bad weather.

It was tea time at the Hall, and Elizabeth and her aunt were seated in front of the crackling log fire, eating hot muffins with their afternoon tea. Elizabeth's appetite had returned and stabilised now. The sitting room curtains had not yet been drawn, and from the warm cosy safety of their fireside chairs, they were able to sit and watch the weather worsening, every minute bringing the storm a little closer.

Outside the wind raged with a fury of its own, its ferocious power sweeping the trees unmercifully, bringing down the loose dead branches like stones and filling up the gutters with debris and leaves. Upstairs, one of the open bedroom windows was heard rattling noisily in its frame, until someone had the good sense to close it against the force of the elements and the rain which would undoubtedly soon follow.

Elizabeth worried over Edward. Unknown to his father, he was at present visiting Rachael at Netley Manor, an occurrence which took place almost every Saturday afternoon now. Although Elizabeth was happy for him, she hoped their meetings would remain a secret from her father, for heaven help Edward were he ever to find out. She twiddled her thumbs, willing him to have the presence of mind to stay at the manor until the storm had passed. The weather was not fit for man or beast to be out in at the moment.

Suddenly the front door slammed and a curse rang out from the man who entered. The two women turned to look at one another. Well, Sir Giles was home at least, for there was no mistaking his voice when he spoke. Grumbling about the atrocious weather and the damage which the high winds would undoubtedly cause, he bid both ladies a polite good afternoon. After warming himself by the fire, he went to sit in one of the armchairs in the corner of the room, turning it round until it stood with its back to them. He had some papers in his hand and it was obvious he wished to sit and work in peace. The old man had declined tea in favour of something a little stronger.

It was growing dark now and with tea over, Charlotte moved to turn up the oil lamp, intent on resuming her embroidery. Elizabeth sat gazing into the fire, lost in a world of her own. Richard had been away for fourteen weeks now; fourteen long, lonely weeks she had spent alone. Her spirits dashed by the endless waiting, she had begun to wonder if he would ever return. She often sought encouragement by reading his poem on the loft window, finding it of great comfort to her. His business in France was obviously taking longer than he had initially envisaged. But soon he would return as he had promised. She simply had to wait.

Charlotte stole a glance at her. Although Elizabeth was pining for Richard and was unquestionably lonely without him, she exuded a radiance which enhanced her beauty as never before. This mystifying glow she had acquired was of great puzzlement to Charlotte. Perhaps it was the hope in Elizabeth's heart which lent her that look of sublime serenity? Thoughts of future happiness which exalted her? Whatever it was, it became her beautifully, and smiling now, Charlotte found it difficult to tear her eyes away from her.

Suddenly the door opened and Edward strode in, his appearance windswept and dishevelled. Moreover, he wore a look on his face which instantly turned both women cold. He approached his sister, his eyes displaying some dreadful inner knowledge. Giles' head was seen to pop around the side of his chair in questioning manner. But, intent on his mission, Edward failed to notice him. Elizabeth was trembling with anticipated fear, her heart pounding heavily in her breast.

'Elizabeth... Elizabeth...' he began, his voice edged with pain.

She rose to her feet, bristling with dread, every instinct she possessed warning her of disaster. 'What is it, Edward? Please tell me!'

'I have just come from the manor, Elizabeth, and... and regret to tell you that Richard has suffered a severe accident whilst in France.' He saw his sister take hold of the armchair for support. Her face had turned white and her expression was fearful.

Charlotte jumped up and took hold of her arm. Meanwhile, the grim, tight-lipped figure of Sir Giles remained out of sight in the background.

'An... an accident? W... what kind of accident, Edward?'

Edward moved forward, hating himself for being the conveyor of such ill tidings. 'It happened at his chateau,' he said. 'Apparently, Richard was in one of the cellars when several barrels of wine fell on him, crushing him. Elizabeth... it is feared his back is broken, for word relates that he was left paralysed from the waist down and is very gravely ill.'

An expression of shock mingled with pity escaped Charlotte's lips; absolute silence from Elizabeth. Edward stared at her anxiously. It was clear that her mind was unable to accept the news, leaving her struck completely dumb. As if matters were not already grave enough, he had more bad news to convey. Gently he took hold of her arms. 'Elizabeth, I must inform you that the accident happened several days ago now and... and as I speak, Richard may already lie dead.'

A surge of pity filled Edward's heart, for the news had clearly devastated his sister. He desperately wanted to comfort her, yet all he could do was stand and stare at her. Elizabeth could not even weep, she was so deep in shock. He watched her eyes close, saw her sway, caught her as she collapsed in his arms. Afterwards came the panic, with everyone moving and speaking at once.

Edward laid his sister on the sofa. Flapping, Charlotte rushed to ring the bell for the parlourmaid, whilst Sir Giles, barely able to comprehend the situation, leapt from his chair making his presence known to Edward at last.

'Smelling salts!' cried Charlotte, ringing for the maid.

Edward kneeled at Elizabeth's side, his face stricken with anxiety. 'Oh, she looks dreadful, Aunt Charlotte! The news has deeply shocked her. Do you... do you think she will be all right?'

Charlotte bent over Elizabeth, feeling her brow. 'Yes, of course she will, dear. Just allow her a little air.'

Suddenly the figure of Sir Giles loomed behind them. He stood purple-faced with anger, openly confused as to what had transpired. 'Would one of you inform me what has happened here?' he spat. 'What is all this about de Ville? And who in God's name told you about it, may I add?'

Edward cast the old man a cold glance. ''Tis none of your business, Father. So kindly stay out of the matter. Elizabeth's health is foremost to me at the moment. Besides,' he added, 'I do not have the inclination to satisfy your curiosity concerning a man whom you openly despise!'

The master stiffened with rage. He was on the verge of retaliating when Charlotte intervened. 'What has happened, Giles, is that Elizabeth has just fainted from shock! Ought not that to be of priority to you now?' She looked at her niece's pale face. 'Can you not see what this has done to her? Can you not imagine her grief when she recovers? Why, the poor child will be inconsolable!'

'Of course I can!' rasped Sir Giles. 'But I fail to understand why news of... of *that man* should be of such concern to her. Did she not terminate their relationship weeks ago? Has she not forgotten his very existence?'

Deeply vexed, Charlotte pursed her lips. What a prize fool her brother was! 'Oh, Giles, are you really such a nincompoop? You believed Elizabeth had forgotten the Count because that is what you wanted to believe! You wanted to believe their relationship was over! You are living with your head in the clouds, Giles!'

Realisation slowly sank in, leaving the master flabbergasted. 'You mean to say their relationship is not over and done with? Are you trying to tell me she still... still cares for him?'

'Of course she still cares, Giles – she loves him! Why can you not bring yourself to understand that? The trouble is, she also loves you. Although Richard begged her to accompany him to France, Elizabeth chose to remain with you because she had promised to nurse you back to health, – otherwise she would surely have left you to go with him!'

Giles was so consumed with shock and outrage that he barely knew how to contain himself. 'Good God!' he cried, then turned to Edward, who met those cold, self-assured eyes with rising scorn. 'Did you know about this?' he questioned savagely. 'Well? Did you?'

Unintimidated, Edward squared his shoulders. 'What if I did, Father? What do you intend to do about it? Tell me, is it your plan to disinherit me again? My loyalty is to my sister. It always has been and it always will be. Perhaps that will answer your question!'

The master was quick to retaliate and began to quarrel violently with his son, ranting and raving at the top of his voice. Poor Charlotte did her best to control the men, but all to no avail.

Amidst the anger and raised voices, not one of them noticed that Elizabeth had begun to recover consciousness. She raised a weak hand to her head. It was throbbing unbearably, aching as never before. Her eyes opened to the bitter quarrel which was taking place in the room and, unable to face it, she closed them again. Edward's bad news flooded into her mind with painful reality. The thought of Richard lying alone and paralysed in France – or perhaps even dead, was more than she could bear. Consumed with grief, she wanted to cry out in her agony – No! No! He cannot be dead! Not he! Not her beloved Richard! Never before had she felt such pain, pitifully weeping as she murmured words of denial. But her cries went unheard, for the family were too preoccupied with their quarrel to notice. Their furious voices rang loudly in her ears, bitter arguing voices which made her head spin. She could bear it no longer. She just had to escape!

Only when they heard the door slam did the other occupants in the room realise she had gone. Unspeakably angry with the two men, Charlotte let her feelings be known. 'Now see what the pair of you have done! And you, Giles, ought to be ashamed of yourself! Can you not spare a little compassion for Elizabeth's feelings? Have you no thought for anyone but yourself?'

'I shall go after her,' exclaimed Giles. 'There is a thing or two I wish to say to Elizabeth!'

Charlotte caught hold of his arm. Her brother must be made to see sense! Goodness only knows what Elizabeth would do in her present state of mind if her father lost his temper with her. 'Giles, listen to me! If you do not wish to become estranged from Elizabeth forever, then be kind to her! For once in your life show some sympathy!'

Without thought of any direction, wishing only to escape the house and all the quarrelling, Elizabeth ran out into the courtyard. The wind was still raging savagely and the first few drops of rain had already begun to fall. A sudden flash of lightning illuminated the courtyard, followed by a loud crack of thunder which shook the very heavens above her. Moments later she dashed into the stables, dishevelled by the wind and beside herself with grief.

Old Ned was startled out of his wits when he saw her. She wore neither cloak nor mantle on this grim, stormy night and stood by the stalls, shaking violently from head to toe. Deeply concerned, he dashed over to her, imploring her to explain what was wrong. Perhaps the master had suffered another seizure. Perhaps he was even dead! 'What is it, Miss Elizabeth? What's 'appened?' he questioned urgently.

She did not answer him. Indeed, he doubted she had even heard him. All she could do was pace up and down the floor, her shoulders heaving from her violent weeping. His kind old heart went out to her, for she made a pitiful figure before his eyes. He knew he must do something to help her, but doffing his battered old cap to scratch his head, the old man wondered what. An idea. Perhaps Master Edward could help? Yes, that was it. He would go and fetch Master Edward.

Elizabeth would have none of it, however, and kept on crying that she did not want anyone. It was untrue, though. She did want someone. She wanted Richard. But he was – was dead! She gave a cry which shook poor Ned to his boots then, barely realising what she was doing, she reached for one of the bridles on the wall. 'Saddle my mare, Ned! Please!' she begged. 'I need to get away from here!'

The old man looked dumbfounded. 'Saddle your mare? But... but I cannot do that, Miss Elizabeth! There's a storm a-brewin' outside which I'll wager is the worst Shropshire 'as seen in a long while. I cannot allow ye to go ridin', Miss, I cannot!'

'Very well, then I shall do it m... myself!' She ran past him for her saddle, weeping bitterly. It was far too heavy for her, although strengthened by her desperation she pulled and pulled until it finally fell to the floor with a thud. She then tried her best to lift it.

'Don't, Miss! Please don't!' cried Ned. 'You'll only 'urt yourself.' He hated himself for complying with her wishes, but felt he had no choice. "Ere, let me. I'll saddle 'er for ye.' And so, against his wishes, he did as he was bid, although still trying to talk her out of her foolhardiness. Ned suddenly shuddered. The master would have him hung if he knew what he was doing!

Elizabeth had taken no heed of him at all, and when the groom had completed his task she snatched the reins from his hands and led the skittish mare outside into the stormy night. Ned's pleas were drowned as she rode off into the darkness unheeding. Rhapsody reared in terror when a flash of silver lightning suddenly lit the sky above them, transforming the house into an awesome, ghostly spectacle. Elizabeth, uncaring of all danger, urged the mare on.

There was no stopping them now. She was punishing herself; making herself suffer the only way she could for allowing Richard to return to France alone. Had she only been with him, then the accident might never have happened. But she had chosen to stay with her father instead – abandoned her beloved for him. For that she despised herself. Her mind could not bear the pain of such a thought, and she urged the horse into a gallop. But no matter how fast they raced, there was no escape from herself or her guilty conscience. Inside she just continued to ache.

In the meantime, Ned had rushed across to the Hall to alert Master Edward as to what had transpired. Edward and Sir Giles had searched the entire house for Elizabeth, having no idea she had even left the Hall. Upon learning what had happened from Ned, the irate master threatened him with a good sound flogging for what he had done, yelling that if anything should befall his daughter, then he would make him wish he had never been born. Poor Ned! He was beginning to wish that already.

'I can hardly believe it!' uttered Sir Giles. 'How can she even think of riding out on such a night?'

'Because Elizabeth is not herself tonight, Father. That is why.' said Edward. 'I doubt she even knows what she is doing!' He was already racing across the hall as he spoke. 'Come, we must make haste to find her! God only knows where we shall begin, though!'

Elizabeth had arrived at Bluebell Wood. How forbidding and unfamiliar it all looked! The towering oaks and the clumps of rhododendron bushes were now fearsome objects which loomed ominously above and around her, whipped into a frenzy of anger and antagonism by the wind. The path had been transformed into a black, twisting snake which took her on towards the centre of the wood. The trees provided very little shelter from the torrential rain which continued to pour down relentlessly, filling the stream to capacity, the wild, violent water consuming everything which lay in its path.

Both horse and rider were soaked through to the skin. Elizabeth's hair hung like rats' tails down her back and across her face after being lashed by the wind, while her dress clung to her body. Pulling the mare to an unsteady halt, she gazed wildly around, shuddering violently at what she saw. Only now did she acknowledge the folly of her actions; only now, when her anger towards herself had dispersed, did she realise what she had done. She let out a cry of anguish, then with her head bent, her body limp from sorrow and fatigue alike, she began to weep again. Suddenly a deafening bolt of thunder shook the very ground beneath her and afraid, Elizabeth knew it was time to go home. Rhapsody took no turning; indeed, her mistress was having difficulty in sitting her now, she was so frightened.

They were still quite a way from the edge of the wood when a flash of lightning suddenly illuminated their surroundings, transforming them into a stage of ghostly phantoms. It then struck a nearby tree, sending a spiral of burning light hissing to its top. That was the last straw for the terrified mare. Leaping forward, she took the bit between her teeth and then bolted through the wood as fast as her legs would carry her.

Elizabeth had become unseated and, unable to regain her balance, clung to the horse like grim death, all efforts to restrain her mount futile.

In sheer blind terror the little mare galloped on, twisting, turning, darting through the trees like an animal possessed. A low branch loomed ominously ahead. Elizabeth pulled harder on the reins but to no avail. Her scream echoed out as the branch stuck her head, then a falling sensation before hitting the ground. After that she knew nothing. No pain, no fear, no heartache. Just blessed unconsciousness which blotted out the torture from her mind.

CHAPTER THIRTEEN

Fortune had indeed been with Elizabeth on that cold, filthy night of the storm. Had not Sir Giles, Edward, and two of the stablemen suddenly caught sight of her frightened mare galloping flat out from the direction of the wood, then she might well have died from exposure. The four of them had split up in their search for her, all calling frantically. Edward had been the one who eventually found her. She was still unconscious. Bitterly cold and soaked to the skin, she made a pitiful sight to her brother's eyes. Yet no-one could have been more relieved than he.

Arriving on the scene, Sir Giles took a small flask of brandy from his saddlebag, then, raising his daughter's head, held it to her lips. Afterwards, with one of the men holding the storm lamp above him as he knelt by Elizabeth's side, he quickly removed his neckcloth and wrapped it around the wound on her forehead, which was still oozing blood. Edward had already covered her up in his own oilskin in an attempt to warm her, for although the rain had stopped, it was still bitterly cold and windy. When Elizabeth showed no sign of regaining consciousness, Giles rapped out orders for his son to ride back to the house with her at a safe speed, with himself and the two other men riding alongside.

Upon their return to the Hall, Edward carried her upstairs, where Charlotte and Annie peeled away her soaking clothes, thoroughly dried her, dressed her in a warm nightgown, then wrapped her up in bed. Some thirty minutes later Doctor Blundell arrived.

Sombrely he examined the patient for broken bones, for respiratory problems brought on by her exposure to the elements, and finally came to the wound on her forehead, which he cleaned and dressed. Afterwards he sat by the bedside with Aunt Charlotte, listening as she related the events which had led up to her niece's accident and the reason why she had ridden off into the storm. Doctor Blundell agreed that it was a shocking business indeed, puzzling the old lady when he added, 'And especially at a time like this.' Charlotte was about to ask him to clarify the remark, when Elizabeth gave a deep groan. She had begun to come round. Oh, what a relief it was when she opened her eyes and asked where she was! Delivered from her anxiety, Charlotte could willingly have wept. Calmly and quietly, Doctor Blundell explained what had happened, but the pain of remembrance was too much to bear and Elizabeth became distraught. Nothing they could say or do would calm her. She was inconsolable.

Sir Giles and Edward heard her cries from the landing and, full of concern, they rushed into the bedroom. When Giles bent over his daughter endeavouring to pacify her, she instantly shrank from him, eyeing him with contempt. She blamed everything on him, condemning him for his bitterness and stubbornness, above all for his complete lack of understanding. Were it not for him, then she would be with Richard at this moment. She had sacrificed the man she loved merely to pamper to the selfish whims of another, for did not her father entertain fanciful ideas that she should stay with him forever? Abandon her own life, her pursuits, in favour of him? Oh, but how she despised him for that!

'Go away, Papa! Leave me alone! I cannot bear to look at you!' she cried.

'But Elizabeth...' he began, looking stung.

'Oh, how you must be gloating now! Gloating to think that the son of your late enemy is... is either d... dead or dying!' She turned her head away and began to sob into her pillow. 'Oh, why did you not leave me to die, too? I may as well be dead, for I have nothing to live for now!'

Eventually Doctor Blundell found it necessary to sedate her, for she had worked herself into an appalling state. Afterwards he told the family that she had suffered a shock to the mind, also a severe chill which he feared might develop into pneumonia. 'She must be watched very closely during the next few days,' he said. 'Keep her warm and quiet, and,' – he glanced at Sir Giles – 'please see she is not distressed.' He cast them an encouraging smile. 'Try not to worry. Elizabeth is young and strong. With God's help, she will pull through.'

Several hours later Elizabeth's condition began to deteriorate. At four o'clock in the morning she was shaking with cold, her whole body subjected to spasmodic convulsions as she worsened. Charlotte remained at her bedside praying for her recovery. Despite the extra blankets which were laid on the bed and the hot drinks which the old lady administered, all efforts to warm Elizabeth failed. A fire burned in the grate, regularly refuelled by Annie, who was assisting Charlotte. Every hour which passed saw Elizabeth worsening, with very little that Charlotte could do but sit helplessly by. She wished Mr. Llani was here, for his presence was so comforting. But due to the storm he had wisely remained in Cambourne for the night. Pacing the floor, her heavy brocade dress rustling with her every step, she considered sending for Giles. But what could he do that she had not already done herself? Nothing! She only hoped that the morning would bring an improvement, for God be with Elizabeth if it did not!

Giles Montgomery was not asleep. Instead he lay tossing and turning the hours away, his mind too disturbed by last evening's events to allow him such solace. How it pained him to know that Elizabeth had not terminated her friendship with de Ville as he had believed! That had it not been for his seizure, then she would be with him now in France. How the news had shattered his illusions; his staunch belief that de Ville was out of their lives for good. Gad, but how wrong he had been! What a fool he had been to think that the scoundrel had yet done with him! The man would do anything to cause him pain – anything! His efforts to entice Elizabeth away to France with him were but a mere beginning.

Propping himself up against the pillows, Giles' lips began to curl in a cruel smile. Well, doubtless the fellow would find all that a little difficult now – if not downright impossible! Paralysed? Perhaps even dead, Edward had said? Well, may God forgive him, but he felt little sympathy! If de Ville was still alive, then his condition would no doubt bring Elizabeth's fondness for him to a rapid end for, being so disabled, what possible use could he be to any woman now? None whatsoever. And if by good fortune he already lay dead, then that would be even better. Sir Giles smiled to himself complacently. His troubles were over at last! For what more could de Ville do to them now?

The following morning, Charlotte warned Giles that Elizabeth had become fearfully ill and that in her opinion she was in for a very rough passage indeed. All through the day the chills persisted, every sign indicating that her condition would develop into a raging fever.

Sure enough, by ten o'clock that night she had become an inferno of heat, her temperature rising alarmingly as the hours progressed. The family took turns at her bedside, with her own faithful Annie in constant attendance, fetching, carrying, glad to be of use to her mistress.

Upon his return, Frederick Llani was deeply shocked to learn what had happened to Elizabeth and proceeded to assist the family in every way he could. The man felt desperately sorry for Elizabeth, unable to conceive the extent of her ill fortune or the full gravity of the Count's tragic accident. He was finding it increasingly difficult to remain civil to Sir Giles, who was undoubtedly the most selfish fellow he had ever associated with. Indeed, it would come as a relief when his appointment here had ended, although he would miss Elizabeth's cheerful company when he left. He only hoped that her luck would change for the better in future, and that Richard de Ville would live and one day return to her.

Doctor Blundell was at Elizabeth's bedside again, concerned over the difficulty she was experiencing in breathing, caused by the inflammation in her lungs. Before leaving, he gave her another dose of quinine, leaving instructions that she must be kept warm and quiet and encouraged to take liquids whenever possible.

Downstairs, Sir Giles persuaded the doctor to partake of a glass of mulled port before leaving. It was cold outside and the drink would help to warm him. The hour was two o'clock in the morning.

Afterwards the doctor prepared to leave. ''Tis quite a long ride to Milfield at this hour of the morning,' he remarked. In the Hall, he turned to address Giles again. 'Try not to worry, Giles – although I know how difficult that will be, with Elizabeth lying so gravely ill.' He rubbed his chin in a thoughtful manner. 'You know, Giles, considering the shock Elizabeth has suffered – to say nothing of her fall, I find it amazing that she has not lost the child.'

Giles stared at him dumbfounded. 'Child? What child?'

John Blundell's expression clouded. Could it be that Sir Giles did not know? 'Well... Elizabeth's, of course,' he replied unsteadily. 'Surely you are aware that she is four months with child?'

Giles looked utterly devastated. He opened his mouth to speak but the words failed to come. For once in his life he was speechless! His heavy jaw hung open, giving him a half-witted look, his wide, staring eyes threatening to pop out of their sockets at any moment.

John eyed him with concern. The news had deeply shaken him. 'Giles... Giles, I see I have shocked you. Perhaps you should sit down for a moment.'

Suddenly Sir Giles emitted a roar of denial which shattered the silence of the sleeping household. 'N..o..o..o.! I do not believe it! It cannot be true!'

'Giles, keep your voice down!' urged the doctor. 'Remember the hour, man!' He placed a comforting hand on the master's shoulder, which was immediately shrugged off.

Giles then raised his fists in the air and began to rant and rave like a lunatic. 'De Ville! De Ville!' he raged. 'That worthless philanderer! The unscrupulous blackguard that he is! I swear that if he is not already rotting in his grave then I shall kill him for this! As God is my judge, I shall! Infiltrating himself into my daughter's presence against her will! Leaving her carrying his bastard!'

'Giles, please! Calm yourself, I implore you! 'Tis not in the least as you think!' The doctor walked beside him as he paced the floor, begging him to listen to reason. 'Elizabeth was not seduced against her will, as you call it. De Ville loves her, Giles. And she loves him! Why, has not the fellow already asked for her hand in marriage? Be sensible, man! Does that sound like someone wanting to take advantage?'

Steely-eyed, Giles turned to face him. 'Allow me to inform you that it is me he wishes to take advantage of, Sir. Me! Can you not see that the man is out to destroy me any way he can?' He gave a constrained laugh, adding, 'And bless me if he has not succeeded in doing just that through my daughter!

Four months with child, you say? I ask you in all earnest, is that not enough to destroy any caring father? The disgrace! The dishonour! The very shame of it!'

Deeply engrossed in their controversy, neither man noticed the presence of a third party who stood silently on the landing above them; someone who bore witness to their conversation. Charlotte had been disturbed by her brother's cries and had gone to see what all the noise was about. Deeply shocked, her hand flew to her mouth stifling her cry. Elizabeth was with child? Oh...!

Visibly overcome by the news, she covered her face with her hands. Poor Elizabeth! No wonder she had taken the news of Richard's accident so badly! To be in her condition and unwed was bad enough. Then having to face the fact that the father of her baby had met with some dreadful accident and was perhaps dying, or even dead, had been more than she could bear. Charlotte chided herself for not having realised what was amiss with Elizabeth weeks ago. Her condition ought to have been as plain to her as the nose on her face; the attacks of nausea she had suffered each morning; her refusal to eat or to ride. Oh, but if only the poor child had confided in her, then she could have been of so much help and comfort! Instead she had kept it all to herself, probably feeling too ashamed to speak of it.

Sadly, Charlotte bowed her head. Richard and Elizabeth lay miles apart from one another, both desperately ill, their child at risk of being lost. Was there anything else left for God to do to them, she wondered?

Next morning, Sir Giles was still in a violent temper, throwing the whole household into a state of fear. He was abominably rude to Stokes when the butler bade him a polite good morning, and caused Annie to drop a jug of hot water on to the carpet after almost knocking her down on the upstairs landing in his haste to find Charlotte.

'You clumsy wench!' he spat. "Tis fortunate for you that you did not scald me! Clean that mess up at once, then get back to your duties girl!'

'Y...yes, Sir!' whispered Annie nervously, then dropped to her knees on the carpet.

Minutes later, Giles stormed into the breakfast room, where he informed Charlotte and Edward of Elizabeth's condition. 'John Blundell gave me a shocking piece of news this morning. Prepare your ears,' he warned savagely, 'for he told me that Elizabeth is four months with child! Can you believe it? With child!' he wailed.

Calmly, Charlotte placed down her teacup. 'Yes, we are already aware of the fact, Giles,' she said quietly. 'I overheard your conversation with John this morning and I have already informed Edward.'

He turned to stare at her. 'And are you not shocked? Are you not completely overcome by the news?'

Charlotte heaved a heavy sigh. 'Of course I am, Giles. I was grieved to hear of Elizabeth's condition and have not slept a wink all night from the worry.' She rose to her feet and approached her brother placatingly. 'I understand how you must feel, Giles; how hurt and troubled you are. But you must forgive Elizabeth. Matters are already grave enough without—'

'Forgive her?' he interrupted. 'Forgive her for bringing shame to my home? Forgive her for allowing herself to be taken by that rascal, de Ville? Hah! Like the devil I will!'

Edward, who had taken the news of his sister's condition like a gentleman, suddenly jumped to his feet to protest. 'It would never have happened had you been sympathetic and allowed Elizabeth and Richard a conventional courtship, Father! If you had given them hope by granting permission for them to marry! But as it was, your attitude forced them to deceive you! Left them with no alternative but to see each other secretly. Well, now you must live with the consequences!'

Giles sneered at Edward with contempt. 'Oh, you are always so eager to protect your sister, Edward! She can do nothing wrong in your eyes, can she? She brings disgrace upon herself and family, and you have the audacity to blame it all on me! That is so typical of you!' He paced the floor, his expression thunderous. 'Well, this time she has gone too far. I refuse to have anything more to do with her! She is no longer my daughter! Tomorrow she can pack her bags and take herself and her disgrace elsewhere!'

Charlotte looked horrified. 'But Elizabeth is ill, Giles. She is not fit to leave her bed, let alone—'

'I care not!' he interrupted. 'I care not what she is!'

Edward grabbed his father's arm in rage. 'Why you insensitive—'

'Oh, stop! Stop!' cried Charlotte in anguish. 'I just cannot take any more of this constant quarrelling.' She began to weep without shame before them, her distress plain to them both. 'Elizabeth's life is in shreds. She has a fever which might well be the death of her – and the best you can do, Giles, is threaten to send her away. Oh, what a heartless man you are!' Picking up her skirts, Charlotte then fled from the room.

'Poor Aunt Charlotte! All this trouble is making her ill. I must go to her,' said Edward, striding after her disappearing figure.

Charlotte and Edward were too preoccupied to notice the figure of Frederick Llani standing in the doorway, his face a mask of contempt. But when Giles turned around he saw him. The master's anger deepened, for it was clear the artist had overheard every word.

'How dare you eavesdrop, Llani!' he growled. 'My family and I were engaged in private conversation. Have you no manners, man?'

'I was not eavesdropping,' stated Mr Llani acidly. 'I simply came to have breakfast. But, I admit to having overheard your conversation, Sir.' He strode into the room and approached Sir Giles, his expression openly hostile. 'Charlotte is right!' he spat. 'You are a heartless man and should be ashamed of yourself! You have a wonderful daughter in Elizabeth, yet all you do is condemn her, concerned for no-one but yourself! You are not fit to wipe her boots, Montgomery! You are not fit to be her father!'

Giles stared at him, outraged. 'How dare you!' he roared. 'How dare you criticise me in my own house!'

Frederick matched his icy stare and continued, unheeding. 'Have you forgotten how Elizabeth nursed you through your illness? How she abandoned her own life and happiness and stayed with you instead? Oh, you were glad of her then, were you not? But now, when she needs you, your love, your support, all you can think of is the disgrace she has brought upon you. Oh, were Elizabeth only my daughter instead of yours, then none of this would ever have happened. Instead, she would be happily wed and in France with her husband now!'

'Get out of my house!' hissed the master. 'Pack your bags and get out! I have had my fill of you, Llani!'

'And I of you, Sir!' replied the artist. 'I know not how I have held my tongue all this time!' He walked back towards the door, then turned to face Giles. 'My only regret is that I must leave Elizabeth when she is so ill. She needs help now, and my advice to you, Sir, is that you give it. Swallow that insufferable pride of yours and act like a human being for once. Be a father to your daughter – whilst you still have her!'

Montgomery was left open-mouthed and staring, Llani's words still burning his ears.

After packing his belongings, Mr Llani went to say goodbye to Elizabeth. Annie was sitting with her, but rose to her feet when the man entered. Elizabeth looked wretched and his heart filled with pity for her. There was no doubt she was gravely ill.

'She's asleep, Sir,' said Annie. 'The medicine the doctor gave her makes her drowsy. But it'll do 'er good. She needs the rest.'

Frederick stood by the bedside, his face masked with sadness. 'Oh, 'tis a bad business, Annie, a bad business indeed.' He heaved a heavy sigh. 'How I wish I had been here when Elizabeth rode off into the storm. I might have been able to prevent her. I could have comforted her in her hour of need.'

'You mustn't blame yourself, Sir,' said Annie kindly, 'I doubt if anyone could have stopped Miss Elizabeth that afternoon. She was beside herself with grief at what 'ad 'appened. I don't think she knew what she was doin'.'

The artist took Elizabeth's hand and held it between his own. 'Look after your mistress, Annie,' he murmured quietly, 'for there is only one Elizabeth – the finest lady I have ever known.' He bent to kiss her softly on the forehead. 'Goodbye, my dear Elizabeth. My thoughts and prayers will always be with you.' Annie saw the tears in his eyes when he turned to face her, reaching into his inside pocket. 'Please give your mistress this letter when she wakes, Annie,' he said. 'Tell her I came to see her, and please assure her of my highest regard.' Then, after one last look at Elizabeth, he quickly left the room, his emotion all too apparent.

Later that day, Doctor Blundell announced that Elizabeth was suffering from pneumonia, and the days which followed saw her fighting for her life. She lay gravely ill, caught in the grip of the raging fever which swept her body with an all-consuming vengeance. Gradually it sapped her strength until there was precious little left for her to fight with. She suffered frenzied attacks of delirium, when she believed she saw Richard walking across the bedroom towards her and would call out to him pitifully. On these occasions she would try to get out of bed, pathetically struggling with anyone who tried to prevent her.

Sir Giles remained with her constantly, his tough old hands holding hers. Wisely he had taken Mr Llani's advice and cast his pride aside, for nothing mattered now but Elizabeth. She was his only concern. Dr. Blundell had warned him that when Elizabeth's illness reached its crisis, he might lose her, and the thought of that was enough to quell all but his love for her. Indeed, during the last few days he had shown admirable concern for his daughter, sitting at her bedside by night and day, praying for her recovery. But all the worry had brought him to the end of his endurance, and now a lonely, crumbled figure of a man desperately willing to do anything in his power to save his beloved daughter, he fell to his knees at her bedside, weeping miserably.

Eyes closed, his palms pressed tightly together, he bowed his head in one last prayer to God. Sir Giles Montgomery promised, and with all the honour and goodwill he could muster, that if the good Lord were to spare Elizabeth's life, then he himself would forgive her for the shame which she had brought upon them. Furthermore, he pledged that he would not rebuke her for her sins, nor ever again speak of her relationship with Richard de Ville. He vowed one last final promise before concluding his touching prayers. Giles promised the Lord that if Elizabeth lived, then he would never again stand in the way of her future happiness – be it what may. This was the pact Sir Giles Montgomery made with God, and might the heavens open and come down on him in fury if ever he broke his word.

That same night, a little after three-fifteen in the morning, Sir Giles' prayers were answered. He had nodded off for a few moments. When he opened his eyes he saw his daughter gazing back at him, all trace of her fever gone. Never was a man more relieved than he! With trembling hands he reached to touch her brow. Oh, but how cool it felt now! How wonderfully, wonderfully cool! Murmuring his thanks to God, he bent over her clutching her to his breast, sobbing for joy without shame. Elizabeth had been delivered from her illness. She would live. Live! Now it was his turn to live up to the bargain he had made.

With Elizabeth well on the way to recovery now, the household was able to slip back into its stride again and once more normality prevailed. Just as he had promised, Sir Giles forgave his daughter for the shame she had brought upon her family, telling her that it was the end of the matter and that never again did he wish to discuss her past relationship with Count de Ville. It was done. Forgotten. Let the past be dead and buried. Elizabeth, however, could not bring herself to tell him that it was not forgotten; that it would never be forgotten. If Richard were still alive, then one day she would be with him again. Nothing was surer than that. But to keep the peace, she kept silent.

Whilst discussing the matter of her unborn baby, Sir Giles had omitted to mention that he had already made plans for the child's adoption; that as soon as he or she was born, then it was to be taken away from its mother to begin a life far away from there. Giles knew that Elizabeth's condition would naturally arouse much gossip among the family's staunch Victorian friends, who would no doubt gloat over the man's unenviable predicament. But he would suffer it – suffer it until that, too, became an issue of the past. Elizabeth was alive and well and, bearing that in mind, he would shoulder anything which chose to come his way.

Charlotte and Edward had been towers of strength to Elizabeth of late, neither one reproaching her for her present condition. Instead they had offered all their love and support. Poor Charlotte! She had wept unashamedly the night Elizabeth's fever had left her, when she had anxiously asked if she had lost her baby. The two had embraced when Charlotte quietly told her that she had not. There had been such relief on her niece's face, making it clear that she wanted Richard's child very badly. Moreover, that she would never have forgiven herself if her recklessness had cost her its life. Edward assured Elizabeth that he was looking forward to the forthcoming event, adding that it would be jolly to have a youngster around the house.

No word had been heard of Richard. However, today brought good news. A trusted servant from Netley Manor had delivered a message to Edward asking him to pass it on to Miss Elizabeth. It was from Rebecca de Ville who, along with Rachael, were at present at the chateau in Bordeaux. Rebecca wrote that Richard was alive and making a slow but sure recovery, the injuries he had sustained being less serious than had initially been diagnosed. Miraculously, his back had not been broken, although his injuries were serious enough and he was having to endure great physical pain. Richard was intent on the agonising task of learning to walk again, defeating his paralysis with courageous determination. How those few written words had encouraged Elizabeth, filled her with renewed hope which would sustain her throughout his absence! She knew for certain now that he was alive, and with God's help he would one day return to her as he had promised. That would surely be a day well worth all the long weeks of waiting.

October the thirty-first heralded Elizabeth's twenty-second birthday. Although she was still confined to bed, she was able to enjoy the celebratory bedside party which Aunt Charlotte had organised. Never before had she received so many gifts, many from the loyal staff who had been so relieved at her recovery. Although never a whisper was heard to pass their lips, warned by the master against idle gossip, they were all aware of Elizabeth's condition and were in sympathy with her against her bitter father.

Elizabeth had been saddened to hear that Mr Llani had left the Hall during her illness, and that she had been unable to say goodbye to him. But she had written him a letter inviting him to visit her whenever he was able. She knew nothing of the words he had exchanged with her father, nor that he had been dismissed. Although Mr Llani had completed Sir Giles' portrait, it lacked the finishing touch of his hand and gave the impression that the artist had abandoned it prematurely – which is exactly what had happened. Sir Giles had sent Mr Llani on his way, and now it was he who must live with his less than perfect portrait of himself.

Ned, who had been consumed with grief during her illness, blaming himself for allowing her to ride out into the storm, had sent her a bunch of yellow chrysanthemums as a token of his respect. Annie had given her an embroidered handkerchief which she had made herself, telling her mistress that life would be 'plainly awful' here at the Hall without her. Sir Giles had bought her a fine leather handbag; from Aunt Charlotte came a fur hat and matching muff, and from Edward an exquisite silver bracelet. He had also presented her with another gift, a beautifully carved crib on which he had spent much time of late. Elizabeth was delighted and, God willing, it would not be too long now before the crib was in use. Doctor Blundell had estimated the first week in March for her confinement. But there was Christmas and the winter to face before then, was there not?

November gave way to a cold December, when the first snow of winter fell upon the peaks of the distant hills, then steadily down into the valleys below, covering the whole land beneath in a carpet of dazzling white. Elizabeth was allowed to leave her bed for three or four hours each day now, and from her bedroom window she watched the snowflakes meandering down to the courtyard below. The sky was grey and heavy today, and for hour upon hour the snow continued to fall, hiding everything beneath. She smiled to herself, recalling those bygone days when she and Edward had enjoyed great fun together on a winter's day like this; days when the two of them had built snowmen in the garden, bombarding each other with snowballs. She remembered how fascinated they had been at the rows of icicles which hung along the stable guttering, their long, spiky shapes such a source of delight to little children.

For them those days had gone, for they must move up the ladder of life to make room for a new, and as yet unborn, generation. Would her own son and daughter play here, she wondered? Or would Sir Giles forbid her to return to her former home with her family after she had left it to marry Richard? Only time would answer that question. But she hoped that Edward's children would have the opportunity of living and playing here, for Cambourne Hall was, after all, Edward's rightful inheritance; an estate which had been handed down to generation after generation of Montgomerys.

Gazing through the window in thought, she wondered if it was snowing in France. She thought of Richard; wondered what he was doing and thinking of at that moment. He knew nothing of the child she was carrying... his child. None of his family knew either. The man had quite a surprise in store for him when he eventually returned to her.

Many miles away at his chateau in Bordeaux, Richard de Ville lay in the four-poster bed, his mind occupied with thoughts of Elizabeth. In spirit he was with her constantly, even through his most gruesome pain. Indeed, during those moments his mind was with her all the more, for she was his hope, and more than that, she was his salvation. Knowing she was in England, just living for his return, was a more potent source of inspiration than all the doctor's daily reports and encouragement, for she inspired him with the will to live; the will to fight his disabling injuries and to rouse up within himself the determination he needed to recover.

Richard had been soundly informed by the most knowledgeable doctor in the land that it would be at least one year before he was able to walk normally again and without the assistance of his crutches – perhaps longer. He was determined to achieve it in six months, and set his hopes on being in England by June of next year. Even that seemed an interminable age to have to wait, with endless hours of pain to overcome before then. His every movement was tortured and laborious, yet despite the pain which gripped his crippled body, he continued to rise to his feet for a few minutes every day, when he would take a step forward with the aid of his crutches. At first the exertion had proved too much and he had toppled to the floor, his crumpled figure a pitiful sight to his mother, who was with him. But he was stronger now and would undertake the task with more successful results, upheld by his determination to succeed. The doctor had warned him that he was pushing himself too far and too soon; that his efforts would rob him of the chance of a full recovery. But Richard had continued regardless, his only concern being to return to Elizabeth. If God was just, then He would see him through.

From where he lay, Richard was able to see out through the window, where he would gaze at the unrestricted view across his land. The scene looked cold and uninviting today, held in the grip of winter, even though the weather was milder here than in England. Indeed, at this time of year it was likely that England was covered by a blanket of snow. He wondered what Elizabeth was doing at this moment. Perhaps she was sitting by the window gazing out across the land? Perhaps she was even thinking of him? He smiled. Whatever she was doing, his thoughts and love were with her... they were always with her.

It was growing dark now. Soon his mother would come to light the oil lamp, after which she would sit chatting to him until teatime. Both Rebecca and Rachael had been towers of strength to him since his accident. This was a grim chapter of his life which he was having to endure. But things would change. The day would come when he would walk again. Then he would return for Elizabeth, and there was not a thing Sir Giles Montgomery could do to prevent him from claiming her.

The thought instilled within him a sudden need to practise his walking. Throwing back the bedclothes, he eased his legs out of bed and moved to take hold of his crutches. It was with visible difficulty that he managed to haul himself up on to his feet, his face masked with the pain which consumed his body. Every little movement was agony, but he cast his pain aside and proceeded with his appointed task, determined to reach the chair in the corner of the room. His efforts were accompanied by audible groans of agony and the occasional mild curse. Beads of perspiration trickled down his face, leaving the front of his hair clinging to his forehead, the knuckles on his fingers showing white from the pressure with which his hands gripped the crutches. Slowly and laboriously he urged his legs into movement... one step...two steps, then having to rest for a moment to recover from the exertion. He was within a few paces of the chair when Rebecca entered the room and her cry of alarm brought her son to an agonising halt.

'Richard! No...! The doctor emphasised that you must rest today! You will only do yourself harm if you continue like this!'

She ran to him, offering her assistance. However, determined to reach the chair, he pushed her arm away and took another step forward. It was too much for him though, and with his strength sapped, he was unable to keep his balance a moment longer. One of the crutches fell to the ground just as Rebecca reached out to support him. He then lowered his head and closed his eyes for a moment, thwarted by despair and frustration.

Anxiously Rebecca held on to him. 'I will ring for help,' she said. 'Claude will come and -'

'No! I do not want Claude's help. Nor anyone else's either!' he spat. 'I must do this alone, so kindly stand away from me and allow me to walk back to my bed!' He had not intended to address her so sharply. It was simply frustration getting the better of him. 'I am sorry,' he apologised, 'I did not mean to be unkind.'

Rebecca smiled. 'I know. And I am right here at your side, should you need me.' Summoning his strength, Richard struggled to walk back to his bed, smiling with inner satisfaction when he eventually reached it unaided. He would rest now. But tomorrow he would walk again.

The festive season saw none of the usual flamboyant parties at Cambourne Hall that year. Christmas was a quiet affair celebrated by just a small family gathering.

On the afternoon of Christmas Eve, Uncle Cedric, Aunt Maud and their ageing bachelor son, Rowland, arrived. They were distant family relatives who announced that they would be staying until Boxing Day. All three were visibly overcome by the shock of seeing Elizabeth's condition and appalled at the news that she was still unwed. Indeed, poor Aunt Maud found it necessary to swoon into the nearest chair, whereupon the smelling salts had to be sent for.

Afterwards, Aunt Charlotte took the afflicted lady to one side and proceeded to enlighten her as to the facts of Elizabeth's dilemma. Nevertheless, being a staunch and highly principled Victorian who considered herself moral to a fault, Maud pursed her lips in open distaste, declaring that Elizabeth had disgraced them all. Furthermore, she knew what she would do if a niece of hers had brought such shame upon them – send her packing to some distant relative and let her make her own way in future! Thus began the most unpleasant Christmas the family had ever known.

On the day itself, when the land outside was still covered by a deep carpet of crisp white snow, luncheon was an equally cool affair. The seven of them sat in stony silence at the table, Aunt Maud and Uncle Cedric still glowering, full of silent condemnation of Elizabeth. Rowland, who barely spoke two syllables at the best of times, proceeded to sit through the meal in grim silence, although his appetite seemed hearty enough – the goose was disappearing at a rapid rate! Edward, bless him, had endeavoured to introduce a little festive joviality to the occasion, but sadly his efforts went unappreciated. In fact, he was left in some grave doubt as to whether they possessed a grain of humour between them, their austere, poker faces never once coming within a threat of a smile. Even Sir Giles lost patience with the three, especially following Uncle Cedric's remark concerning the unfashionable length of the master's Dundreary whiskers, referring to them as being 'untidy'. Just who was he to criticise, anyway? Oh, what an abominable nerve the fellow had!

Thankfully the thorny trio saw fit to depart the Hall at three o'clock that afternoon, their excuse being that further snow storms looked imminent. Suffice it to say, it was one of the clearest skies which December had ever seen, but oh, what a relief it was to see the back of them all!

The New Year of 1887 was here already, and the third week of January brought an unexpected spell of the most glorious winter weather imaginable. Although the nights were bitterly cold and crisp with frost, the days were incredibly sunny, the evenings ushering in the most magnificent molten orange sunsets one could ever wish to see.

It was during this pleasant spell that Edward suggested taking Elizabeth for an afternoon drive. She had not been out at all since the night of her accident, and although she had regained her health, Edward believed the change would be of benefit to her. After some initial reluctance, Sir Giles eventually agreed. So, dressed in her purple woollen dress with its pretty apron effect, her fur-trimmed mantle, hat and muff, she set out with Edward on their afternoon drive.

Oh, but it felt wonderful to be outdoors again, the winter air so refreshing after being cooped up in the house for so long! She had almost forgotten what it was like to breathe in its sweetness and in no time at all her cheeks had turned into a healthy pink in place of her earlier pallor.

'Where would you like me to take you, Elizabeth?' asked Edward pleasantly.

Elizabeth's reply was spontaneous. 'I would like to go to Netley Manor, please, Edward – if you do not object?'

'Of course not, my dear, although apart from the staff, there will be no-one there. The Marquise and Rachael have been in France for weeks now nursing Richard.'

'Yes, I know, Edward. I simply wanted to see the house from the roadside, that is all.'

Understanding, Edward smiled. 'Very well, Elizabeth. Then we shall go.' He glanced at the clear blue sky. 'As it is such a glorious day, I suggest we drive the long way to Netley, over the Long Mynd – if the carriage tracks are clear – then down through Milfield. Would you like that?'

'Oh, yes, I would indeed, Edward!' she replied enthusiastically. "Tis such a long time since I was last up the Long Mynd.'

Soon they were driving up the bumpy road which led to the very top of the range of hills. The scenery from up there was spectacular, the most breathtaking view which Shropshire had to offer. On a clear sunny day such as this, one could see for miles in every direction: the neighbouring Welsh hills to the west, the outlying counties to the north, south and east, and in the near distance the Caer Caradoc hill, where it is said that Caractacus made his last stand against the Romans.

Crisp snow still covered the ground, although the carriage tracks were clear enough and they were able to travel without too much difficulty. The view was indeed that of a winter wonderland; an expanse of dazzling blue-white for as far as the eye could see. It was cold up there too, and Elizabeth was glad when they had reached the valley at the other side, for it was so much warmer down there.

Through the village of Milfield they drove, past Doctor Blundell's charming stone cottage and the 14th century church, then on through the neighbouring hamlets towards the Netley road. Elizabeth's cheerful chatter had become subdued by a deepening sense of nostalgia. She was recalling that fine summer day when she and Edward had driven to the manor for Rachael's birthday party, both deliriously happy, she excited to the brim at the prospect of spending one whole afternoon in Richard's company. It seemed such a long time ago now, and so much had happened to them since then, she reflected sadly.

Edward drew the carriage to a halt outside the gates of Netley Manor. Tears sprang into Elizabeth's eyes as she gazed at Richard's home again. It had not been her intention to be so heavy-hearted; she simply could not help it. But for her father's seizure and Richard's accident, they would be together now, wed and happy, awaiting the birth of their first child. Instead he lay in France a crippled man, whilst she was alone, and at a time when she needed him most. Tears began to fall as she gazed at the house which should by now have been her marital home. Seeing her wretchedness, Edward placed a comforting arm around her shoulders, murmuring words of consolation. But, for all his good intentions, her brother's words were of no consolation at all. That would only come with Richard's return, and every night in her prayers she asked the good Lord if He would please make it soon.

Elizabeth cast her mind back to the afternoon of the party, recalling those precious moments with Richard on the lake... then afterwards in the clearing when they had given their love to one another. It had been the most wonderful day of her life, a day she would never forget. The lake would be frozen now.

In fact, the whole place looked cold and distant in its setting of stark white snow, the trees which lined the drive now leafless skeletons in this, their winter's rest. Even the house looked desolate and abandoned.

A veil of depression shrouded her as the fear that she would never see that house again implanted itself in her mind. No amount of reason would dispel it. Elizabeth shuddered, suddenly feeling cold. She turned to her brother. 'I think I would like to go home now, Edward,' she said. 'Thank you for bringing me here.' As her brother urged the horses forward, Elizabeth took one last look at Netley Manor, her mind so full of Richard. Somehow she knew that her very last thought this side of the grave would be of him.

CHAPTER FOURTEEN

On the twenty-seventh day of February at precisely 5.18 a.m., Elizabeth gave birth to a beautiful baby girl. A few days premature, it had been a difficult birth, with many anxious moments before the child finally made her way into the world. But now it was over and all was well with both mother and child.

Earlier, Sir Giles had looked so worried as he paced up and down the landing floor – just as he had when Elizabeth herself had been born. Although he had shown the most admirable concern for his daughter during her confinement, he stubbornly refused to go anywhere near his little granddaughter, refusing even to look at her. The whole household had made up for him, though, with everyone taking turns to steal a peep at the child. Charlotte said she was beautiful. Edward announced she was adorable, and Elizabeth, so proud in her new role of mother, declared that she looked like Richard.

Edward bent over the crib, his fingers curled around the baby's tiny hand. 'Indeed, she does,' he agreed. 'But believe me when I tell you, Elizabeth – she also looks like you!'

A name for the child was discussed, with Victoria emerging as favourite. Elizabeth, however, announced that the baby was to be called Emma Louise, simply because it pleased her and that she believed it would please Richard too.

Sir Giles was adamant in refusing to see the child, and on the ninth day after her birth he suddenly dropped his unexpected bombshell.

'Adopted?' Charlotte looked shocked to her roots. 'What on earth do you mean – adopted?'

Giles stiffened. 'The word is plain enough, is it not?' came his crisp reply. He took a pinch of snuff, then sat behind his desk in the study, Charlotte standing before him. 'Some time ago I found a family in London who were willing to take the child and give it a good home. Elizabeth must be told, and she must accept the fact.' Avoiding Charlotte's reproachful eyes, he turned his head away from her. 'I did not wish to distress Elizabeth with my decision following her illness, and purposely kept the matter to myself. But the time has come when she must know, for I will not have that man's b -'

'Giles! For pity's sake!' cried Charlotte.

'... That man's... offspring in my house,' he corrected.

Charlotte was so angry she felt like shaking him. 'Firstly Giles,' she began, 'the child is not an 'it'. She is a little girl – your granddaughter, your own flesh and blood when you care to remember it! How can you even think of giving her away?'

Giles' icy stare matched her own. 'I am not giving it... her away, as you call it. I am having her legally adopted, Charlotte.' He pursed his lips. 'As for her being of my flesh and blood, might I remind you that she also has de Ville blood running through her veins?'

'Yes!' retaliated Charlotte, 'and that is the truth of the matter, is it not, Giles? Your pride has been offended because you and Rebecca now share the same granddaughter!' She gave a contemptuous laugh. 'Oh, such poetic justice after all these years!'

'Desist!' he cried. 'Rebecca de Ville has nothing to do with the matter! Nothing!'

'Humbug, Giles! She has everything to do with it! The whole wretched business arises out of the fact that she rejected you all those years ago! Admit it, Giles! Be honest for once!'

Purple-faced and seemingly lost for words, Giles jumped to his feet and stormed from the room.

Elizabeth bore the brunt of his anger when he strode into her room a few minutes later, informing her in no uncertain terms of the plans he had made for little Emma. Consternation flooded into her, the smile fading from her face. 'No, Papa! I beg of you! You... you simply cannot mean it!'

Giles paced the floor, his hands clasped tightly together behind his back. 'Believe me, Elizabeth, it is for the best,' he said firmly. 'The Bilseys are fine upstanding people who will give the child a good home and upbringing. That is the most important factor, is it not? Besides, given time, I am convinced you will forget about her.'

It was enough to make Elizabeth cry out with shame and indignation. 'Forget about her? My own daughter? Why, I have never heard such a monstrous statement! Shame on you, Papa, for saying such a wicked thing – and I would rather die than give her up!'

Giles looked equally determined. 'I am afraid my mind is made up, Elizabeth. You have no say in the matter.' The old man began to walk to the door, addressing her over his shoulder. 'Might I remind you that the Bilseys will be here first thing in the morning to collect the child? So kindly be good enough to have her ready. My forbearance in the matter is at an end.'

Elizabeth began to weep hysterically, and in her blind, bitter anger spat out words which made her father recoil in his steps. 'One of these days

Richard will come and take me away from here – and his daughter, too! I ask you in all sincerity, Papa – do you really want to face him with the news that you have given her away?'

'Silence!' he cried. 'I told you I never wished to hear that name mentioned in this house again!' Eyeing his daughter with fury, he approached her bed. 'He will never come back for you, Elizabeth! Never! The man is, after all, a de Ville, and if nothing else, he is proud. Do you honestly believe he would present himself to you in the condition he is in? No. Not he! Besides, his insidious seduction of you in the first place was most certainly to get back at me! I guarantee it had nothing to do with cherishing any affection for you, Elizabeth!'

His daughter gave an anguished wail. 'Oh what a wicked and heartless thing to say, Papa! Richard does love me! And one of these days he will come for me! You will see!'

The sound of their raised voices suddenly woke the sleeping baby, who began to scream at the top of her voice, considerably disturbing her grandfather. Elizabeth had turned away from him and was sobbing into her pillow whilst the child continued to scream. Giles looked uncomfortable, dearly wishing someone would come to attend her. On and on she cried. Eventually, unable to bear the noise a moment longer, Giles moved cautiously towards the crib. His grim, unsmiling features were stern and hard, his heart as cold as ice. A moment later, however, a most amazing transformation took place. Upon seeing his little granddaughter for the very first time, the old man's expression began to soften. Seconds later his face lit up with sheer delight. Oh.... but how beautiful she was! How utterly sweet and adorable!

With eager, trembling hands he stooped to pick up the small, cuddly bundle, his lips curling in an undisguised smile. Gently he held her against his shoulder, whispering words of comfort in her ear. Her crying immediately ceased, along with that of her mother, who watched the two with bated breath. Still smiling, Sir Giles stole another peep at her little face, marvelling at her likeness to Elizabeth at that age. She had been blessed with the same dark curly hair, bewitching blue eyes, round, delicate cheeks and the same little mouth. Oh, but it was as though the clock had been turned back twenty-two years and this was his own dear Elizabeth he was holding!

His expression suddenly clouded as unwelcome reality flooded into his mind. But this was not Elizabeth. This was the child of his most hated enemy – and illegitimate into the bargain. It was with an unfathomable look on his face that he returned the child to the crib, then left the room without so much as a word or backward glance.

The following morning, Aunt Charlotte and Edward took their stand beside Emma's crib protectively, determined not to allow Giles to take her.

At that point the man himself walked into the room. Without a word, he strode over to the sleeping child and picked her up. Elizabeth's hand flew to her mouth in fear. Had the Bilseys arrived for Emma already, she wondered? A moment later her unspoken question was answered when Annie suddenly entered the room in a state of panic, announcing that the Bilseys had indeed arrived.

Sir Giles made no move whatsoever. He simply stood there with his little granddaughter in his arms, an unreadable expression upon his face. No-one spoke and the air was rife with anxiety. Sir Giles then moved with the baby to her mother's bedside. Believing the moment had come when she must part with her child, Elizabeth screamed out to Edward in terrible desperation:

'Edward! Please do not allow Papa to take her! Please, Edward!'

Swiftly he moved to the doorway, determined to block his father's path. Oddly enough, Sir Giles paid no heed to his son or his actions. Instead, he smiled at Emma's sleeping face, then handed her to her bewildered mother. His words astounded them all. 'Kindly convey to the Bilseys that I have changed my mind, Annie.' He smiled tenderly at his daughter. 'Tell them there is no unwanted child in this house. Bless me, but no granddaughter of mine shall be adopted!'

Sir Giles Montgomery was a changed man. No-one would have believed the transformation which took place in his character during the first few weeks of Emma's life. She and she alone was responsible for bringing about this amazing change in him, for her presence in the world proceeded to give him more happiness than he would ever have thought possible. The child had succeeded where everyone, with the exception of Elizabeth herself, had failed. Now he showed tolerance and understanding; had established himself as friend instead of foe, Emma having redeemed his character for the better.

These days he allowed Edward more and more freedom to run the estate, whilst he spent time with his granddaughter. Oh, but he almost drove Elizabeth mad with his old-fashioned fussing over every little thing! Was Emma too hot or too cold? Was she wet? Was she hungry? Was she thriving? Indeed, had not his daughter been so overjoyed by the transformation which had softened her father's hard old heart, then she would undoubtedly have wearied of him. But she took it all in good spirit, for the man had certainly excelled himself in kindness towards herself and her child of late.

Upon his orders, the guest room next to Elizabeth's bedchamber had been made into a nursery, displaying everything a child could possibly need. Following a shopping expedition into Marbury, he had returned with a carriage-load of toys, clothes and nursery furniture, delighting them all with the splendid wooden rocking horse which he had had especially made for her. How they had all laughed! It would be at least five years before she had grown big enough even to climb up on to the thing! Giles was so proud of her too, and often carried her to the stables, delighting old Ned when he introduced her to the family horses, telling her he would buy her a pony of her own when she was older. Great happiness and an air of blissful contentment now reigned throughout Cambourne Hall, with every servant on the place delighted at the master's amazing transformation. All was well at last.

April heralded an early spring, bringing a profusion of tall, yellow daffodils to the woods and gardens around the estate, with almost every vase in the house filled with them. The trees and shrubs suddenly burst forth into life again, offering colour, scent and beauty to a landscape which had been brown and drab for so long. Sunshine and clear blue skies replaced the cold grey winter, the weather already hinting at the prospect of a long hot summer. A thick carpet of bluebells had already pushed their way up in the wood, and next month would see them in their full glory.

A deepening sense of excitement had begun to pervade Elizabeth's spirit, a growing premonition that became stronger and stronger with every day, until she was convinced beyond doubt of the fact that Richard was coming home. Somehow she sensed it, felt it, knew it! She was convinced enough to convey her feelings to Aunt Charlotte one morning, but the old lady had reacted sceptically, telling her not to build her hopes up. Richard's accident had left him with the severest of injuries. It could be months before he had recovered enough even to think of returning to England. Elizabeth had refused to be dismayed, however, for she had grown to have faith in her heart and its predictions. Richard was returning home as he had promised. Of that she had no doubt.

That same evening, before tucking Emma up in her crib, Elizabeth sat with the child on her knee, telling her that her papa was coming home to them; that very soon now they would all be living happily together at Netley Manor and that none of them would be separated from each other again. Guilt stabbed at her conscience as she thought of her own father. Sir Giles adored Emma; he worshipped her. What would become of him after the two had left, she wondered? When the house was emptied of their presence, never again to be filled by the sound of her baby's touching cries? Poor man! How desolate he would be, lonely and broken, with nothing in the world to give him joy any more. But it was of his own making, was it not? It did not have to be like that. If he could only overcome his pride and hatred, then life would be so different for him. Elizabeth looked thoughtful. Perhaps he would change. For had not Emma touched his heart in a way which neither she nor Richard had been able to achieve? Perhaps his love for Emma would help him overcome his hatred of Richard? Allow her parents to marry at last? Life would indeed be sweet for them all then, with no need to deprive any one of them of the others. She smiled, hoping that this would be the course of things to come, then kissed her baby's cheek before laying her down to sleep. They would not have to wait much longer now either.

Today was the fifth day of May, and that afternoon found Elizabeth in the library. Since waking that morning she had been plagued by a strange feeling of restlessness, excitement mingled with unease; a most peculiar sensation which had naturally puzzled her. It was with her now as she stood on a chair browsing through the many books which lined the shelves, looking for something to take out into the garden to read.

Suddenly Annie rushed into the room, waving an envelope with tremendous excitement. She was talking so fast that she was barely understandable at all.

'Oh, Miss! Miss! You'll never guess what!'

'What is it, Annie? What is the matter?'

'It's this letter, Miss! It's from 'im! 'Im!' Her eyes were all but popping out of her head as she spoke.

'Him?'

'The Count, Miss! 'E's back! A messenger from Netley Manor 'as just passed this on to me sayin' I must give it to you straight away!' She then thrust the letter into her mistress's hand.

Jubilation flooded into Elizabeth, who was suddenly so happy she barely knew where to put herself. 'Oh, Annie, I knew it! I knew it! I have known for days now that he was returning! Now he is back! He is home!' She quickly ripped open the letter, feasting hungry eyes on the words she had so longed to see.

Netley Manor
May 5th
In the Year of Our Lord 1887

My dearest, dearest love,

No words can truly convey the feelings in my heart as I write. Where should I begin, my love? With my deepest, deepest sorrow at being parted from you for so long? With my joy, my overwhelming happiness at being home again and near you? No, my dearest Elizabeth, for of these sentiments I am certain you are already aware. But what you cannot possibly know, my love, is how very much I have missed you during my long months of absence. The longing in my heart every day for you, to touch you, to hold you, to look upon your face again and to make good my promise to return to you. Oh, Elizabeth dearest, the thought of you kept me alive all those months, sustained my spirit, my determination to recover and come back to you. Now I am here, and nothing in the world can keep me from you.

This evening, at six o'clock, I shall come for you as promised. Be waiting, my love. Rid me of the ache of being without you for so long. Marry me and make my happiness complete. There is so much more I wish to say to you, Elizabeth, so much I wish to tell you, but I regret that time does not permit. Before I close, my dearest, allow me to convey how much I love you, Elizabeth.

I love you. May you always be assured of that.

Until we meet this evening,

I remain your ever loving servant,

Richard

Tears of joy ran down Elizabeth's cheeks, and at that moment there were no words able to do justice to the feelings in her heart. Richard was home and he loved her. What greater happiness could she have wished for than that? Laughing and weeping at the same time, she closed her eyes and clutched the letter to her breast, thanking God for delivering him safely home again. She noticed he had not mentioned anything about their child in his letter and could only assume that as yet, he did not know. Although news of her illegitimate baby had reached just about everyone's ears in Shropshire, no respectful servant worth his salt would presume to enlighten his master with tales that he had just become a father. So Richard was indeed in for a surprise when he arrived at the Hall for her that evening. Oh, just thinking about it filled her heart with the most incredible elation!

She glanced at the clock. Heavens above! It was almost four o'clock already. She must hurry if she was to be ready and waiting at six. Only then did she realise that Annie was still standing there waiting. Last year, when she and Richard had planned their escape together, he had told her that she might bring her maid along to attend her. Now, with little Emma to look after, Elizabeth needed her more than ever.

Hastily she explained matters to the maid, instructing her to run upstairs and pack their clothes at once. 'But not too many, Annie,' she added. 'Just a valise for Emma's things, and naturally your own. I shall return to collect mine at the earliest opportunity. That way Papa will be assured of my intention to return to visit him, for I am unwilling to leave him without hope.'

Suddenly the door opened and the man himself entered the library. Afraid he would see the letter in her hand. Elizabeth quickly reached for the nearest book, opened it, then stuffed the letter between its pages.

The book was still in her hands as he approached the two women. His eyes strayed to it and he looked pleased. 'Ah, the Holy Bible, I see. Very commendable, my dear.' His eyes fell upon Annie, who was looking extremely nervous in the master's presence. 'Annie... what business brings you into the library at this hour of the afternoon?'

'Annie has come to tell me that... that Emma has woken, Papa,' replied Elizabeth, on her behalf. 'So if you will kindly excuse me, I shall go up to her.'

'But of course,' he said pleasantly. 'You will bring her along to see me, Elizabeth, for you know how dearly I love to see her?'

'Of... of course, Papa,' she replied, already consumed with guilt. 'You know I will.'

Because Sir Giles remained in the room, Elizabeth thought it prudent to leave the letter lying in the Bible, for it would be disastrous for them all were he to see it. She must remember to collect it before she left the Hall that evening. As things turned out, however, she never did.

Upstairs, she informed Edward and Aunt Charlotte of Richard's letter, and also her plan to leave home that night. Both were overjoyed to learn of Richard's safe return, although afterwards Elizabeth saw an expression of dismay on her aunt's face. Charlotte knew that Giles would be left broken-hearted, a fact which caused her great sorrow. At all costs he must be absent from the house when Richard called that evening, for she knew her brother would not allow him to take Elizabeth and Emma from him. Giles had vowed to kill Richard for his sins and, given the chance, Charlotte knew he would do just that.

Elizabeth went on to say that she would despise herself for evermore if she were to leave her father without so much as a goodbye, but her aunt told her she had no choice in the matter. If she wished to leave peaceably with Richard tonight, then for all their sakes she must do it secretly. It was the only chance she had. Charlotte promised to speak to Giles after their departure, and to try to convince him that the only way he would ever see his daughter and granddaughter again was to swallow his pride and make his peace with the de Villes. By doing that he would gain a son as opposed to losing a daughter. The choice was up to him.

Edward conceived a plan to entice his father away from home at the appointed hour of six o'clock. He would arrange for them to visit Squire Ridley on a fool's errand; a pretence that the man wished to see them on a matter of importance. Edward knew he would be made to suffer for his crime, but assured Elizabeth it would be worth it. All alone with his sister, he put his arms around her in an affectionate embrace. 'Take care of yourself, my dear. I shall miss you both dreadfully, but despite that I wish you all the happiness in the world. Rest assured, I shall visit you and Richard often.

Indeed, I shall be proud to,' he said.

After one last brotherly hug, he was on the point of leaving the room when he suddenly turned to her. Edward Montgomery was never sure what prompted him into saying what he did. 'Elizabeth... thank you for the love and kindness which you have always shown me. Even at a very early age, I knew you were trying hard to compensate for Father's lack of affection'. He smiled. 'I just wanted you to know how much I appreciated it. God bless you, my dear.'

Elizabeth was left with tears in her eyes, unaccountably sad all of a sudden.

At Netley Manor, Richard de Ville was preparing for his journey to Cambourne Hall. His valet had just left the room after assisting him to dress and, all alone now, Richard stole a glance at himself through the mirror on his dresser. He wondered how Elizabeth would see him within the hour. Would she perhaps see a pitiful figure of a man who had endured great physical pain and mental torture during the last few months? The scars left behind by that pain and the scattering of grey hairs which had not been present before? Or would she see the same man who had left her all that time ago, tall and upright and without impediment?

He squared his shoulders and, at the cost of some difficulty, straightened his back. It still ached like a bad tooth and would go on doing so for quite some time, so the doctor had said. In addition, his right leg had still not fully recovered and he found it necessary to walk with the aid of a stick. But he had achieved his goal. He was back in England one month ahead of the time he had allowed himself, attributing it to sheer determination and willpower. Now he must make good his promise to Elizabeth: take her from her father's possessive clutches. At the same time, Richard knew his task would not be easy.

Downstairs Rebecca and Rachael awaited his presence in the sitting room. Rebecca was visibly distressed at the prospect of her son's impending mission to Cambourne Hall. The three of them had only arrived home from France the previous evening, and he had not allowed himself time to recover from the long, arduous journey before informing them of his intentions. Rebecca had done her utmost to sway him from his decision, begging him to delay the matter until he was stronger. But he had refused to listen, determined to make good his promise to Elizabeth. Although Rebecca admired his courage and determination, she knew he was incurring grave danger in even thinking of taking Elizabeth away from her father. Sir Giles Montgomery would lie down and die before allowing his beloved daughter to be stolen from him by a de Ville. She sighed with despair. The matter was in the hands of God now, and in Him they must all put their trust.

Rachael looked much happier. Being young and carefree, her head filled with romantic notions, she viewed her brother as a heroic knight in shining armour venturing to rescue a damsel in distress. She was oblivious of the fact that something might go wrong. He would drive off for Elizabeth, snatch her from under her hateful father's nose, then return with her to where the two would be married and live happily ever after. To Rachael, that was really all there was to it, the danger element being of very little consequence at all. Her fanciful ideas simply led her to believe that love would conquer all.

The misguided young lady jumped eagerly to her feet when her handsome brother entered the room. 'Oh, Richard, I cannot tell you how much I am looking forward to having Elizabeth here. Indeed, I can hardly wait! Please hurry for her, Richard. Mamma and I will be waiting.'

'Would you kindly leave the room for a few moments, Rachael,' said Rebecca sombrely. 'I wish to speak with Richard alone.' When Rachael had gone, she endeavoured yet again to dissuade him from going to Cambourne Hall. 'I implore you, Richard, postpone your visit for a while. Allow Giles time to think the matter over. If you ride to his home uninvited, then his reaction...'

'I care not for his reaction!' rasped Richard stubbornly. 'As for allowing him time to think matters over, has he not already had almost twelve months in which to contemplate? Has he not been aware of my intentions since last year, when I warned him at the ball what I would do? No, Mother.' He shook his head. 'The man has had plenty of time for all that.' He turned to her, his eyes softening. 'You may pray for Elizabeth and me this evening, Mother – but do not try to prevent me from going to her.'

Rebecca knew his mind was made up. Nothing she could say or do would sway him from his decision. She clasped him in a warm embrace. 'Then go, Richard,' she said quietly. 'And may God go with you.'

CHAPTER FIFTEEN

At five-thirty that evening, Elizabeth watched her father and brother ride up the drive and out of sight, on their way to Squire Ridley's home as arranged. Tortured by conflicting emotions, she felt sad and guilty at having to leave behind her father's back, yet filled with overwhelming joy in the knowledge that she would soon be with her beloved again, whom she longed to see with all her heart. Her happiness quickly overpowered her sadness, and all she could think about now was Richard; Richard, whom she loved and had waited for all these months.

She ran along the landing to her room, where she fussed over her appearance. This evening was so special and she wanted to look her best. The rose pink dress she wore became her beautifully, and pinned to the stiff lace collar was her treasured cameo brooch. Emma looked delightful in pink and white lace, her dark curly hair peeping from beneath the brim of her matching bonnet. The little girl was all ready to meet her papa at last. The valise containing her clothes and toiletries stood in readiness at the side of Elizabeth's bed. Annie was downstairs somewhere, saying goodbye to all the staff.

Uncontainably excited, at ten minutes to six Elizabeth returned to the landing window with her daughter in her arms, watching and waiting for Richard's arrival. Emma was gurgling happily, blissfully unaware of the situation which she and her mother faced. At precisely the hour of six, the grandfather clock downstairs began to chime the hour. One... two... three. At that very moment a carriage appeared at the far end of the drive, travelling at a brisk pace as it headed towards the house. Elizabeth gave a cry of joy. Oh, he was here!

She rushed along the landing to alert Annie. The maid was just coming up the staircase as her mistress appeared at the top. 'Quickly, Annie! Count de Ville has arrived! We must make haste!'

Elizabeth proceeded down the stairs with the child in her arms, Annie close behind her. In the hall they stood waiting for the knock at the door. When it came, Elizabeth jumped. She then watched Stokes in the pursuit of his duty; saw his astonishment upon opening the door. Count de Ville was the last person in the world he had expected to see. Elizabeth then heard that deep familiar voice informing the butler that he was expected that evening. Hurriedly she turned to pass Emma, who had now lapsed into slumber, over to Annie, who stood in the near background. She then watched her beloved make his entrance into the hall, beholding his eyes in an engulfing look of love. Deeply moved by the moment, by his very presence, all she could do was stand and gaze at him in a spirit of worship. Oh, but he was as tall and upright as she remembered, although she noticed that he carried a cane which supported a visible limp. But apart from that he was still the same, just as handsome and as masculine as he had always been. She marvelled at the way he had overcome his crippling injuries, for less determined men would undoubtedly have abandoned hope and been confined to a bed all their life. But not he! Not her Richard!

His eyes worshipped her in return... the woman who had inspired and encouraged him to recover from his injuries. Tenderly they whispered each other's name, both venturing a step towards the other. Then Richard held out his arms to her and with an impassioned cry she rushed towards him.

Just how long they stood there locked in their tight embrace they never knew. It was the most moving moment of Elizabeth's life.

Overcome by emotion, she clung to him desperately, laughing and crying at the same time. 'Oh, Richard, Richard! You are home at last! I have missed you so much! I...j... just cannot begin to tell you...'

Her face was wet against his as he whispered how much he had missed her in return. 'Thank you for waiting for me, Elizabeth. For being here. I love you so much! So very, very much!'

Their touching reunion brought tears rising to Annie's eyes, and had the same effect upon Aunt Charlotte, who stood watching from one of the doorways. It was a most tender scene that they witnessed. Neither woman could possibly have known that the couple's happiness would be so rudely shattered a few moments later. Sir Giles and his son had only reached Platter's Barn when the master's horse had stumbled, throwing him off. In desperation, Edward had implored him to take his horse to Squire Ridley's but shaken, Giles had decided to return home, leaving Edward to walk the lame horse.

Suddenly his dishevelled figure appeared in the hall, startling everyone. Indeed, it was difficult to know just who was more shocked, he or his dumbfounded family.

Immobilized, he stood with his mouth hung open, eyeing Richard as though he were looking at a ghost. 'Wh... what the deuce...?' he began.

With the exception of Richard, everyone looked fearful, all wondering what had gone wrong with Edward's carefully laid plan to keep Giles occupied elsewhere. Although decidedly staggered by Richard's presence,

Giles quickly recovered. Then he strode across the hall towards the couple, his face a mask of hatred. His voice was razor sharp as he addressed the Count, although he spoke more at him than to him.

'So, like the devil he returns! Hah! One would have thought that God had punished him enough already! But, no, like the blackguard that he is he returns for more!' Giles eyed his enemy contemptuously. 'Damn you, Sir! Damn you to eternity! Have you any conception as to what you have done to this family? You are a fool! A fool for ever returning here, for I vowed to kill you for your sins against my daughter!'

Unmoved, Richard looked back at him with equal contempt. 'I, the fool?' He gave a cutting laugh. 'No, Sir. You are the fool for believing you could keep me from Elizabeth. I warned you months ago that I would return to take her from you. Now I am here, and I intend to be as good as my word.'

'Oh! Take her, indeed!' cried Giles with mocking scorn. 'I declare your phrase most liberal, Sir! For did you not "take her" prior to your departure for France? Take her in every sense of the word? Why, you diabolical scoundrel! Deserting her after having had your way with her!'

Puzzled by the remarks, Richard frowned. 'Deserting her? I do not understand?'

'Liar! Liar!' spat Giles. 'I put it to you that you understand only too well! Leaving her with your –'

'Papa! Please!' objected Elizabeth. 'Richard knows nothing of... of...' Her voice trailed away, for she was too distressed to continue. That was no fitting way for Richard to learn about their child.

As though on cue, Emma suddenly began to whimper. Only then did Richard notice Annie standing in the background with the child in her arms. He stared at the small kicking bundle and frowned. He then shot Elizabeth a questioning glance. 'Whose child is that, Elizabeth?' he enquired.

When she failed to reply, he asked again. 'Whose, Elizabeth? Please tell me.'

Elizabeth cast him the most loving look, her voice tender when she spoke. 'She is your child, Richard... yours and mine. Her name is Emma Louise.'

The exclamation of shock that escaped him rang out across the hall and his astonishment was clear to them all. 'Oh, Elizabeth... words fail me..'

Giles Montgomery was quick to interrupt the touching scene. 'But not me, Sir!' he volunteered. 'You must be made to suffer for your crime!'

As he took a step towards them, Elizabeth attempted to push Richard towards the door, fearful of what might transpire. 'Quickly, Richard! We must go! We must leave here at once!'

But the man refused to move a muscle, compelling her to cry out again. 'Please, Richard! Please...'

'Stand back, Elizabeth!' ordered Giles. 'Stand back, I say!'

He then grabbed Elizabeth's arm and pulled her away from Richard, infuriating the other man. Richard immediately took hold of him and a scuffle ensued between them. Suddenly Edward appeared, puffing and panting, having run like a man possessed from the stables. He immediately caught hold of his father and dragged him away from the Count, then continued to maintain a tight hold on him. Great commotion followed, with Sir Giles snarling abuse at his son for interfering. Edward called out to the couple to leave the place while they still could. Aunt Charlotte was physically and verbally urging them through the doorway, with Elizabeth calling out to Annie to bring Emma.

Richard was difficult to persuade, however, and angrily protested against leaving in such a manner. 'Damn you, Sir Giles! I have never turned my back and run from a man in my life! I will be blessed if I shall do that now!' He heaved an exasperated sigh. 'In God's name, why must you persist with this unreasonable behaviour? Would it not be of advantage to us all if we sat down and discussed the matter amicably?'

Montgomery was quick to disagree. 'No, Sir, it would not! I would rather go to my grave than come to any amicable agreement with the likes of you!'

Richard shook his head in despair. 'Yes, I do believe you would,' he said. 'Well, Sir Giles, I have done my best to make peace with you, but all to no avail. Whatever happens now, be it upon your own head. My forbearance with you has expired!' He clasped Elizabeth's hand. 'Come, let us go, Elizabeth, for your father wearies me.'

Giles began to struggle violently, yelling at Elizabeth to 'come back.'

The couple were already in the outside porch, being urged and pushed by a desperate Aunt Charlotte. Annie was behind her mistress, her face white with fear. Edward was still calling out to them to hurry. Suddenly, Annie cried out that she had forgotten the valise. It was still upstairs where she had left it! Charlotte begged them to leave it behind, but Elizabeth said that Emma would need her clothes and toiletries. It was she who offered to run upstairs and collect it.

'You take Emma out to the carriage, Annie!' she said. 'I shall go for it myself!' She turned to Richard, squeezed his hand. 'You go ahead, my love. I shall be but a moment before I return!'

He opened his mouth to protest; tried in vain to pull her back. But her fingers slipped through his and she was already running across the hall. Worried, he followed her inside, watched her as she dashed past her angry father, then onwards towards the staircase. 'Elizabeth! Elizabeth!' he called.

She paused, then turned to look at him, casting him the most enchanting smile he had ever seen. He smiled back in response, their eyes locked in a deep look of love. It was a very intimate moment between them, when nothing and no-one else mattered.

'Hurry, Elizabeth!' he urged.

'I will!' she said, then was gone.

Giles had been watching them and, incensed by the look which they had just exchanged, he struggled with greater determination. Just as Richard disappeared through the doorway on his way outside, Giles wrenched himself free of Edward's hold, yelling that he was going to kill de Ville. However, torn between carrying out his threat and running after Elizabeth, the man hovered for a moment, unsure of just whom to tackle first. During his moments of indecision, Edward rushed along to the gunroom and quickly locked the door for, without a weapon, his father would be unable to kill anyone. Seconds later, Sir Giles was running up the staircase after his daughter.

Upstairs in her bedchamber, Elizabeth was about to grab the valise when her father suddenly rushed into the room, distressed beyond words. His face was ashen and he was holding his chest as though in pain, his breathing ragged and desperate.

'Elizabeth... Elizabeth. I... I beg you! I implore you not to do this! Please do not rob me of the two most precious things in my life...yourself and Emma! It would destroy me, Elizabeth, destroy me!'

Feeling wretched and deeply sorry for him, Elizabeth endeavoured to assure him that this was not her intention. 'Oh, Papa, I do not wish to rob you of anything, and I certainly have no wish to destroy you. I love you dearly, Papa, but I also love Richard! I love him and I need him! Can you not see that, pray?'

Giles caught hold of her arm in desperation. 'But you do not need him, Elizabeth! This is your home! You can live here for as long as you wish! You do not need de Ville at all!'

Elizabeth frantically rejected this. 'But I do, Papa! I want to marry Richard! I want to be his wife!'

Whilst they were arguing, Sir Giles was pushing his daughter closer and closer towards the open French windows. Moments later they were standing out on the balcony, their voices ringing out across the courtyard in bitter conflict.

'If you do not wish to lose us, Papa, then cast aside your bitterness and make peace with Count de Ville! Do it for me and your granddaughter, if not for yourself! Please, Papa, I beg you!' she implored. She took hold of his hands, still weeping uncontrollably, offering to beg on her bended knees if it would bring about a change of heart in him. 'Please, Papa! I beseech you not to stand in the way of my happiness!'

Giles immediately recoiled, for her words reminded him of the promise he

222

had made to God. Had he not promised the Lord on that cold, bitter night last October that if He only spared Elizabeth's life, then he would never again stand in the way of her future happiness – be it what may? Oh how that promise haunted his conscience now!

Plagued by inner torment, he considered what life would be like without Elizabeth and his cherished granddaughter to cheer it. How desperately he would miss their happy faces; Elizabeth's contagious laughter and her baby's touching cries. Without them, he would have nothing in the world to live for. His life would be meaningless and empty. He might as well be dead!

Giles began to weep without shame before his daughter. Were Elizabeth's lover any other man but de Ville, then he would undoubtedly have honoured his promise to the Lord. But to sacrifice his beloved daughter into the hands of his most hated enemy was completely beyond him. Tormented by the most wretched guilt, he knew he could not do it. He would have to break his word.

He closed his eyes in anguish and raised his face to heaven, letting out an almighty cry to God. 'No..o..o! I simply cannot do it! I refuse! I refuse!'

Startled, Elizabeth shrank away from him until she was leaning heavily against the balustrade. Slowly but surely it began to give way. God in His fury had already set the wheels of justice turning. The master of Cambourne Hall would have to pay.

Sir Giles, now a pitiful sight to behold, was unable to look his daughter in the face a moment longer and turned his back on her. It was then he uttered the last words she would ever hear from him. 'Oh, forgive me, Elizabeth! Forgive me! As dearly as I love you, I cannot bring myself to deliver you into the hands of my enemy! I will never make peace with de Ville, Elizabeth. Not even for you will I do that!'

There came a loud crack as the balustrade gave way and Elizabeth's piercing scream echoed out across the courtyard. The next thing she knew, she was falling... falling... falling.

She felt no pain, only a numbness of the body and a strange acceptance in her mind of what had happened. It was all over now and she knew it. Perhaps she had always known that she was destined never to have a life with Richard. There had been dreams and premonitions enough to warn her of it. She managed a weak smile. The days she had spent with him had been the sweetest of her life. They had been her joy, her greatest happiness, and she thanked God for at least allowing her that.

Vainly she tried to move, but only her arms were free of the numbness which had claimed her legs and body. The cobblestones were a hard bed to lie on, although they felt smooth beneath her fingers as she stretched out her hand to touch them. Through dimming eyes she looked up at the evening sky, watched the sun disappear behind a luminous, silver-edged cloud, felt the wind sweep gently across her face. Elizabeth was free of pain and at peace with herself and the rest of the world. Lying there on the cobbles, her life slowly slipping away, what more did she have to ask for?

Suddenly she heard shouting, panicking voices, and the next thing she knew was that someone was bending over her, desperately crying her name. It was Richard. His face was a mask of anguish, touching Elizabeth's heart. She wanted to tell him that she felt no pain and that he must not worry. But then Charlotte and Edward appeared, smothering her with grief at what had happened. All three knelt by her side, Richard gently raising her head and cradling her in his arms.

She slipped a weak arm around his neck and held him in return. He was weeping emotionally. 'Oh, Elizabeth! No! No...!'

'Please don't, my love,' she murmured. 'I feel no pain... truly.'

Edward looked up at the balcony; saw the broken balustrade. 'How did it happen, Elizabeth?' he asked desperately. 'How did you come to fall from the balcony like that? It was so strong...so safe...'

'I do not know, Edward,' she replied. 'It...it just happened, as though I had no control over it at all. It was the strangest happening...'

'We must get her into the house!' cried Charlotte desperately. 'Doctor Blundell must be sent for at once!'

But when they tried to move her, she cried out. It was no use. Elizabeth was dying. There was nothing anyone could do for her now.

Weeping pitifully, Charlotte and Edward held her close before reluctantly standing back to allow her a few minutes alone with Richard, Edward still unable to understand how his sister came to fall. She smiled at them in turn as they left her, never to see either of them again.

Elizabeth asked to see Emma, whereupon Annie, who was standing by sobbing without shame, moved forward with the child in her arms. 'Sh.. she is 'ere, M... Miss Elizabeth,' she wept, falling on her knees beside her mistress. Annie blamed herself for what had happened. Oh, if only she had not forgotten the valise!

Richard raised Elizabeth's head so that she could see their child.

Gurgling happily, Emma was wide awake and looking directly back at her mother, ignorant of her fate. Smiling tenderly, Elizabeth touched her little cheek then, overcome by weakness, laid back her head again.

A misty veil of darkness had begun to descend upon her and, knowing she had but a few moments to live, Elizabeth told Annie to go to Aunt Charlotte. 'And Annie...' she said weakly, 'please do not blame yourself for what has happened. It was not your fault.'

Alone together, Richard held her close in his arms, fighting back the tears which threatened to overpower him again. How in God's name had this happened to Elizabeth, he wondered? How had she come to fall from the balcony?

Elizabeth raised her eyes to his. 'The most difficult acceptance of all, my love, is... is knowing that I am to be taken away from you. That is the worst pain to bear.'

His arms drew her closer. 'Oh, never, never, Elizabeth! Wherever you are I shall find you! I do not believe that even God Himself would deprive me of that!' Despite his anguish, he smiled reassuringly. 'I have already told you, I would not want to live in a world without you.'

'But you have Emma now, Richard. Tell me, dearest, what do you think of our daughter? Do you find her pleasing?'

'Pleasing? Oh, indeed I do, Elizabeth. Why, she is the most adorable daughter a father could wish for.' He kissed her softly in gratitude. 'Thank you for making me so proud, my love. My only regret is that I was not by your side when you needed me. Please forgive me.'

Suddenly Elizabeth began to cough and her whole body felt as cold as ice. Afraid, they clung to each other tightly. Richard found the words she whispered strangely comforting. 'If God were to grant me one last wish, then with all my heart I would wish for a chance to relive the days which I spent with you, for without doubt, they were the sweetest, most wonderful days I have ever known. I would gladly die a second time to be with you, Richard.'

'Then wish, Elizabeth! Wish as you have never wished before and *believe* and have faith in what you ask for!'

Gazing into his eyes, Elizabeth felt inspired and encouraged by his words. She smiled a loving smile. 'Then I will,' she murmured. 'Kiss me whilst I wish, my love.'

Tenderly his lips met hers and exalted, she reached out her heart to God in silent prayer. Elizabeth Montgomery made her wish. At the end of the kiss she was gone.

A spirit amongst them now, with God's grace Elizabeth was able to witness the events which took place following her death. She saw Richard in his agony still holding her body in his arms, weeping bitterly. By his side were Edward, Charlotte and Annie, all comforting one another as best they could. Suddenly she saw the figure of Sir Giles come rushing from the house like a man possessed. His face was as white as a ghost and he was shouting, 'Elizabeth! Elizabeth!'

Upon reaching the grief-stricken group, he savagely pushed Richard away from her body, then fell to his own knees beside her. She watched him cradle her in his arms, beseeching her to speak to him, crying wretchedly from pain and guilt. 'Elizabeth... Elizabeth, speak to me! Oh, forgive me, Elizabeth! Forgive me!'

Richard moved quickly forward, his own voice wretched with grief. 'She cannot speak to you, old man! Can you not see that she is dead?'

Overcome by horror, Giles began to shake his daughter. 'D... dead? No... No.! She cannot be!' He began to shake her lifeless body, his face a mask of disbelief. 'Elizabeth... Elizabeth! Oh...! Oh...!' he wailed. 'Forgive me! Please forgive me!'

Incensed with anger, Richard grabbed hold of him and pulled him away. 'Leave her alone! It is too late to beg her forgiveness now, Sir! She cannot hear you!'

Sir Giles tried to push him off, but in his fury Richard gripped him tighter and began to shake him. 'You despicable excuse for a human being! Are you satisfied now? Satisfied at knowing that Elizabeth has sacrificed her life for your cause?' His grip tightened. 'Why, I ought to kill you for what you have done! But that would be too good for the likes of you, Sir! 'Tis my belief that your own guilty conscience will eventually be the death of you!'

Montgomery was choking and spluttering alarmingly, unable to speak at all. It was Charlotte who implored Richard to release him, crying that this was neither the time nor the place to air their differences with poor Elizabeth lying dead at their feet. Complying, Richard flung the master away from him, spitting out his hatred of the man.

Edward, who had been standing helplessly by, moved to face his father. 'How did Elizabeth fall from the balcony?' he questioned menacingly. 'Did you push her? Did you? I swear I will hang for you if you did!'

Nervously, Giles caught his breath. 'Of...of course I did not push her. What kind of a man do you think I am?'

'Do you really want me to answer that?' sneered Edward bitterly.

'You might not have pushed Elizabeth from the balcony,' spat Richard. 'But your hands are still stained with her blood!'

Sir Giles was quick to retaliate – and to pass the blame. 'You blame me for what has happened here tonight?' he snarled. 'Such effrontery! Why, 'tis you who have brought all this grief upon our heads! Interfering in our lives... your persistence in pursuing my daughter!' Giles stared at her still, lifeless body and gave a wail of despair. 'N... now she is dead! Dead! Oh, confound you, Sir, but I swear I shall make you pay for this!'

Striding the few paces which separated the two, Giles struck Richard across the face with the back of his hand. Gasps of shock came from those who watched. Charlotte's heart was in her mouth. Edward knew what was coming. 'I challenge you to meet me in duel, Sir! I trust you will accommodate me?'

'Name the time and place!' came Richard's prompt reply.

'Very well. At dawn tomorrow in Hangman's Wood. I trust the time and place are convenient to you?'

A vestige of a smile appeared on Richard's lips, almost as though he welcomed Giles' challenge. 'Indeed it is, Sir. You have my word as a gentleman that I shall be there.'

Before saying his goodbyes, Richard held his baby daughter in his arms for a few minutes, whilst Sir Giles returned to his own daughter's side.

'Should anything befall me tomorrow, then you will take care of Emma for me, Charlotte? See to it that she has a good Christian upbringing?' He managed a weak smile. 'I would also be obliged if you would tell her about Elizabeth and me when she is old enough to understand. Assure her of the love we shared together.'

'Of... of course I will, Richard,' replied Charlotte emotionally. 'But you speak as though you have already lost the duel?'

'Perhaps I have,' he said, his eyes heavy with sadness. Perhaps that is the way I want it, Charlotte.'

She looked appalled. So did Edward, who said as much. 'But you must fight him, Richard! Fight him and make him pay for what he has done!'

'Oh, he will pay, Edward. Never fear of that. But there are different ways of paying, are there not? Your father's punishment will come – but not at my hand, I regret.'

The two men embraced, with Edward promising to be in the wood tomorrow morning at first light. He stated quite plainly that he refused to be his father's second. Some other fellow would have to oblige.

Aunt Charlotte wept when Richard put his arms around her in affection.

'Thank you for your past kindness, Charlotte. Elizabeth and I were fortunate to have had you to help us. God bless you.'

'And God bless you, Richard. Rest assured, my prayers will be with you tomorrow.'

Richard then returned to Elizabeth's body, and to the man himself. 'I trust you will allow me a few moments to say goodbye to Elizabeth?' he asked.

The old man rose unsteadily to his feet, too distressed to object any more. Weeping emotionally, he walked towards his family with his arms outstretched, seeking their comfort now. But, unable to forgive him, they closed their hearts and turned away from him. Sir Giles Montgomery stood alone, a pitiful, desolate figure of a man who had no-one to blame for his predicament but himself.

Richard fell stiffly to his knees beside Elizabeth's body, where he cradled her in his arms for a few moments. 'I shall never stop loving you, Elizabeth ...

never,' he whispered. Whatever happens, I know we will find one another again... somehow... some day. Until then, my dearest love.' He kissed her lips for the last time, then allowed himself one last long look at her. Even in death she was beautiful.

The scene was grim in Hangman's Wood at dawn the following morning. It was cold and the land around was rain-swept, the weather adding its own touch of solemnity to an already very solemn occasion. The distant hills were shrouded beneath a heavy blanket of mist, and not a single bird was heard to sing on that grey, dismal morn. Amidst the gloomy setting, Elizabeth's spirit was there amongst them.

Both participants had already arrived on the scene: Sir Giles Montgomery deep in conversation with his seconds, whilst his son conversed with the Count.

'Good luck, and may God be with you, Richard,' he said. 'Although the man is my father, I shall never forgive him for bringing about my sister's death yesterday. Shoot to kill!' he urged, 'or as God is my judge, I shall be sorely tempted to put an end to him myself!'

After the Count had removed his black coat, Sir Giles his Chesterfield overcoat, the two men were instructed to stand back to back in the clearing. Upon being given the call, they would proceed to take the customary ten paces forward. Richard glanced at the heavy overcast sky, arousing the curiosity of several of the onlookers who wondered what he was thinking about at a time like this. Whatever it was, no-one knew but he.

They were ready. The count began and the two men moved away from each other, the atmosphere rife with expectation. Montgomery's jaw was set firm and determined, his eyes already glinting with the sweetness of revenge. The moment he had been waiting for had arrived and there was no wavering, only hatred in his heart for his opponent.

In comparison, Richard's expression was altogether kinder. His heart was filled with thoughts of Elizabeth, recalling the enchanting smile she had cast him in the hall yesterday evening. It was a smile which inspired him now; one which held the promise of a new beginning. Richard felt comforted, for he knew he would be with her again very soon. He felt no fear as he heard the voice call out: ... 'nine, ten, turn... fire!'

The two men now faced each other, and just for a moment their eyes met and held across the clearing. Then Sir Giles raised his pistol and took deliberate aim, whilst Richard's hand remained by his side. Without a moment's hesitation, Sir Giles Montgomery shot the younger man, grievously wounding him near the heart.

Although Richard was severely injured, he remained in a standing position.

Then, with a satisfied expression on his face, he raised his own pistol and took careful aim. Montgomery began to perspire, his heart quaking as never before. The man was within an inch of losing his life and he knew it! It seemed a lifetime that he was made to stand and wait for his opponent's shot. Eventually it became too much for him to bear and he shouted at the top of his voice. 'In God's name what are you waiting for, man? Shoot me if you have a mind to! But for the love of heaven get it over with!'

Richard smiled complacently, then pointed his pistol towards the ground and fired it into the rich brown earth. There followed gasps of shock from the bystanders; an even louder gasp from Sir Giles' own lips. Satisfied, Richard eyed him across the clearing. 'I told you, Sir, dying is too good for you. Living will be your punishment, I fear!'

It was over, and everyone was quick to move at once. Not a single fellow was seen to approach Sir Giles, however, and he was left to stand all alone in his moment of glory, his moment of sweet revenge.

Eventually, Edward walked over to him, but it was not to congratulate his father on his victory when he spoke. 'You shame me beyond words, Father! After my dear sister's death yesterday, I had hoped you would find some degree of compassion in your heart for a man who has already suffered so much. You do, after all, share the same grief, the same loss, do you not?' His face twisted in a contemptuous sneer. 'Oh, but knowing you as I do, I should have known better! Well, Father, I confess I have had my fill of you, and from this day forth I vow never to speak another word to you as long as I live. For your sins against Elizabeth and Richard, I shun you! And may God have mercy on you now – for no-one else will!'

Sir Giles stared at his son, dumbfounded. He opened his mouth to speak but from sheer shock the words failed to come. The young man turned his back on him and walked away. Edward Montgomery kept his promise. He never uttered a word to his father again.

Although greatly disturbed by his son's statement, Sir Giles did not intend to be robbed of his moment of triumph and, looking extremely self-satisfied, he approached his fatally wounded opponent. Considering his injuries, Giles found it remarkable that the fellow was still on his feet. Indeed, a lesser man would doubtless be lying dead now. Well, if nothing else, de Ville certainly had guts. Montgomery admired him for that.

His voice was proud and complacent when he addressed him. 'Well, Sir, did I not warn you that I would punish you for your sins? Did I not say all along that I would make you pay for your deeds against me and mine? 'Tis done now, Sir. Concede!'

Despite his pain, Richard smiled. Before he fell, he uttered words which would haunt Sir Giles Montgomery until his bitter end. The master of

Cambourne Hall would be reminded of them every day until, unable to bear them ringing in his ears a moment longer, and plagued by the burden of his guilt, he would take his own life on Hangman's Tree only a few short weeks from now.

'Indeed you did, Sir. And I do concede that it is done – at least, for Elizabeth and myself. However, there are two questions I wish to ask before I' – he smiled – 'before I leave you. Firstly, although you no doubt feel complacent in your victory today, gratified that you have finally avenged yourself against my mother for rejecting you all those years ago and that you have done your worst to us, knowing what you do, Sir Giles, I wonder – was it really worth the price you had to pay?'

Giles flinched as a look of realisation masked his face.

Richard continued. 'Finally, because your hatred of my family not only cost Elizabeth her life yesterday, but today will make your granddaughter an orphan at your very own hand and that one day you yourself must explain her parents' deaths to her, I ask you in all sincerity – how will you go on living with the knowledge of what you have done?'

It was the morning of the funeral. Elizabeth's spirit was still there amongst them during the couple's last journey to the village church at Netley. Outside the iron gates the funeral cortège belonging to the two families drew to a halt, brought together on this, the saddest occasion of their lives. It was Rebecca de Ville herself who had suggested the double funeral and, although Sir Giles had agreed, too consumed with sorrow to object, he had, however, refused to allow the couple to be buried together.

He gave orders that Elizabeth was to be laid to rest in the Montgomery family grave, and that it would be sheer hypocrisy on his part to allow de Ville to be buried with her.

Outside the church gates stood a large gathering of men, women and children, these being not only villagers from Netley itself but from every village around. It was only understandable that they should wish to pay their last respects to the couple who had lost their lives so tragically that week. They bowed their heads as the funeral parties arrived, with many of the women weeping when the pallbearers, Edward Montgomery amongst them, stepped forward to lift the two coffins from the carriages.

Considerable booing broke out amongst the crowd when Sir Giles alighted from his own carriage. The old man was in such a deep state of grief, however, that he barely appeared to notice. His face was ashen, his eyes sunk deep into their sockets, their lids red and swollen from the extent of his endless weeping. No man or woman present disbelieved the master's sorrow, and it was clear to all that he was now a finished man. Gradually the booing ceased and once again respect prevailed. Leaning heavily upon his sister's arm, Giles and Charlotte made their way into the church, the de Villes close behind.

Inside, the Reverend Michael Stedly had expected a good turn-out on this sorrowful occasion, but never in all his life had he expected anything like this. The little church was packed to overflowing. Those who were unable to find a seat formed standing rows at the back, and those who were unable to squeeze inside all gathered around the open doors.

There were many familiar faces in the pews, with not a dry eye amongst them when the coffins were placed side by side before the altar. Immediately behind the Montgomery family and their many friends and relatives sat the staff of Cambourne Hall and its estate. Among them were Granville Stokes, Annie, who was sobbing bitterly into her handkerchief, and dear old Ned who sat with his head hung low. His expression was perhaps the saddest of all, for today was, without doubt, the most sorrowful of his life. Never again would he hear the sound of Miss Elizabeth's bright, cheerful laughter about the stables, the joy she used to bring to his drab old life. The Hall would never be the same without her either, forever haunted by the memory of her tragic demise.

In the very back pew sat the desolate figure of Frederick Llani, his face a mask of grief. Word of the couple's deaths had reached him in neighbouring Wales where he had been staying, and the fellow had driven with all speed to get here for their funeral. Like everyone else, Mr Llani had been deeply shocked to learn what had happened to Elizabeth and Richard, finding it impossible to understand how Sir Giles could have allowed such tragedies to take place.

Standing at the back were many of Sir Giles' rebellious labourers, here to pay their last respects both to Miss Elizabeth and to the man whose kindness and fairness had brought a little hope into their miserable lives. Unknown to them all at this moment in time, they would soon be reinstated at Cambourne under the employ of Master Edward. Netley Manor and its estate would shortly be sold off and, following Sir Giles' suicide, all would be well in their world again.

On the opposite side, in the very front pew, sat Rebecca de Ville and her grieving daughter. The poor young woman had been distressed beyond words at the death of her brother and friend, and had besought her mother to sell the estate so that they might return to France where they would be well out of reach of Sir Giles Montgomery's hatred. Rachael cherished a secret hope that one day Edward might wish to join her. But as things turned out, it was never to be.

Directly opposite the two women, Sir Giles was on his knees in prayer.

The man suddenly opened his eyes and inclined his head sideways to steal a look at the woman who had initiated his hatred all those years ago. It was the first time in over thirty years that he had seen her. Rebecca felt his eyes upon her and turned to look at him. Giles saw the anguish which masked her beautiful face, the pain and the sorrow in her eyes. Giles cast his mind back to the days of their betrothal and his heart gave a turn in his chest. He had treated Rebecca diabolically and had sworn his vengeance against her for rejecting him. Well, he had taken and relished his vengeance – but at what cost? Because of it, Rebecca had lost her only son, whilst he had lost his own beloved daughter who had been his very life. Moreover, he had lost her by trying to cheat the Lord Himself in breaking a sacred promise. As Giles stared at her, Richard's last words flooded into his mind to haunt him – 'Was it really worth the price you had to pay?'

The old man groaned with anguish and turned his head away from her, weeping emotionally from shame and guilt. Oh, God, what had he done? Why had he not swallowed his stubborn pride and made peace with Rebecca and her family? His hatred had succeeded in destroying them all. Oh, but it was too late now!

It was the most intensely moving service that anyone could remember, with the Reverend Michael Stedly delivering his moralistic sermon to the assemblage of mourners. He began, 'I am fully aware of the tragic circumstances in which these two children of God lost their lives, and beseech you all, let not your hearts be filled with the evils of revenge, for revenge is mine sayeth the Lord. Instead, let your hearts be filled with love and forgiveness for your enemy, forever to walk in the path of righteousness and honour. To love thy neighbour as thyself.' Finally he concluded, 'for the meek shall inherit the earth, sayeth the Lord. Amen.'

After the service the mourners gathered together around the two open graves. Sir Giles was so overcome by grief that he had to be supported on either side by Edward and Charlotte. As the Rector stood to deliver his last address over the two coffins, Charlotte moved forward to place a bunch of wild bluebells on the lids of each. Reverently she bent her head as she stood between them and, although she was weeping, the old lady managed a smile. 'God bless you, dears,' she whispered. 'Every spring I promise to bring you bluebells from the wood in remembrance of you both, and will cherish the memory of you in my heart until I die.'

Still watched by Elizabeth's lonely spirit, one by one, the coffins were lowered into the earth. The Rector then stood looking down into her very own grave, in his hand a clump of rich brown Shropshire earth.

'Earth to earth... dust to dust... ashes to ashes...'

As the handful of soil struck the lid of her coffin, she saw no more.

Elizabeth Montgomery's spirit had been called. She was no longer amongst them now.

CHAPTER SIXTEEN

The first thing she saw when she opened her eyes was old Ned sweeping up the courtyard below. Relief flooded into her. Just for a moment she had thought...

She was still feeling dazed when she called out to him. 'Ned, oh Ned!'

Puzzled, the old man looked up at her. He raised his cap and began to scratch the top of his head. She smiled. It was a mannerism she had seen many times. It was so familiar to her.

The old groom called out to her, his words shattering her world. 'But... but my name's Ben, Miss.' He gave a chuckle of laughter. 'Ned was my grandfather... remember?'

Her breath caught in her throat and she suddenly felt dizzy. She closed her eyes tightly, refusing to believe it. No! No! It couldn't be...? She couldn't be...?

The old man called out to her again, asking if she was all right. She couldn't speak. She couldn't say a word! Panic threw her mind into unbearable chaos and she was afraid to open her eyes from fear of what she might see. Eventually she had to. When she did, reality faced her – the modern stables, the concrete courtyard, her own clothes. She was back in her jeans, her white cotton blouse and open-toed sandals. The sickening truth flooded into her... who she was. She was no longer Elizabeth Montgomery, Elizabeth who had lived and died in the eighteen hundreds. She was Catherine Shepherd again, and very much a part of the twentieth century.

Frantic, she gave a cry. 'No... !' She didn't want to be Catherine Shepherd! She didn't want to live in this age! She was Elizabeth! She was! She was! Oh, but she had been so happy in the age she had come from. It was her age. She belonged there...with him.

Deeply tortured, she covered her face with her hands and began to sob. Everything made sense to her now. She had been brought back to the house where she had once lived, loved and died in order that her dying wish could be fulfilled. With God's blessing, she had been allowed to return in time, to re-live the days which she had spent with Richard de Ville.

The good Lord had heard her prayer that evening and in His mercy He had granted her wish. After all those years, His recompense to Elizabeth

234

Montgomery had been fulfilled. Now it was done. It was over.

With her mind so full of Richard, her beloved Richard, she wanted to cry out that it wasn't done. It wasn't! How could it be? He was in another place, whilst she was here. Despite everything, they were still separated! The pain of remembrance became too much to bear and in her agony she called Richard's name, which echoed across the courtyard. Her cry alerted Ben, who was on his way back to the stables. He turned to stare at her, shaking his head in puzzlement. Who might Richard be, he wondered?

Beside herself with anguish, she ran inside to the bedroom where she flung herself into a chair and wept emotionally. Never in her life had she felt so tormented. God had allowed her to return in time to be with her beloved again; allowed her to treasure those memories in her heart and mind, only to face the harsh reality of her loneliness now. Desperate, she gazed frantically around the room, shuddering as she recalled the last time she had been here – the night she had fallen from the balcony. Ironically, the valise was still there where she had left it. Had it not been for that, then things would no doubt have turned out very differently. Oh, but for the valise...

The tears began to fall again. She wanted to be with Richard so much! But how? How? Sitting there, deeply afflicted by those bitter-sweet memories of yesteryear, she suddenly recalled the ghost of Cambourne Hall. Alistair had said it was Richard's restless spirit seeking his beloved Elizabeth. Catherine thought about it for a moment or so. Richard had repeatedly told her that he would never rest in a world without her – even in the afterworld, he had said. It was then she remembered, and cast her mind back to July, 1886, when they had spent their very last day together in Bluebell Wood. Now... what was it he had said to her? 'If for some reason I ever lose you, Elizabeth, I promise I shall wait here in the wood for you, remaining for as long as it takes for you to come to me.'

A spark of hope lit Catherine's eyes. Was it possible? Was it really possible...? Suddenly she knew where she must go if she ever wished to find him again.

After one last look round, she left the bedroom to hurry along to Emma's flat. As she reached the portraits on the landing, she paused. Oh, but it was so clear now who Sir James reminded her of, for he bore a remarkable resemblance to his dear father, Edward. Her eyes rested upon her own father. How very unnecessary it had been for them to part the way they had! If only Sir Giles had been a more forgiving man, how very happily things would have ended! She kissed the end of her finger and held it against his cheek. 'Rest in peace, Papa,' she whispered tenderly, 'I forgive you.'

Proceeding with her train of thought, she wondered how she was going to explain her return to the past to Emma. Would it all prove too much for her?

Should she even consider trying to explain what had just taken place in Elizabeth's room?

Catherine carefully considered the matter. Perhaps God would not want her to speak of the wish she had prayed for on that evening in 1887. Perhaps it was meant to be a secret known only to Himself and to her? It was difficult to know what to do.

Catherine need not have worried over Emma's curiosity, for the burden had already been lifted from her shoulders. Earlier, when she had left her, the old lady had slipped into a sleep from which she would never wake. Emma Montgomery had been allowed to live for ninety-four long years, and at the very end of those years she had been favoured, by the grace of God, with the gift of her extraordinary meeting with Catherine Shepherd – Elizabeth herself. Now Emma's time had come.

Upon entering the flat, Catherine saw that she was still sitting in the chair where she had left her, her eyes closed as though in sleep. She looked so peaceful. Indeed, Catherine had no idea that Emma had passed away. She smiled tenderly. The last time she had seen her, she had been but a child in Annie's arms. Oh, but even now the whole thing almost staggered belief! After one last look at her, Catherine quietly placed the keys upon the coffee table, then left her. She must go to Bluebell Wood without delay!

Downstairs in the hall, she saw Lady Montgomery busily arranging flowers in a vase. Remembering that her employer wished to question her that evening, Catherine endeavoured to slip quietly past her, unseen. But, upon reaching the front door she came face to face with Sir James. He looked startled by the encounter and, as he gazed at Catherine, he grew uneasy. The man sensed a change in her this evening. There was something about her face, her eyes, which caused him mild alarm. Yet he found it difficult to analyse just what it was.

As Catherine stared at him, she found herself smiling tenderly. It was as though she were looking at Edward.

Frowning, James asked, 'Catherine, what... what is it?'

In that unguarded moment, Catherine found herself replying, 'Oh, Sir James, I know who you remind me of now. You are the very image of my dear brother, Edward.'

She could not have shaken him more if she had deliberately tried, and his shocked expression brought home to her the apparent foolishness of her statement.

Lady Montgomery had overheard Catherine's chilling admission and now turned to stare at her in amazement. Two pairs of questioning eyes were upon her, silent in their demand of an explanation. Both had turned quite pale. Indeed, Catherine would never forget the look on their faces at that moment, for they were staring at a ghost. Their fears had become reality.

Completely lost for words and unable to face them a moment longer, she quickly brushed past Sir James and ran out into the garden. In her haste, she decided it would be quicker to ride to Bluebell Wood, so headed straight for the stables. Ben Sykes laughed when she asked him for a horse, believing her to be pulling his leg. He had been concerned for her earlier, never having seen a woman quite so distraught before. Ben wondered how she had come to be standing out on the forbidden balcony, for no-one had stood out there since Elizabeth Montgomery had fallen to her death some time in his grandfather's day.

'An 'orse, Miss?' He chuckled. 'But you told me you couldn't ride!'

'Forget what I said, Ben. Now, any horse will do – and you don't need to saddle it. I can manage!'

The poor chap looked perplexed. Lifting his cap, he began to scratch the top of his head. Catherine smiled. How she would love to have told him that his old grandfather used to do that, too.

Ben mumbled under his breath. 'The young lady doesn't just want an 'orse, but she means to ride it bareback into the bargain. These Canadians are strange 'uns!' he reckoned. His eyes almost popped out of their sockets when he saw her leap on to its back from the old mounting block, then ride across the courtyard as though she had been born on a horse. He would never be able to understand women! Ben had just returned to his duties when Sir James and Master Alistair came rushing over to him. Both were out of breath and the master looked as white as a ghost. Whatever was up, he wondered?

James Montgomery might well have looked white. Following Catherine's amazing statement that he reminded her of her brother Edward, it had not taken him long to acknowledge that which he already felt in his heart. Catherine Shepherd was a reincarnation of Elizabeth Montgomery – and what was more, she knew it. James had cast his mind back to their very first meeting, when Catherine had asked him if they had met before somewhere. That afternoon, she felt that James was familiar to her, but this evening she knew for sure. From that he concluded that something must have happened to enlighten her. That surely would explain the change which he sensed in her earlier. It all made sense to him now, with those awkward little pieces fitting perfectly into place. The reason why she had come here was clear to him, together with her strange behaviour and her insight about the lake at Netley Manor. James knew there had been something odd about her all along, especially after her avid interest in Elizabeth and Richard. Sarah had felt it too, and from the first moment Catherine had entered the drawing room for her interview. Had she not said that she felt Catherine had more right to be at Cambourne Hall than herself? Oh, the irony of that little statement! Poor Sarah! He had left her in a state of shock in the drawing room.

Alistair had been told, and although he had not exactly laughed outright, James had some difficulty in convincing him that he was serious. Eventually, after carefully considering all the facts, Alistair had been compelled to agree with his father. Both men said that Catherine must be found and tactfully questioned without delay.

James' voice sounded anxious when he called out to Ben. 'Have you seen Miss Shepherd about, Ben? Has she been this way at all?'

'Aye, Sir. She 'as!' The old man nodded. 'She wanted an 'orse. Rode off like she'd been born on one, she did!'

Alistair glanced at his father. 'So she can ride! She told me she had never been on a horse in her life!'

'In my opinion, Catherine was telling the truth, Alistair. I don't think she has ever ridden a horse in this lifetime. But she would certainly have had enough practice as Elizabeth,' he said in quiet undertones.

'The young lady gave me a bit of a turn earlier, Sir,' said Ben. 'To be truthful, I felt a bit worried about 'er.'

'Gave you a turn? In what way, Ben?'

Ben cleared his throat. 'Well, Sir, I saw her standing out on the old balcony. And... and she was crying. She seemed very upset.'

'The balcony?' James gasped. 'Are... are you sure, Ben?'

'Aye, I am, Sir. She didn't look 'erself at all. Kept on calling me Ned. Ned was my grandfather, Sir. 'E worked 'ere in Sir Giles' day. Any'ow, when I told 'er I was Ben, she got 'erself into a right ol' state, weepin' and wailin', callin' out to someone called Richard.' The old groom frowned. 'I couldn't understand it, 'cos there was no-one else around but me.'

'Good God!' uttered Sir James. He turned to Alistair. 'I wonder who gave her the key to Elizabeth's room? It couldn't have been your mother. She would have told me.'

'I bet it was Aunt Emma!' exclaimed Alistair. 'They were very close, you know. In fact, I believe Catherine intended to visit Aunt Emma this evening.'

'Emma. Of course!' said Sir James. Looking thoughtful, he stroked the end of his chin. 'I wonder if Emma knew?'

'You mean, that Catherine is a reincarnation of Elizabeth?'

'Yes. There must have been some reason why she gave Catherine the key.' A troubled look began to darken James' face. 'I don't like any of this, Alistair; Catherine being out on the balcony, crying and calling for Richard. The whole thing is making me uneasy.'

'Let's go and see Aunt Emma now,' suggested Alistair, 'we simply must find out what has happened.'

238

'Later. We must find Catherine first. When I saw her in the hall a short while ago, she... she appeared different somehow. It was the expression on her face, the look in her eyes – a look of revelation. I'm convinced something happened to her this evening. Come along, we'll drive to Netley Manor to see if she's gone there. I have an awful feeling in the pit of my stomach that Catherine is in danger!'

Back at the house, the telephone rang. Lynette informed Lady Montgomery that a Miss Jenilee Harris was calling from Paris asking to speak to Miss Shepherd. Sarah still hadn't recovered from the shock of learning that Catherine was Elizabeth Montgomery's reincarnation, and that somehow or other she had found her way back to Cambourne Hall, the house which had once been her home. How had she found her way back here? And how had she discovered that she had once been the ill-fated Elizabeth? Sarah recalled the evening when she had taken Catherine to meet Emma, remembering their strange reaction to one another. Had Emma sensed who Catherine was? Is that why she had wanted to meet her so urgently? Sarah decided to question Emma right away. But first she would speak to Miss Harris.

'I'll take the call, Lynette,' she said, still deep in thought. A moment later she was speaking to Jenilee. 'I'm afraid Miss Shepherd is out at the moment. I'm Sarah Montgomery. Can I... can I take a message, Miss Harris?'

'No, I don't think so,' said Jenilee. 'Will Cathy be long? I told her I'd call this evenin'.'

'I...I have no idea,' began Sarah. 'Catherine didn't...didn't say where she was going.'

A prickle of unease feathered down Jenilee's spine. Something in Lady Montgomery's voice caused her concern. 'Is there somethin' wrong, Lady Montgomery? Is Cathy all right?'

'Yes, of course she is, Miss Harris. Catherine is very well. But...'

'But what?' questioned Jenilee. 'I wish you'd tell me!'

'Miss Harris...are you a close friend of Catherine's? Have you known her long?'

'Yeah. Cathy and I've been friends for years. We're almost like sisters. We share an apartment in Vancouver, and we recently came to England together on vacation. I went on to Paris to visit relatives. Cathy shoulda come too, but she wanted to go to Shropshire instead. So we split up in London and went our separate ways.'

'Why? Why did she want to come to Shropshire?' entreated Lady Montgomery.

Following a short, uneasy silence, Jenilee replied, 'I'm afraid you'll have to ask Cathy that, Lady Montgomery. I can't help you.'

'But you do know?' persisted Sarah. 'You do know what urged her to come here?'

It was obvious to Jenilee that Lady Montgomery was growing suspicious of Cathy, and she wondered if something had happened. She must warn her to be careful when she spoke to her. 'I'm afraid I must go, Lady Montgomery,' she said. 'Would you tell Cathy that I'll call her at nine-thirty this evenin'. Please tell her to be there.'

Sarah sighed. She knew Miss Harris was covering up for Catherine in some way. 'Yes, I will tell her, Miss Harris. Thank you for calling. Goodbye.'

Oh, but it felt so wonderful to ride again, to feel the power beneath her as she urged the gelding on! As she rode, her thoughts strayed back to her own dear Rhapsody. How she had loved that plucky little mare, so long dead and gone now, although it only seemed like yesterday when she was with her.

She remembered the way to the wood without any trouble at all, but oh, how very different it all looked now. The narrow winding path of yesteryear was now much wider. It had also been gravelled to accommodate the tractors and trailers which were used on the estate. Almost all the hawthorn hedges had disappeared, with stout timber fencing replacing them. Many of the beautiful trees which had once lined the path to Lower Coppice had also gone, although she was pleased to note that several young trees had been planted in their place. Great corrugated iron barns had been erected in many of the lower pastures; ugly blots on the landscape which had once been so pretty.

A dreadful thought occurred to her. Suppose the wood wasn't there any more? Suppose it had been ripped up along with so many of the other coppices around the estate? The thought caused her to panic. She would never find Richard then! It urged her into pushing her horse on.

During the next few minutes her heart was in her mouth, hoping, praying that the wood would still be there. Then her eyes beheld a familiar sight, there in the distance – Bluebell Wood. She almost wept when she saw it. It was still there! It was! It was!

But arriving at the entrance she found the wood a mere shadow of its former glory, now overgrown with brambles and scrub and not in the least as she remembered it. In Elizabeth's time there had been a mass of beautiful rhododendron bushes growing here. But not now. There was not so much as a trace of where they had been.

She found it difficult riding along a path so thick with thorny brambles, and eventually found it necessary to dismount. After securing her horse to a tree, she then set off on foot towards the centre of the wood. As she progressed, a tremendous sense of excitement was building up inside her.

When she finally arrived at the stream, still there after all those years, she could have cried with joy. It was somewhere along here that she had first met and fallen in love with Richard. Oh, how the memory of that warmed her heart! She paused for a moment to gaze around. What would she find, she wondered? Indeed, what did she expect to find? Him? Still waiting here for her as he had promised? Was she perhaps a little mad even to consider such a possibility? A sudden thought: supposing he was here? How could they be together again when both existed in two separate worlds? She did not know. It was all beyond her. She was simply following the callings of her heart. But wasn't she forgetting something? Wasn't she forgetting that the reason she was here in the first place was because of God's grace and will? Had He not granted her wish and allowed her to return into time to be with Richard again? Bearing that fact in mind, shouldn't she have a little more faith in Him now? Encouraged by the thought, she felt happier.

Eventually she arrived at the clearing where she and Richard had been accustomed to meet, although it had become so overgrown, it had lost all familiarity now. Catherine found a fallen log and sat down. How very peaceful it was on this warm summer evening, with only the sound of the birds to break the silence. Her mind was everywhere at once, for it was a strange situation, sitting there waiting for a man whom she had known and loved in an earlier existence. Glancing at her wristwatch, she saw that it was seven o'clock. There was still a couple of hours before darkness began to descend on the wood.

As time passed by, she lost herself in the memory of their last meeting, when she had lain dying in his arms in the courtyard. His words came flooding back to her: 'Wherever you are, I shall find you. I do not believe that God would deprive me of that.' She recalled her own words to him: 'I would gladly die a second time to be with you, Richard.' How vivid the memory of him was in her mind! She could almost see him before her, his tall, dark handsomeness, his shining black hair and those crystal blue eyes. She loved him now every bit as much as she had loved him then... she always would.

The waiting seemed endless, and reality suddenly pricked at her mind. Why was she torturing herself like this? It was just too cruel! Richard wasn't here at all! How could he be? How could he? Hope abandoned her, and in that moment she recognised the futility of waiting for him. How foolish she felt, believing that Richard would find her again after ninety-four long years! He was gone! Gone! Gone! Gone! And she was left alone with her memories. Desperately unhappy and tortured beyond endurance, she covered her face with her hands and wept bitter tears. She just could not bear the pain any longer.

How long she sat there weeping, engulfed in her own misery, she did not know. Then gradually the most wonderful feeling began to creep over her, a spiritual, uplifting feeling which touched every part of her. She ceased to weep, gave a sigh as she allowed herself to be consumed by the glorious peace which had overcome her now. Afterwards there came a deep sense of awareness. It was as though Richard was near...she could *feel* his presence in every fibre of her being, filling her heart with the most tremendous joy.

Barely a breath passed her lips as she slowly lowered her hands and opened her eyes to look around. Oh...but what a beautiful sight faced her now! The sun was shining through the trees in full, dazzling glory, filtering through the leaves and branches casting its silver light all around her. The whole wood had taken on an ethereal look, as though touched by the very hand of God.

Reverence stole over her and she closed her eyes again, and it was at that moment that she heard a voice calling her softly.

'Elizabeth, Elizabeth...'

Her breath caught in her throat and a tremble feathered down her spine, her whole body alert with hope. The voice addressed her again: 'Oh, Elizabeth...did you really believe I had deserted you?'

She gave a cry. It was such a familiar voice. 'Oh! Richard! Richard...'

There was no trepidation when she opened her eyes to look at him; no fear in her heart at what she might see. Only happiness and a deep sense of wonder filled her now. Had she expected some ghostly apparition, then she could not have been more wrong for, taking on human form, Richard de Ville was exactly as she remembered him on their very first meeting here in Bluebell Wood. Dressed in the identical clothes – black trousers, high black riding boots and that frilly white shirt – he was the same breathtaking man he had always been.

Spellbound, she gazed at him, whilst he was smiling back at her, reflecting her love.

'Richard...' Her voice was but a breath. 'Oh, Richard...'

Smiling tenderly, he walked towards her, his eyes filled with love. 'Did I not promise that I would find you again, Elizabeth? Did I not promise to wait here for you until you came to me?'

She rose to her feet, her arms outstretched to him. 'Oh, yes! Yes, you did! I should never have doubted you, Richard.'

He was standing before her, but made no move to touch her. Perhaps such contact was impossible, she thought.

'My beautiful Elizabeth,' he murmured, 'you are the same as I remember. Only your garments are unfamiliar to me. Oh, I have missed you so much these long, lonely years. I have longed for you to return to me. I love you, Elizabeth, I love you!'

'Oh....and I love you, Richard! I have never stopped loving you! Now that

I've found you again, I never ever want to lose you!'

He gazed deep into her eyes, his voice questioning now. 'Do you remember our last meeting, my love? When you were lying in my arms in the courtyard that evening?'

'Yes, I remember. How could I forget? Leaving you was the hardest part of dying.'

'And do you remember telling me that you would gladly die a second time to be with me?'

She smiled softly. 'Yes, I remember,' she murmured.

'Were you sincere, Elizabeth? If so, do you still feel the same?'

'Need you even ask, Richard?' she replied tenderly. 'Believe me when I tell you that my life is meaningless without you. It means nothing to me. My happiness, all my memories and everything I cherish in my heart belongs with you. I belong with you, my love. I would willingly forfeit my life here on earth to be with you again. Does that perhaps answer your question?'

His smile robbed her of breath. 'Then we shall be, Elizabeth. We shall be! Oh, you have brought me such peace at last. Trust me as we go to our new beginning.' He took a step closer and held out his hands to her. 'Take my hands, and have no fear, my love. Remember I am with you all the way.'

Clasping his hands, she smiled at him enchantingly. 'I have waited so long for this moment, Richard. All I ever wanted was you. I will follow you wherever you take me.'

After all those years, Elizabeth Montgomery had finally achieved her heart's desire. She was with her beloved Richard, and no-one would part them again. She felt no fear at all.

It was almost dusk when Sir James and Alistair arrived at the wood. The two had searched everywhere for Catherine, but to no avail. Indeed, had it not been for Sarah remembering her interest in Bluebell Wood, then they might never have searched there at all.

They found her horse, still tethered to the tree, and making all haste the men began their search, both calling out as they proceeded. After a good twenty minutes or so it was Alistair who finally spotted her. 'Look! Over there!' he pointed. 'By the fallen tree. It's Catherine!'

Relief transformed Sir James' worried face, for a nagging fear had convinced him that Catherine was in some kind of danger that evening – if only from herself. But there she was, sitting quietly on the ground with her back to them, leaning against a log.

Lengthening his stride, it was Alistair who reached her first. 'Catherine! Oh, Catherine, thank goodness we've found you! Did you not realise how very worried -' He stopped abruptly in mid-sentence, his expression aghast.

'Catherine? Catherine?' he cried anxiously.

When she failed to respond, he reached out to touch her. 'M..: my God! I don't believe it! She's... she's dead!'

The men fell upon their knees beside her, both shocked beyond words. Her body was in a sitting position, with not a mark to indicate just how she had died. But the most startling thing of all was her face. Both men gasped when they looked at it, for in death she wore the most enchanting smile. It was almost as though she had welcomed her tragic demise.

James Montgomery stared at her questioningly. Looking at her face, her smile, it was not difficult to imagine that she had seen... someone. Perhaps she had, he thought? Perhaps Catherine – Elizabeth – had seen her beloved Richard again? His spirit had always remained here, waiting. James bowed his head in sadness. Alistair did likewise.

'It's my belief that something happened to Catherine today,' said James quietly. 'Something which undoubtedly changed the whole course of her life.' He heaved a heavy sigh. 'But we shall never know. Only she was in possession of that secret and sadly she has taken it to the grave with her.' James took her hand and held it between his own. 'I wonder what it was?' he said.